STRAYBORN

DRAEV GUARDIANS

BOOK ONE

E E RAWLS

To my grandmother who encouraged me, and my mother who supported me

Summary: Cyrus Sole, a half-human girl with weak wrists discovers she can manipulate metal, but then has to flee when the Argos Corps are sent to kill her… Aken-Shou, the last Scourgeblood, discovers he can create lava, and something more dangerous… The Draev Guardian Academy is their only sanctuary. But training to become a Draev won't be easy. Cyrus has to hide her human side, as she gets placed in Floor Harlow with the outcast students. And with creepy Corpsed on the prowl, and whispers of her possibly being a reborn Princess, both she and Aken find themselves caught in a web of secrets, racial tension, and an old legend with enemies that could spell their untimely demise…

ISBN 978-0-9985569-0-1

[1. Fantasy. 2. Coming of Age—Fantasy. 3. Ability—Fiction. 4.Orphans—Fiction. 5. Magic—Fiction.]
www.eerawls.com

Printed in the U.S.A.
First edition, October 2019

Titles by E.E. Rawls

Earthaverse:

Draev Guardians Series

Strayborn (1)

Storm & Choice (0.5)

Dragons & Ravens (1.5)

Strayblood (2)

Alteredverse:

Frost, Winter's Lonely Guardian

Portal to Eartha

Beast of the Night

Madness Solver in Wonderland

Coming Soon:

Straypath (3)

Secret projects ;)

Find out when the next books are releasing, and get exclusive content, by following my newsletter at:

eerawls.com

GOUBELIN
BERGVOLK
Mondburg
Diviso Sea
HIGHLANDS
KIN
D
Backbone Mount
Greater
Magica
Forest
Kingdom
Valley
Haunt Marshes
Grin Chasm
Lesser
Magica
Forest
ARAH SANDS
SALMU
BARIS
Noncello river
HUMA
OF
XOTIPHOS

SIVORTSKA

DRAETHVYLE
Lake Doroth
Outer Woods
Clover

ELDFJÖLL
OM OF
ETH
RĂSĂRIT
Morbid Dungeons
Tantō
Mountains
ELVENSTONE
Suez's
Skull
AKATSUKI
HIGASHI
ORESTABELLA
EPUBLIC
OTIPH
ARTHA

If you made it to this page, congratulations. You get a cookie.

Will I tell you who I am? No.

Maybe.

If and when I feel like it.

But until then, I'll let you work your brain muscles and figure it out for yourself. All you need to know right now is that my account of this tale is factual and thoroughly researched to the best of my superior ability.

I was there to witness many of these events first-hand. And for those events which sadly lacked my humble presence, I was able to interview and record the words and thoughts of those who were.

But first, before you continue reading, if you are one of those humans from Earth, then there are a few things you need to know.

You've probably forgotten the existence of the Altered in your world—select humans whose genes were altered during the first age. You might know them as fae, goblins, elves, vampires, kitsune and other such names. They once shared Earth with normal humans, such as yourself, until prejudice and fear forced many of them to leave.

They left through one of several hidden portals, and came into a new world: a world similar in size and atmosphere to Earth—a second Earth, you could call it, where they were able to thrive. It is also important to note that a few human outcasts snuck in among them.

As the Altered races flourished, and countries and nations developed on the new planet Eartha, among the most powerful became the Vemparic Empire and the Xotiph Human Kingdom.

The humans had discovered a great power, known as the Pure Light, and their royal line, the Swans, guarded it closely while their kingdom prospered.

But one day, when a new Pureblood came to rule the Vemparic Empire, he desired to steal this great power from them—and there was only one Swan princess left, named Cyrus, who could stand in his way. This day became known as The Disaster, the day when the world was forever changed.

If reading the prologue is depressing, well, that's the point. But the real story begins with a little redhead girl on planet Eartha, who has a sense of humor and a bad case of messy hair, and a boy with big dreams, who are both about to be caught up in the old legend that surrounds the Pure Light…

PROLOGUE

THE DISASTER OF 0 AD

The Swan Princess staggered back, not wanting to believe the sight before her eyes. "You…you killed him!" she cried.

The Pureblood Emperor turned a cold smirk up at her, his clothing stained, chin and cheek spattered red. A bloodied sword clattered from his grip to the floor, to rest beside a lifeless body. His blue eyes were cold flames, a twisted soul craving power. There would be no end to his thirst for bloodshed, no end to ravaging the nations and tearing the world apart. He had become a ruthless being, so unlike the person she once knew.

"He was in the way," the Emperor's chilling tone replied.

The Princess trembled, her knees ready to buckle beneath her. "He was your best friend… Why would you do this?" she screamed. "How could you betray us!"

"Best friend…as were you, once," he murmured, though more to himself than to her.

Two guards came rushing through the broken-down doors of the sacred room, their swords raised. The Emperor smirked, and with his bare hands seized both weapons by the blade. He threw the swords back in their faces and in an instant had them both gripped by the throat.

They screamed as the color and life drained from their skin, until their bodies were no more than shriveled, lifeless husks. When he released them, they collapsed to the floor as bone and dust.

The Emperor faced the Princess once more, and step by step he drew nearer across the holy room.

She glanced over her shoulder to the sacred pedestal where the Pure Light hovered, floating like a swirl of white swan feathers—the great power that was her sworn duty to protect.

"Now, be a good little princess and hand me," the Emperor growled, "that *power*."

Cheeks damp with tears she could no longer feel, she turned away from him, wincing against the pain. With what strength she had left in her feeble body, she scaled the stairs, racing toward the sacred pedestal and its ethereal light, her scarlet hair fluttering back from her shoulders.

"NO!" The Emperor's shout rang out and his footsteps charged up after her, striving to stop her before she could take hold of the Pure Light first.

The floor quaked suddenly and fissures separated the tiles, as if the ground were crumbling beneath them. Chaos roared beyond the room's grand windows, shaking the walls.

The Princess panted, her hand stretched out. Desperation filled every fiber of her being as her hand reached up toward the glowing power.

Her finger brushed it.

Her palm wrapped around it.

"That power is *mine!*" the Emperor screeched, catching up to her.

The Pure Light awakened, casting rays as bright as the sun over her and filling the room.

All the world around them disappeared into white. The

floor, the decorative columns, the vaulted ceiling, and her own legs beneath her disintegrated into the ethereal, blinding light.

The Emperor's hand reached out to grasp her arm as he crouched within reach, staring up at her through wild, glowing eyes before he, too, was overcome and vanished into white nothingness.

He ceased to be. She ceased to be.

And the world forever changed…

The Emperor comes
King of Evil awakes
Who will win,
Whom shall the world take?

There awaits the guilty throne
Crown of Pureblood borne alone.
Will it save or will it kill?
Hatred longs to have its fill.

Beware the cloaks of night descend
A shifter seeking for revenge
Behind young faces monsters lie
Twisted secrets, the Impure Nights.

Arise, three Ghosts of distant past
Save us with the Pure Light vast,
War has begun, the dice are cast
The Swan must live, or none will last.

For good or evil is yet to be seen
The one who wills to destroy the king,
Yet if a change brings hearts to unite
Only then may Eartha stand and fight.
Crown of Pureblood borne alone
There awaits the guilty throne.

The Emperor comes
King of Evil awakes
Who will win,
Whom shall the world take?

—*"Song Of The End"*
Prophecy, 1st Oracle

PART 1
CYRUS

1

2,008 Years Later (2007 AD)

Seven-year-old Cyrus Sole picked up the white swan feather, twirling it between her fingers. This week was going to be a bad week, she could tell. Her gut always felt uneasy before something bad was about to happen.

"Don't mess with my feather collection."

Cyrus put the feather down and picked up the brush instead, combing it down her older sister's auburn hair. Heily sat admiring herself in the metallic mirror, and adjusted a clip once Cyrus finished.

"Your hair's so pretty, long n' soft. Wish mine was, too," said Cyrus.

Thirteen-year-old Heily chuckled. "It is rather nice, isn't it? All the boys compliment me daily," she said with a pleased blush.

When Cyrus's downcast face reflected in the mirror, Heily turned on her rotating chair. "Don't go getting all depressed, *Miss Cry-a-lot*. Not everybody is meant to have hair like mine."

Cyrus glanced away, scanning Heily's modern room, which had all the latest fashion and tech that Elvenstone Town could offer. "I know," she replied. "I just wish I was pretty—a little pretty. Anything besides *this*." She gestured to her short, bright-as-cherries hair and simple face. "So kids won't say I look like a boy all the time," Cyrus added, and grimaced down at the floor, her small feet shuffling.

"Well," Heily thought for a moment. "Growing your hair out sure didn't work." A giggle slipped free as she recalled Cyrus's hair poofing like a deformed tomato. "*Ahem*. Sorry, but it really was the funniest thing I ever saw. Your hair grew *out* instead of down."

Seeing the pout on her step-sibling's face, Heily calmed her mirth. "You're just a child, Cyrus. I'm sure your hair will change once you hit puberty. But it'd help if you dressed up more nicely: a touch of lipstick, a cute dress, and not to mention if you behaved more like a girl, instead of frolicking about in the dirt. What do they call that game? Longball, *ugh*!" She sniffed. "Only unruly boys play such games. Seriously, act more like a girl. Not some tomboy."

"You're saying I shouldn't be *me* anymore?" Cyrus folded her arms.

Heily shrugged. "I'm just trying to help. Do you like kids making fun of you and calling you *Cherry-top* and *Tomato Boy*?"

Cyrus stuck out her lower lip. Some other humans had red hair, and they weren't teased. But she knew her hair wasn't the real reason why kids teased her.

"You wanted advice, and I gave it. Now go do what you want," Heily said and stood, stretching her arms and smoothing her skirt before heading out the door. "Don't forget to wash the dishes! It's your turn, and it's starting to stink in the kitchen."

Cyrus watched Heily go, eyeing the tight waist of her dress, wondering how a person could breathe in such tight clothing. Were some girls born without lungs?

Cyrus chewed her lip. She liked games, liked being outdoors. It was fun. She didn't want to wear dresses and makeup every stinking day. Maybe once in a while, but not like Heily did.

Sigh. But how nice it would be to get the positive attention perfect Heily constantly got? Endless compliments about what a "wonderful young lady Heily was growing up to be." Then those same people would turn and see Cyrus and then quickly pretend they hadn't—because she was a half-blood.

Dad never said it out loud, but it was clear he loved Heily more. And Step-mom Narcissa made no effort to hide her favoritism; Heily was her real daughter, after all. A bitterness hung unspoken between the woman and Cyrus, and for more reasons than just that Cyrus wasn't biologically related.

No one liked Cyrus because her real mother had been a vempar—the race humans hated, the enemy they'd spent hundreds of years fighting. Vempars were strong, and they preyed on humans and other races in order to quell their hunger.

Elvenstone was a risky town to live in, up here in the northernmost reaches of the Human Republic of Xotiph, the closest town to the border that met with the Vemparic Kingdom of Draeth. Elvenstone was a human outpost, in a way, to monitor the vempars' movements and make sure borders weren't crossed.

Most people in town wanted nothing to do with Cyrus, even though she had taken after her dad's human genes. To look at, she was practically human—no fangs, no bat ridges in her ears, no Healing capability. But the blood of Mother flowed somewhere in her veins, and that was enough for the townspeople to shun her.

Mother… Cyrus could barely remember her, except that she'd had beautiful long, wavy hair the shade of scarlet roses, and that she'd loved Cyrus very, very much. Much more than anyone had since.

Mother had died when she was two years old, found murdered. They suspected it to be the work of other vempars, but in a world where people disappeared often, nobody bothered to investigate. It left Cyrus feeling only half of a self, the vempar half of her an unknown and foreign gray area.

Why did Mother have to die? Where was she buried? There was no grave in Elvenstone, and no one she asked would talk about it.

Cyrus chewed her lip as she studied her reflection in the mirror.

Maybe, tomorrow, she should try doing as Heily suggested…

Next morning found Cyrus paused at the front door, the outside world of Elvenstone just beyond and waiting to laugh at her.

She had on a cute blue dress; a touch of makeup colored her cheeks and lips, hairclips held down unruly curls.

She felt ridiculous, like a ladybug trying to pretend it was a fairy! But if it could make people treat her better, then…

"If you keep standing there, you'll be late for school," Narcissa reprimanded from across the kitchen.

"Give her time, Mama. I dressed her up myself. And I must say, for a child, she almost looks pretty!" Heily wore a satisfied smile, as if she'd managed to create something from what had once been a mud pie. "Don't be shy! Go out there, and do your best to act *lady*-like."

Heily shoved Cyrus out the doorway and onto the white paved street.

Cyrus panicked, looking frantically about at a passing bicycle and the haze-trail from a cargo carrier's engine. Heily followed her out, saying something about making sure Cyrus wouldn't chicken out and run back home.

Heily's friends arrived a few seconds later, all lip gloss and glittery fabrics. They giggled at the new sight of Cyrus for several torturous moments, before stealing Heily away and leaving Cyrus to follow in their wake. The older girls chatted, gossiped and giggled, quickly forgetting about the tag-along child on their walk to school.

What were they always *giggling* about? Cyrus pouted, watching them disappear over the street's slope. Alone, the air felt nice and quiet around her…until three teenagers zoomed past on rollerboards, sending up dust that made her nose wrinkle.

She followed the diamond pattern mosaics that ran along the sidewalk. There were mosaics everywhere in town—rimming streets, fountains, and the walls of structures.

Terraced hills rose to one side above the town rooftops, green and pleasant above the maroon, four-sided roofs and whitewashed walls. As she walked, she wished she could wander up there among the crops instead of facing people at school today.

Her nervousness escalated when she finally reached the white columned school, making her feet drag slower than a snail. Kids all around were scrutinizing her new appearance as she passed by.

Reaching her desk, she sat on the edge of her seat. Children in the room snickered and began whispering to one another. Chins nodded her way, making it obvious who they were talking about.

It wasn't until recess, though, that she really wished invisibility was her superpower. Classmates circled her like beady-eyed vultures.

"What? It's been a *girl* all this time? Who knew! Hahahaa!"

"Who could know, with that silly cherry-top head?"

"Bahaa. Cherry-top! Cherry-top!"

They jeered and chanted, and she pouted back sourly.

"Can I have some whip cream with that?" one boy joked,

scrubbing a hand through her hair and messing it up.

"Stop it!" She jerked away.

"Did you think changing your clothes and painting your face would make you one of us?"

"*Teehee*, as if!" laughed a smirking brunette.

"Cherry-top is just a girly boy who's confused. Vempar blood does that to people, y'know," tutted another, and they laughed harder.

Clenching both fists so hard they turned white, Cyrus marched away, past the ridicule and taunts, past the playground, to the farthest edge where it was muddy and smelly from last night's rain and where she could hide among the tall bushes in peace.

So much for *that* plan. She never should have listened to Heily! She kicked at the soggy grass.

She'd always be a half-blood, and always be targeted for it. "I wish...I wish I hadn't been born in this stupid town."

She listened to the hum of the town's single airship as it slowly rose, propellers whirring. If only somebody would accept her just the way she was...but some dreams were too much to dream.

"No," came a voice behind her.

She squeaked and turned around, coming face to face with a pair of gleaming copper eyes, flecked with blue like sprinkled rain.

Huntter, a boy who was a year older, stood there. He was cute with thick, fluffy brown hair that jutted bangs down his forehead, except he always wore a glare that could make rocks tremble.

Sometimes she would catch glimpses of his shadow during recess or as she walked home. But whenever she met his eye or tried to draw near, he would melt back and vanish, elusive as a wolf.

He went to the Argos Corps Academy, and had on their olive-colored uniform, training to one day become an Argos and protect humans from enemies, such as vempars.

"What do you mean, *No?*" She tried to smooth back strands of stubborn hair peeking out from perturbed hairclips.

"You shouldn't wish for something different," Huntter stated bluntly. Those intense copper eyes held her frozen. "Don't be what other people want you to be. They call you names to hurt your feelings, but they're just empty idiots trying to satisfy their need for attention. Ignore them."

She gaped, speechless. Not only was he talking to her, but giving advice? And the way he spoke was so grown-up.

Huntter's mouth hesitated, his gaze fidgeted. "I know what it's like to be…different. But stay the kind girl you are. Don't let mean people change you."

Cyrus's wide eyes showed her surprise better than words could. Before she could speak, though, Huntter shrunk back and sprinted away, vanishing once more into the street shadows.

She let her outstretched hand fall back to her side, and tipped her head up at the pale sky. A solitary cloud drifted its shadow slowly over the town's curved roof tiles.

"Don't let mean people change me…? Why does Huntter care?" she asked it.

That boy really was a mystery.

Her wrists began aching again, and she rubbed them.

2

A current of warm air wove through Elvenstone Town, carrying with it the scent of spring. Years had passed, and Cyrus would soon turn thirteen come summer. She held her arms out, knees bent, ready during a game of longball-tag.

"Catch it! *Catch it!*" a scruffy boy shouted her way.

Cyrus ran into a leap—grabbing the longball out of the air before her feet landed back down.

"Touchdown!" She waved the ball in triumph, all sweaty.

Her team hollered in victory, waving their arms and making faces at the losing side.

"I can't believe she caught it," a gangly boy commented.

"Heh, just like a *boy*," added another.

They snickered at their little joke.

Cyrus tossed the ball over her shoulder without looking. The ball bounced off the gangly boy's head and into his friend's face. Both groaned, holding an aching head and sore nose.

Cyrus hid a smirk; longball-tag was great fun. But it was also hurting her wrists more than before. She adjusted the fingerless gloves that wrapped around her wrists and hands, keeping them stiff and safe. White lines like scars now zigzagged around each wrist like a bracelet, hidden beneath the glove fabric. There was no explanation for it, and it wasn't something she could openly talk about.

The thrill of the game still bubbled inside her, but deflated when she glimpsed Heily walk past the field—a disapproving frown clear on her pretty face. Cyrus grumbled under her breath.

As Cyrus left the field and followed the sidewalk home, her thoughts strayed to the future. She couldn't stay forever in a town that didn't want her, could she? Some boys might let her join in on games, but that was the extent of her social life. No one wanted to be associated with her.

'What is it you want me to do, Lord God?' she prayed silently to the Creator as the sun dipped below the terraced hills. *'What am I supposed to do with this life? I can't just stay here and... I want something meaningful.'* She wiped off a frustrated tear.

Once back home, she dumped the trash into the pickup bin and watered their small garden, before finally taking off her shoes and heading inside into the kitchen. She grabbed a seat and opened a container of crackers, munching them over the counter.

Narcissa strode past, switching on the oilpowder stove to begin work on dinner. She fingered the engraving on the wall that represented Suez, a god in folklore whose body some believed had formed their continent.

It made the woman angry that Cyrus had a different belief, following only Lord God.

"I thought I told you to take a shower before coming in the kitchen," said Narcissa.

Cyrus looked down at her clothes, which had some dirt smudges and wet spots. "I will, I'm just grabbing a snack."

Narcissa made a sound through her teeth. "Always playing games, always dirty..." she muttered, adding a Néos curse. "Is it that vempar half of you that keeps you from being dainty and clean?"

Cyrus chewed, swallowed. "You make me do most of the chores—how could I be clean? Sorry I'm not another Heily."

The human woman barked a laugh. "No, you're most certainly not, tainted the way you are."

A cracker broke in Cyrus's grip. "My mother was different—not *tainted*."

Narcissa lowered a slab of meat into the soup pot. "All vempars are monsters. And the sooner you realize that, the better. You should focus more on your human half."

Anger heated Cyrus's face. She lowered her hand to the counter.

Her mother had never been a monster. No matter what this town thought, or what this human woman said, it wasn't true!

A sharp gasp made Cyrus look up. Narcissa had frozen, staring at the counter.

Cyrus followed her stare to the metal spoon Cyrus's finger was resting on—only now, the spoon was melting itself into a blob. She watched as the blob of liquid metal drifted over, into her palm, and there re-molded itself into the shape of a knife.

A scream tore from Narcissa's throat, and Cyrus flinched away from the knife, letting it fall to the floor where it clattered solidly.

"Elemental Manipulation." Narcissa pointed a trembling finger at what Cyrus had just done. "You've inherited that evil magic from your mother's blood!"

Cyrus backed away, not understanding.

Narcissa shouted, "Get out, you witch! *Get out!*"

Cyrus dodged a thrown plate and hurried outside in a panic as her step-mother's shouts followed after her. What had just happened? Her pulse was racing. She ran. And she didn't stop running until the house and the woman was out of her sight.

She found and sat on the curb by the town's bookshop, with fear and a mix of emotions churning in her chest.

A pretty mosaic of vines ran under her seat along the white street walk, and she traced the leaves absently with her gaze.

Passersby gave her stares after a while, so she decided to go hide inside.

The shop was one of the places she used whenever she needed somewhere to hide. The rows of books were a comforting maze.

Mother had an Elemental Manipulation Ability, or so Cyrus had heard from town gossip, though she never fully understood what it meant—only that it was something townspeople labeled as dark magic.

Cyrus searched through the Science aisle of the shop, until she found a curious book titled: *Vempars, & Their Ways.*

She browsed through its worn pages.

Ability: the gift that a select number of vempars are born with, also known as Elemental Manipulation. It is the power to manipulate certain elements via the wielder's essence (a form of life-energy).

In most cases, a vempar's Ability is awoken during an emotional outburst or stressful situation…

She paused. That didn't quite sound like dark magic or anything evil. More like an unusual life-energy that some vempars could put to use.

She recalled how angry she'd felt before the spoon shifted, then read on.

According to the book, it seemed that in most cases Ability was passed down through blood, though not always.

These gifted vempars were taken and trained to be made into Draevs for the Draev Guardian League—the elite fighting force of the Vemparic Kingdom.

One page showed a list of Ability classifications:

Terravis (Eartha)
Blazevis (Fire)
Liquivis (Water)
Aerovis (Air)
Metamorvis (Transformation)
Armavis (Weapons)
Electrovis (Electromagnetic)

Cyrus sat back, taking in what this could mean for her, if she had the power of a Draev. Would the town find out? Would she be arrested, or worse?

She didn't want to go back to the house, but there was nowhere else for her to go. Maybe Dad could reason with Narcissa and gloss this whole incident over...

She placed the book back on the shelf and made her slow trek back home.

She tiptoed through the door, only to find that Narcissa was in a fit, ranting at Heily about the ordeal, while the step-sister stood looking confused and afraid.

When Narcissa spotted Cyrus, she began pointing and shouting, "May the god Suez burn the evil that's inside you!"

Dad was there, and he gripped the woman's arm and raised his voice. "Stop shouting, and calm yourself! What happened today was a fluke, nothing more. Understand? No one needs to know of it. Don't ruin the Sole family name any further than it already has been."

Narcissa snarled under her breath. Heily remained uncomfortably silent.

"You won't let this dark fluke happen again. Will you?" Dad turned to Cyrus. She nodded feebly. "Good. I don't want to hear it ever mentioned again. It's time for dinner."

As they went to the table, Cyrus instead slumped her shoulders and went upstairs to her room, losing all appetite.

She sat on the floor before the window, watching dusk as it gradually veiled the sky with its starry cloak.

She had prayed for a purpose, something important to do that would make people stop judging her, but now things were worse than ever. Being half-vempar was bad enough, but now she had the power of a Draev too?

'Why did you make me this way, Lord?' she cried.

She didn't care about ruining the Sole name, but this Ability, or whatever it was, had to be kept secret, no matter what. Cyrus had once overheard Dad talking with members of the Argos Corps: the specialized combat division and protectors of humankind, the exterminators of vempars—in particular, of Draevs. And they'd been talking about *her*.

"Contact us if she begins showing any vempar traits, or anything like the Ability her mother had," they had said.

The Argos didn't exactly say what they would *do* to Cyrus if she did have Ability. But she knew what they did to vempars down in the town's square... Her gut turned queasy. She sat there as night crept in through the window, wrapped up in her battered emotions.

The next day came and went, and then several more, and Dad didn't contact the Argos Corps about her Ability. She still feared there was a chance he might, one day. Whether it was guilt over Mother's murder keeping him silent for now, or social status, how much longer could it last? Surely it wasn't for love; he'd never loved her.

Meanwhile, there was a constant undercurrent of tension in the house. None of them talked during breakfast, unless necessary, nor met her gaze. Narcissa avoided her like a poison that might corrupt them if they got too close. The woman's frown was disdainful each morning when Cyrus passed through the kitchen on her way to the door, and each late afternoon when she came home. Cyrus wasn't sure how much more of it all she could take.

She used to wonder how Dad could hate vempars so much when, in the past, he'd gone and married one. But Heily had given her the answer one evening, years back, while doing embroidery on a scarf. Cyrus thought back to that memory now:

"Dad didn't know your mama was a vempar then, Cyrus. She'd kept it secret. And by the time he discovered the truth, they were already married, with you on the way."

Something about that felt off, and Cyrus had voiced so.

"I'm just telling you what my mama told me," replied Heily, threading the needle.

She didn't feel like Heily was lying, but something about the story was fishy. How could Dad *not* have known what Mother was?

The story continued that when Dad didn't want anything more to do with Mother, instead of divorcing her (he wouldn't forsake the vows, and shame himself further in front of the town) Mother had been allowed to stay and live in a cabin just outside Elvenstone's wall.

Cyrus imagined how hard life must have been for her. Maybe much like how it was for herself, now, without friend or family, isolated…

Another school day passed, as she held these thoughts close, and she stayed after to join a group of orphans in a game of longball-tag. Younger orphans didn't care as much about what she was, at least right now, and she enjoyed playing with them.

Mist rolled along the terraced hills beyond town as the day grew late. Cyrus finished one last game before heading home, and she breathed in the calming scent of moisture-filled air.

She decided to take the long route home. There was plenty of time before dinner, and the cloudy day with its damp, cool air and earthy scent was beckoning her to stay outside.

She let it wash away thoughts of the past and problematic Abilities, and let it soothe her soul.

Strolling white street after street, she curved through town following a line of orange mosaic flowers. Teens on rollerboards zipped by. A small cargo carrier full of jars rattled past, and chatter from an open tavern drifted across the sidewalk. Melody from the town's bell tower sounded out the evening hour, spooking a flock of pigeons.

There was no sign of Huntter's shadow today. Usually she spotted him when she left the school building, though he never hung around to talk. He must be off on a training exercise with his mentor...

"Hit him!"

"Slimy monster. *Haha*, try and reach us if you can!"

"Do you know why you're caged up like an animal? Because that's what you and all your kind are—*animals*."

Taunts were echoing through a side street that opened onto the Town Square. She spotted the group, who were throwing sticks, rocks and whatnot at a hanging death-cage—one of several lined up; cages of rough black silver bars and straps bolted together, suspended in the air by rope and thick T-cross poles. There was no escaping one of those. Black silver was unbreakable, except by dragon fire, as far as she knew.

Death-cages dotted Town Square, showing off criminals and caught vempars for the public to scorn as they starved and rotted away. She always avoided going near the square. It was a haunting sight she didn't need. But now, against her better judgment, she was venturing close, drawn in by those taunts.

Squinting, Cyrus spied the death-cage currently under assault: a male contained within its bars. He had pointed ears, with ridges similar to a bat's lining the insides.

A vempar.

The prisoner's hunched body looked gaunt beneath the

ragged clothes clinging to him; his head dirty under a mop of long, oily black hair and grime. Dark circles under his eye sockets made them look sunken, his skin drawn and parched. The result of no food or water, and nothing but rain from the sky for a shower; and a lack of *essence*—the life-energy vempars fed on. Bruises and welts covered the exposed flesh the rags couldn't hide, and his bony hands gripped the black silver bars.

Cyrus felt a pang of sympathy in her chest, and couldn't stop her feet from guiding her closer. His body wasn't Healing, probably due to lack of *essence*.

Did the man deserve this fate? Just for being born a different race? If he was a murderer, then she'd understand, but most dangerous vempars were killed on the spot—not brought back to the cages. Most likely this person had been caught trespassing through human lands.

"Hey!" Cyrus called to the group taunting him. "There's no reason to throw rocks. Leave him alone."

The group turned, all eyes fixed on her.

Uh, did she just say that? *Out loud?* When she was one girl, and they were seven boys?

Oh crud.

"Well, look who's come to greet us." The tallest boy flashed an unpleasant grin.

It was too late to back down now.

"I guess their kind come in packs," laughed another boy. "Where *one* is, there's bound to be *more*—not unlike cockroaches."

Cyrus searched for something to say.

The group drew near.

Her breath hitched in her throat. She almost took a step back before catching herself. She dashed forward, instead, and placed herself between the gang and the death-cage. "Vempars are people. They have feelings, same as you," she argued.

The imprisoned vempar raised his head slightly.

She didn't know what she was doing, only that she couldn't stand to see someone being tormented.

The boys edged closer. "Puh-leeze. Don't try and get us with that cheesy *They've got feelings and emotions* stuff. We don't care. They're all murderous scum who feed on us," said the tallest.

"You don't know that!" she protested.

He grinned. "How about *you* come play with us instead? You motherless tramp."

Her hand gripped the pole that held the death-cage, trying to keep her balance, her mind racing.

The group moved in, circling, cutting off any escape.

Heart pounding in her ears, she struggled to think. How had she manipulated the spoon?

Was there anything metal she could use now?

'Pull...stretch...remold the metal...'

Her eyes cast about, searching for something, anything.

The scrape of the gang's footsteps drew closer...then halted.

Cyrus glanced over to see why.

The boys stood motionless, the whites of their eyes showing and their jaws hanging slack.

It was so startling. She followed their stare—down to where her left hand was gripping the iron pole.

Strips of iron had peeled away—liquefying, elongating, reaching out like fingers with knives for nails.

Then the knives flung free, heading for the boys.

They shrieked, all of them ducking and diving aside.

"She's got freak powers like *them*!"

"Quick, call the Argos!"

The gang split and sprinted off in different directions before Cyrus could react.

The Argos? No, *no no no*, not them!

They'd kill her. They'd sentence her to a death-cage!

Where could she run? Where could she hide?

None of this was supposed to be happening!

'What should I do, Lord God?'

Tears stung her eyes as dread overcame her.

This would be the end. There was no hope left…

"Girl!"

Cyrus jumped at the husky voice at her back, and half-turned toward the cage, lifting her chin to meet the vempar's intense gaze. He wasn't speaking in human Néos, but Inglish: the Common Tongue she'd been learning in school.

"Girl, set me free and I can take you away from here." His words came out parched, yet life gleamed like a spark in his eyes.

Away *how*? The Argos Corps would track her down! And could she really trust this person, a captive vempar?

Despite her doubts and concern, Cyrus imagined the cage's bars bending out. Eyes shut, and right hand splayed against the pole, she *felt* through the pole's metal up to the cage's metal…and willed it to bend.

Brrreeee—Kk!

The black silver bent outward, enough for the man to wriggle out between the bars and drop down, landing on his bare, starved-thin feet with a painful grunt.

"Well, that's quite an Ability ya got! Able t' bend black silver 'n all." The gaunt vempar stumbled from having gone who-knew-how-long without using his legs. His vempar Healing kicked in though, rejuvenating his body—an average person would have collapsed in agony.

"I thought your Healing wasn't working?" Cyrus asked.

"I've been savin' the last bit of it up for an escape," he replied.

Cyrus gawked, wishing she'd inherited *that* from her mother. "You sure you can run?"

He waved her concern aside. "I can handle myself without

essence for now, missy." He grabbed her arm and pulled her down the nearest alley, quickly ducking into the shadows. He spoke low, "You know this town better than I do. Guide me to the edge, and I'll take matters from there."

A chill ran up Cyrus's spine. She was speaking to a vempar, and he was gripping her arm. This was all happening too fast. When she woke this morning, she didn't think it'd be her last day in Elvenstone. That she'd be running for her life, leaving everything familiar behind. But she had to, or the Argos would kill her.

Cyrus gave a small nod and took the lead, making sure to keep to narrow, dim alleys and pathways through town as they fled. There was one place she had to stop by first, though. If she really was leaving Elvenstone for good, then there were important items she had to bring with her.

Stopping in the shadowed space between two houses, she requested, "Wait here, please?" before climbing a short oak tree to reach her bedroom window. It was cracked open to let in air, easy to lift and squeeze through. Below, the vempar made a surprised, frustrated sound and paced back and forth.

Cyrus didn't waste time: quick grabbing a backpack and throwing on a hooded cloak over her T-shirt.

She picked up the old stuffed-animal bunny on her nightstand. Its cheerful face smiled up at her, just like it always had—the first and only thing Mother had made for her. The only thing she had, besides a ruby pendant necklace, to remember Mother by.

She stuffed both securely in the backpack before shouldering it. Heily's laugh sounded from the adjacent room suddenly, and Cyrus froze.

Was she really going to do this? Leave forever?

"You're such a good daughter, Heily," spoke Narcissa's voice.

Cyrus pressed her ear to the wall and listened.

"I don't know how you put up with having that tainted half-blood for a sister."

"It's the right thing to do, Mama." Heily sounded pleased. "Show kindness to her, just as we would any stray. And besides, if things become too scary, I know we can trust Dad to take care of it. He can contact the Argos Corps anytime."

Cyrus pulled her ear back, her heart hardening in a knot.

She didn't belong here. She *never* had.

With resolve flooding through her veins, she climbed back out and down to the waiting vempar.

As they hurried down the next alley, she couldn't help but glance back at the house one last time, murmuring one silent goodbye to the life and family inside.

Shouts echoed off the whitewashed walls they passed, seeming to come from every direction at once—the Argos Corps were searching for them. They ducked behind a parked cargo carrier while it was delivering produce.

Cyrus's dry throat couldn't swallow.

Heart thumping like a frantic rabbit's foot, she ran in a crouch across the last street, with the vempar close behind. The low wall that encircled the town lay ahead, just ten yards away. She pointed it out to him. The vempar gained a new burst of speed, then, and pulled her along by the elbow.

As soon as they approached the wall's stone face, shouts rang behind them, fervent and furious, in a race to stop the two criminals' escape.

We've been spotted!" Cyrus yelped, and darted a quick look back. Humans in olive uniforms were filing through the streets and scaling rooftops, their belts holstering weapons, and feet clad in thick-tread boots—the Argos Corps.

Those on the roofs were taking aim with the barrels of their gunswords.

"Move!" the vempar growled at her side. And before she could react, he picked her up and tossed her with great strength onto the wall top.

She caught her balance and gathered herself together, then turned to reach and help him climb up as bullets chipped the stone, barely missing him.

Chut-chut-chut! Kk-pm-pm!

He didn't need much help, digging his bare toes into the wall and lunging upward, catching the edge and hoisting himself onto the wall top.

They barely had time to duck and fall over to the other side before a volley of bullets passed where their heads had been.

Landing on cushioning grass, Cyrus and the vempar made a dash for the tree line, ducking low, sprinting across the stretch of ground between them and the shelter of the woods.

Two bullets grazed past, nicking red across her companion's upper arm. But then no more came. The Argos would pursue them on foot now.

"Don't stop!" The vempar panted, gripping her hand tight in his and practically dragging her to keep up with him.

Don't stop? As if she didn't know that! For a starved, lanky person, he sure was fast.

A gust of warm air whipped her bangs across her vision, and a sudden burst of excitement rose within her chest. Running wild and free without bounds across the green expanse toward freedom—and a new life—sent a thrill through her. She was really leaving Elvenstone behind. Leaving the past and pain behind to rush forward into an unknown future, which beckoned like a hand reaching out to her.

She was *free*…

And then the hum of engines came.

3

Argos bladecycles pierced through the woods, veering around trees trunks and tall ferns—gliding over the ground via twin sets of ducted fans, in place of wheels, tilted in a V for stability. Cyrus could hear their humming engines approach as the vempar kept her running in a low crouch.

"I suppose we can't outrun the darn things," he muttered, looking frustrated. "Wait here," he then told her.

She crouched under a fern, and watched as he inched his way toward a trunk and straightened his back, hiding behind it. She was about to question what he was doing, when a bladecycle zipped past the trunk and he launched himself at the driver—knocking the human unconscious and off it in one swift shove.

The vempar plopped onto the bladecycle's seat, grabbed the handles and clumsily steered the V-tilted fans in Cyrus's direction. She hopped onboard, wrapping both arms around him from behind, and the engine sped them away through the underbrush foliage.

A shout rang out as they were spotted, and the hum of more bladecycles came in pursuit. The vempar steered them into the thick of the ferns. Fronds slapped at them; he grunted against the whip-like stings and Cyrus hid her face behind his back.

The plants grew taller the farther they went, arching over their heads until they were concealed from the Argos' sight.

Cyrus wasn't sure how long it was before the hum of bladecycles diminished and they seemed to have finally lost their pursuers. The vempar didn't pause, however. He drove on for as long as he could, just to be sure they were truly alone and safe.

When they did stop for a break, Cyrus's arms peeled off stiffly from around him, and he flexed his aching hands.

"Name's Gandif," he said after a moment of rest, and held out a hand. "Thanks for helpin' me out, 'n sorry ya had to run away like this." His odd Inglish accent wasn't consistent.

She shook the hand. "I'm Cyrus. And don't worry, it was time for me to leave anyway."

"Oh?"

She turned her face away, not wanting to talk about it.

"You speak perfect Inglish for being so young. I've gotten rusty with my human Néos."

She shrugged. "We learn early. Everybody's supposed to know the Common Tongue."

"Welp!" Gandif rose and stretched. "We can spend the night here, or keep goin'. What do ya think?"

"Keep going," she said firmly.

He glanced down at her, then shrugged.

Several more hours passed riding through the trees, leaving Elvenstone farther behind. Gandif kept the speed steady enough so he didn't have to keep both hands firmly on the handles.

They kept to the fringes of the thick, mysterious Magica Forest, where it was safer and easier for travelers to navigate—or ragtag runaways. The Argos would give up tracking them, now that they'd left human territory.

Night soon came, like an enveloping cloak turning the forest into a world of glowing fungus, blinking fireflies, and nocturnal calls.

"I'm headin' back to my home city. Yer welcome t' join me, missy, but you don't have to," Gandif told her, once they'd stopped for the night, stretching first his arms then his bony legs.

Cyrus looked sidelong up at his scruffy chin. Now that she was free of Elvenstone, she didn't know what to do. The thought of venturing into the Vemparic Kingdom chilled her to the bone; but if she didn't stick with this guy, she'd be left here on her own—and she had nowhere to go and zero navigational skills. "What city is it?" she asked.

"Draethvyle, the capital itself."

Cyrus poked at a glowing mushroom. Draethvyle was where she'd heard her mother was from.

"I'll come with you a bit longer," she said.

"Do whatever fancies ya, missy." Gandif shrugged without concern.

Cyrus let her weary head rest against a patch of cushioning moss, its green glow warm on her cheek, and her body sank fast into sleep. The vempar kept half alert, resting back on a tree stump, as if wary of what might be lurking in the dark forest's recesses.

～

Swirls of fog fingered the surrounding birch trees, which stood white and silent as ghosts. Someone, somewhere, was shrieking.

Cyrus lifted her head out of the dirt tunnel and saw the encircling trees like silent ghosts. Something was slumped on the ground, something that had red hair like her mother's.

'*Who is that?*' she thought.

A charcoal hand materialized from the fog, and she shrank back. A mouth opened wide, black and bottomless, dripping blood.

Swannn!

Cyrus woke, sweat dripping down her neck. It was the same nightmare, again. She rubbed her temples and calmed her chest. Gray dawn had arrived, and not too soon for Cyrus's aching head and empty stomach. She saw Gandif was already awake.

They rode on through the dim haze as it lit the trees. And when they stopped to hunt out berries and clean water, the light got snuffed out by rain clouds.

She rinsed off the dirt still clinging to her in a clear pond. Gandif had to strip to his underwear before he could clean off the stink and grime of death-cages. She kept behind a mossy boulder meanwhile, not looking, munching orange colored berries and some lemony leaves he said were edible.

Once finished, he searched about and went over to a boulder that had a massive dent in its side. She watched as he crouched down and yanked something out from underneath it: clothes.

When he saw her staring, he shrugged. "Never know when ya might need clothes. I like t' keep a few things buried around, just in case."

She didn't have the nerve to ask what sort of person keeps spare clothes buried about the woods.

He finished shouldering on a trench coat, and donned boots, belt, and a wide-brimmed hat—a gold chain from his pocket he laced around the hat's base. She watched curiously, but didn't ask.

"We'd best go on foot from here," said Gandif. "Wouldn't want people t' get the wrong idea, us ridin' a human-style bladecycle."

She nodded, and he stuffed the bladecycle against the same boulder, piling leaves and branches over it along with his dirty clothes.

They left the forest, coming into woodland, which soon thinned to white birch trees as she followed Gandif onward, the white bark summoning thoughts of the nightmare, which she quickly pushed away. The trees then fell away and the ground sloped down into an expanse of grassland, stretching far as the eye could see. Cyrus paused at the edge, taking in the view. Gray clouds swirled patterns across the sky, and drizzle rain speckled the open land and her cloak.

She blinked away droplets condensed on her eyelashes, and raised her hood, in case there were any watchful eyes lurking nearby.

Beside her, Gandif turned, his hollow-from-hunger eyes emitting a green-leaf glow in the gray light. "So, yer a fellow hybrid, eh?" he said.

"Fellow? You're half-human too?"

"Meh, only a fraction. Not as much as you."

True, he could Heal and he looked nothing like a human. Life must have been easier for him, being able to blend in with his own kind, instead of wondering which half of himself he belonged to.

"How did you get caught?" She'd been meaning to ask, but hadn't been brave enough to talk about personal problems.

"Ohhh." He combed through his long, curly hair. "Fell into a trap, ya could say." Fear clouded his brow suddenly then. "Clover's gonna have my hide when she finds out I ended up in another death-cage…" He swallowed.

Cyrus almost asked what he meant by *another*, but instead asked, "Who?"

"My wife. I can hear her lecture now, callin' me all manner of impolite names." Gandif hunched his shoulders and shook his shaggy head. "Anywho," his chin tipped her way, "I won't even begin t' wonder how-under-the-sun *you* could happen in Elvenstone. A vempar and a human livin' in a town full of Argos? *Pah!*" His hands perched on his hips. "What confuses me most, though, is how you've inherited Elemental Manipulation Ability." His expression narrowed and he leaned closer. "You ought t' be trained to use that Ability right, missy."

She shied away.

"Only a Draev Guardian can teach ya. And, well, seeing as you've got no home or place to go…"

She swallowed, knowing what he was getting at.

"…Draethvyle could be a great place for you," he said. His head tilted with a lopsided grin, as if this were a special opportunity and not some death trap. "There's a school there that teaches Ability users. You'd fit right in!"

Cyrus's eyes widened. "Fit right in with *vempars*? Live in a whole city full of them?"

How could she possibly— It was crazy, *suicidal*! The first vempar she met would either enslave her or consume all of her *essence* until she was a crusted corpse. That wasn't on her Survival To-Do List!

"Listen, kid." The ragged man brushed a handful of curls back from his temple. "Without a home or place to belong, you're easy prey for anybody—and I don't just mean vempars. Any outlaw lookin' to make fast cash would be more than happy t' sell you into slavery, or worse." He twirled a finger. "Harsh truth."

Cyrus's chin sunk. He was right. She couldn't take care of herself. And not just anyone would accept a stray Ability user in their home. Her options were limited.

'*You're not a little girl anymore, Cyrus Sole. Toughen up!*' she thought to herself and slapped her cheeks, even though a grown woman would faint at the mere thought of such a foolhardy plan.

The Vemparic Kingdom—the place where humans were hated, where humans were viewed as slaves and a source of food. And the place where she could start a new life, discover the gray area that was her vempar half…

Was this really what Lord God had planned for her?

"A tad afraid, eh?" Gandif gave her a toothy smile.

She pouted sideways.

"I can understand if y' are. I wasn't exactly happy myself when I was taken by humans." He moved down the grassy slope in long strides, toward the stretch of open, endless green before them.

She scurried after him.

"Listen, Cyrus missy," he said once she caught up. "If you're nervous, you can hide yer identity n' pretend to be a vempar. All you'll need is a pair of fake fangs, and keep those human ears hidden behind that bushy hair. The fact you've got Ability should in itself be enough proof t' fool anybody."

"But…" she bit her lip, "if someone *does* find out…"

Gandif quirked an eyebrow down at her. "Ya don't have t' come, missy. The forest faeryn might take you in; they're mostly nice…though they'd dislike yer Ability."

She watched the damp grasses bending underfoot.

"Nothing 'll come of yer power that way, though, and what a wasteful shame that'd be!" He grunted, scratching at the stubble along his jawline. "There are too few with Ability nowadays."

Was he trying to make her feel obligated to train?

Maybe living with the faeryn wouldn't be so bad. But if another incident with metal happened…

"I guess I could give it a try," Cyrus said, and her stomach flipped on the verge of nausea. "But I'll have to escape if things get—*you know*—dangerous."

If she'd be able to escape, that is. Could a human outrun a vempar?

Despite the danger, mastering her Ability could prove useful. Maybe Mother had trained there; maybe this was her chance to learn about the world she had come from?

Cyrus spotted a satisfied curl on the man's lips, and she frowned up at him.

"There's one more thing I should probably mention," Gandif said, and tipped his head up to the frothing clouds overhead. "The Draev Guardian Academy can be your teacher and temporary home, but…"

There was a long pause, and Cyrus tensed.

"…The school is mostly for boys."

There was a longer pause, and then she exclaimed. "WHAT? You're telling me this *now?*" Grass caught at her shoe, tripping her.

Seeing the look on her face, Gandif cleared his throat. "*Ahem.* Sorry, missy, but Elemental Manipulation mostly happens in males. Rarely is it in females, which makes you quite unique." He rubbed his nose.

"I don't want to be *unique.*"

"There's one or two girls born with Ability, now and then. You might see some at the school. But if ya really want t' blend in with the crowd and not draw attention to yerself, then I suggest you pretend to be a boy."

Cyrus balked. Could he not see how terrifying this was? It was bad enough kids teased her for *looking* like a boy, but now she was going to play *being* one?

"And anyway, you'll be safer as a male." Amusement lit in Gandif's eyes. "The last thing you'd want is some vempar boy falling in love with you." He laughed then, as if it'd be the funniest thing, and she scowled at him.

Like it or not though, he was probably right. The better she blended in with the students, the safer her half-human secret would be.

"Fine. It shouldn't be too hard for me. I always got boy roles in school plays. I must be a natural at it," she muttered.

"That's the spirit!" He slapped her on the back. Then he raised a hand, pointing beyond the sea of grass. "There she is, the beauty herself: Draethvyle City!"

Cyrus squinted to see through the gathering mist. There it was: wall, towers and spires rising from the land like a decorative crown. The city was built upon the only thing that could be considered a hill in the expanse of grasslands.

She inhaled.

This was it, a new beginning. No turning back.

She strode with determination in her steps.

A strange fallen statue among the lulling sway of grass caught her attention as she passed it—the clay head of an eagle.

PART 2
AKEN

4

"Hmm hm-hm *hmmm~*"

Seven-year-old Aken-Shou hummed a lively tune as he made his way along the snow-covered path through the woods. The chill breeze brushed his sun-bright hair about his shoulders, his bangs falling over his left eye as the rest pulled back in a half-ponytail.

He glanced up at the trees which were dark in the fading light, their limbs like arms and fingers reaching through the shadows. Snow floated down silently, one snowflake landing on his eyelashes. Blankets of white had already caked the ground and now reflected an eerie light as twilight drew near.

Aken shuffled down the path as it curved and lowered. A small lantern swung back and forth on the ash pole propped across his shoulder. He continued humming the cheerful song, lantern swaying.

"Taters taters, I dream in my head

They float around as I lie in my bed,

Hot and mushy with buttery sauce

Before they eat you, gobble them hot…"

Krnch.

Aken paused at the sound, and his pointy ears twitched to listen behind him. Stories about the Wandering Wraith and other myths filled his head, making fear bubble inside him.

He turned to see what had made the sound, but nothing was there. Only snow and the silent woods.

"…Huh." His brow furrowed. "C'mon, keep focused," he told himself. "I gotta get home with these herbs before Mom gets mad." He patted the bundle tucked inside his winter coat, then tugged the wool scarf closer around his chin. "*Man*, my fangs are gonna fall off from all this stupid, freezing cold. I hate winter!"

Krnch.

The sound came again, from the right.

Aken looked through the corner of his right eye, but still nothing was there.

A chill brushed up his back. Earlier on his trek to the herb grower's house, the woods had been nice. But now that daylight was almost gone…

'*I just gotta hurry,*' he thought to himself.

Skrnch-chnk.

Again the sound of someone—or something—approached from behind.

He nervously looked left.

Trnk.

He spun around.

K-krrk.

He shifted back, pulse racing. Creaking twigs and crunching snow seemed to be coming from every direction at once.

He turned round and round, gripping the lantern pole like a weapon, scanning the trees.

And then, it jumped out at him.

"Uwah!" Aken stumbled back and held the pole ready for attack.

A black squirrel sat there, pawing the snow at his feet, and it cocked its head and blinked dark eyes up at him.

His grip on the pole relaxed. He suddenly felt very stupid.

All that fear over a squirrel.

The furry critter tilted its big fluffy ears, and made a chattering noise like laughter, before bounding up the nearest tree to perch on a branch. It seemed to be grinning down at him. Aken pouted, and was tempted to grab a rock and throw it. "Cheeky rodent, I oughta make a scarf outta that furry tail of yours."

The squirrel chattered more laughter, and with its tail flicked snow off the branch at him.

"*Gah!* Why you—"

A dark shape grew out of the corner of Aken's eye, and he stilled. He wasn't alone.

Aken leaped to the side, away from the shape. But his foot slipped on a layer of ice and he fell backwards, landing against the base of a trunk, scraping his elbows on crusty roots.

"Ah—ah! Stay back, I'm warning you. I'm a scary vempar!" Aken shouted at the wraith-like shape, and struggled to get back on his feet, gripping at the roots behind him for support. "I'm warning you!"

The looming form wrapped in black shrouds waited before him, a wraith come to steal his life.

"Now, now," spoke the wraith, "Surely a child like you wouldn't harm an old, traveling faeryn like me, *reh?*"

Aken scrambled up to his knees and blinked to clear his vision. The black shroud fizzled to a dark cloak with the hood drawn up, tattered and worn with age—just like the hunchback beneath it. The hunchback's voice creaked and wobbled, either trying to cackle or chuckle, but it sounded like a cat trapped in a trashcan.

A faeryn, not the Wandering Wraith? The old man's skin was blue, and he looked ready to fall over from the slightest passing breeze, now that Aken could see him clearly.

But appearances could be deceiving; he wasn't about to let down his guard.

"Why's your skin blue? I've never seen a blue faeryn," Aken questioned.

"That's because my kind are rare now. I'm a moonlight faeryn. But don't go telling people about it," insisted the elder through a croak. "What is your name, child?"

The black squirrel chirped suddenly, bounding from the tree to land on the faeryn's creaky shoulder. A bony hand offered an acorn, which the squirrel snatched up without hesitation.

Aken frowned. "It's Aken-Shou...erm, sir."

The man's already wrinkly forehead wrinkled deeper, and his face of blue-lake skin cracked a smile. "So, it *is* you," he breathed.

Aken cocked his head.

"The False Guardian, whose destiny is tied with the Swan Princess," he furthered, with a distant look to his eyes.

Aken waited, then made a sound in his throat, and the moonlight faeryn's far-away look returned to the here and now.

"I am a *watcher of the stars*, a listener of Lord God. And I have been sent to return something to you, lad."

The squirrel's tail flapped like a furry flag on the old perch.

Aken blinked. "Okay?" Was this man growing senile as well as old? *Return something.* What, and from who? Nobody cared about him.

"Keep this." A blue hand held out to him a leather-bound book, in surprisingly good condition for how yellowed and ancient the pages were.

Aken took and examined it curiously. It was thick, with a title marked on the spine.

"A Bible?" He blinked. "Uh...well...it's, *erm*, I mean... I'm pretty sure this never belonged to me. So I don't know what you mean by *returning something*. And anyway, my parents'll get mad."

He felt the leather gingerly, a series of questions running through his head.

An older kid at school had said the Bible was one of several books of ancient history from another world, and that it was written by the Creator, Lord God. It sounded cool. Dad got mad at the very idea, though, and called people who believed such things idiots.

Why was a faeryn traveler giving him this?

The hunchback held a finger up to his cracked lips, "Let this be our little secret."

"Not to be rude, but you aren't making any sense."

"It does not have to make any sense, right now." The man opened his other hand, where a tiny glass orb shone in his palm, as if a star had been trapped inside it. "A spark of light, a star to guide the way through the darkness in your mind, Aken-Shou. With this, you will find the reborn princess."

The orb rolled into Aken's hand. "Sure..." he said as he stared at its clear, glossy surface.

"Best hurry home, now, lad! It's getting dark," the faeryn said, drawing his hood closer, pulling Aken's attention away from the orb. "And do bring a more, *reh*, dangerous weapon with you when traveling alone." He eyed the lantern pole, clearly amused.

Aken sniffed in protest, even if the comment was accurate. "Do you live around here?"

"No, no." A blue finger rubbed the squirrel's head. "I doubt you'll be seeing me again, any time soon."

"Oh. How come?"

The man's smile tilted down a fraction. "My time as Oracle is done, my part to play in this world finished. My gift will pass on to another, soon—a young moonlight faeryn, like me," he said.

Aken cocked his head. But the man motioned with his hand, "Hurry on home. You will understand all of this when the time is right, when you are older."

The squirrel gave another laughing chirp, grinning and flapping a paw to mimic its humanoid companion.

With both items stuffed in coat pockets, Aken waved uncertainly to the old hunchback before hurrying on through the snow-packed path, lantern bouncing behind him. The cool, dark of dusk shrouded all else.

Huff-huff-huff. Aken-Shou tried to run through the deepening snow sucking at his boots, plodding up to the door of a wood-shingle, two-story house. It stood among a jumble of other wood houses, stalls, and tent structures that made up the Outskirts—a ramshackle district hugged against the city's eastern wall.

Draethvyle, capital city of the Vemparic Kingdom, was made of decorative stone, spires and peaked rooftops. But the Outskirts wasn't inside the city, everything here was wood, tent or crude brick—not pretty stone. Plain and bland, built for practical use instead of beauty. Simple homes, just like the one before him that looked ready to crumble from rot.

Aken eyed what bit of the city's high, seamless wall he could see from the dirt street that wound its way to the eastern gate. His house sat near the dividing line of the wall, where durable stone melted into wooden unkempt structures, and nice roads became dirt streets and dusty paths.

A white flake tickled his nose. The snow was drifting heavier through the thickening sky now. He looked up one last time before opening the crude door.

Aken entered. To the left, the combined little kitchen and dining room had the woodstove burning—warming the chill air that followed him inside.

"It took you long enough," came Mom's voice from the kitchen corner.

He placed the bundle of herbs on the scuffed dining table—a plain, rectangular slab. Dad wasn't there, again.

"Sorry, Mom."

She marched over, ladle propped across her narrow shoulder. "I couldn't get dinner started without these! To think I had to wait for a lazy lout." She picked through the herbs, tight-lipped.

Mom was blond, with pretty features—Aken's coloring and eyes took after her. But she was a busy woman who didn't waste time on things or people, and affection wasn't in her nature.

"Here. Drink." She set a glass of red-colored liquid on the table, a little spilling.

Aken pulled off his gloves and drank obediently. "Mm, can I help you pick berries next time? If the juice is this good, the raw berries must be even *more* good!" He attempted a cheerful smile and waited for a response.

"...When you're older," Mom said through a breath. Then she focused on adding herb leaves to a soup pot boiling over the stove.

"Will Dad be back soon?" he asked. "There's lots of snow outside. It'd be fun to build a snowman or something."

"No. Even if he was, he wouldn't have time to play games with you. Life is more important than play."

Aken hid his disappointment. He reached a hand inside his pocket, to show her the cool glass orb the old faeryn had given him, then thought better of it. She either wouldn't pay attention, or would think he was making up another fantasy tale.

Instead, he trudged up the creaky staircase to his room in the attic. The ceiling slanted on both sides with the roof, making the small room feel even more cramped. There wasn't much but simple furniture, and a sunken bed against the wall under a square window.

He set his lantern on the side table, and opened the

top drawer. His collection of tiny clay figures rattled inside. He placed the Bible in with them. Seeing the clay made him sigh and brought back a memory from several years ago:

"Mommy! Look, look what I made!" Five-year-old Aken said excitedly, tugging her over to the side of the street where he had molded figurines from the wet dirt. They were supposed to be birds, but rather lopsided and lumpy. Still, he held one up.

"Look! Watch dis, when I focuses in it." He positioned his free palm behind the bird, and thin strings of glowing *essence* connected from him to the clay. "I cans make da birdie move! See see?"

The dirt wings made awkward flapping motions, and Aken was grinning with pride. But Mom…she slapped the bird away.

"We don't do things like that, Aken-Shou! Do you want to bring unwanted attention?" she snapped, eyes alight. "We can't have that! We can't have eyes on us right now…" Her shout faded to a strangled mutter under her breath. Then she eyed him once more.

"To have power is to be shunned and feared, you little idiot." Her mouth tightened. "Behave, and keep this strange thing with clay to yourself. I better not catch you doing this again."

And with that, he remembered her kicking away the other dirt sculptures he'd so carefully made before marching off.

Now, eyeing the glass orb in his palm one last time, he put it with the clay figurines he'd made since that day and kept hidden.

Aken climbed over his bed to reach the window, settling down, resting elbows on the windowsill, chin in hands. From here, he could see over the wall into the city, and could just make out the palace towers, and the spires of Draevensett: the elite Draev Guardian League Academy.

Draevensett was a school of high prestige, well known throughout the kingdom. A school only Ability users could attend, so you had to have Elemental Manipulation Ability. Aken longed to go there, to train and become a Draev Guardian, become a powerful protector of the kingdom and vempar kind. Draevs were feared and respected for the unique power they possessed.

Mom had called Aken's strange gift with clay useless, something not fit for Draev Guardian training. She and Dad would never let him go to Draevensett, and it felt like his dream was slipping away.

"I won't give up," he murmured.

He would practice with clay, no matter what they said. He would find a use for it.

He stared beyond the foggy glass to the quiet world of dusk beyond, snowflakes dancing like little pixies as they gently floated from their heavenly home in the clouds.

'False Guardian…Swan Princess…' Aken wondered at the hunchback's words and what they could mean.

5

Years later, a cool autumn breeze found twelve-year-old Aken-Shou at the edge of the school playground. Kids were either on rickety swings, jumping rope, or sharing the latest gossip, while he was busy shaping clay into birds, and soaking in the colorful leaves and dappled sunlight.

His peers were keeping at a distance, just like always. They didn't talk to him unless it was to say something rude, and the adults eyed him with suspicion.

Scourgeblood many called him and his parents. He didn't understand why, and neither Dad nor Mom would explain; they just kept to themselves, secluded, and warned him never to make a scene.

Mom had been adamant he stop using clay because it would draw attention and bring the Draev Guardians. When Aken tried to ask her why having the Draevs' attention would be a bad thing, she just shook her head.

"Everybody respects the D.G. League," Aken argued. "If I could join them, it'd be a good thing!"

Dad, who was at home for once, fixed him with an iron gaze that made him fall silent. "Not for you, it won't," he said, and Aken shrank back. Dad huffed, as if bothered having to explain this. "Our blood is different from other vempars, see? And it makes them fear us. The city would never accept you as a Draev. We're—" Dad stopped short and shook his head. "Just do as you're told, Aken-Shou, for our sakes. You'll understand when you're older."

Aken didn't ask again, but he kept thinking about it. Even today, as he molded clay.

"Hey, pretty boy!" hollered Denim.

Oh *great*. Aken groaned. No school day could be complete without the second cousin to the prince harassing him.

Denim was a lean kid with gelled-up black hair, and was a real magnet charmer with the girls. He swaggered over, a group of followers tagging along like faithful puppies on his heels.

Why Denim's family lived in the Outskirts, and not the city, he didn't know or care. Rumors said they'd gotten themselves swamped in debt, and this was their punishment.

"What're you doing?" asked Denim when Aken didn't respond. He'd adopted some of the Outskirts' slang. "Oh wait, that's right. You're doing what ya do best: being an odd-ball."

The groupies laughed at their leader's joke, as if it were the funniest thing on Eartha.

Aken said, "I thought I smelled something spoiled rotten. Now I know it's just an aristocrat."

Denim clenched his mouth shut for an angry second. "You're just jealous. One day, I'm gonna leave the Outskirts behind, and you'll still be stuck here in the dirt." He leaned forward, squinting down at the ground. "What girly art are ya making this time, anyway? Another rubber ducky?"

The group laughed harder, slapping their thighs. Aken gritted his teeth, letting his side bangs hide his face.

"Seriously dude, you look just like your creepy mom with that hair. Does she make rubber duckies, too?" Denim gestured. "Is that how your parents get money? Or is it dirty criminal work they do?"

Aken's fist hit Denim's face so hard the boy slammed into the ground before he knew what had happened.

The groupies leaped back, gasping in shock.

Denim swayed, dazed for a moment, then pushed back up to his feet, refusing any help. "*You little* punk!"

"Bring it on." Aken stood ready, motioning with a hand. "Since your mom hasn't been whacking your behind, I'll do it for her. You're long overdue for a spanking, baby."

A kid in the group laughed, and Denim glared at him with boiling rage, wiping his red nose. It was the last straw.

"Roahhh!" Denim charged, and Aken met him head-on.

Dust clouds rose as they rolled and kicked, punched and yanked.

Kids hollered all around, chanting and urging them on.

The battle was soon pulled apart by an adult who'd rushed over—a parent of one of Denim's lackeys. But by then, they were both sorely bruised and black-eyed.

"You Scourgeblood!" spat Denim. "I heard about your kind. Everybody hates you—you're monsters. You and your parents should've died with the rest of them!"

"Shut up!" Aken shouted.

"Freak!" Denim said over his shoulder as he was forcibly led off the playground, and the group scurried after him. They added their own insults to echo his:

"Freaky-freak!"

"Freak of nature!"

"Go back to the princess fairytale ya came from!"

"Oh, that was a good one."

"It was, wasn't it? Thanks."

That evening found Aken-Shou getting a scolding by Mom, as she went off on another rant about "not drawing attention." Someone had tattled about the fight, and now Aken sat at the table staring at the floor and hoping Denim was getting what he deserved too.

"You're grounded for a month! Do you hear me?

No more playground mischief for you!" Mom declared.

Aken made a grumbling noise and crossed his arms tightly. "What did Denim mean by *Scourgeblood?*" he asked, changing the subject. "I keep hearing that word, and you never bother to explain it. What's it mean?"

Mom moved back and forth, busying herself cleaning, and the silent seconds ticked by.

"You're too young to know..." he heard her murmur. And then she half faced him, hands still busy cleaning a table that could never get clean. "We're different," she said. "Our powers are... *unique*, and to most people terrifying. You see, our kind did many bad things in the past, and for that they were hunted down. Only you, I and your father are left, now."

"You mean, there's no more? Just us?" he exclaimed. "Why? What *bad things* happened for everybody to hate us?"

She paused. "Do you remember that old story about the Swan Princess?" He nodded. "The Emperor in that story was a Pureblood, or what people now call a Scourgeblood," she said.

"That evil Emperor was a Scourgeblood?" Aken's fingers gripped together. "So it's true then, we're monsters. I'm related to a monster..."

"Never mind that, Aken-Shou. Both I and your father have worked hard to be accepted into this vempar society, and we have a place to call home. We mustn't use our powers for anyone to see—ever. Your blood powers haven't awakened yet, and won't for some time, but this Ability you have with clay isn't good to show off. It'll only frighten people, and we can't risk the D.G. League coming to take you away." She held his gaze. "Do you understand?"

Aken half-nodded. "But I still—"

"Good. Then stop being an idiot, and stay in your room."

Alone upstairs every day after school now, Aken kicked his legs back and forth on the bed. This boredom was brutal, and this claustrophobic wooden box of a room made him want to shriek!

He opened the window, gazing out at the splashes of autumn across the Outskirts and distant grasslands. Stalks were still green where they peeked out from underneath piles of leaves. A vine creeped up the opposite house, its heart-shaped leaves glowing as if dipped in blood, burnt around the edges.

With a defiant huff, he climbed onto the narrow windowsill, then twisted around to grab and climb the slanted shingle roof, eventually reaching his favorite perch up by the chimney.

Twreeee~kreeee!

From the rooftop, Aken's eyes skimmed the clouds until he spotted them: swallows, like little black arrows, swooping and soaring through the sky. One of the fastest birds in the world was the red-chested swallow.

No predator would it not out-maneuver, no storm would it not soar through, no gale would it not face. Amidst lightning and thunder, while other birds hid in their shelters, the swallow flew on, with the wind currents speeding its fearless flight.

Aken leaned against the brick chimney, resting his arms across it while he watched the small birds fly through a melting crimson sunset sky toward a gold-rimmed horizon. He wished he could follow them there, wherever *there* led. Nothing was as free as a bird in the sky.

Moisture welled in his eyes. As the sleek creatures shrank smaller and smaller into the sun, he listened to their fading calls, his chin on his arms.

Kreeee…Kwreeee…

Draev Guardians were free like that, too. They didn't have to hide their powers, or put up with bullies.

They could go anywhere, and face anything.

A shape moved across the distant rooftops off to his left—it moved with ease, with a short cape flapping behind. It must be a Draev out on patrol, checking that all was secure and no enemy humans in sight.

The hatred between vempars and humans was one spanning centuries—maybe even longer. Despite being physically weaker than vempars, humans were smart and used their resourceful intellect to create formidable weapons.

Aken rubbed his nose. Vempars needed *essence* to survive, and taking it by force was the only way to get it—none would willingly donate the stuff. The humans would rather wipe out vempars from existence, first, and the other races would be more than happy to help.

He'd heard snippets of gossip while wandering the daily Outskirts markets: talk of the Vemparic Kingdom attempting a truce with other races.

Aken wasn't holding his breath over it. Vempars would always need *essence* to survive, and no one wanted to give it to them freely. Instead, rogue humans were threatening to raid their villages and detonate explosives like terrorists. What truce was there to be had? The idea was as absurd as trying to get sabercats and wolves to be friends—a picnic between the two would never end well.

Aken watched as the Draev figure faded from sight. He wondered if it could be Draev Master Nephryte—one of the greatest Ability users and defenders of the kingdom, the hero who had saved countless lives and battled goblins during the Goblin Shadow War. He and the other elite Draev Masters were those who had kept the goblins away, and who now kept the humans' technological weapons at bay. He wanted to be a great hero like that, like Master Nephryte. Be seen and acknowledged by people, instead of shunned and treated like a monster.

"*Hnn*, I'm tired of this." Aken stretched. "I'm not gonna stay here just cuz I gave some kid a pummeling he was looking for!"

Aken leaped off the roof, and despite it being two-stories high, landed somewhat gracefully on the ground—well, on his head, but at a perfect angle, and he quickly recovered thanks to his body's fast Healing.

He thought of Denim's words. "I don't look that much like Mom, do I?" he muttered grumpily at no one, and went for a stroll through winding dirt streets as the last bit of color from the sinking sun struggled to hold on.

He wandered aimlessly down a narrow alley, hands in his worn pockets. "Some important guys have longish hair. I don't see anybody making fun of *them*." He kicked at a pebble.

He huffed and flopped down on the pebbly dirt, head resting back against the brick of whatever building was behind him. Trash bins littered the alley, his nose noticed.

Chr-crnk.

Something rustled from behind one of those bins.

Aken slowly got up and approached the noise, careful not to crunch any glass or paper with his shoes.

The rustling stopped, and he froze, scanning for the culprit.

Yellow eyes glowed from the bin's shadow. Aken kept still as twin long teeth followed by whiskers and a pair of paws emerged.

His breath caught. It was a sabercat! A large cat species of the continent. They usually kept to the forests, feeding off anteleer, boar and such, and sometimes livestock. Farmers hated them, and many feared them. But despite the cat's wild ferocity, up-close, it was a truly beautiful creature. And this particular one was a small kitten.

Gold-brown fur marked by dark stripes and spots, ears turned up with long furry tips, white painted around the eyes and muzzle—it was like an adorable painting. A fuzzy, striped tail brushed the ground, and soft paws stepped toward him without a sound.

Aken knelt and spoke softly. "Hi there, little kitty. Where's your big, scary mom?" He craned his neck around to make sure nothing was creeping up behind him. "Or maybe you got lost? You couldn't have wandered in here on your own, could you?"

The kitten stared up at him, then approached. He held out his hand, half nervous it might bite. Even though he'd Heal, pain wasn't pleasant.

The kit paused and looked ready to hiss, but he kept very still, and several patient seconds passed.

A cold, wet nose touched his hand, then rubbed against it—a cat's way of greeting.

"*Awww*, you're all alone and need a home, don't you?" He rubbed its furry head. "We've got a lot in common, you and me." He smiled. "Misunderstood, alone, branded as monsters... How about you stay with me?"

He leaned forward, a finger pressed to his lips, and gave a sly wink. "But we'll have to keep it a secret."

6

Sabe was a bundle of fun, but keeping a wild animal from being discovered wasn't as easy as Aken had hoped, even with Sabe's small house-cat size. Especially when he kept clawing up stuff in his room.

"What in the world ruined these curtains?" Mom demanded.

Aken pretended it was him, that crazy battle dreams had him kicking and clawing imaginary opponents in his sleep. As proof, he scratched his fingernails into the side table—biting his tongue as wood dug under his nails.

Mom seemed to buy the act, stomping off angrily, and he turned an eye to where Sabe was hiding. "You better appreciate this," he hissed.

Sabe purred.

He didn't want to lie, but he was afraid what Mom might do to a saberkitten. He kept Sabe in his closet during school hours, then played with him out in the grasslands beyond the Outskirts, and Sabe followed him on trips to the herbalist in the woods. He caught grasshoppers, snakes and other critters on his own, so Aken didn't have to worry much about finding food. He shooed Sabe out of sight whenever people were near, and the kit seemed to understand that not every person was nice.

Sabe was a handful, but soon became his best friend. The kit trotted along, white paws keeping up with Aken's stride as they navigated through the undergrowth one day, the Outer Woods painted autumn yellow around them.

"Wish I could fly instead of walk all this way, y'know? How totally cool would that be!" said Aken.

Gaps of sky poked through the leafy canopy, and Aken pointed up at the birds sailing past. "Like those swallows. That's what I want to do, soar like the wind!"

Mew. Sabe was shaking his head with a pinched look—his way of strongly disagreeing.

Aken laughed. "What, you're afraid of flying? But having wings would be so cool."

GRraow.

Aken's ears twitched; his merriment cut short.

That growl wasn't from Sabe...

Throaty rumbles interrupted the woods' peace, and Aken stumbled to a halt, staring ahead at what suddenly stood in their path.

A pack of feroces.

Hungry. Blood red eyes. Long muzzles brimming with sharp teeth, eager to eat him in one bite. A predator far worse than any sabercat.

Wolf-like, each beast as huge as a bear, four muscular legs. Furry hand-like paws with long claws. They were as good at climbing as they were running, too. He really wished he could sprout wings and fly, right now.

The first feroce stood erect on its hind legs, towering over Aken and Sabe, claws raised for the kill.

Great. Aken should've been paying attention to his surroundings, instead of goofing off! Oh well, no use whining now.

The pack of feroces moved forward as one, and he jumped back—there was no time for plans!

He scooped Sabe up in an arm, ducking the feroce's

claws, before veering in the opposite direction of death at a fast run.

Paws galloped and scraped across the woods floor after him. He didn't dare glance back. He knew he was mere inches from being sliced open. Even with Aken's unnatural speed, they were gaining on him in long, panther strides. And there was no haven to run to.

'I thought I'd live longer than this,' Aken thought, and almost laughed.

Suddenly, a voice that was not a voice spoke, from nowhere and everywhere at once: *Use your gift*, it said.

Aken's head jerked, searching for the voice. *'Gift? How can I…'*

Aken wasn't sure what his hand was doing, or how—he just did it.

Feroce breath approached hot on the nape of his neck. Dread filled Sabe's liquid eyes. Aken tugged out a clay swallow he'd made and kept in his pocket, and focused: channeling *essence* through his fingertips into the clay. He tossed the swallow up in the air.

The clay began to grow and stretch midair, until its body became bigger than he was.

The feroces growled, and the first one lunged to wrap its jaws around and snap his neck.

Aken leaped for the swallow—*thwmp!*—landing on its clay back. And he willed it to fly.

Sabe clung to his chest as he clung to the clay. Branches whipped past them, leaves snagging in his hair, as the clay bird flapped and soared upwards. The green canopy broke, and they sailed into the sky, leaving behind the feroces who snarled in confusion.

Aken let out a breath.

No longer in danger of being eaten, he took a moment to gaze around in awe at the woods below his feet and the big sky overhead.

He was flying.

"Wow…" The air rushed past him as the bird beat its wings. "This is…awesome!" he shouted, fists waving high.

Meeow!

Sabe clung to him, claws digging in, as the swallow veered toward home, and Aken laughed, filled with pure excitement.

Stopping the ride short of reaching the Outskirts, Aken hopped off and channeled the *essence* back through his hand into his body.

The clay shrunk, and the bird was once more a little sculpture in his palm.

"The freedom of flight, the realm of the birds…I have it!" He grinned. His strange talent with clay could become *more* than just a curiosity, after all.

Shoes poised on the edge of the roof, with Sabe pacing back and forth nervously at his heels, Aken tossed the clay bird, channeling a string of *essence* into it.

The bird's wings spread, growing until it hovered riding-size in the air before him.

"C'mon!" He hopped onto Limitless—the name he'd given the clay swallow—and pulled fearful Sabe along with him. "Away—*we*—go!"

The swallow flapped forward. Aken's breath caught in his throat as currents of air washed past him, and a nervous excitement burned inside his chest. As the city's steepled rooftops began to shrink, cool night wind whipped at his hair and sleeves.

Sprinkled stars and a full moon glistened brightly, more than they ever had from the ground. Exhilaration filled every fiber of his being. With so little holding him up, a simple mistake and he'd fall into death's embrace.

But he found himself laughing, and higher and higher the

bird went, tilting nearly vertical. *'Up! Faster!'* he willed and held on, one hand grasping each wing, legs dangling freely behind him.

Sabe dug every little sharp hook-claw into the bird's back, his fur stuck up like a hedgehog and eyes wide saucers, yowling at the crazy boy beside him.

The swallow was a sky rocket, climbing up, up, *up*…until they touched the tips of silver clouds, and darted like a dolphin through wispy silver oceans.

On the other side of the ocean clouds, Aken had the bird level out and glide steady for a moment, pausing to catch his breath in between laughs.

The spherical moon glowed brighter than a pearl dipped in sunshine, and the distant craters filled his vision. "So, this is what we ground-dwellers miss out on, huh? This whole other view of the world."

Wet rimmed Aken's eyes, though he grinned. Sabe's now frizzy head tilted with a worried look. "Let's try something *more* daring," Aken shouted.

Meeyow! Sabe shrieked. The vempar boy commanded "Down!" and the swallow lurched forward and tilted.

He and Sabe held on tighter, *tighter*. The bird nose-dived, true as a falling arrow. Speeding to the world below, splitting the air in two. Down, *down*.

Aken's wild laugh fought against the wind, and tears streamed from their eyeballs against the rushing, stinging air, their legs waving like flags behind them, arms and paws clinging for dear life.

Then, on a whim, Aken let go…

MreeeoW! Sabe screeched, watching him fall.

Falling through a world held by nothing but air, Aken turned his back on the approaching ground to face the wide, deep sky around him—a night ocean of sparkling diamonds—ignoring all else but that beautiful sight, which none but those with wings ever beheld.

Rooftops were so very small, and the moon above so big, as if time and gravity had come to a complete stop. Though, in reality, he was falling to his death. It felt more like gliding than falling.

Arms spread out either side, he closed his eyes, soaking in the feel of undulating air against his back and the serene calm surrounding him. His heartbeat hummed. His mind floated in bliss.

Ba-thump.

The rooftops neared, the ground grew.

Ba-thump.

Roof tiles closer, patterns more defined.

Ba-thump.

A patch of ground reaching up, ready to touch him. Blades of green reaching to brush his hand…

Underneath his falling body, the clay swallow swooped—landing him on its back, while the bird maintained its speed a mere five feet off the ground.

"Whoa!" Aken rolled over on his stomach, the air knocked from his lungs, and directed the bird to slow down a few notches. The young sabercat growled, glaring up at him with the most enraged, upset face a kitty's features could muster.

"*Aw,* c'mon, Sabe. I knew it'd catch me in time. I wasn't gonna die. Really! I had it all planned out." He tried to appease, but Sabe turned his little nose up and away.

"Don't get all haughty and mighty with me, *you.*" He reached down and tickled Sabe's furry tummy.

Meuwww! The kit tried to dodge his hand, running in circles on the bird. Aken giggled, rotating on his knees, chasing after Sabe.

7

As winter drifted by, the cold put a limit on flight time; it was a relief when spring finally blew in. Aken continued practicing flying, daring to venture through storms that came with the seasonal changes, wind and rain pounding like pellets against him, blurring vision, thunder rumbling the air.

He also continued sculpting clay, completing a five-foot tall eagle—the symbol of courage. Sabe's tiny claws helped make markings that resembled feathers. It stood out in the grasslands, where people would be less likely to bother it.

Thoughts of Draevensett still whirled in his mind. Despite what his parents said, he still believed becoming a Draev Guardian would be a good thing. Everyone admired the city's protectors. People wouldn't label him *monster* or *Scourgeblood* if he became one of the kingdom's heroes!

Aken shook his head, and with a yawn fell asleep on the lumpy pillow on his bed.

He woke to a gloomy overcast sky on the verge of rain, the next morning. And when he opened the closet, Sabe was gone.

Panic filled his chest. He searched the room, then every corner of the house. Sabe never left his room; only once or twice in the past, when he'd forgotten to shut the closet door all the way. But Sabe had always come right back.

Then he noticed the window partially open... 'Darn it.'

Morning passed as he searched the streets, alleys, the park, the school yard. Until there was only one other likely place left: the grasslands beyond the city, where the eagle sculpture stood.

"Sabe?" He called out across the endless waves of grass. "Buddy?"

Aken paused to scan the wide, open space. The eagle was missing.

No—the sculpture had fallen over on its side, cracked. Worry welled in his stomach. Why would it fall? It was too heavy for the wind to push.

"This blob is yours? I figured as much."

He whirled around at the cocky voice. There stood Denim and his lackeys. They were tossing rocks in their hands.

"I thought I'd teach you a lesson about defacing public property. You're not supposed to spread your *art* all over the place, Scourgeblood." A smirk split Denim's face, his right hand flipping the rock as if it were a coin.

"Last I checked, the grasslands were free for all," said Aken.

"Ha! Monsters don't have rights. And last I checked, that's what you are."

Aken's hands clenched. He tried not to look at the eagle.

"Did you hear the good news? I've just been enrolled in Draevensett. Turns out I have Ability." Denim held out his palm and a sheet of ice formed around the rock. "Guess I'll be leavin' you and this dump behind. A grand destiny awaits me!"

Aken's jaw twitched.

"That aside, you'd better get outta here real quick," Denim continued. "We just finished off a sabercat, and who knows when more'll come. I shouldn't warn a

Scourgeblood, but since I'm such a generous soul, it's my duty," he said with mock honor.

"Sabercats!" One of the lackeys whimpered and shook. "That mother'll be comin' for her kit soon. She'll eat us! We should leave—*right now.*"

"Knock it off! We're goin' soon, okay?" Denim shoved the boy. "It's not like a cat could kill us."

"It can if those long teeth rip your head off!"

"Whatever," Denim spat.

"A...kitten?" Aken's forehead creased, then darkened. "What did you do?" His hand flew out, grabbing the nearest boy by the collar and shaking him. "The kitten: WHERE is he?"

Startled, the boy in his fist pointed a shaky finger over toward the sculpture.

Aken forced himself to look where the boy indicated. It took a moment before he could make out the lump of brown curled in a ball at the eagle's head. "Ah—!" he exclaimed, and threw the boy aside as he ran to the spot.

Reaching the brown lump, he stopped, heart a pounding hammer, fear gripping his stomach.

'No...no, not—' He knelt down.

It was Sabe. Injured, curled up in a little gold-and-brown ball, slanted eyes tight in pain. "No...Sabe..." He couldn't speak through the lump in his throat and the tears drowning his chest.

Gently lifting Sabe—his only friend—he cradled him in his arms, slowly rocking back and forth. "It's okay. You're gonna be okay, buddy." He swallowed. "I'm here. I'm h-h-he-here..." He fought a rush of tears. Sabe's wounds were bleeding, broken areas, as if hit by rocks. For such a small animal, rocks were dangerous bullets.

Sabe's heartbeat felt slow against him, the kitten body so frail in his embrace. He held his breath when Sabe opened his glossy eyes a crack, staring up at him, his friend. The look on his furry face…Sabe seemed to be smiling, one last time.

Then his gaze went slack and furry body fell limp.

Aken stared at the lifeless form in his arms. Speechless. Shaken. Broken. His chest feeling like someone had crushed it with a hammer.

Did Sabe really…?

Tear after tear pattered, leaving damp marks on the kitten's fur.

"Sabe." He choked as he hugged the kit to himself. His only friend, the only one who cared. Gone.

'I need him.'

What would Aken do now?

'I'm all alone.'

Rocks. Who had thrown those rocks? They said they'd just finished off a sabercat…

Aken's shoulders shuddered, rage replacing tears.

When he gently laid Sabe back down, he turned to face the cluster of boys, who now had their backs turned as they fast walked away before any other sabercats could show up.

"Afraid of a sabercat…" Aken growled. "I'll give you more than *that* to be afraid of."

His vision grew dark, almost red, as anger enveloped him. "You," he shouted, his fists white-knuckled, "You *killed* my friend!"

He screamed with such fury that Denim's group stopped in their tracks to look back.

A deep hum began rumbling through the eartha beneath their feet.

"Hey, w-what is that?"

"An earthquake?"

"Is that Scourgeblood doing something?"

The boys looked to Denim, but the aristocrat shoved them. "Get back to the city." There was an uneasy look in his eyes. "*Go!*"

Aken's whole body trembled. A red aura swirled around

his arms and the ground rumbled harder. He opened his hands and thrust out both palms in a shout.

"*GRAAH!*"

Soil burst up from the ground in a showering fountain of hot red. The burning spout receded only to be followed by another—closer to the boys now running away. Another, and another.

The boys looked back with open horror as spouts of dirt flew up, heated and melted, becoming lava midair.

Denim flung out his hands and ice crystals dusted the air, but it was nothing compared to the lava's heat, and try as he did no more ice would form. "Run!" Denim's shout rang needlessly. The group ran faster than frightened dogs back toward the city. Dirt-to-lava spouts burst up, chasing after them. Boys tripped and tumbled over themselves, swatting at singed sleeves and pants in their struggle to get away.

Once the bullies were no more than tiny ants in the distance, the fiery aura dimmed and the tension left Aken's body. His hands trembled.

He couldn't be amazed about what he'd just done. His heart was aching bad. Sabe was gone, and it was his fault. He should've been there for Sabe when he needed him, should've taken better care of him. Should've, should've...

Wet trails glistened down his burning cheeks, as he walked back to where Sabe lay. He sat there for who knew how long, numb and staring at a future with his friend that no longer existed. He'd died so fast—there hadn't been time to Heal him. Aken wasn't even sure how to Heal grave injuries like that. An adult could have, if one had been around.

If...should've...

Aken dug a grave at the fallen eagle's head; no place could be better. "You were the best, y'know?" He talked while he worked, lumps burning his throat, thinking back to their adventures. That was the only thing keeping him together right now: the memories.

Finished, he put wild flowers—lemondrops, daisies, bluebells—on the upturned earth. "You've got this nice eagle, here, that we made together. An eagle," his voice broke, "cuz you were an amazing and courageous little friend."

He wiped damp cheeks with the back of a dirty hand. "B-but I'll see you again. I know I will. Lord God's taking care of you; He cares about the things He creates—even little animals. So, I know I'll see you again, in Heaven."

He stood, wiping blurry eyes and runny nose on a short sleeve.

KH-FOOMmmm-Mmm-Mm!

Aken jerked as a blast echoed through the air, humming and rippling across the ground.

It faded to a growling rumble as he stared about in alarm. "What the?"

It came from the city, from the Outskirts. Flashes of flame and smoke wafted up from one spot among the housing, but he couldn't tell what had been hit. The echoes of shouts could be heard.

He saw several dots in the distance hurry into the woods, away from the city—most likely rogue humans, who'd lashed out against vempars for hunting their kind, again.

But rogue groups hadn't been able to make a successful attack against Draethvyle in years.

How did they manage to get that close to the city and set off an explosive—or whatever it was—without the Draev Guardian League detecting them?

Where was that famous hero Nephryte, the one who was supposed to be among the greatest of Draev Guardians?

Feeling as empty as a hollowed-out shell, Aken started to walk back, his face a mess of tear trails and dirt. He should get home before Mom or Dad noticed, even though every fiber of his being screamed to stay with Sabe.

Ah, what was he going to do without him? Why bother with this miserable world anymore?

'*Change the world,*' whispered a voice. Yes, it had to be changed. If he became a Draev Guardian, he could do that. He *would* do that.

Aken's feet carried him without him barely noticing, taking him up the dirt street as it wove into and through the Outskirts. People were hurrying past, running in the opposite direction or grabbing buckets of water.

Cold worry trickled down his spine, and he made his pace quicken.

When he reached and turned the final corner that opened up to his house, a blazing inferno met him.

Waves of heat thrust out, forcing him back. "What—?" he mouthed. Fire rose where his home should have stood, a skeletal ruin now filling his vision.

He stumbled back, arms limp at his sides. Numbness made the heat and pain feel far away though he could smell it, see the pillar of smoke and yellow frothing.

This couldn't be real...

Body refusing to respond, he stood there, slack, watching the blaze consume the last remnants of what once had been home. Glass shards reflected the scene as buckets of water fought to drown the inferno.

'*Mom...Dad...*'

8

Two things had survived the fiery blaze of his home that day.

When a northerly wind brought in rain from the mountains, and the cool air let him get close enough to step inside the charred, skeletal house, nothing had been left but metal bits like the stove. Not even a body.

Neighbors had confirmed that Mom and Dad had been home at the time. Black soot and ash must be all that remained of them.

Why couldn't they have escaped? Why couldn't this have been prevented? Where was the great hero, Master Nephryte?

Navigating around collapsed ceiling beams, Aken had spotted charred remnants of a bedside table: the one from his room—the second floor now a littered mess across the foundation. There inside the top drawer, safely intact, was the small glassy orb and old Bible—the items from the hunchback.

How those had survived…there was no logical explanation. Yet there they were, and now he kept them close, along with the clay swallow in his pocket. Possessions of a life now gone. His new life as an orphan just beginning.

Something dark stirred inside him, something restless and

angry. His goal and dream were distant shards of another lifetime—he could almost forget he'd ever had a dream. Almost.

Today, Aken kept alert as he wandered the stands, booths and pavilions of the market scattered throughout the Outskirts; his clothes felt dirty as rags, his soul a bundle of calluses and frayed edges.

He'd had to find food and shelter on his own for days, now; no one wanted to take in or help a Scourgeblood. Aken kept a sharp eye out for any vulnerable produce—apples or bread would make a good meal.

People along the street gave wary looks as he moved past. They knew what he was, and they knew what he was up to.

Letting bangs shadow his eyes, Aken surveyed the area ahead: Two people were purchasing loaves from a baker's stand, distracting the vendor and leaving the other loaves unattended: delicious baguettes cooling from the oven, aroma filling the air.

This was his chance.

Tensing his muscles, Aken sprinted toward the stand in a burst of unmatched speed, his right hand snatching a loaf.

He knew it was wrong. Lord God said never to steal. But his stomach wanted that bread, even if his spirit starved for something more than food, and he was too angry to care.

"You—!" the vendor shouted after him.

Aken paused and looked over his shoulder calmly. Too calmly.

The overweight vendor twice his age hesitated before Aken's icy glare. A glare that dared him try and take back the baguette.

The vendor didn't move. "You've no right to have that, Scourgeblood!" he said, fear tinging his voice.

"Is that a challenge? And here I thought everybody was afraid of monsters." Aken snapped his fingers.

Handfuls of dirt shot up into the air, floated and landed

upon the bread-laden stand where it *crackled* into lava-born flames.

Customers gave a start, backing away from the scene and the strange Ability at work.

The vendor scrambled to put out the blaze, and Aken hurried on up the street, ready to take a bite out of the warm *essence*-filled loaf.

Behind him a gust of wind picked up, blowing down on the burning lava, cooling and smothering the flames instantly.

The vendor watched with puzzled relief, and when he realized what was happening, a grin spread across his face.

The same cool gust blew Aken's hair back, and he squinted against the pressure as he walked. A tall silhouette blocked the path suddenly, making him stop. The gust faded to a breeze, and Aken stared up at the vempar man.

Fair brown hair rippled to the shoulders, and bangs framed a clean-shaven face. His upturned eyes were as blue as rivers. He stared down at the unruly boy in his path, with a stare that could shake any criminal.

The loaf fell from Aken's hand behind his back, where he then tried to hide it behind his shoes.

'*Did he see me steal?*' Aken had to shake his head to look away from the river-eye currents, focusing instead on the clothes: A blue swallowtail jacket, and on the open collar perched a rank pin: a silver fang with one curving bat's wing. The rank pin of a Draev Master.

The shoulder cape fastened around him was a pretty thing—dark blue, silver lining, light-weight—but more importantly had an identity pin on the right shoulder, depicting silver wind currents blowing across a moonstone cloud.

The marks of the Draev Guardian League. Their coat-of-arms no doubt embroidered on the cape's back, if only this guy would turn around so he could see. But that identity pin, could this be…?

Aken couldn't stop staring, and wasn't sure what he should do, or if he should speak.

"Did you find him?"

The call tore his stare away, as an older boy trotted over and posed casually at the Master's side. Face smooth as wax, he eyed Aken curiously, and Aken swallowed. His maroon hair, with striking red highlights, was cut at odd lengths and angles. Eyes a mulberry shade glowed from under his hooded lids and random bangs.

His white collared shirt had been rudely sliced up to become a vest; detached black sleeves and white cuffs dangled on both forearms as he crossed them over his chest. Ripped-up pants, and shiny shoes, it was as if the boy's wardrobe had undergone surgery—one that had gone tragically wrong.

Aken frowned at the vertical scar carved from the base of his right eye down his cheek. Deep red, vicious, edged in charcoal black.

A scar? But vempars Healed from almost anything…

"Aken-Shou Bloodre."

The Master spoke, his voice smooth as a river. "I am Draev Master Nephryte. And this," a hand motioned to the boy beside him, "is Mamoru, one of my students-in-training."

It was *him*, Master Nephryte. The hero he used to admire and want to be like, the hero who should have been there to protect his home before it burned to ashes.

"Aken-Shou." The Master's greeting turned serious, and his gaze flicked toward the loaf on the ground. "I cannot allow you to wander these streets disrupting commerce and damaging property. There's trouble enough beyond these walls without you adding to it here." He indicated the city wall with a chin nod before staring him down again. "How old are you?"

"I'm gonna be thirteen," said Aken, giving his own serious look, which wasn't easy. "Why?"

"Good. You are to come with me and receive proper training," Master Nephryte announced. And then his back turned, and he started away, assuming—no, *expecting*—Aken to follow along and do as told.

Anger replaced any trace of intimidation. All of the blame he hadn't known what to do with for the past week had been directed at the D.G. League and at this person.

It was *his* fault a group of humans had slipped a weapon into the Outskirts—destroying his home, his parents, his life.

If this *Master* had been doing his *Guardian* job, he wouldn't be here homeless and starving. Some hero.

"No!" he shouted at the man's back.

The Master paused, then turned.

The scarred boy beside him clucked his tongue, amusement in his eyes.

"No? Why do you refuse, Aken-Shou?" Nephryte's river-smooth voice almost made Aken question why, too, but he caught himself and vigorously shook his head.

"Because it's *your* fault what happened! My home got burned up because you didn't protect us," he growled. "I won't trust a false hero."

Nephryte's expression softened a fraction. "The house that burned…that was your home? A very tragic case," he said. "I would have been patrolling the Outskirts that day, but an incident elsewhere had drawn me away… The Draevs on duty saw no sign of an attack coming, not before it was too late. You have my deepest apology." The Master bowed his head. "I come to offer you a new home, at the D.G. League's Academy, Draevensett."

Aken's chest pounded.

"It is an offer I advise that you accept." Master Nephryte paused before further adding, "You must. Or face the consequences, by order of the law."

Aken swallowed. "What does *that* mean?"

"It means, if a vempar born with Ability misuses it—causing harm to fellow citizens, not heeding warnings—then he is to be either destroyed, or locked away in the depths of the Morbid Dungeons. That is the rule," said the Master. "You are a Scourgeblood, and you appear to be running rampant with your Ability—that is a dangerous combination. If you are uncontrollable, then..."

"I'm not running rampant!" Aken protested quickly. "I just—I just did that because I was hungry. I wasn't trying to hurt anybody."

Nephryte's mouth closed, considering.

Draevensett, a new home, sounded much better than a dark cell or death. Aken's childhood dream was within reach. And yet, could he put all his anger aside? The back of his mind was itching.

Anything was better than a dark cell.

He didn't like being told what he must accept, though. Stupid law.

"How do I know this isn't some trap to get rid of me? You'd all be glad if the last Scourgeblood was dead. Admit it!" Aken threw up his hands, and the dirt street erupted in lava.

It wasn't much, a small pool—he didn't know how to use Ability that well—but people did shout and scurry. He couldn't resist a pleased grin at that. Fear was a form of respect, after all.

Master Nephryte, however, raised a single finger.

The air around him condensed, turned moist, then covered and smothered the lava—extinguishing its life with a searing *hiss*.

Aken gawked. And then a growing wind rose around him and lifted him clear off the ground.

"*Wha*—AH!"

His hands swam, trying to grab hold of something—*anything*—legs kicking at air. He tried to create more lava, but thick-as-rope air currents wouldn't let him move as they pinned both arms tight to his sides.

He struggled, determined to get free by sheer force of will. He couldn't let himself be so easily defeated!

The hint of a smile touched Nephryte's lips while observing Aken's vain struggle. "A very determined and stubborn soul, with great potential. If only you would listen and do as you're told."

Aken glared down from where the air held him suspended, trying to spear the vempar with his furious gaze. Nephryte appeared not to notice.

"A vempar of your power cannot be left alone, or who knows what damage you'll inflict upon yourself and those around you. Aken-Shou, this is not a trap to get rid of you." He tapped his lower lip thoughtfully. "Yes. I have decided to take you with me—whether you like it or not."

With that, the Master turned once again, and the older boy fell in step with him.

"Huh?" Just as Aken began wondering what they were up to, the air ropes constraining him began to pull his body forward, following after them. "Hey—! Y-you let me go, right now!"

All he could do was kick and shout like a caught animal. It must have been an amusing sight for the market crowd: a boy dragged through the air like a balloon on a string, feet a whirring propeller. He could hear their snickers and laughter.

"Jerks! Son of a warthog, stop flying me around, or I'll— *Yaaaahg!*"

The air ropes shook him.

Aken yelled and kicked the whole way into the city. He didn't even notice their leaving the Outskirts behind until the grand school came into view. Then he saw, and then he fell silent, staring up at the rising towers, star-struck and jaw dangling.

The air ropes released and he landed clumsily on his knees with a grunt. The Master and Mamoru shared a smirk before continuing up to the iron gate.

They knew he would follow. And follow he did. It was either that or be dragged the rest of the way—and he really didn't want anybody from this grand place seeing him *like that*.

Aken put on a wide frown, masking his awe behind it, and plodded toward a new life and an old dream.

Aken stood within Draevensett's courtyard and turned in place. He was finally here, to study and train for the D.G. League—the first step toward becoming the greatest Draev Guardian. His anticipation battled with guilt, though. It was only because he'd lost Sabe, Mom and Dad that he was here, now.

Master Nephryte—who he preferred to call *Mentor* rather than a heroic *Master*—let his student Mamoru give Aken a brief tour of the school and introduce him to the dorm floor boys he'd be living, learning and training with.

Aken put on a casual smile as he faced the group.

"This is Aken-Shou," Mamoru gave introductions. "He'll be a part of Floor Harlow from now on. He's the—"

"The Scourgeblood, so I've heard. Figures he'd end up on our Floor," spoke one of the boys. He had the look of a noble snob about him and leaned his head back so that he looked down his nose at Aken.

The other boys shifted, fear or distrust showing in their body language, and Aken held back a lump in his throat.

"Enough, Hercule," said Mamoru. "Aken-Shou is our comrade, now. You can't call him names."

The noble turned his head aside with a snort.

"Does that mean he has crazy monster powers?" asked another: a too-merry boy with orange spiky hair. "I'm Bakoa, by the way!"

Aken frowned at him, the word *monster* stinging. "Hercule. Bakoa. *Hmph*, good to know the names of my enemies," he said coolly.

Bakoa's grin fell in fright. "Eh?"

Mamoru intervened, "Let me show you to your room, Aken, and then we can head down to the dining hall."

After that, the word *Scourgeblood* floated through the halls and classrooms of Draevensett. Denim was at the school, and had made sure everybody knew by the following day. As Aken tried to eat lunch in the cafeteria, students made a show of avoiding the table he sat at.

After a while, Aken slammed his hands down on the table. The sound rang through the room, and he rose and fixed his gaze on the crowd of students. "Yes, I'm the last Scourgeblood, that's right! And you know what? That's not all I'm gonna be. One day, I'm gonna become the greatest Draev Guardian ever, and kick all of your behinds!"

There was a pause, then bursts of laughter filled the air.

"The greatest Draev Guardian ever?" one student guffawed.

"What a joke! Everybody knows Master Nephryte is the greatest. That twerp thinks he can beat him?" said another.

"Maybe he plans on using some evil power. Why's a Scourgeblood being allowed here, anyway?"

"Because they have to control him. They can't let a monster run loose through the kingdom."

Aken grabbed his tray and marched out the doors.

A month passed by, feeling as slow as molasses, and the same looks of distrust and unease people had given him in the Outskirts were repeating here. But he was determined not to give up; the stubbornness inside him wouldn't let him.

It hurts. So cold…

He was having more trouble, though. A void of loss and pain kept digging at his heart—a void that wouldn't go away but grew. All consuming, dark, wrapping around him like a vine.

So cold, so dark…

Something stirred restlessly. If grief, pain and anger were a living thing, then it was scraping every part of him with its claws. And one night, that pain and darkness in his dream took on a face—a face identical to his own. It stood before him like a dark reflection in a mirror, growling like a madman and whispering: *So cold. Crush them all…*

Aken jolted awake, slick with sweat. He stared around his room, though there was nothing but furniture and shadows.

So dark. Crush them, heheh. Crush them all…

He tried to ignore the thoughts of that dark reflection, but couldn't go back to sleep.

The next day, Mentor Nephryte pulled him aside, confronting him at eye-level in the stairwell. "Aken-Shou, I can tell something has been weighing you down. Talk to me; I can help you."

Aken tried to leave.

"If you won't talk to me, then focus and pray about your troubles before they grow worse. Lord God hears the words of a sincere heart," the Mentor insisted and took him by the shoulders. Apparently Nephryte was one of the few in the city who followed the faith in Lord God, instead of the red goddesses.

"I know it's been hard for you to adjust here, but things will change and get better as long as you keep trying. Have you been reading the book Job, as I suggested, how he suffered a great deal and overcame it?"

Aken pushed away. "Why would I listen to you?" he growled. "I used to think you were a great hero, but it's your fault I'm an orphan!"

He ran past him, heart pounding. A part of him regretted exploding like that, but he just couldn't take it anymore.

Entering the commons hall, he climbed up and sat on one of the window's cold, clammy stone sills—his perch of solace.

Once he'd calmed down, he let his mind drift, and suddenly the hunchback's words from that long ago day came to him:

"A spark of light, a star to guide the way through the darkness in your mind, Aken-Shou. With this, you will find the reborn princess."

The starlight orb shone in his pocket now. He fished it out with a finger and eyed its glowing surface.

He was about to put it back when an image flashed and faded.

Curious, he held it up close.

An image surfaced like swirling ink deep within the orb: the face of a girl.

He straightened.

Her ears were round—a human. Scarlet hair curled down narrow shoulders, framing a petite face. She was beautiful, like a princess. The inked lines waved, making it look as if she were moving and smiling…before the image blurred and dissipated. Gone.

He tucked the orb back.

That was weird.

The image of the scarlet princess continued dancing on the surface of his mind, and he wondered who she could be and why he bothered to care.

Below, none of the students looked his way as they bustled about the commons, content to pretend he didn't exist.

I should make them acknowledge me, the madman inside cackled. How about a few more pranks? Force them to look at him…

The door to the hall swung open.

He glanced in the direction briefly, then straightened, as someone new walked in.

Someone with scarlet hair.

Part 3
The Harlow Strays

9

The southern gates of Draethvyle City loomed before Cyrus as she and Gandif approached. Armed guards carried rifle-axes over their shoulders and eyed the stream of people shuffling along the stone walk. She tried to avoid their piercing eyes, sinking back in the hood of her cloak.

There was a check by the gatekeepers that their faces weren't on any of the Vemparic Kingdom's criminal lists, next jotting their names in a logbook and asking the reason for their visit.

Her shaggy friend was good at giving convincing answers; he tossed an arm around her. "It's my nephew's first time here!" he said, "And I just had to bring him t' see the festival."

Cyrus frowned, but the guards let them pass after Gandif paid an entry fee—he must've hid a bundle of dels in with his spare clothes.

Cyrus rubbed the fake pair of fangs in her mouth with her tongue. Gandif had carved them from white birch for her, fang caps that fit snug over her real canines. Though uncomfortable, it worked for now, until something better could be found. *Eck*, the taste of wood was unpleasant.

As they passed under the gate's archway, she tipped her head back to see the symbol on the center stone: two hands, palms up, beneath a bat-winged crown. "That's our kingdom's crest," Gandif whispered. "Best you know that one."

She nodded as they came through to the other side, and there, she beheld the city.

Draethvyle spread like a wonder of fluted stone, scrolling patterns and gothic designs. Gandif led her by the hand up a wide paved street, turned a corner that melted into narrow cobblestone, before shifting back again to pavestone.

The streets were a mishmash of textures and sizes—from five-carts wide, to barely one—crisscrossing the lay of the city in a maze. Trees grew at intervals along sidewalks, petunias dripped from windowsills, and bridges arched across the river Noncello running through the city's heart. She caught glimpses of courtyards—secluded spaces with mini gardens and turtle ponds. There were piazzas, with shady trees and iron-lace benches, and open plazas, showing off large fountains.

A pigeon shied away from her shoe, pecking at crumbs.

Fountains were masterpieces, depicting mythical creatures and scenes from legends. Heroes slaying monsters, lovers dancing, mermaids singing, sagas unfolding. Her busy gaze soaked everything in.

They passed a quaint café and a luxury fabric shop. Turrets and spires rose above the rows of peaked rooftops and parapet balconies, rising into the sun. She watched as a stream of swallows circled the highest towers, and pigeons roosted in the masonry among eyeless stone gargoyles and glass windows.

Cyrus let Gandif pull her along while she marveled, and he navigated street after street. "Now listen, miss. Here's a fast rundown of the place," he told her. "The city's divided into three districts: Uptown, where the rich folk and structures of grandeur reside—full of those fancy colonnades, and mansions with their floral gardens and trimmed hedges. Then Downtown, that's the heart and soul and lively buzzing place of commerce, entertainment and daily living—where we are now."

Cyrus eyed the shop-lined streets and plazas, wonderful-smelling bakeries and pubs.

"Then lastly there's Lowtown, the place of warehouses and construction, and the lower class dwelling apartments. Some would call the Outskirts the fourth district, but it's outside the east wall, and has all manner of poor and strange folk."

He pointed, "At the center of the city's the palace, home to our ruling monarch King Magnovska. The Church of Draeth is that steep and spired thing towering high nearby it. And not far away is Draevensett Academy! Oh and don't forget the big clock, Tall Tim; he's useful when yer lost."

Cyrus nodded, though she doubted she could remember it all.

Mother had once roamed these streets. What had it been like for her growing up here? Had she been happy? She tried to imagine a young image of Mother skipping up the street.

She was following in her footsteps, in a way, heading toward the Ability school Mother had most likely attended. This was the closest she would ever get to her. There was no grave in Elvenstone; no one seemed to know where her body lay, a fact Cyrus found hard to live with. But here, she could almost feel her presence, almost touch the past.

Cyrus pushed her hood back to see better, then felt self-conscious. Her cherry red hair caught people's attention. She made sure to hide her human ears in its tangled mop. She'd streaked their insides with charcoal lines like a bat's, to resemble vempar ears, but trusting in a simple disguise was more than unnerving.

A carriage rolled past—an odd thing with two large wheels and one smaller wheel at the front, giving it a triangular look. Some sort of engine propelled it forward.

Technology here was different, old fashioned yet sleek.

A man in a long coat and cravat crossed the walkway in front of them, two young girls following at his heels. At first she thought they were daughters, but their clothes were dreary gray and worn, and they kept their heads down as they carried purchase bags. Cyrus realized with a start they were humans—his slaves. Her heart clenched.

Finally reaching the end of the street, Gandif indicated a series of rising towers with a chin-nod. "There she is! The famous Draev Guardian Academy, Draevensett."

Her eyes widened. It looked more castle and mansion combined than school.

She adjusted the fingerless gloves she kept on, and her hands shook like leaves as they stopped before the looming iron gate. Its rods curled and weaved like a dark fairytale, and stone posts either side bore roaring winged lions with horns. Gandif wore a lopsided grin as he pushed open the left gate half and took the lead, up a wide paved path.

"Go away, go away!" Something squeaked at them.

Cyrus started.

It had a head of cotton fluff, and leaves for arms and legs and a series of wings. "Go away!" the small creature repeated, flying about and swatting at their hair.

"That pixit's still here? Darn thing," muttered Gandif, ducking under his hat.

The pixit snarled, showing a mouthful of pointed teeth. "No belong, no belong!"

"Yer what don't belong!" Gandif shouted and hurried up the path. Once the gate was behind them, the pixit stopped following and went back to its nest in the wall. "Stupid thing acts like it owns the place," he muttered.

Cyrus followed him up the slope and they passed underneath the arch of two connected towers. She took in deep, calming breaths, and caught scent of something sweet and floral in the air. Beyond the arch, the path became a flagstone drive and circled a fountain before the school's main entrance. The fountain's statue was another winged lion, this one looking solemn and grand.

The castle-mansion school towered high. Tall leaded windows and tracery, fluted spires crowning each tower, all curves and points, grand and intimidating. Gandif stepped up to a door tucked beneath the colonnaded walkway running the length of the school's front.

"Remember now, you're a vempar boy. Don't go slippin' up," he muttered at her ear before knocking on the door.

She swallowed.

At a brisk "Come in!" they entered. The place was a jumble of rooms, something like a doctor's quarters and a biologist's lab rolled into one. Bottles, vials, and equipment filled every table and shelf, along with bizarre potted plants. She poked at a spongey purple one.

"Zushil?" Gandif asked, peering around.

"Yes, I'm here— Oh. If it isn't an old acquaintance."

A face poked out from a side room, weighted under black hair that stood up like too-tall grass. Zushil came over and set down a blue pot on a counter space, his quick eyes behind glasses taking them both in. His narrow, long features showed both surprise and disgruntlement, and he smoothed his lab coat. "Finally come to request a favor of me, hm, Gandif? That's the only reason you'd show up after so many years."

Gandif's grin tilted and he nodded, clapping a hand on Cyrus's shoulder. "That's right. A favor for this girl, here, Cyrus."

Girl?! Her eyebrows shot up.

"She's got Ability, and wishes to master it." Cyrus was prepared to yell at him, when he added: "She also wants her female gender t' be kept secret."

Gandif leaned sideways to her ear, his breath tickling her cheek. "He's the school doctor. There'd be no foolin' him about your gender. Better to say it upfront now," he explained.

She pouted but couldn't argue.

The doctor quirked a long wiry eyebrow at Gandif. "Still speaking with that lame accent you call *bounty hunter talk*, I see?" he muttered.

Gandif rolled a shrug, ignoring the rebuke.

Zushil adjusted his glasses, then bent to peer down at Cyrus. She instinctively stepped back, and the doctor grimaced.

"Shy? Well, either way, Ability rarely happens in females. So you're going to have to prove to me that what you have is, in fact, Elemental Manipulation Ability. I refuse to trouble myself in—"

"You still owe me for savin' yer life. I've never asked for anything, until now," Gandif interrupted.

The doctor's brow pinched, and he removed his glasses, setting them on the counter for a moment as he rubbed his forehead. "Who *is* she to you?"

"Someone I owe a favor, and I'll say no more. C'mon, I've seen her use the gift. Will ya let her enroll or not?"

Zushil considered them both as if calculating something, then let out a huff through his thin lips. "All right. Show me what you can do, tween."

"Huh? Oh!" Cyrus jumped, and looked around for something metal to manipulate, and spotted a spoon near Zushil's elbow. Concentrating, she let her hand reach toward the spoon, touching it, imagining her *essence* pouring over and into the metal…*twisting*…

K-krrrrk!

She heard a gasp from the doctor and looked up.

In his palm were the glasses he'd set on the counter, only now they were melted and twisted—the frames resembling a distorted snake. Somehow, she'd accidentally touched them instead of the spoon.

Zushil's face soured as if he'd lost something expensive, and Gandif's stubble jaw puckered, trying not to laugh.

Cyrus cringed at the mistake.

"I...um..." she began to apologize.

The doctor looked bitterly comical, setting the once-fine glasses gingerly on the counter, his narrow mouth a perpetual grimace. He harrumphed, then faced her again.

"I see you do, indeed, have a rather special—if not horrifyingly *destructive*—Ability. Terravis class."

She winced, inching back at each word.

"We cannot have such a terrifying thing running loose through the kingdom. Who knows what manner of destruction you'll cause if you don't stay put here where you can be properly supervised? For that reason, I will approve that you are eligible to enroll in Draevensett."

Cyrus blinked. She was accepted? Just like that? "Wow!" Thrilled, she clasped her palms together.

"I'll go inform the principal," said Dr. Zushil. "In the meantime, you may go to the commons hall and get acquainted with your new classmates—most of them do homework in there. And yes, I'll keep your *gender-whatever* nonsense a secret." He briskly went to the door, "Come!" expecting her to follow promptly.

Back outside in the damp open air, Cyrus did follow, until she noticed Gandif's stride slow and swerve off to the side. He came to a stop at the shimmering fountain, and she deviated from Zushil toward him. She paused two steps back, until he finally turned to face her. Reluctance clouded his grin, and her heartbeat quickened in fear.

Zushil, farther ahead, halted once he realized no one was following, and he grew more irked by the second, waiting.

Gandif offered Cyrus a smile. "Well, missy, I guess this is where we part ways."

Ah...that's right. She should've expected this. It wasn't like they were family or anything; he had his own life. But it tugged at her heart strings to say goodbye to the last link she had left of her old life—painful as it was.

Cyrus suddenly felt more nervous than ever. Without him, what would she do if something went wrong? Who would help her? She really would be on her own, now.

Gandif shook his shaggy head, as if reading her thoughts. "Now, now," he clucked, "Don't start gett'n the heebie-jeebies. Everything'll be fine! You'll see."

He gave her a wink before half-turning away, and offered one last comfort. "I'm sure this place is where yer meant t' be, kiddo. They'll treasure that Ability of yours. And who knows, maybe I'll catch ya later sometime, eh?" Dull light caught in his toothy smile.

With that, he left. And Cyrus watched until his back faded from view beyond the gate, her stomach in knots.

She was alone.

In a foreign kingdom.

With those who hated humans.

"Will you *kindly* hurry and move your hindquarters up here?" snapped Dr. Zushil, still waiting and tapping a frustrated polished shoe. "I'm a busy man, you know—*quite busy.*"

She jumped with a start and hurried after him.

A new figure approached on her left as she did, and she turned her head. A tall vempar with eyes as blue as a flowing river passed her by. The river current within them caught her for a brief moment, studying her, before releasing its hold.

She felt her lips part. But before she could speak, he vanished through the colonnade.

The doctor tapped his shoe again, and she hurried. He led her up a series of steps to the school's grand main doors: tall, arching rosewood panels with bat-wing scrollwork and the Draev Guardian coat-of-arms at the top, and lion heads for door knobs. She followed Zushil across the threshold and into a white-and-silver marble foyer. Her footsteps echoed indoors off the vaulted ceiling and delicate columns lining the walls. At the center of the foyer stood a great marble statue of a man, cape rippling out behind him, his strong hand extended to welcome those who entered the school. Cyrus paused, tilting her head back.

"That is Protector Draev, the founder of the D.G. League and of this school," spoke Dr. Zushil, pausing for a moment. "He was the greatest vempar to have ever lived."

She noted the way an invisible wind seemed to blow the statue's hair, and she added the founder to the list of things she'd have to remember from now on. The doctor continued walking, and she followed him up one of two grand staircases curving along the walls; her hand trailed along the polished rail. Decorative leaded windows stared at her as they reached the top and passed through hallway after hallway, their patterns playing shadows across the tile floors. Now and then a banister snaked away from their path to meet with a floor above. Lamps of oilpowder hung unlit at intervals between scenic paintings and niches of rare pottery and plants.

It was a small relief to see they used oilpowder, same as back home—a substance with the unique property of glowing bright once lit, and reusable, the fuel for engines and many other things.

The doctor halted before a door, catching the handle and opening it for her to step through. She steadied her breathing, clenching at her backpack's shoulder straps.

'Time to meet my new classmates. My vempar classmates.'

A ken-Shou adjusted his perch on the commons hall windowsill—stained-glass blues, reds and yellows painting him in gaudy splotches.

I should make them acknowledge me, the madman somewhere inside him cackled. *Make them, make them...*

Aken tried to block it out.

The main door to the hall swung open with a *creak*, and Aken's eyelids lifted halfway in response. Students about the hall paused what they were doing, looking toward the sound.

A young vempar rounded the door with care, short red hair in loose messy waves, and eyes the shade of lilac flowers. Her gaze was low, avoiding any eye contact, and Dr. Zushil towered beside her wearing his typical sharp frown.

Aken's breath stilled. It was *her*—the princess he'd seen in the starlight orb!

Or at least a girl who very much resembled her. The princess had been human, though, not vempar.

"*Ahem*, everyone! Your attention, please! This is Cyrus," said Zushil. He bent to the girl in a whispered conversation before straightening again. "Cyrus Sole, to be exact. Your new classmate, who's come from a distant farming community."

In the hall, she looked like a warm ray of light through an overcast, frigid day. Aken could feel the madman draw back into its cage within the deep recesses of his mind.

He grinned as a thought hit him: This could be his one chance to make a real friend, one who wasn't from around here and who didn't know about Scourgebloods.

Cyrus forced herself to look up from the floor at the numerous faces—vempar faces—staring at her. She wanted to dissolve into mist and blow away.

Avoiding any direct eye contact, she swept her gaze from the hundred-plus group to look at the ribs of the vaulted ceiling. It was a pretty ceiling. So were the row of colorful windows with stained-glass designs.

And there in the rainbow shadows glowed a pair of blue eyes.

She gave a start. The eyes belonged to a boy, who sat watching her, his side bangs casting shadows down the planes of his face.

In one smooth motion he bounded down off the sill and crossed the table-littered expanse, coming to a halt before her. She took a step back. His hair was blond as the sun, and his irises like the sky. He had on dark pants and a maroon lace-up shirt.

The boy held out his hand and gave a bright smile. "Hi, Cyrus! I'm Aken-Shou; plain Aken for short. How old are you? I'm gonna be thirteen in July."

Cyrus gave a small, insecure smile back but didn't take his hand. "Hi. Um, I'll be thirteen in August."

"Cool, so we're in the same grade."

Dr. Zushil harrumphed. "Now that you're so *happily* acquainted, Aken, why don't you go and show Cyrus around Draevensett?"

"Sure thing, Doc," Aken saluted.

The doctor's features pinched in distaste. "Quit calling me *Doc*, you miscreant! It is either Doctor, or Dr. Zushil."

Aken tilted his head with an edge of mischief. "How about Doco the Zush—that's got a cool ring to it? Or Doc-a-doodle-doo." He imitated the guy's tall, stood-up hair with a hand, like a chicken's comb.

Snickers and laughs circled the commons hall.

"Quit that, this instant! *This instant!*" The doctor stomped, and the student body fell silent. "I'll never understand why Master Nephryte tolerates an unwanted stray like you, but you'd better learn your manners before he changes his mind." Zushil stalked out the door.

Cyrus watched as Aken gave a shrug, waving the matter aside and turning back to her with the same smile. "So anyway, how about I show you around this place?"

She nodded faintly, though she wished it were someone else. This boy seemed like the type who sought attention through troublemaking, and she didn't want any part of it.

"Oo-oo! Me too, *me too!*"

Something bounded out of nowhere to her side, and she started in fright. The *something* was another boy, who winked merrily. Taller than Aken, he had wild orange, spiky hair and sandy-green eyes in a very expressive face. His beginning square chin was cute, and he rocked up and down on his heels. "Welcome to the school, Cyrus!" he said.

His clothes reminded her of desert sands: a black tank, baggy canary pants that poofed out before squeezing the ankles, and shoes with up-turned toes. He resembled a skinny genie, and his skin was the shade of light mahogany.

"Butt-out, Bakoa. *I'm* giving the tour," said Aken.

Bakoa squinted. "I can help, too. Why do you care so much, anyways?"

Aken snatched her hand and began leading her away before she realized it. "Hey, wait up!" Bakoa hollered after them.

⤴

The two boys showed Cyrus through hall after hall, stairwell after stairwell and staircase, classroom after classroom, until her head was spinning and body careening—and there was still more to cover!

From what Aken explained, the student body was divided into five Floors: Harlow, Tathom, Smart, Harcourt and Earnest. Each had their own dorm floor and a banner with their Floor's crest at the entrance.

Aken and Bakoa led her up to the top fifth floor, where a banner hung bearing the crest of an elaborate sun with wavy rays and a falcon flying through.

"This is our Floor, Harlow," Aken answered before she could ask.

"Oh." She wrung her fingers together. "And who's in charge of Floors?"

"Each is supervised by a Draev Master."

"What's a Master, exactly?"

"Masters are the highest ranking Ability users in the Draev Guardian League," he explained. Masters were just below that of the Grandmaster, who governed the elite fighting force, and they all had combat experience in leading Draev squads out on missions and in defense of the city.

The five Draev Masters who chose to give their time serving the League's Academy hoped to pass on their knowledge to future generations, to create the next wave of Draev Guardians who will defend the Kingdom of Draeth. Here, they acted as both dorm leader and mentor, responsible for honing their students' combat training, lifestyle, and overall good behavior while students attended daily classes.

"Five Draev Masters, five groups," Cyrus contemplated. "How do I know which Floor I'll end up in?"

"Simple." Aken shoved his hands in his pockets. "You either get picked by a Master, or placed with whoever the principal decides. I was forcibly picked by mine."

'Great,' Cyrus thought, who in their right mind would want her? She was a new weakling. She'd end up with some lame Floor, no doubt about it.

"Our Master——" Bakoa began to say, with bubbling enthusiasm.

"Mentor," Aken interjected.

"——is *Master* Nephryte. And he's the best of the best!" Bakoa finished.

Aken's jaw tensed.

"He's smart, kind, and the totally coolest, *greatest* warrior ever!" Bakoa went on. Shining stars of admiration swam in his sandy-green eyes. This Nephryte Master must mean a great deal to him.

"He is not." Aken cut in again, this time raising a determined fist. "And I'll prove it. I'm gonna be the first ever to defeat him!"

Bakoa cocked his head to the side, then squinted, rubbing a finger over his cleft chin.

"I will, you'll see," Aken insisted sharply. He veered his attention back to Cyrus——hooking one of her arms around his to steer her away. "So, what do you think of the place so far? Pretty grand, huh?"

His shoulder brushed against hers; she wanted to pull away. Never had a boy been so close——they usually kept away like she was the *plague of death* itself. As a matter of fact, most everybody did. It was a shock to suddenly feel physical contact. She freed her arm, trying to act casual.

Aken watched her as if waiting for something, and she remembered his question. "Oh, yes, it is. I think it's beautiful. Enchanting," she answered.

Bakoa grinned and nodded.

Aken glanced at the floor and murmured, "A lot like you

are."

Her breath choked in her throat. What the heck did he just say? She bristled before she could stop herself. "You've got a screw loose if you think I'm pretty. And just so you know, I'm weird and nerdy, and I don't plan on changing." She pinched her gloves.

After a pause, Aken laughed. "Who isn't a little weird? You're fine just the way you are, Cy."

Heat rose to her cheeks. Cy—she had a nickname, and it wasn't Cherry-top.

On her other side, Bakoa reached for her arm. "Do you want to see the library? I can take you."

"Don't even, *Baka*. I'm her guide," Aken objected.

"*Wuh*, how come I can't be included? I'm tired of being left out all the time!" The desert boy sniffled.

Cyrus looked back and forth between them, her lungs iced over. *Her...?* Did Aken just say *her*?

Oh no. How could he tell? Nothing about her screamed *girl*!

She had to hide it—she couldn't afford to stand out in this school as a rare female Ability user! The more eyes on her, the more likely her half-human secret would be found out. A half-human Ability user would be fun to experiment on, or use as a slave—providing they didn't execute her as a spy, first. Blending in as just another boy was her best defense.

Fear made goosebumps down her arms, and she instinctively touched her throat.

"I..." Cyrus tried to say.

Both boys stopped arguing to look at her.

"I—I'm actually a boy."

There, she said it. And silence reigned.

Aken's eyes grew the size of dinner plates, and the desert boy's jaw dropped to the floor.

Somewhere beyond a window, a cicada chirped, serenading the awkward moment. *Chirrrrup. Chirrrrrup.*

Aken turned away, gripping the sides of his head.

Bakoa leaned forward, peering closely at Cyrus's face. "Are you sure?"

Cyrus took a step back. "I would know myself, wouldn't I? Anyway, is Aken upset?"

"He has emotional issues. Best not to ask about it," he whispered.

Aken returned, shoving Bakoa aside, and gave Cyrus his finest cool-guy smile. "Of course you're a boy." He gave a laugh that sounded too forced. "We knew that. This was just a bit of friendly teasing. Right, *Baka*?"

"Fibber." Bakoa wiped his nose with a wrist and stuck out his lower lip. "There you go being mean t' me again. The word *baka* means *idiot* in Hanasu. You're calling me an idiot every time you say that!"

"Am I?" Aken asked with a tell-tale smirk.

"Bakoa is an island name, and it means *bow to the warrior*."

Aken shrugged up his palms. "Okay. Anyway, no harm was meant, Cy. It's obvious you're a guy. You've got a real, *erm*...masculine figure!"

Cyrus should have been pleased they fell for her bluff, but a flicker of anger sparked at that last comment.

"Where's the restroom?" she asked, fed up with this conversation and with this troublemaker.

Aken blinked. "Oh, that way." He pointed to a door in the entryway: Harlow's restroom & shower room. She was about to go inside when she saw it was for *boys* and that Aken and Bakoa were coming in with her.

Eek, no way was she going in there with them!

She spun back around. "Never mind! I'm fine. I just wanted to know where it was—ahahaha." She gave a strange laugh before dashing off in the opposite direction, leaving both boys behind.

Exiting Harlow by way of the stairwell, she sprinted like an anteleer, leaping down three steps at a time, backpack bouncing behind.

'So embarrassing!'

There must be another restroom, somewhere. *'Hurry, HUrry, HURRY. Agh, I really gotta go!'*

The floor below had better have one—*It better!*

11

The principal of Draevensett raised one bushy eyebrow across the mahogany desk at Doctor Zushil, who looked quite miffed about something—then again, he always looked miffed about something the way his mouth seemed permanently chiseled in a displeased frown.

Principal Han was feeling his centuries-worth of years today, gray and white hair frizzed around his robe's shoulders and stole. He had retired from being Grandmaster of the D.G. League to take up the task of running this school and producing quality new generations of Draevs. He relished it, though some days were more weary than others, like today.

Han patiently listened to Zushil's grudging recommendation of a boy recently found to have Ability: Cyrus Sole, able to manipulate certain metals while touching them.

It suddenly dawned on Han why the doctor was wearing a pair of old, discolored glasses, and he stifled a throaty laugh. "Well, I do accept your recommendation, Dr. Zushil," Han said once the doctor had finished speaking. "It's not as if we can be picky these days. Even those with a fraction of Ability are prized gems."

Han turned his head to the four Draev Guardian Masters

also present in the office room, opposite Zushil. "Now then, as for where to place the boy." His hands folded and his lips parted, when suddenly the door flung open and the fifth Master walked in.

"Principal Han." Moving with fluid grace, the vempar took a stand alongside the other Masters, even as they shot glares at his tardiness. Master Nephryte faced the principal. "I hear a new student is joining us. Please, Principal Han," he bowed his head formally, "allow me to take him under my care."

Han's brow lifted.

"What?" one of the Masters exclaimed. "You don't know anything about the boy, and already you're trying to snatch him up?" accused Master Deidreem. Younger than Nephryte, Deidreem was a charming viper when temper didn't get the better of him. His arms were crossed and lips sour. The bay window's light touched the dark curls spilling from beneath his top hat, and his skin the deep gray of a stormcloud dipped in charcoal threatened to bring a heavy downpour.

Nephryte stopped himself from rolling his eyes. "I was not aware this was a competition. I am the Master with the least amount of students; therefore, the boy should fall to me. Master Deidreem, it is simple logic."

"Logic, *tch!*" Master Deidreem pinched the hat's brim, his epidote-crystal eyes glowing under its shadow. "You and all your great logic—"

"Enough," Master Eletor cut in. His languid lids were half-asleep from pulling an all-nighter. "You're worse than bickering chipmunks." He lazily ran a hand through his bedhead of aqua hair.

Deidreem's mouth twisted but kept silent.

"Haven't you enough on your plate, though, Nephryte?" Eletor's arms lifted with a yawn and he craned back his neck. "With that kid, I mean. Aken-Shou." He made a face. "It took a full week to undo that last prank of his."

Dread clouded the room at the memory: Every student's and Master's hair had turned a horrid bright green from hidden dye in shampoo bottles.

They recoiled at the reminder. Master Seren-Rose touched her black hair protectively, and old Master Brangor carefully stroked his red beard. Nephryte shut his eyes—no doubt remembering Aken-Shou skipping through the halls, laughing and pointing at everybody's green hair and shouting "Broccoli head!"

Deidreem's frown lifted into a smirk. "You've really got your hands full with that one. A piece of work, he is."

Nephryte coolly ignored him. "He's not a bad kid. Whatever else he may be, it is *not* that. And I can assure you his punishment cleaning the bathrooms was severe."

Principal Han shook his head, marveling at Nephryte's determination and patience with a boy who, from day one, had been nothing but trouble. How did he manage, especially when the boy despised him so? It was by his and Han's mercy that the last Scourgeblood was allowed to stay and train. But a day would come when the boy's blood power would awaken, and then...

"Perhaps this new student will be a good influence on Aken-Shou," Nephryte continued to implore. "He looked out of place when I saw him. I can tell he's not from the city. Does he have any family?"

Han shook his head.

"Then I can be of help. Most of my students are orphans. What is his name?"

"Cyrus Sole. From the northern farming communities?" Han glanced over at Zushil, who confirmed with an impatient nod.

"Cyrus Sole..." Nephryte repeated.

Han drummed his fingers on the desk, thinking, as the room awaited his decision.

Cyrus paused at the mouth of the door leading into the third floor, and scanned every which way. This was the north wing, teacher and staff offices, if she remembered correctly. There had to be a restroom.

Hopefully that Aken wouldn't come looking for her. Why did he have to be the first student she met?

Immersed in her search and thoughts, she rounded a set of antique lobby chairs and almost bumped into a tall, ultramarine shirt. "Ah! Excuse me!"

She tilted her head back for a quick look at the person, then stilled. It was the vempar from earlier, the one whose river eyes had followed her so intensely after she parted ways with Gandif.

"That's quite all right, student Cyrus," he spoke, voice smooth as water, a river that was calm and sure of the course it took. Light from a row of windows played in his eyes.

Fair brown hair framed his unblemished features in waves, stray bangs tucked behind a pointed ear. There was an air of knowledge and books about him.

Wait, how did he know her name? Was the whole school talking about her already?

"It is a pleasure to meet—" he began, when she blurted out: "Where's the restroom?"

He paused and blinked.

She didn't mean to say it like *that*. How embarrassing!

He raised one long finger, pointing to a door on her right bearing the label *Restroom*.

Her face colored. Why didn't she see that sooner? '*Nice first impression, stupid-head,*' she screamed in her skull and darted for the door.

Inside the restroom, her shoes squeaked to a halt. Three boys were standing at "wall toilets" or whatever those things were called. She shielded her face with a hand and carefully avoided looking their way. If she was going to start living here as a boy, she'd have to get used to this. *'I'll be fine as long as I avoid those wall things.'*

Trying to appear inconspicuous, she slipped into one of the stalls.

Thankfully the students soon left, and she washed her hands in silence, letting out a breath.

Her reflection in the mirror above the sink caught her eye: that fluffy short hair and small frame. She could hear the old jeers in her head: *"Cherry-top! Cherry-top!"*

No, here she wasn't that pitiful, made-fun-of kid. Here, she could be someone else, someone better. Leave the past behind.

Hefting her backpack and exiting the restroom quietly, she bit back a yelp when she spotted the vempar man still standing there, waiting for her.

"May I speak with you, now?" His gaze caught her like a lasso, and she nodded timidly. "I am Master Nephryte," he extended a hand. "It is a pleasure to meet you, Cyrus Sole. I am to be your Draev Master during your stay."

She blinked up at him. This mystery man wasn't some creeper, but her new Master? And he was the powerful one Bakoa had mentioned, which meant her Master wouldn't be someone lame?

'Thank you, Lord!'

Cyrus lightly shook his hand, hoping a vempar couldn't sense human blood through touch. His skin was warm, as warm as the smile he gave, long hand engulfing her cold fingers.

"You have nothing to be nervous about, student Cyrus. I am certain my other students will grow to like you."

'Like? Hopefully not as in taste,' she thought wryly.

He released her hand, and she nodded politely. "It's nice to meet you, Master."

Hyah!

A shout rang out of nowhere, startling the flesh off her bones, and she whirled sideways to see the top of a potted tree behind the Master move. Something leaped out, diving like a bird of prey, soaring fist-first and aiming a blow to the back of the Master's head.

It happened so fast, she barely had time to register the assailant as Aken—a battle grin splitting his face.

The Master coolly lifted his index finger, not even bothering to look, and Aken came to a sudden halt mid-soar. He squirmed, suspended in the air by nothing.

Cyrus let her jaw dangle open.

"Not again," whined a voice. Bakoa was peeking out of the stairwell and shaking his orange head.

"You—" Aken began. But before he could get another word out, Master Nephryte's finger moved in a circular motion, and Aken was sent spinning across the lobby like a whirring tornado.

Wind whipped hair into Cyrus's eyes and she tugged her hood up before Aken finally came to a crashing halt—head first—into the tiled floor. *Chnk!*

This Draev Master must be very powerful to use his Ability so easily, without hardly moving. She stared in awe. It was one thing to see yourself using the gift, but quite another to see someone talented like Master Nephryte use it, a genuine professional.

The Master's face was the picture of worn patience. Apparently this was not Aken's first attack attempt—and probably wouldn't be the last. What the heck was he thinking? How immature was this boy?

"Yu-yu-you..." Aken stammered, trying to stand straight after falling flat on his face, nose bloody and swollen. Like a drunken idiot, he ran into chairs and walls trying to steer toward them.

Master Nephryte showed no concern whatsoever, but she cringed, until Aken's nose began changing color. The purple and red damage faded, Healed—his face soon restored to its previous charm. Spooked, Cyrus drew back.

Aken wiped leftover blood from his nose, and turned his fury up at the Master.

Master Nephryte gazed coolly back in return. "That was quite a sad attack plan. Or were you throwing a tantrum?"

Aken raised his right hand, pointing at the Master. "One of these days, I'll win against you. Just you wait."

The Master did not flinch a centimeter.

Aken pointed a thumb to his chest, blazing with determination. "I'll become the greatest Draev Guardian ever to exist! I'll surpass you and everybody in the D.G. League, even the king. And when I do, I'll fix this broken, messed up world. You wait and see, I'll make this world soar through the dawn into a new age!" he stated, chest puffing out.

Aken's name was the picture of a bird soaring into the dawn—Cyrus thought that's what it meant in Hanasu. But he was an overconfident idiot to have such a lofty goal. Determination radiated from him like the sun, daring the odds to defy him. It was almost contagious, making her wonder if she, too, could defy the odds set before her.

The evening lamps glowed to life around them, and he looked almost regal in their golden glow.

"Then I suggest you start by getting better grades." Master Nephryte sliced through the moment like a knife, holding up a test sheet from a folder under his arm: a big, red *F*-beside Aken's name.

A look of dread crossed the boy's features, his glorious moment spoiled, his chest a deflated balloon. But the Master wasn't done yet.

"Is this how you plan to surpass the D.G. League? The king himself? By getting the worst grades in school? Because you've most certainly done that." He confronted the withering boy, point-blank. "If you really want to accomplish something, work on yourself first. And while you're at it, start thinking more about what Lord God wants you to do, instead of only what *you* want to do." He rolled the paper up and *bopped* him over the head with it.

Aken's chin hung in humiliation.

Cyrus thought she saw the hint of a grin at the edges of Nephryte's lips before the Master turned to her, all courteous once more.

"It's already time for dinner. Cyrus, would you care to join us?"

Join for *dinner*? She dreaded to think what dinner might consist of. Did they eat anything besides absorbing *essence* from living things? There were rumors among humans— things she didn't want to consider right now. Then her stomach growled loudly, answering the question before her mouth had a chance to.

"That was the next place we were gonna show you, Cy." Aken's pointed ears perked. He appeared beside her so fast that she jumped. He snatched her backpack off and left it in a chair. "Follow me!" He winked, all humiliation forgotten.

Cyrus had no choice as he swiftly caught her hand and pulled her with him into a run. "M-maybe—!" was all she managed to say before her lungs gasped for breath.

Bakoa hurried after them. "Hey! Wait for me, you guys!"

12

Draevensett's dining hall was grand: capped by a domed ceiling, and ringed with depictions from the League's history. Long-plumed birds, dragons, and warriors reached out of the paintwork into sculptures—giving a three-dimensional illusion as if they were alive and stepping free of the walls and ceiling.

Cyrus's gaze roved. The dining hall was divided into five sections. Narrow fluted columns and paper screens made barriers, one section per Floor.

Aken led her to Floor Harlow's, where four other boys were already seated at a long table.

"It's cool you're on the same Floor as us, Cy." He looked over his shoulder with a smile.

Cyrus couldn't fake a smile back, nerves froze her every facial muscle.

She barely noticed Bakoa rush in to take the chair between two empty seats—a clever plan to sit between them—and Aken shooing him off.

"Yo, Harlows!" Aken greeted the group, and presented with a grand sweep of an arm, "This is Cyrus Sole, from one of those remote farming communities, our new floormate!"

Four faces turned to stare.

Cyrus swallowed, and sweated as a silent second ticked

by.

Then they each rose.

The first boy kept his chin down, as if too shy to meet her gaze, same age as her, though he was short by a few inches. He peeked from beneath a too-big Bladeer hat, his eyes pale as blue ice. "Z…Zartanian," he said, soft-spoken. Raven bangs framed his fair cheeks, and the rest of his curly mop was gathered in a low ponytail.

He quickly sat back down, readjusting the blue collared coat around his narrow shoulders and dress shirt. His dark pants were tucked into high-laced leather boots. She offered a small smile and nod, but Zartanian ducked beneath the hat away from her sight.

"*Hmph*. Hercule Dragonsbane," said the next boy, dripping with aristocratic pride, his pearl-gray hair and layered bangs combed to one side. The air around him gave off a rich, earthy lavender scent to match his lavender vest, white dress shirt, gray cravat and slacks.

His golden eyes burned like that of a dragon's, almost belittling her, and she fidgeted, quickly looking to the next student.

The tallest and oldest student among them craned his neck her way. "Lykale," he said briskly. White hair rose around his hairline like an unmown lawn. Rectangular glasses perched on the bridge of his long nose, aqua eyes glowing behind the lenses. He flashed a smile that lacked any warmth.

A stylish tan coat and khaki pants made him fashionable, except for the black choker around his neck with a padlock pendant.

The fourth member rose from his chair to give a cordial bow. "A pleasure to meet you, Cyrus Sole. I am Mamoru." Lamplight lingered in his red highlights. He winked, and her cheeks flushed.

His smile tugged at a vicious scar cut down his lower right

eyelid and cheek.

A scar on a vempar?

She almost curtsied but caught herself, bowing her head like a boy instead.

He had a bizarre sense of fashion. His olive skin showed where fabric chunks were missing. "Welcome to Floor Harlow," he said. "We're an *interesting* group, to say the least, but I hope we can still get along."

She glanced at his black-and-white shoes and bowtie, formally out of place amidst the fabric chaos. "Thank you. I'm sure we will," she said politely.

What did he mean by *interesting*?

Before Cyrus took a seat at the edge of the table, she peered beyond the paper screens to see the rest of the dining hall. Chatter echoed and plates clacked throughout the wide space. The other Floors were larger compared to Harlow— having forty or more students compared to only seven.

She could make out a few adults: one vempar man wearing a top hat, and a lady in a sleek dress with serpent patterns.

Gandif had said it was rare for a female to have Ability, but that it did happen. The lady stood out like a bejeweled thumb in the hall. It was a fearful reminder to Cyrus why she was faking her gender. She couldn't afford to stand out in a crowd like that.

Carts rolled in through a pair of swinging doors at the far back, loaded with silver trays, as servants steered one to each table throughout the hall. At that moment, Master Nephryte arrived, taking the head seat left of Cyrus.

Their dining cart arrived, and Aken jumped up. "I'll get it!" he said.

The Harlow group stared at him as if feathers were growing out of his head.

"How come when Master Nephryte asks you to get the trays, you never do?" Bakoa began to say.

"Here!" Aken's fingers splayed, and the biggest tray on the cart suddenly lifted and floated over to the table. With a *thump* it landed, and a brown blob came out from underneath. The rest of the trays followed suit—more blobs coming out from under them: little clay cranes, she realized.

She watched as they flew into Aken's palm, where they shrank and he pocketed them, his grin a picture of pride. The other boys shot wary looks his way.

Master Nephryte glanced from him to her, taking mental note of something. He nodded, "Thank you, Aken-Shou." A faint smile tilted his lips.

Aken's proud grin faltered.

Cyrus pretended to mind her own business as Aken went back to his seat, and let herself be distracted by the polished trays now lined down the table center.

The thought of food was cheering. But then she had to worry what would be beneath those polished lids, and what she would do about it.

What did a vempar...

—Master Nephryte lifted the first lid—

...eat?

A roasted bird bedded in potatoes, sliced carrots and zucchini, stared up at her. Other trays revealed bread rolls, breadsticks, a heap of fruit salad and lettuce. Cheesecake, cream-filled tarts and croissants for dessert.

Food. Edible food. Delicious food.

Drool threatened the corners of her mouth. How long had it been since her last meal? Her hands darted out like ravenous bird beaks to fill her plate, and she snatched the slab of meat Mamoru carved—ignoring a twinge in her wrist. Plate piled high, she dug in, stuffing her mouth and eating like a starved skeleton, not even letting the fake wood fangs slow her down.

The Harlow boys watched in silence. It took several seconds before Cyrus noticed, and she halted her feasting.

That growling stomach of hers had failed to notice no one else was eating yet. Letting down a roll and drumstick from her hands, her shoulders slouched sheepishly.

A laugh carried from one of the neighboring paper screens. "Wow, is there a famine we should know about?" A pair of blue-green eyes watched them through a gap in the screens. "I see the strays have gotten themselves a new Floor member, eh? Tell me, is the redhead normal, or a total weirdo like the rest of you?"

Aken stood, chair shoving back. "Shut your pie-face, *jerk*, or I'll do it for you!"

"Bring it on, *blond toots*! Just don't let that Scourgeblood of yours get out of control." The speaker's head emerged, pushing aside the screen. Aken growled. Both boys looked ready to leap across the floor space at each other.

Master Nephryte raised one index finger, and both froze at the warning. "That is enough of *that*. Denim, Aken-Shou, sit down and eat your dinner, and be grateful for it." His voice was hard ice.

Aken glared before sitting back down. The other boy slouched away from the screen and back to his own crowded table.

Master Nephryte clapped both hands together, the sudden noise making Harlow jump in their seats. "Now then. Let us pray before we eat," he said.

Pray? Oops. Cyrus had forgotten her manners completely. Though to be fair, she didn't know if vempars prayed, or what they believed. "...M'sorry..." She chewed and swallowed.

The Master gave a reassuring nod. "It's quite all right, Cyrus. This is your first day here. You already have far better manners than Aken-Shou has ever had—perhaps you could teach him."

Aken made a sound through his nose before settling back in the chair, still glaring at the paper screen enough to burn holes through it.

Mamoru poured from a sparkling water pitcher, its crystal surface catching lamplight. He bent to her ear as he filled her cup—the scent of amber oil surrounded him. "Those two have been enemies since childhood, back when they lived in the Outskirts," he whispered. "Denim's a bully, and he's related to the prince, you see, and has quite a following wherever he goes."

Mamoru moved to the next cup, and as he did, a sad familiar feeling washed over her. So, bullying happened even among vempar kids. *Cherry-top.*

Once Mamoru finished filling the cups, Master Nephryte said a prayer, thanking God for the day. "…And we thank you, Lord, for bringing Cyrus Sole into our Floor household. I ask that You guide Cyrus and each of my dear students along the path You have set before them; that You keep their souls safe and encouraged, close to You, that they may grow to know You more.

"In John 15, You called us *Your friends*—we, the creatures You created. As selfish and sinful as we are, yet You chose to love us. You provide salvation for any who will accept it, even for a hated race like us. I am grateful to You. You are the Savior of our souls and the true Master of all. Amen."

The students dove into the aromatic food, though far more dignified than she had. She considered the deep prayer as she chewed. It seemed that Master Nephryte shared the same Bible faith as her. So many humans in Elvenstone were against the faith. Of all the Floors to end up in, she happened to be in one with a believing Master. Gnawing on a breadstick, she let her attention rove across the table.

Bakoa started laughing about something, and Mamoru used a fork to fling a pea at his nose, but the pea bounced off and into Lykale's glasses. Aken guffawed, and Zartanian hid his mouth behind a hand.

Cyrus found herself grinning for a moment, then

smothered it. The scene reminded her of a misfit family. But she didn't really belong here, and the thought of family was a sore spot. She was just here to train her Ability.

She worked on cleaning her plate, getting lost in the wonderful tastes and smells. If vempars ate regular food, how did they get the *essence* they needed to survive? Without realizing, she mumbled to herself, "Do vempars get any *essence* out of this?" and licked her fork.

The table fell silent, and she gave a start.

"What do you mean?" The Master's brow furrowed, though he didn't look at her directly, while sampling the lettuce.

Fear rattled her rib cage. She fumbled for an explanation. The silence was deafening, their waiting looks piercing.

And then Aken broke in, "Well, I'm not sure how they do things in your neck of the farming community woods, but here we—" he reached over and snatched Lykale's glasses—"*Hey!*"—setting them on his nose and speaking in a mock-intelligent voice, "—we take the gathered *essence* of select organisms and infuse it into our produce. *Ngah*—!" Lykale snatched them back.

"If you're trying to prove you have a brain upstairs, then that was pathetic," the older student replaced his glasses. "You're as much a scientist as an ape in a lab coat."

Aken shooed the insult aside. "In *normal-people speak*, it means Draev groups go out, gather *essence*, put it in containers, then put it in our food. There ya have it!"

It…was in the food? Select organisms—in other words, the *essence* of faeryn, humans and other races.

Cyrus almost dropped a potato. But *essence* wasn't blood. It was a form of life-energy. So…it should be safe to eat? At least her cover hadn't been blown.

"Harvesting *essence* is a dangerous job. Encounters with Argos are frequent lately," the Master spoke, swirling a glass of sparkling clear liquid.

How was *essence* harvested? She'd heard rumors. But Master Nephryte looked kind, refined, not like someone who could...

"Harvesting is not fatal. I have never had a casualty," the Master set down the glass after a sip, as if reading her thoughts. "But some Draevs are careless, taking too much and not valuing the lives of other races. That's why people hire Argos to protect them." His gaze darted to Aken, who was making a little clay crane fly back and forth around Mamoru's head.

"Sounds like we shouldn't harvest, then," Bakoa commented.

"It's necessary for Draevs to harvest, Bakoa," said the Master. "Vempars live here because of the abundance of *essence*-filled food. Otherwise, every vempar would be out hunting for themselves and spreading fear, which could start a new war—as it did in the days of old, the Time of Wandering, when our race were scattered wanderers. Things are different today; the kingdom unites us, and the Draev Guardian League oversees our needs.

"Our only worry now is earning money—which is a far easier worry to handle and less life-threatening," he added. "Being citizens of a kingdom, forced to obey set laws, has brought stability and made vempar kind into a true civilization."

"*Blahhh.*" Aken thumped his head against the back of his chair. "History equals *boring.*"

"How's harvesting done?" Cyrus asked. "I mean, back home at the farm I never had to, and it wasn't talked about much..."

Master Nephryte turned in his chair to face her, and placed a hand on her left shoulder. "Harvesting is done through Touch," he said quietly. "Micro-receptors in the palms of our hands can draw out a living thing's *essence.*"

A nervous twinge crept up her back. They used their

hands, not *fangs*? She'd better be more careful. At least her act as an ignorant country boy was proving useful—no one seemed suspicious that she lacked knowledge.

Master Nephryte shifted to address the rest of the boys around the table, raising his voice, "A powerful vempar can use Touch against other vempars, as well—to weaken or drain them of life. This is how criminals are executed: weakened first, so they cannot Heal properly, then hung. Of course, beheading is more efficient…"

Bakoa dropped his fork and clenched his neck with a frightful squeak.

"However," the Master furthered, "taking *essence* from fellow vempars is otherwise prohibited—except in cases of self-defense. You should be wary, young students. Vempar outlaws won't hold back in killing a Draev in this manner. One day, you will have to battle such outlaws as part of your duty to protect the kingdom."

Her body gave an involuntary shudder, suddenly cold. Becoming a Draev was sounding more and more unappealing.

'I'll get out of here once I master my Ability,' she told herself. There was no reason to stay, once she was sure she could survive on her own out in the world. She sipped the glass of water.

⤳

"This will be your room."

The Master halted before one of several doors lining Harlow's dorm; a rug ran the length of tiles quieting their steps. Coming in from the stairwell, the entryway branched into two corridors: to the left student rooms, to the right a study and the Master's living quarters.

"You're next to mine!" Aken said, and swung an arm around Cyrus's shoulders, which she attempted to evade. "We're gonna be neighbormates! Like *roommates*, but neighbors.”

“Yeah, I figured that out.”

As she reached for the doorknob, Master Nephryte asked, “Your suitcase?”

“Oh, this is all I have.” She indicated the backpack slung over her arm. A flash of sympathy crossed his face—the kind you give a runaway. Though it was Aken who carefully asked: “Do you have any family?”

“Not really.” She looked away.

Aken gave her shoulder a squeeze. “That’s okay, buddy. Neither do I. In fact, none of us Harlows do.”

She gaped. “All of you are orphans?”

He nodded. “That’s why people call us strays. Me, Bak, Zartin, Lyk, Maru—all five of us. Well, except for Herc,” he thought again. “But his parents are self-absorbed noble snobs, so I’m sure he *feels* like one sometimes.”

She stifled a laugh at the odd nicknames. “Was it because of humans?”

“For me, it was. But the others are orphans for different reasons—not that they’ve bothered to share much about their pasts with me.”

Listening, Master Nephryte glanced at a pocket watch before interrupting. “The hour is late, and I have paperwork to look over, so I’ll leave you to get accommodated. I hope you find everything to your liking, Cyrus. My room is down at the other end, if you should need anything. Sleep well.” He patted Aken’s shoulder, to which the boy grimaced.

She dipped her head as the Master left, then, breathing in, she pushed open the door with her elbow.

The bedroom was bigger than her old one back in Elvenstone. An olive-green bed against the right wall, a backless sofa against the left wall by the window, and green curtains framing a view of Draevensett’s steep rooftops and towers piercing the sky. She went over to the window; below was an open courtyard—a circular garden at the heart of Draevensett. Around it circled a spiral walk, connecting all floor levels.

"What's that floor opposite us?" She indicated the rest of the fifth floor across from them, on the other side of the moon-shaped courtyard.

Aken scratched his jaw. "Floor Tathom." He said it like the name gave him a sour taste.

She ran a hand along the cedar wood chest at the foot of the bed. Other furniture included a dresser, side table and nightstand. A brass lamp sat beside a clock in the shape of a cat, and a second lamp attached to the wall near the ceiling.

Shelves stood ready and waiting to be filled, and a built-in closet left of the door was deep enough for an amount of clothes she'd never owned in her life. Opposite it, a small alcove held a sink and mirror.

She surveyed the perfect room for a moment, imagining a new life, a new start. As soon as she let herself feel excited, though, a sadness crept in. It was all finally catching up to her, all in a rush. One day waking up inside a familiar cramped human room, the next standing in an old fashioned dorm in a foreign city…

"It's just like my room, only my bed isn't against the wall," Aken said, his voice cutting through the dreary waves threatening to swamp her. He surveyed the beige walls. "You can borrow some of my art prints, if you want."

She poked at two items found laid out on the bed: patch-like things in the shape of symbols. "What's this?"

Aken tapped the large one, "That's Draevensett's and the D.G. League's coat-of-arms." A fang bearing bat wings, with two white feathers crossed underneath, and a large shield for a background.

"And this," he tapped the smaller sticker, "is Floor Harlow's." A yellow sun with rippling sunbeams and a bird in flight. "You put them on your shirt. It's so we don't have to wear school uniforms. Don't worry, they stay on and don't get messy."

"Oh." They felt silky between her fingers.

Aken studied her sideways, as she dragged her backpack over to the bed, letting it drop on the green rug. She slid down with it, resting her head back against the bed, knees drawn up.

He sat down without a word beside her.

After a long moment of feeling awkward, she worked up the nerve to speak. "I guess I'm feeling overwhelmed. It's all so much to take in—so many different sights, rules, people…all at once."

Chased away from her hometown, spending a fearful night in the woods, struggling to adjust to a different culture, and pretending to be someone she wasn't—that's what she really wanted to say.

Gaining some energy, Cyrus forced herself back up on her feet and began to unpack.

The few contents of her backpack plopped onto the bedspread—including the ruby pendant necklace and stuffed bunny. She fingered each.

"Those look special." Aken sat up on his knees to see.

"Mementos." She held the bunny in her arms for a moment, "…Of my mother." Tucking the necklace inside a hidden zipped pouch in the bunny's back, she propped it against the pillow. Her knuckle involuntarily rubbed a damp corner in her eye.

Aken reached out to touch the bunny's ears. "She must've loved you very much."

"Yep. The only person who ever did. This was the first thing she made for me. And the necklace is just something she used to wear a lot, because her hair was bright red and it made the color stand out… I guess she was proud of it." She chuckled. "Maybe I should be, too."

Aken nodded, "Red hair is awesome." His lips hesitated a fraction, as if searching for the appropriate words, before asking: "Do you have many memories of her?"

Memories. Cyrus swallowed to keep her voice even. "I remember her hair—my hand reaching out to touch it. It was long, and I think I mistook it for spaghetti once and tried to eat it."

"*Pfft*—" Aken laughed into the edge of the bed. His reaction made her chuckle, too.

She failed to mention the *other* memory she had of Mother, though—a memory or a dream. Of red hair, a woman running, overwhelming fear, desperation, white trees standing around like ghosts, a dark underground tunnel…and then screams…

She shook off the shiver running up her limbs, pushing the images out of mind. It had to be just a nightmare, she kept telling herself. Not a memory. Those images had no basis in reality.

Why was she telling Aken any of this, anyway? He was annoying. Somehow he'd made her drop her guard a little, and now she was sharing past stories like an old lady.

"It's been a long day, and I'm tired," she said, dropping the hint for him to leave. Aken nodded and picked at his fingernails, not seeming to understand. "I'm going to bed," she said more forcefully.

He looked up, realization dawning, and got to his feet. "Oh, okay. Um, goodnight then."

She closed the door behind him, and exhaled.

Pajamas and a spare shirt were on the bed. She thanked whoever they were from; it'd be nice to sleep in something clean.

Her heart pounded as she changed and sank beneath the covers of a new bed. Moonbeams played through the window, while her mind stirred restlessly. A new world, a new life and disguise, could she really do this?

She must have dozed off eventually, because a rapid knock on the door woke her at the break of dawn.

13

The rapid knock on Cyrus's door was followed by someone bursting into the room without waiting for an answer.

"Wake up, Cy! It's almost breakfast time, and we're gonna have a *special* one." Mischief twinkled in Aken's eye.

Cyrus sat up, startled awake before recognizing it was him. She checked the time on the cat clock, and her mouth yawned in protest. Then the realization hit that a boy was in her room while she was in pajamas. "*Eep!*" she squeaked and drew the bed covers up to her chest—not that there was much to hide.

"What?" Aken tilted his head at a curious angle, and she flinched. "Wow," he pointed, "You have the worst case of morning hair I've ever seen! Is that a bird's nest?"

She threw a pillow at him, then pressed her palms around her head, smashing down the wild hair strands. A mischievous grin was inching up Aken's face; she didn't like it. "What do you mean by *special* breakfast?" she asked.

Minutes later found them sneaking outside along Draevensett's stone façade, warmed by the dawn, coming up against the kitchen quarters. Aken took the lead, ducking under windows and letting grass muffle their steps.

"What special breakfast? Is there a picnic out here?" Cyrus

was asking.

Aken halted below one window so fast that she bumped into him. "Aha!" he exclaimed quietly and peeked over the sill—careful not to let more than his eyes and nose show.

Wondering what he could be up to, she followed his gaze and spotted a pie: steaming, gold and delicious on a small table within arm's reach.

"Operation: Snatch Breakfast, now commencing."

"Are you seriously planning to take that pie? That's stealing, you troublemaker!"

"Pie? No way, buddy." Aken shook his head with a serious frown. "I'm aiming for the mega prize. *The Tray of Golden Heaven*, itself."

"Huh?" Looking again, she saw another tray: wide and stacked high with swirls of dough and cinnamon and icing, cooling on a countertop not far away. She exclaimed.

"Raiding food from the school I live at isn't stealing. They've got plenty."

"Is too! What are those things, anyway?"

"Cinnamon rolls. How can you not know that?" Aken was already over the sill and sneaking across the kitchen floor, crawling on knees and forearms toward the *Tray of Golden Heaven*.

The staff inside were preoccupied with hurrying about the network of kitchen rooms, preparing the day's meals. That is, all except for one woman: heavy-set ,with a stern, piggish face and poodle-hair sticking out from under a large chef's hat. She strutted about the labyrinth kitchen, surveying progress—and she was headed their way. Cyrus waited for Aken to get caught and punished.

The head chef lumbered toward the large tray. Cyrus watched between her fingers, as Aken flattened his body against the floor and managed to squeeze underneath a counter table just in time before the woman arrived.

"Mm-*hm*." The woman's beady eyes scanned, evaluating

the cinnamon rolls' golden hue, breathing in the scent. Cyrus kept low outside the window, then craned up just enough to see Aken pull something long out of his pocket: a clay snake.

The snake darted across the floor. It was swiftly followed by a shriek that rang through the entire complex.

The head chef screamed and danced—yelping and leaping about the floor, doing anything she could to get away from the slithering snake as it wiggled after her ankles. The staff scrambled left and right, trying to catch it.

In one quick motion Aken got to his feet and snatched up the tray, balancing it on a shoulder. He leaped over the windowsill as graceful as an anteleer, and tossed a look back at the head chef, giving her a wink.

The woman's cheeks burned fierce red, a steel carving knife in her hand above a now chopped-up clay snake. "YOU AGAIN."

"Whoops. Time to leave! Hop on, Cy!" Aken tossed a clay swallow into the air, and she watched as it grew big enough to seat two. He smoothly hopped aboard its back. The woman came charging out the window like a maddened bull, somehow managing to fit her bulky form through the gap. Without time to think, Cyrus got onto the swallow.

Before the woman could grab them, they were airborne, and Cyrus clung to Aken's chest from behind. The head chef below stomped and waved vein-popping fists in a tirade.

"Whoo, was that fun or what?" Aken's chest shook with laughter against her arms, as his knees steered the swallow away—the *Tray of Golden Heaven* held securely in his hands.

"No! You're terrible!" She wanted to slap the back of his head.

Landing the bird in a thick copse, underneath a willow far back in the school grounds, he set the tray on the grass. Cyrus's empty stomach growled as delicious aromas wafted up and the inviting sight of golden dough became overwhelming. "If you don't eat now, there won't be anything until lunch," said Aken, and he dug into the cinnamon rolls, stuffing one at a time into his mouth.

Cyrus gave in and sampled one. The doughy sweetness and cinnamon made her heart flutter. Cinnamon rolls, this was one vempar dessert she could get used to. "Don't expect me to raid kitchens with you, ever. Or I'll turn you in myself," she warned. He flashed a grin covered in icing.

Afterwards, a pond in the copse made for a place to wash away the evidence—or try to. Her stomach was nauseous, not used to so much sweetness in the morning.

"Good breakfast, huh?" Aken said and patted his bulging stomach.

"Shut up. Should I dare ask what you do for lunch?" She groaned.

He looked at her and laughed, falling over onto his side and unable to get back up. A breeze rustled the tray, empty of all but stray crumbs.

The stomach ache must have put her to sleep, because when her eyelids opened, a narrow face with glasses filled her vision.

Dr. Zushil's judgmental gaze bore down on both her and Aken as they lay on the crumb-littered ground.

Aken leaped up to run.

"You're not getting away *this* time, you miscreant!" said Zushil. "For dragging new student Cyrus along in your unspeakable acts, raiding the kitchens *again*, youuu," he waggled a finger, "you shall pay! Rotten little—"

Before he finished the sentence, Aken threw the tray *smack* in his face.

"*Guh!*" Zushil's hands flung up to shield his nose, and Aken grabbed Cyrus's hand, pulling her with him into a run out of the copse.

Zushil shouted and chased after them across the school field.

After a while of running, someone called out from up ahead, and Cyrus saw Master Nephryte waving them over. Looking back, as angry bull Zushil was gaining on them, Aken sped up and leaped into the safety zone that was behind the Master.

They ducked low. The Master, perplexed at first, must have caught on to the situation from the icing bejeweling Aken's shirt, because he frowned deeply.

"Th-tha-that BRAT!" Zushil came to a panting halt before them, and she and Aken peeked out from behind the Master's tall waist. The doctor pointed a quaking finger, "He massacred the school's weekly supply of cinnamon rolls! Whole wonderful, beautiful rolls gone—*wasted*." Zushil's arm shook, head ready to explode off his shoulders.

"They weren't wasted. I made sure to cherish every moment I had with them," Aken argued from around the Master's hip. Master Nephryte tilted his neck and gave him a look: a *Not-another-word-out-of you* look.

Aken shrunk like a wilted weed.

"Control him," Zushil demanded. "I won't take much more of this, Master Nephryte, and neither will anyone else! If he is uncontrollable, then I say do what needs to be done. Scourgebloods never did deserve to live among us."

Aken stared at the ground bitterly. Why did they call him *Scourgeblood*? Nothing was worse than feeling unwanted, a piece of trash to get rid of, exactly how hometown humans had made her feel. Is this what Aken was facing here?

Master Nephryte shifted so that he stood between her and Aken, placing a hand each on one of their shoulders. "Aken-Shou and Cyrus are my dear students. I will not take kindly to any threats against them." He gave each a brief fond look. "They belong here. Aken-Shou deserves to live the life Lord God has given him."

Aken lifted his head, jaw slack.

The doctor took a step back and waved his palms in defense. "Threat? No, no, no. I only meant...*erm*..."

"I'll see to it that Aken-Shou is taught better behavior." The hand on Aken's shoulder squeezed, making the boy cringe. "Although I can make no guarantees it will work," Master Nephryte admitted. "His ignorance puts all blonds to shame."

Aken's cringe morphed into a glare.

Zushil departed, muttering to himself, while the Master headed them both back to the school.

At the front paved path, the Master halted and faced them. He leaned forward ominously, hands on hips, hair sweeping across his collar in the spring breeze. "Allow me to take a guess," he said, "A repeat of my lecture won't change a thing inside that thick pudding-head of yours?"

Aken looked away, jaw set, hands fidgeting behind his back. "Sorry," he mumbled. "But it's not like anybody expects good from me, anyway."

Master Nephryte regarded him for a moment, then shook his head. "So, you want to prove them right?"

Aken's face heated. "No, that's not what I'm saying."

"Then go use that stubbornness of yours and prove them wrong—prove their fears and doubts about you are mistaken, as they see you become a hard-working and self-controlled Draev."

Aken shoved his hands in his pockets. "Sounds like a pain in the behind."

The Master rolled his eyes, and turned to Cyrus.

From a pocket, he took out a cashcard—an alternative to paper-and-coin. He held it out for her. "I just finished an early city patrol shift and was coming to lend you this. Since most of my students are orphans, I take it upon myself to provide for them what parents or guardians normally would. Go buy yourself a new wardrobe, school supplies, and any other items you need. Show me I can trust you and that you're not a troublemaker, like this one. And do make sure Aken-Shou doesn't use it." His gaze darted pointedly at the boy.

Aken pouted, crossing both arms sulkily. "It wasn't my fault last time it exceeded the cashcard limit or whatever. Like I even know what that means."

The Master held in a sigh.

"Thank you, Master Nephryte," she said, graciously taking it, aglow that she could finally get some decent clothes that didn't look like she'd ran half-a-day through woods in.

The Master waved them away. "Be back here by noon for Ability practice. Harlow will be getting a mission at some point today, so be ready. Mission grades are important." As they headed away, he added: "And no getting into mischief, Aken-Shou! There will be an apology essay waiting for you to write, and you will assist the head baker in the kitchens."

"Fine, fine!" Run-skipping down the path, Aken twisted around to stick out his tongue before they vanished out the gate. The cotton pixit yapped at them.

Exasperation lined Nephryte's face. "That boy…"

14

Bright sunshine kissed the picturesque city stones as Aken led the way into Downtown's lively district. They hopped aboard the back of a passing tram and rode into Main Street, where shops lined both sides up and down the length of the river Noncello. Fanciful arched bridges connected the sides.

Aken hopped off and she quickly followed. "I hope you're not planning on us being friends," she said. Aken's feet stumbled. "I don't need friends who enjoy causing trouble for others."

"What? Wait," Aken waved his hands. "The whole breakfast thing was a mistake—I admit it. I wasn't thinking clearly. I'm addicted to cinnamon rolls and sweets and every unhealthy thing. Some days I just can't control myself." He pleaded, but she remained stoic. "I won't get you into trouble again—promise! Please, can't we be friends?"

She stared at him while he fidgeted uncomfortably, then said, "No more troublemaking."

He nodded vigorously.

She huffed and walked on. Cyrus noticed that in most parts of the city, rivulets flowed in place of gutters, where rainwater gathered. Minnows swam in their mild currents, and she leaned over a low stone rail to watch for a minute.

It was peaceful, as were the trees lining the walk, each ringed in delicate metal fences. Vines climbed up several wallfaces. Stone grotesques of strange creatures and griffins perched at the corners of roofs, as if eyeing the citizens.

Two bikes and a motor carriage rolled past; the engine had a musty scent like wet rock. "Oilpowder engines," Aken waved steam puffs aside. "At least it fades fast."

"Smells like a field of flowers to me," she murmured. In Elvenstone, you could detect the compost that burned alongside oilpowder in engines. But here they must be adding some sort of fragrance to neutralize the odor. Aken gave her a questioning look. "Compared to farm villages, I mean—they smell much worse," she reworded quickly.

He gave her a funny look, then a child crying for ice cream distracted him. She readjusted her fingerless gloves and turned in place, surveying the shop windows and pedestrians.

Another fancy motor carriage steered past, bearing some aristocrat. Workers on a five-wheel contraption, called a rumbler, delivered goods and produce to shops. Most vempars who walked about wore an array of fashion foreign to her—waistcoats, lace shirts, shoulder-pad jackets… But the younger ones had a more modern flare, almost a mix of human-style. Her nerves bristled when one of them passed by her. She kept feeling like they were eyeing her from behind, searching for her locked up secrets, though she was probably just being paranoid.

Mother had been one of them, once. She felt only warmth when thinking of her.

'I can conquer the fear.' She set her jaw.

Aken's hand tugged hers. She winced at the small twinge of pain it sent to her wrist. Her hands had been feeling better lately, and she hoped it would last.

Aken steered her into a shop, *Fashion Sense Pro*. Small on the outside, but one step inside and the store became extensive rows of hangers and brimming shelves, a section each for different ages and styles. There were beautiful ladies dresses to the right, but Aken navigated her opposite into the boys clothing.

"Lykale! Figures you'd be here. Can you help Cy out with a new wardrobe?" Aken found the older Harlow boy there shopping.

Lykale adjusted his glasses and peered down at Cyrus. "Normally, I'd refuse. But what this redhead is wearing goes beyond criminal fashion offense. I'm not living in the same dorm as *that*." He gestured to all of her.

"Gee, thanks," she muttered.

Lykale scanned through the rows, picking out possible items that would match her petite frame. "Just as long as nothing's skin-tight—I can't stand skin-tight," she added.

A shelf of plaid shirts and angular-cut vests caught her eye, very similar to some human designs. She pointed them out to Aken.

"Well, just because we don't like humans, doesn't mean we don't like their fashion. I may hate them, but I gotta admit they have a sweet sense of style." Aken held one up. "They're so futuristic! Old-timers hate it, but teens are loving it."

The words *I may hate them* circled her ears like little stabbing daggers.

In the changing room, Aken wanted to try on things for fun, and she had to slam the door in his face before he could come in with her.

"Okay, yer shy, I ged it—you don have t' kill my nose wid de door. I'll go in de other one." He rubbed his nose. "Just trying t' be economical n' save space."

In the end, she ended up with good casual and dress shirts, jackets, legwear, a cap, human-like sneakers and leather boots. Also a suit and top hat—which Lykale said were required for formal occasions. It was much better than shopping with prissy Heily; she even got to try on outrageous getups just for laughs. If she'd done that with them, Narcissa would've exploded like a cork out a bottle and Heily fallen in a faint. It was good to be free of them— and a part of her felt guilty for feeling that way.

Cyrus involuntarily snorted a laugh when Aken tried on bike gloves and too-big goggles, winking over the rims at her. "Now *that* makes you look like the troublemaker you are," she stated.

Off to the left, a lady was trying on a green dress, twirling its many-layered skirt and matching floral scarf. It was so fancy, so much lace on a gown. Had Mother worn things like that? A part of her actually wanted to try it on.

"*Ah*, your words just stabbed my heart!" Aken said, clutching his chest.

She shooed him away so she could hand the cashcard over to the clerk. "You're worse than a two-year-old. Lykale, thanks for helping me out!"

Lykale nodded coolly and continued on with his own shopping. "At least Harlow won't be punished for murdering fashion."

Once she and Aken finished getting all the supplies she thought she'd need, the sun was hours higher in the sky. They strolled the walk overlooking the river, shopping bags carried on the back of Limitless, the clay swallow trailing them.

She licked at a three-scoop high ice cream cone he insisted she try, from the city's best Gelatteria.

"So, what are these grade missions the Master was talking about?" Cyrus asked.

"Oh, those. Students are grouped into teams, and every week get a mission from the D.G. League to do," said Aken. "They're missions that let us practice our Abilities, and develop combat and team skills—all that stuff. We're young, so we don't get the seriously dangerous missions, yet. We're also graded on our team performance."

"Hm…when's our mission?"

He savored a lick of cookie dough ice cream. "Could be anytime, whenever the call comes in."

Cyrus nodded her chin. "I keep noticing people putting up white feather decorations. What's that about?"

"The Swan Festival's coming up."

That's right, she'd forgot; Elvenstone would be getting ready for the celebration too, by now.

"That reminds me, you're new to the city, so you don't know about the Festival Duel, do you?"

Cyrus shook her head.

Aken explained, "Every year, Draevensett organizes the Festival Duel, where two students face off against each other, and the winner is granted one request from the king. I really want a spot in the Duel—Herc and Bak do, too. But we have to complete all group missions successfully, first, and then we can compete with the other students for a spot."

"A spot?"

"Only two students get chosen for the Duel."

"Out of the whole school?" she exclaimed.

"I wouldn't say the whole school—just those who want to be in the Duel."

"So, if I mess up on a mission, none of Harlow will get to compete?" She cringed when he nodded.

Aken laughed, "Don't worry about it. Hey, you're growing an ice cream mustache." With a napkin, he reached to wipe the hazelnut and cream mustache off.

She spooked. "I can clean it off myself," she murmured hastily and grabbed the napkin. He cocked his head, probably wondering why her face had gone red.

Twree! Twree-kree! Swallows played above the river water. They skimmed the surface like little black arrows, scooping up drinks in their beaks. Aken grinned, "C'mon!" grabbing her free hand.

Down a flight of steep stone steps, they reached a river landing. Little waves lapped against the stone dock. Iron-lattice benches there faced the water on a raised platform.

They both sat on the sun-warmed edge of the dock and dangled their shoes over the water, finishing up the ice cream. She admired the serene view of the river and arched bridges. A breeze tickled her nose with the scent of petunias, and hot pretzels baking somewhere.

No more cares in the world, the view and scent seemed to promise. *Not today.*

The opposite bank mirrored theirs, dotted in unlit streetlamps. Why couldn't she have been born here? With Mother married to a vempar who would have loved her, and Cyrus not a half-blood? It wasn't fair…

"Aaaken! Cyyyrus!"

A holler tore out of the blue, defiling the peace.

Aken's face became a puckered grimace and tilted up, just as Bakoa trotted over the arching bridge above them, waving down from the balustrade. "Yeah, yeah, we hear you *loud* and clear," said Aken.

Cyrus kindly waved back. "Hi, Bakoa."

Pleased as a hyper otter on caffeine, Bakoa hollered down, "It's luuunch time, and Master Nephryte says to cooome baaack!"

A bell gonged, sounding out the noon hour.

"See? Even Tall Tim is saying so!"

Cyrus spotted the tall clock tower rising over the rows of rooftops, a large intricate clock face on two sides.

"Oookay," Aken mock hollered back. "But watch out for the raaain, Sand-dude."

Bakoa tilted his head back to check the sky. "I don't melt in the rain—how many times do I gotta say that? And it's not even close to raining now, you fibber." Bakoa's lower lip jutted out.

Cyrus didn't understand the joke, but coaxed Aken to get

up. She didn't want to keep everybody back at Draevensett waiting, especially her being the *new kid*. Aken's expression said he had no desire to hurry back, whatsoever, but he forced himself up anyway, leaving the river and tranquility behind.

Cyrus hurried across the school grounds to the Harlow group already there waiting. She had on a new change of clothes—a collared brown shirt with sharp angles and capris. Draevensett's coat-of-arms sticker on her shirt back, and Floor Harlow's on a short sleeve.

Hercule, the boy with pearl-gray hair and dragon gold eyes, shot a disapproving frown. Lykale drummed his long fingers on his crossed arms. Cyrus made herself small and stood by Mamoru and Aken.

Master Nephryte had a curious shoulder bag looped around his arm. He ordered, "Now that we're all here, form a line and hold hands."

Cyrus tried not to flinch when Aken took her hand on one side and Mamoru the other.

The air around the lined-up group, with the Master at the head, began to stir, turning and rotating, faster and faster, until a whirlwind formed, lifting them up without warning. Cyrus gripped the hands holding her, trying not to scream, ignoring shooting pains in her wrists.

F-woosh! Shaped like an invisible hand, the whirlwind carried all eight of them through the air, over and beyond Draevensett's spires.

"Whoa." Bakoa's sandy-green eyes went wide with thrill, his orange hair whipping like living flames. "Master Nephryte, you're the most totally awesomest mentor I've ever had!"

"He's the *only* mentor you've ever had," retorted Hercule. "And *awesomest* is not a word!" The wind shoved hair in the aristocrat's mouth, and he choked.

Cyrus squinted, trying not to see how far above the ground they were. After several minutes, the carrying hand of wind faded from underneath them, and with a start she saw the land fast approaching below.

Master Nephryte landed smoothly on his feet with grace, and Mamoru followed, equally perfect. Hercule landed in a kneeling position, Lykale and Bakoa stumbled behind him. Shy Zartanian had to catch his hands on the ground for support. Aken landed flat on his face.

Cyrus flapped her arms in an attempt to grow wings, and would've smashed her head in if not for a rope of air catching her shoulders and setting her upright. She straightened, panting.

Aken raised a dizzy head and scrambled to get up, grass in his ears. "Y-you did that to me on p-purpose!" His glare shot off-kilter daggers at the Master.

Master Nephryte shrugged, indifferent. "It isn't my fault if you haven't been practicing the Landing Technique I taught in E.M. Study. Aken-Shou, the fault is yours alone." Ignoring the boy's glare, he nodded over to Mamoru, "Perhaps later, if you would be so kind as to help Cyrus and…Aken-Shou…with Landing?"

Mamoru gave a nod. Sunlight caught the black edges of the scar down his cheek. Cyrus stared at it, until he turned and winked. She quickly looked elsewhere.

"Exercise first, then lunch. And remember to use your Ability techniques—that's the whole point." Master Nephryte plopped the bag from his arm onto the meadow grass.

Cyrus surveyed where they'd landed: a grassy slope parting the woods, rolling down to a beach of fine sand. They'd left the city premises entirely.

She watched the boys race each other down to the sand, flinging shirts, shoes and socks off before charging through the warm water lapping the shoreline. It was her first time seeing so much water gathered in one place: stretching beyond the horizon to kiss the sky above.

Master Nephryte must have noticed her awe because he stood beside her, taking in the view. "Lake Doroth, one of the Kingdom of Draeth's beauties," he said.

She tilted her head back; he was so very tall compared to her.

He smiled down and lightly patted her head. "You'll grow up soon enough, Cyrus—don't be in a hurry."

She gaped. "I was thinking of the lake, not my height," she mumbled, and continued watching the lake.

"Cyrus, come on!" Aken waved for her to join them.

She hesitated, staring at them shirtless in the hot sun. She hoped they weren't expecting her to do the same. *'Young vempars have fine muscles,'* she thought. Then noticed Hercule still had his shirt on, and Zartanian had kept his hat.

She trotted down to the sand, cheeks hot—from the sun, nothing else.

"I vote for volleyball," said Bakoa, hands in the air and a silly otter grin on his face.

"You get way too excited." Aken hefted a leather ball in one hand and turned to her. "What sport do *you* wanna play, Cy? You choose."

"Um…" Fidgeting with her gloves, she tried not to watch as dappled light played along his sleek chest. To her left, Mamoru was even more impressive. "I like volleyball," her voice squeaked. She took off her shoes and socks.

"Volleyball it is!" Aken raced over to a net already set up. "And you're on my team."

Bakoa squinted. "Volleyball's what I suggested. But when Cyrus says it, then you want to? Nobody ever listens to me!"

"*Baka.*" Aken made a goofy face from the other side of the net, puffing his cheeks and crossing his eyes.

Mamoru moved to take the left corner position, and as he

did, bumped Aken's head with a fist, "Don't call names."

Both Lykale and Hercule moved to join Bakoa's side of the net.

"Two out of three!" Aken called out, rubbing his head, and struck the volleyball high.

Two? The game would be over in no time! And wasn't someone missing? Cyrus pressed her lips together.

Zartanian. The quiet boy sat in the shade of a round-leaf tree with roots snaking out of the soil, his knees drawn up to his narrow chin. The scene reminded her of a little *Cherry-top* who, not long ago, had done the same thing during group activities. Sympathy panged in her chest. She watched Master Nephryte make his way over and kneel beside him, speaking too quietly for her human ears to hear. She shifted her attention back to the game.

The volleyball sped toward Bakoa. The goofy boy watched it come, a lopsided smile across his face. A strange calm and focus overtook him, and then he moved:

Bakoa's right hand lifted, poised above his left shoulder, ready to slash the air. The ball came within reach, and he slashed—but what had been his arm and hand was now a huge hammer of sand, and it sent the ball flying back.

Cyrus's jaw hung. The volleyball sailed past her left ear. Behind her, it was struck up and back over the net by—

What in the world was *that*?

Mamoru tossed what looked like a piece of amber rock, and it grew, shifting in midair like a cage releasing a prisoner, and a dark form leaked out from the rock. A being landed on the sand, on two wide feet.

It stood many heads taller than its owner, and when it moved, the being looked made of rubbery wax. A pear-shaped body, dangly long arms and legs, and elephant-ish feet. It whipped one long rubberband arm and struck the volleyball over the net. Far, *far* over.

Hercule shouted as the ball soared, "It isn't fair when you

use that puppet!"

Puppet? Now Cyrus could see the hair-thin strings, like liquid-gold sap, pulsing, connecting from Mamoru's fingertips to the being. More like *seeping from* than *connecting from* as the strings seemed to be a part of his flesh—melding from the skin of his fingertips as if they, too, were sap.

Mamoru moved his fingers like he was playing a musical instrument, composing a song he had long memorized. "Scurro," he coolly corrected Hercule, his mulberry-colored eyes slitted. "It has a name."

Hercule made an expression that he could care less.

"Way to go, Scurro!" Aken pumped a fist.

But Bakoa's sand-hammer arm lengthened, stretching far back and catching the speedy volleyball; he prepared to throw it back at them.

A tiny clay bird flapped up to Bakoa's waist and exploded in a burst of lava, burning his sand arm. "*Agh!*" He quickly doused his arm in wet sand, snuffing out the burn, and the volleyball dropped.

The ball descended—inches from touching the ground.

Lykale bent sideways, diving his hand down just in time to scoop the ball and hit it back up—attaching *something* to it in the process.

That something blew up in a cloud of smoke as the ball soared back over toward Cyrus. She and her team coughed as the cloud impaired their vision.

The ball made a *thud* on the ground. Round-one lost.

Waving to clear the haze, Aken called out, "Foul! Foul! That was a *foul!*"

Lykale folded his arms with a satisfied smirk. "We're supposed to use our Abilities; and creating weapons through chemistry *is* my Ability. I'm Armavis."

"You just carry stuff with you and mix it together. That's not *real* Element-whatever Maniputation," Aken shot back.

"The *knowledge* of how to do so is." Lykale sniffed

indignantly. "An Outskirts bumpkin like you couldn't figure out a tenth of what I know."

"Dude, a childhood in the Outskirts doesn't make me a bumpkin. It's not the ol' countryside beyond the wall."

"You could have fooled me with the way you talk," Hercule interjected. "You sound like a high born one moment, then a countryside dimwit the next! *Dude* and *ol'* are not proper words," he lectured. "Learn to speak more consistently, won't you?"

"Ooh." Aken posed with one hand on a hip, waving the other at Hercule prettily. "Mr. Fancy Proper-pants don't like the way I speak, does he? Well, here's what I think of that…" Turning his back and bending over, he slapped his behind at the fancy boy and stuck out his tongue. "*Blehhh!*"

Hercule's face turned flaming crimson, and Cyrus covered her eyes.

"I'M GONNA MURDER YOU!" Hercule charged.

"Shouldn't that be '*going to*'?" Aken remarked before zig-zagging away down the beach, kicking up water. Hercule lunged after him.

Cyrus peeked between her fingers. That troublemaker…boys were so immature. Did they ever grow out of it?

Mamoru raked a hand back through his bangs, but instead of getting involved, he turned back to the game, directing puppet Scurro to pick up the volleyball. "You give it a try, Cyrus."

Scurro plopped the ball into her hands. She stared at it. Using Ability was still a foreign thing to her, and she remembered why she'd stopped playing volleyball. Last time, her wrists had ached badly for days. But it was too late now, and there was no telling what they'd do if they learned their new member had a defect.

Instead of using her wrist to hit, Cyrus swung her fist, punching the ball clean over the net. Her fist tingled; it'd hurt later on.

"Sweet shot!" voiced Bakoa as he jumped to catch it. His other flesh hand crystalized into sand and widened, hitting the ball back.

Cyrus dove—sliding on her knees, hands clasped together in a fist, ready to strike the ball up before it could touch ground, when a stab of pain made her left wrist twitch.

"Heads up!" came Bakoa's shout. The ball glided overhead, and without time to think she reacted—springing up, right hand in a fist, striking with all her might.

The ball flew and struck Bakoa full-force in the head before he could duck or turn into sand. He fell like a plank to the ground.

Cyrus gasped.

They all stared at her—even Aken and Hercule, who'd paused. Why they were staring and not helping Bakoa made her look down at her fisted hand, which oddly wasn't hurting from the hit.

Gleaming metal covered the surface of her hand, wrist and glove. Metal. She'd coated it with metal, like something out of a magician's tale!

Thrill pumped in her chest. "Oh, poor Bakoa!"

Aken guffawed, while she raced to the sand boy's side.

"Baka, *erm*—I mean, Bakoa, are you okay?"

The boy raised his head, blinking dizzily. "Sure, n-no problem. It'll p-pass..."

Something crawled up his spiky hair and onto his forehead. "Spider!" she shrieked. Her metal hand slapped the pest away—slapping Bakoa again in the process. His eyes rolled back into his head. "Oh no! I'm so sorry!"

Aken skid to a halt by her shoulder, laughing. And Hercule, too exhausted to chase after him anymore, sagged and doubled-over.

"I've never seen a hit like that. Cy, that's some awesome

power you got going on." Aken clapped her shoulder. "I knew you were keeping some big secret from us." He winked.

"'*You have.*' It's '*you have*'—not '*you got*'." Hercule's weary fist pounded the sand.

She watched as the metal faded back to skin and glove around her hand. A woozy feeling washed over her body, forcing her to sit.

Someone touched her back and a new surge of energy moved through her bones, making her straighten. The Master moved past her. "I believe you used the iron in your blood to cover your hand in metal," he said. "The downside is that it will make you weak and anemic. I suggest you use outside sources, and keep something metal with you at all times."

She dipped her head. So that's why she felt tired; and somehow his touch had restored her energy? Cyrus studied her hands. If she could continue encasing them in metal, she could use them without fear of pain. Imagine that, being able to live like a normal person without pain.

Master Nephryte helped Bakoa to his feet. "We'll pause for lunch. How does that sound?"

Bakoa grinned groggily, "Food sounds yummylicious."

They toweled off before tugging shirts, shoes and socks back on. Bakoa conveniently absorbed the sand that was on him.

A whistling noise trilled sharply. She looked about then watched as the Master plucked a communication device from his belt to hold to his ear. "Yes?" He listened to a voice she couldn't hear for several moments, then ended the call and refastened the comm device to his belt.

"It seems lunch will have to wait. Harlow's been given a mission," the Master told them, and their heads raised. "A dragon is on the loose."

Cyrus peeked through the bush and into the field beyond. A fence carved out a wide circle of pasture for flocks of sheep. Nearby sat the cluster of farm houses. And there, grabbing up a baaing sheep in its jaws, was a small dragon—if you could call a dragon three-times a man's height small. Farmers were holding all sorts of metal objects as weapons, and kids were throwing rocks. The dragon paid them as little attention as a gnat.

Master Nephryte had Harlow huddle together for a moment. "You'll need cover to get close—Lykale, you provide that. Cyrus and Zartanian will be responsible for getting the people and sheep away to safety, while the rest of you work to scare off the dragon," he ordered. "The goal is to scare the dragon so that it never comes back. Most would probably say kill it, but I don't feel that'd be right." He backed away. "This is your mission, and whether you fail or succeed will determine if Harlow can enter the Festival Duel trials this week. I'll let you figure out the rest of the plan on your own." He vanished into the trees, and the students were left facing each other.

"Me and Bakoa can pin down the dragon long enough for you to get everyone away safely," Mamoru said, nodding to Cyrus. "Aken, Hercule, Lykale—you be the barrier between the dragon and the farms, in case we fail to hold the dragon long enough. Then we'll work to scare it off with Hercule's flames and Lykale's concoction. Got it?"

They nodded, though Cyrus's brain had trouble following. There wasn't much time.

Lykale crouched and left the cover of the trees to make his way into the field. Cyrus looked from him to Mamoru to Hercule. They seemed ready and sure of themselves. She swallowed her fear, and met Zartanian's gaze—he patted his hat firmly down, turned his back and began edging away from their hiding bush.

All of Harlow was already out on the field, she realized, and crawled after them, keeping low in the tall grass. By the time she reached the pasture fence, a series of *Poof* sounds started and fog filled the air—Lykale's cover.

The dragon raised its head, a sheep crying in its jaws as the large lizard turned this way and that, trying to see through the billows of gray.

She heard a whistle, and Mamoru's puppet Scurro came out of the fog and grabbed the dragon from behind. At the same time, Bakoa's sand arms shot out in front of the dragon, grabbing it by the jaws and forcing its mouth open.

Cyrus tried not to panic and followed Zartanian into the pasture while Scurro and Bakoa wrestled the dragon. The beast's growl rumbled through the ground, and its loud hiss seared her ears. Zartanian unlatched the gate before moving opposite her along the fence. Circling the sheep from both sides, together they clapped their hands and pushed at the flock to get them running towards the now open gate.

The sheep cried and bustled out the pasture, heading towards the barns where farmers hurried to guide the terrified animals away. Several kids continued throwing rocks that didn't reach the dragon. "Don't do that, you have to get to safety," Cyrus urged them. The kids, not much younger than herself, wouldn't listen, and Zartanian tried to shoo them back without getting close, making shooing gestures.

Bakoa's sand arms began to break apart from the strain.

"Take them and go!" Cyrus grabbed one girl by the arm and shoved her at Zartanian. But instead of taking her and forcing her to leave, he shied back and drew his hands in, as if she were diseased.

From the dragon's jaws, the single sheep finally got free and fell. Cyrus dashed forward and herded the bleating animal away. A vicious hiss made her glance back. The dragon writhed, flopped down and rapidly rotated its body.

Scurro's arm came loose as the dragon rolled and twisted free. Up on its limbs, it came charging towards her and the sheep.

"Oh crud!"

Zartanian and the kids saw, and they bolted for the woods.

Hot air licked Cyrus's back as the raging dragon gained on her. The shadow of jaws was almost above her. She dared to glance back and saw the dragon's open mouth come.

Then a clay bird exploded at its snout.

The dragon roared, claws pressing in the ground to halt its momentum as a shower of clay exploded, cutting it off from Cyrus and the others as they fled.

"How do you like that noseful of lava? Shorty dragon!" shouted Aken.

But one kid hadn't been so quick to get away, and Cyrus didn't notice until the dragon lunged and had the girl in its jaw—her hair and shirt caught on its teeth.

Cyrus's heart stopped. There was nothing she could do— nothing anyone could do in time.

Streaking across the field in a blur, and in one leap reaching the dragon's jaw, Aken grabbed the kid and let his momentum carry them out of the mouth before it closed. But not before a dragon's tooth sliced down his back.

Aken tossed the kid Cyrus's way then circled the creature, luring it away from them. The dragon's attention latched onto Aken. A blast of smoke shot from its snout as it prowled towards him.

Aken backed up, coughing.

Cyrus held the girl close, shocked. If only she could have done something, like Aken had—used her Ability to help, instead of watching helplessly.

ROar! The dragon charged. With a shout Aken turned tail and ran. "Okay, I take back the Shorty comment!" He headed back into the pasture, the furious dragon close behind. It took in a deep breath and opened wide as a stream of fire shot from its jaws.

The burst of fire singed Aken's hair and shoes.

A second blast of fire shot across the field: this one aimed at the dragon and blasting the dragon's flames off course. From the safety of the trees, Cyrus watched this new stream of fire, which blew from Hercule's mouth.

Aken turned to face the dragon alongside Hercule, adding clay birds to the mix, and Lykale threw something that exploded in a red cloud of spice.

The dragon gagged and snorted, disgusted by the smell. It tried to snap at one of the boys, but between the lava blasts, fire, and spice cloud, it hissed in frustration and flapped its wings, lifting up into the sky. Clay birds antagonized the dragon until it finally sailed away.

"Woo, mission accomplished!" Aken pumped a fist, the cuts on his back Healing, as they watched it leave.

Hercule confronted him. "You were supposed to lead the dragon to me—not go veering off who-knew-where!"

"Cool your flames. I had things under control," Cyrus heard Aken reply as she approached. The kids were now hurrying back to the farms, and she helped the girl who was still in shock from her ordeal move her feet. Mamoru was inspecting the damage done to his puppet, and somehow made the puppet shrink and melt back inside an amber rock.

"Stop being full of yourself! How can we act like a team if you don't follow the plan and keep trying to take the spotlight for yourself?" Hercule jabbed a finger at Aken's chest.

"You'd rather me stick to the plan than save someone's life?"

"That's not— You know what I mean! You could have saved her and still kept to our plan." Hercule fumed. "Listen here, I have a spotless record of $A+$ in every class, all except for Missions. And do you know why? It's because you're bringing my grade down!"

"Sorry, okay, but you can't blame it all on me."

"You're just saying that because we're the ones bringing your grade *up*! Every class, other than Missions, you're barely above failing."

"Well, sorry I wasn't brought up with a fancy education like you! Everything wasn't served to me on a silver platter."

"You think I had it easy? That I didn't have to work my backside off? How dare you—"

"Um, guys?" Cyrus interrupted. Their intense expressions turned her way and she jumped. "The sheep are running loose all over the place. I think we should help..."

The farmers were struggling to regain control of the animals, and only Zartanian and Bakoa were helping.

The Master appeared behind Aken and Hercule, making them both jump. "Failure to contain the sheep, and poor communication within the team... I give Harlow a *C* for this mission, and only because you did manage to scare the dragon off."

Steam vented between Hercule's clenched teeth.

Aken shrugged and backed away, "That's a good grade, right? We're qualified to enter the Festival Duel trials, right?"

The Master tutted. "You qualify, but just barely."

Cyrus rubbed at her wrists. And to think she was worried *she'd* be the one to make Harlow fail.

As half an hour passed of chasing sheep, the last of the animals were finally herded back into their pasture, and Cyrus wiped her sweaty brow.

An old farmer thanked her, patting her hand. "We would've had t' sell our farm and home if the sheep had been lost. They're what we live on. You saved us."

The young girl they'd rescued also thanked them as her face went red with shame. Even though she was vempar, if her head had been severed or her heart bitten through, she would have died.

Cyrus had a moment of revelation. Was this why Lord God had brought her here? Having a strange power and running away to a foreign city wasn't part of her expectations for life or goals, but she could help others and save lives now. Here, her Ability could have a purpose and make some difference.

Harlow departed, making their way beyond the pasture and into the rolling hills.

"We can have lunch out here, if you like," the Master suggested.

"Yes! My stomach is dying," said Bakoa.

Kreeeah!

Aken shook his head. "Wow, I can hear it. That's some stomach death cry."

"No, that wasn't me..." His brow furrowed.

Kreeeah!

Cyrus turned towards the unearthly sound as it came from the woods.

A shape emerged from the shadows of the trees, a hulking mass of limbs and claws. Shreds of black fabric and dark metal plates made a body. Six limbs protruded, with dark gray skin and bone, and a too-large head swung their way. Black fabric flapped in the breeze like hair, and the face like a mask of bone stared at them, mouth gaping.

Cyrus stood frozen.

"What the——?" Hercule began.

"Get back! *Now!*" the Master shouted.

An arm wrapped around Cyrus's waist as Aken carried her and grabbed Zartanian, running to the Master's side with both of them in tow.

The grim creature lumbered toward them.

"Hold hands in a line!" Master Nephryte ordered.

Each student grabbed the hand nearest them, and Master

Nephryte channeled the wind to lift them up. They rose as the armored corpse-like creature moved to where they'd been standing, and it watched them as they landed in a tree far on the other side of the field.

Master Nephryte lifted the comm device to his lips, "Emergency Report: a Level 2 Corpsed has been found near the Bewely's farmland, same location as the dragon-removal mission Harlow was given earlier. Requesting immediate backup." He turned to the students. "I have to stop the Corpsed before it nears the farms. Wait here, no matter what happens. Mamoru, you're in charge of them."

"Wait for you—?" Aken shouted after the Master as he glided out of the tree. Mamoru blocked Aken's chest with an arm.

"No one leaves this tree. Stay put, or I'll glue you down with my sap Ability," Mamoru warned.

Cyrus watched as Master Nephryte hovered in the air before the grotesque Corpsed. The bone mask's distorted eyes rolled toward him and its mouth stretched wide; a blast of darkness shot out—a black beam of energy. The Master flew to the left, dodging the beam as it streaked past and hit the ground. Where the black energy hit, the grass shriveled to dust, as if the darkness had swallowed every ounce of life from the spot.

The Master slashed his hand through the air and a sword of air struck the Corpsed. It stumbled back several feet, but managed to swing two long limbs made up of multiple joints at him.

Nephryte raised his hands and a shield of air deflected both blows.

The Corpsed turned and began crossing the field, heading for the students, and fear gripped Cyrus.

Wind picked up across the grass, making the trees groan, building into a rotating funnel that the Master flung and wrapped around the Corpsed, halting its progress.

The big Corpsed rotated inside the funnel for one long moment, then screamed and wrenched itself free of the battering winds and launched into the Master.

Cyrus yelped, watching as the Master narrowly evaded the many sets of metallic claws slashing for him. The Corpsed moved against each slash and blow of air which knocked it back, and shot another beam of darkness from its mouth. Nephryte hit the creature with a wall of air, then thrust a palm of wind at one of the limbs.

The limb froze, motionless in the shackle of air, and the creature fought to break free.

Master Nephryte performed the same motion again and again, as he dodged, until every limb of the Corpsed was shackled in air. The head, however, spun round, following his movements.

Sweat dabbed the Master's brow as he flew, circling the Corpsed, the dark beam following after him. Cyrus realized he was trying to get behind the head where he could then shackle it. But the Corpsed's head rotated just as fast as the Master could fly. He looked weary, maintaining air shackles around the many limbs as the Corpsed shook and strained against them.

Cyrus looked to Mamoru, then back. She wanted to help, do something, but they were untrained middle-schoolers. If Master Nephryte, one of the most powerful Draevs in the kingdom, was having trouble with this creature, then they stood no chance.

Cyrus silently prayed, and in that moment heard a loud *Crack*.

She opened her eyes in time to see a new vempar arrive, bringing down a heavy blade on the Corpsed's mask from above. He wore the Draev uniform, and behind him three more Draevs leaped into the field.

The Corpsed hissed, and Master Nephryte used the distraction to get behind the masked head and shackle it still with air.

A rain of blows from Abilities and Draev weapons of the group assaulted the mask, until cracks appeared in the bone-like substance.

And then, the mask shattered.

The Corpsed's limbs slumped to the ground.

Cyrus couldn't be sure from where she knelt in the tree, but as the mask pieces fell, she could've sworn there was a second, smaller face—a humanoid skull—behind it.

The Corpsed folded in on itself, until there was nothing but a pile of fabric shreds and metal parts left.

Master Nephryte reunited with Harlow beneath the tree, each of the students brimming with questions. Bakoa couldn't keep still, and Zartanian was hugging his arms as if chilled to the bone.

"What was that *thing?*" asked Aken.

"One of the greater dangers the D.G. League faces to keep this kingdom safe," the Master said, dusting his tunic and cape. "We call them Corpsed, and they're worse than Argos to deal with. That metal on it is black silver, which as you know, impairs our Healing. There aren't many Corpsed in existence—as far as we know—but they're powerful, and are centuries old."

"What *are* they, though? And what were those dark beams it shot out?" Aken continued. "I've been out in the woods and grasslands my whole childhood, and never seen anything like that."

"You're fortunate you have not. There are theories as to what they could be, but we don't really know. The only thing you young ones need to remember is to stay away from them, and report to us right away if you see one."

"That's not much of an answer," said Bakoa.

Master Nephryte patted his back. "Don't worry over it; I

doubt you'll see another one for many years. Now, it's past lunch and I'm starving. How about we relax in the park?" He shouldered the bag he'd brought with him.

Cyrus would've liked more answers, too. If she became a Draev Guardian, would she have to combat monsters like that? She wasn't sure she had the nerve… Then again, she'd probably leave the city by then.

Harlow held hands as the wind carried them over the landscape. This time, Cyrus could see more of Lake Doroth, the distant villages ringing its waters, and Draethvyle to the south.

The city's towers approached, and then the many peaked rooftops. Her leg muscles tensed as they passed over a high iron fence, and her feet plopped down to grassy ground.

She rubbed her temples to rid a nauseous feeling and her ears popped; she let her hands drop to see the city park they'd landed in: stone paths curved along stretches of grass and trees, benches and shady niches, ponds with handrails and little bridges. Somewhere, birdsong mingled with the strumming of a mandolin.

Nearly every tree was lavished in cherry blossoms, so much so that the breeze rained down showers of petals. They floated like feathers of rosy sunlight, filling the air with a rich sweet scent.

Captivated, Cyrus twirled in place, arms outspread as if to soak it all in. She caught Aken watching her silly moment of delight, and stumbled to a halt, her cheeks feeling as pink as the blossoms overhead. She tried to laugh it off, tucking bangs behind an ear—then, remembering her disguised human ears, hastily undid the tucking.

Instead of using one of the lattice tables, Master Nephryte spread a large blanket out on the grass underneath a gnarled cherry tree. From the shoulder bag he pulled out a basket filled with sandwiches, salad, slices of cheesecake and raspberry tarts.

"Master, you really are the best!" Bakoa's face lit up.

The sights and smells were calming after the encounter with the Corpsed. Master Nephryte said a prayer of thanks, then they dug into the food. Bakoa snatched the salt shaker, and Cyrus watched as he made a blizzard on his sandwich.

"Ew, that is disgusting." Hercule leaned away.

"Wha?" Bakoa said around a bite. "It gives flavor—I like flavor. Salt's the best flavor!"

Hercule squinted at the sandwich, his face turning green. Bakoa dashed on some extra salt, and the noble had to get up and leave with a hand over his mouth.

Cyrus nibbled, and tried to ignore the heavily salted bread being swallowed across from her. Maybe his sand Ability had messed with his sense of taste.

After finishing a raspberry tart, the memory of that morning's cinnamon rolls turned her stomach. And after watching Bakoa grab for a second sandwich, she was a swirl of nausea and had to stand.

Aken gestured with his hand, urging her to follow him away from the picnic and deeper into the park. "Don't get lost!" he laughed and suddenly raced ahead of her, weaving through the paths of trees and petals.

The scenery eased her stomach, her being, and she breathed in the sweet nectar air. Thrusting her feet forward with each step at a run, she tried to catch up. But with so many petals swirling like a shower of spring snow, she could barely see, and in the downpour lost track of him. She slowed to a halt under a hefty, tangled tree and caught her breath, resting back against the bark. Sunlight pierced down between gaps in the canopy, and orange and indigo birds trilled. She eyed a cicada, its abdomen making a low rattle.

Here, she could almost forget about the past and half-blood problems and her wrists. If she rested her head back, there was no such thing as pain. The world was warm and sweet and paradise.

Something rustled, and her head jerked up. She could sense eyes crawling up her back.

Slowly, Cyrus turned to face the source. But there was nothing but empty grass. Furrowing her brow, she turned back around and almost bumped into a head hanging upside down.

A scream caught in her throat.

"Guess you did get lost," said Aken, hanging upside down like a bat from the branch above, his nose almost touching hers.

She jumped back, pulse racing. He looked ridiculous, pointy ears and hair dangling, and he made it worse by dancing his arms and head about. She accidentally snorted a laugh, then threw a playful punch when he laughed back at her.

She climbed up the tree after him, careful to put weight on her feet and elbows instead of her wrists. The world was nothing but blue sky and cherry blossoms up here.

"Aken, do you ever feel fear?" she asked once she found a secure enough perch.

He folded his hands behind his head, leaning precariously on a thin branch. "Sure I do. Everybody does."

She frowned. Remembering how he'd faced the dragon, she doubted that. "I want to help people, and use my Ability, but...I don't think I could face something as scary as that Corpsed."

Aken's lips pursed in thought. "Don't let it get to you, Cy. We won't be fighting those things until we're older. And hey, I've got your back." He winked.

She half-smiled, and tried to put the gruesome incident out of mind.

⁓

Near the picnic, Nephryte leaned against the old tree's knotted base, watching the two far-off students play about.

A breeze brushed hair into his eyes.

Student Lykale approached, also observing the duo who were now climbing trees like squirrels. "Is it right to let them be so carefree?" said the eldest boy.

Nephryte kept silent for a moment. Sunlight dappled across the surface of his vision. "Taking time to appreciate life is also a part of training, Lykale. It will remind you of what it is we're fighting for."

Lykale glanced at him sideways, then made a sound through his nose before returning to the picnic desserts.

15

Dusk was a stretch of black velvet sky studded with a trail of stars beyond Cyrus's window as she returned to her dorm room. She and Aken had spent the evening writing an essay-long apology to the bakers, and then an hour in the kitchens slicing fruit and rolling out pie crusts. Aken still smelled like baked apples and cinnamon.

"Are you adjusting okay?" he asked her. His back rested against the bed frame as they sat on the rug. "Moving from the Outskirts to here was a lot for me, sort of like culture shock. So I get it if you're feeling overwhelmed."

Cyrus smirked, doubting he could ever understood her situation. "Hm, I'm fine... What was your life like in the Outskirts?"

Aken hesitated and scratched his arm. "My mom and dad were busy or away most the time. Our neighborhood was rough. They didn't want us there, and I couldn't make any real friends."

"I thought you were an orphan?"

He picked at the rug. "I am, now," he said. "My animal friend, Sabe, got killed by Denim's group. And on that same day my house was targeted by humans and burned to the ground—with my parents trapped inside."

A part of Cyrus went numb. She fought back a sudden

lump in her throat.

"Nephryte should've been doing his job that day—been the hero there to save them. I can't forgive that, or forgive the humans responsible. *Wicked creatures*," he growled.

Cyrus winced. It stung—a reminder she didn't really belong, that she was an enemy in their eyes.

"Not to change the subject, but what is a Scourgeblood?" she asked. "I heard Denim call you that."

Aken's gaze fell away, his features overcast by invisible clouds. "It's just…something people called my family."

Cyrus waited, but he said nothing more; maybe it was a touchy subject. To be honest, it was surprising he'd shared anything about his past with her. What did he have to gain by befriending an awkward redhead? She really didn't want to be involved with a troublemaker, and yet, he probably had more in common with her than anyone else here.

"How about you? What was life like?" he asked.

She felt a little compelled to share something. "My mother was killed when I was little," she said finally. "I was left with my dad, a spoiled step-sister and bitter step-mom. They never liked me, and I never had any friends. Like you, I was bullied."

"Why would they not like you?" He looked stunned.

Her shoulders lifted to her ears. "Because they didn't like my real mother. She was…an outcast. But anyway, when my Ability awoke, people were terrified, so I ran away."

Her voice sounded cold, even to her own ears. She couldn't care about relatives who were no doubt glad she was gone. How could Aken miss his indifferent parents?

The room fell silent. Beyond the walls, faint chatter and padding footsteps echoed the rhythm of school night life.

"It puts a hole in your heart, doesn't it?" Aken said, and watched a moonbeam as it rippled across the floor. His tone sounded heavy—the kind of heavy when your soul has been crushed to pieces for a long time.

"Yeah, it does."

Aken's gaze shifted to her, suddenly intense, and her cheeks heated. He grabbed one of her hands, wrapping his pinkie finger around hers. "Let's make a pact."

She swallowed, trying to inch away. "You mean, a promise?"

"Yes. A promise that we'll keep moving forward, despite everything. That we'll never let the past weigh us down. That we'll look out for each other, to the end."

He waited expectantly, and she almost gave a nervous laugh.

"Okay. To the end of this Draev Guardian business," she added.

Pinkies shook.

Aken hopped up on his feet. "Hey, wanna do something fun before calling it a night?" He gave her a mischievous wink.

"Like what?" she asked, uncertain of that wink.

He unlatched the window and a flood of cool, damp air breezed in through the room, pushing hair back off his shoulders. Climbing up onto the windowsill, he made the clay swallow Limitless appear.

He turned, held out a hand for her to take. "Come fly with me?"

She eyed the clay skeptically, but his eyes—deep-as-sky eyes that made anything seem possible—drew her in like a moth to the flame.

She took his hand and he closed his fingers around hers, pulling her up onto the sill with him. He stepped out across the air onto the swallow's back—a steep drop to the courtyard beneath them—then pulled her onboard and seated her behind him, showing her how to grip the clay-feathers like the pommel of a saddle.

Limitless flapped forward.

Cyrus's chest tightened as she gripped the spongy

feathers. Fear and thrill raced her pulse. She'd once wondered what it was like to be a bird, nothing to weigh you down, no shackles to the ground. But it was almost too free. And Aken's eager grin was making her second-guess this decision.

"Hold on," he said. "Away—*We*—Go!"

Wings beat hard as the bird took off and soared over Draevensett's steep rooftops and dark, piercing spires. Their hair whipped back in a tangled mix, and she squinted against the rush of wind.

"*Woo*-haa!" Aken spread his arms, his shout almost drowned out. Wind stole her breath away as the bird veered up, up, and *up*.

Her ears popped as they reached above the cloud line; thin clouds rolled in waves across a starry sea, and the half-disc moon bobbed ahead.

The swallow dipped in and out of the fluffy ocean, and Cyrus drew her hand along the milky white, feeling misty condensation.

They approached a group of bats out hunting the skies. Purple flesh wings glowed in the moonlight. One bat screeched and swerved aside as she tried to touch it.

Aken glanced back at her, and she nervously looked elsewhere. He continued to laugh, arms raised—wind filling his shirtsleeves as if they were wings of his own.

～

They landed outside the city in the grasslands, and sprawled on their backs atop a low rise. Clouds gathered on the horizon, though overhead remained clear.

Aken had brought her to his favorite viewing spot, a place without city lights interrupting the night's splendor. Where staring up at the ethereal expanse was like peering into a whole other world just beyond reach.

"Look." Aken pointed up at a curving line of stars, "The

wings of Cyrus the Swan—just like your name."

Cyrus furrowed her brow. "I didn't know I was named after a constellation."

Aken looked at her. "Really? Then you don't know about the legend that goes with it?"

She shrugged, "Just vaguely."

Aken shifted to one elbow so that he faced her, a mysterious gleam in his eyes. "The legend says Cyrus was the keeper of the world's Pure Light—the special energy stuff left over from the planet's creation after Lord God created it, an immeasurable power. Cyrus was the princess of a great human kingdom, and also the guardian who watched over the Pure Light.

"But when the Pureblood Emperor learned of the power, he came up with a plan to steal it. He activated a weapon that was capable of obliterating whole cities, and as it worked to create havoc across the world and distracted everyone, he went to where the Pure Light was kept, determined to rip the power from its sacred pedestal and use it for his twisted desires.

"Only the Shoshana Prince blocked the Emperor's path, and their duel was bloody, but the Emperor eventually defeated him. Before he could lay his hands on the ultimate power, though, the Swan Princess came and grabbed the Pure Light and absorbed the power into her body, where it melded with her very being. And then, she willed it to take her life.

"The princess disintegrated in an explosion that killed the Emperor and took the Pure Light away from this world with her, away from evil's hands, forever..."

Aken drew out the last word dramatically, his arms outspread toward the starry heavens.

Cyrus blinked. "That's...depressing," she finally said, playing out the story in her mind. "Do you think there's any truth to it?"

His shoulders shrugged, and he tucked his hands back behind his head. "Who knows. It'd be cool if there was!"

"Why call her Swan? What's the meaning behind it?"

"Mm, I think it's something to do with the Pure Light resembling swan feathers, or something like that. But who really knows?"

"So, let me get this straight: we celebrate the Swan Princess for taking the Pure Light away with her as she died, even though the world got ruined anyway by the Emperor's crazy weapon?"

"Ah," Aken held up a finger, "The world got ruined, but not obliterated. Life survived to rebuild, all because she didn't let the Emperor get his hands on the ultimate power."

Cyrus's cheeks dimpled in a sour smile. "Why in the world was I named after *her?*"

"Hm," Aken's mouth puckered, thinking. "Maybe your mom saw you as a Pure Light to the world? Cyrus the Swan is seen as the world's great mythical hero."

She tilted her gaze back, considering it. "And maybe it was Mother's favorite constellation?" Pieces of Mother she never knew. What other things had she loved? She wanted to collect those pieces.

Birch trees…scarlet hair…panicked footsteps…blood… She shut out the nightmare's flashing images. Thinking of her must have brought them up again.

"What do you think the Emperor was? What is a Pureblood?" she asked.

Aken's mouth opened, then closed, halting whatever he'd been about to say. Instead, he mumbled, "Who knows. People with anger issues."

The gathered clouds on the horizon mounted higher, carried on a spring wind that started to pick up around them. Soon, the stars would be obscured.

"The Swan Festival starts this week," Aken reminded. "The Trials that'll decide who gets to be in the Duel are

Monday, and the day after is the Festival Duel itself." There was a giddy edge to his voice. "I have to pass the Trials. I *have* to."

"One step towards your dream of becoming the greatest Draev Guardian?" she asked with a smile.

He nodded. "I don't care about the king's request part, but I really want to be in that Duel and win."

Cyrus shook her head, having no desire at all to be part of some crazy battle.

Aken picked a sprig of grass, twiddling it between his fingers before touching it to his lips. He blew, and a whistling tune carried across the firefly-speckled grasslands. A mystical tune, a melody reminiscent of something far gone and forgotten. She knew the lullaby from somewhere, though she couldn't place how, or from when.

Night birds in the distance whistled back warnings as the wind picked up.

Then came a different sound.

Kreeeah!

Cyrus sat bolt upright at the eerie cry. She tried to see through the vanishing moonlight. "What is that? Is it a Corpsed?"

Aken peered across the sea of grass, his night vision better than hers. "There's something moving," he said. "But it doesn't look big like that freakish thing we saw earlier. I doubt it's anything." He craned his head, "We can go, if you're worried."

Cyrus nodded, rubbing her wrists.

Kreeeah!

As they road Limitless away, the cry echoed after them.

⁓ం

Cyrus held a pen to the diary's blank page. Stretched out on her stomach on the bed, she pondered what to write as wind beat at the windowpanes beyond the lamp.

Birch trees flashed again inside her mind…rippling red hair…the patter of running feet in her ears. Desperation. A death-chilling scream in the dark…

She rubbed at the sudden shiver in her arms. Why did she keep thinking of that nightmare? It couldn't be real, yet it played on repeat when it chose, as if to torment her.

The nightmare still bothers me, though I try not to remember it during the day. So far, most people here have been nice. I know it's only because they see a young vempar and not the real me, but it's been a refreshing change not to be made fun of day in and day out. I'm finally living a normal life—well, as normal as an Ability user can get.

I wanted to ask the principal or Master Nephryte if they knew my Mother, and if she'd attended this school. Problem is, they might figure out my secret if I ask. If anybody knew Mother and knew she'd married a human, they could figure out the truth about me.

I can't take that risk…yet.

With a yawn, she finally laid the diary aside for the night.

It was dark. Cold. A cool winter gust lacking snow.

Damp. A dirt tunnel laced with roots.

Cyrus struggled to move, to crawl in the tunnel, but stark terror immobilized her knees in the soggy, rotting leaves that made up the ground. She couldn't see. There was nothing for eyes to grasp onto. She tried feeling around with her fingers.

There were sounds. Dripping sounds. Cruel chuckling sounds.

Then a shrieking wail trembled the air—so loud, so piercing, her head stung with needles. She attempted to cover her ears and blot out the noise, but it refused to be muffled or ignored. Over and over, it shrieked. She trembled from the pain, from the vibrant horror her body could feel coming from that voice. It wouldn't stop—*It wouldn't stop*. She had to find it. *Had to end it.*

Through utter blackness she crawled toward the cry—mashing leaves and mud with every move on hands and knees—and a dim tunnel mouth took form up ahead. It drew her forward like a beckoning light, until her head emerged on the other side into billows of mist. The scene of a forest met her wide gaze through the haze.

Moisture clung to the dim atmosphere. Swirls of fog fingered around birch trees, who stood white and silent as ghosts. The shrieking had stopped.

Where had it come from? *Who was it?* A distance from where she looked out into the woods, a bush began to rise. No, not a bush. It was a person, a dark silhouette, willowy like a graceful vulture. And there was something slumped on the ground at its feet—something with red hair.

Who...? She squinted to better see through the mist.

It was a woman on the ground, with red hair like Mother's.

The silhouette raised its head. What dim light there was fell across its face, and two agate gray eyes turned towards her.

Swannn! A mouth opened wide, black and bottomless, twin dagger fangs dripping blood sprinkling onto the cold grass. It was coming toward her.

A strangled gasp escaped her throat.

Legs unable to move, she braced herself and shut her eyes as the gaping mouth swallowed her whole...

The world went silent and still.

She dared to open one eye.

A cloud of fog had enveloped everything, and strange ink shapes came and went in the milky whiteness. She watched as one of the shapes became more solid, and something like arms came reaching out. A torso, a face, took form.

"Cyrus…"

The call was a whisper.

That voice, she knew it, and like a veil the fog parted.

Eyes like deep rivers pierced through the white, and his brown hair flowed as if underwater. Master Nephryte's calm gaze turned slowly to her.

He looked younger, much younger.

What was that on the collar of his shirt? A splash of something.

The closer he drew toward her, the more red that *something* became, and the truth of what it was gripped her like a vise.

Blood.

Cyrus sat bolt upright. She grasped at the bed covers, hands slick with sweat, and screamed.

It was dark. Everywhere. *Everywhere was dark.*

16

A ken-Shou covered a yawn, while he continued reading through *Daniel* in the old Bible from the hunchback faeryn. He hadn't read it since the day his parents died, but tonight he felt drawn to pick it up and read again. A part of him had felt abandoned by Lord God that day, but now he wasn't so sure.

Daniel was one of his favorite tales: about a man who was persecuted for his beliefs, and about his three friends who were sentenced to die in a blazing furnace because they worshiped Lord God.

Notes were written across and in between the old wrinkled pages by the book's previous owner—whoever that was. He skimmed a few of them; the owner seemed very interested in the lions den Daniel was about to be thrown into.

Looking up from the pages, Aken rolled the starlight orb in his palm, staring into its glassy depths. Would he ever see the mysterious human princess again?

But why did he want to see her? He hated humans.

She had looked so much like Cyrus, though, it was unnerving.

Cyrus—he felt a twinge of guilt for not being fully honest with him about what a Scourgeblood was, and for brushing it off like it was no big deal.

He focused harder on the orb, hoping to summon up some image…

And then a scream split the silence.

In one swift tumble, he was out and in the hallway and forcing open the door to Cy's room, rushing over to the bed, where he found Cyrus huddled and clawing at the bedsheets, shivering all over.

"Cyrus?"

The boy's lilac stare went straight through him as if he wasn't there.

Aken wrapped one arm firmly around Cy's shoulders and tapped the other hand against the side of his face, brushing red hair and sweat back from his temples with a thumb. "*Calm down*, Cy. You were dreaming," he said, trying to get him to recognize where he was.

Cyrus's shaking gradually ceased and he took several deep breaths before scanning the room—as if making sure what he was seeing was real. "Ak…Aken."

Aken let out a relieved sigh and put on an encouraging smile. "Must've been one heck of a dream you had there."

Cy's stare met his for a brief second, then dropped, and he rubbed his arms as if to rub away the nightmare.

"How about I sleep over tonight?" Aken offered, "I've got some picture books we can read. Nephryte hates it when we stay up past bedtime, but whatever. I think the situation calls for it."

Aken moved to get up, but halted when a hand caught the hem of his shirt.

Cyrus opened his mouth. "An…old nightmare," he breathed.

Aken slowly turned back around.

"I…have it now and then—the dream, I mean. In different ways. But it felt more real this time. And…"

Cyrus's voice trailed away, but inside she was thinking: '*...And it's the first time I saw a face I recognized.*'

What did Master Nephryte have to do with her nightmare? Why would his face show up beside her mother's body?

He was a new person in her life, and a little intimidating for someone as small and weak as herself. So perhaps her subconscious was simply displaying those feelings in a visual outlet. That's what she wanted to believe, anyway.

She saw Aken about to ask something, and quickly spoke up first, "It's just a nightmare. I don't want to think about it anymore."

Aken's mouth closed, concern clear in the crease of his forehead, but he respected her wish—and it made her feel guilty for snapping at him. In a softer tone, she added, "But I would like something good to read."

With a spreading grin, Aken dashed off. But not before turning and eyeing her curiously, "Is something different with your mouth?"

With a jolt, she remembered her fake fangs weren't in— she took them out to sleep. Instead of saying anything, she gave a shrug and pretended not to understand, masking the frantic beating in her chest and hoping his sensitive hearing wouldn't notice.

He didn't press the matter. She fast grabbed the wood caps from a small box and put them on when he left. That was close; she had to be more careful. One simple mistake like that, and she'd be found out...

For much of the night, they huddled before an oilpowder lamp, reading *The Green Gulk* and other fiction hero tales. They had just started *The Twelve Legendary Knights* when footsteps passed by the door. They covered the lamp, silent as mice until the coast was clear again.

The dark, gruesome remnants of the nightmare eventually faded. Those dreadful images were nothing more than figments—a result of trauma from losing Mother, and for never learning the reason *why*, and not even having a grave to visit.

None of it could be real, because if she *had* witnessed Mother's death, then she wouldn't be sitting here, alive, to ponder about it—she would've been killed by those murderers along with her.

Cyrus began to yawn; after so much reading, her eyelids were drooping…

The hour on the cat clock ticked late.

Aken glanced sideways, chin in hands above the book they were currently pouring over. He watched as Cy dozed, settling into a peaceful sleep.

He wondered what sort of nightmare it had been, and why Cy kept having it. Poor guy.

Well, at least Cyrus looked to be at peace now. Putting books away, he drew the bedcover around Cy before yawning and sprawling himself out on the backless sofa by the window, dreaming of Gulks, magical hammers, and thunder.

Kh-Kroomm!

Rumbles like that of an angry giant rolled along the rim of Aken's subconscious. The quiet intervals in between grew shorter and shorter. A series of flashes streaked across his closed eyelids, followed by a ground-shaking boom that rumbled louder than any giant could manage.

Kah-Kr-BOOM!

Aken and Cyrus both jolted awake.

It took a vague, fuzzy moment before his brain could

register the noise as a thunderstorm, and not giants. Rain pounded the windowpanes, clinking the glass like pebbles.

Lightning carved and played in the sky like a wild concerto. It was as mesmerizing as it was terrifying. He watched for a long while.

Something dark and cloaked rose from beneath the rain-pelted windowsill as Aken watched the storm. The dark shape rose until it filled the glass and blocked out the view.

A pair of blank calcite eyes glowed at them.

Krah-BOOOMMM!

Lightning outlined the shape's shredded fabric and two corpse-like hands gripping the window frame. One hand reached to the glass, forcing the window panel open. Bony fingers extended toward them—toward Cyrus.

Aken dove forward, slamming the panel shut with his shoulder and knocking the creature off the sill.

"A Corpsed!" Cyrus screamed. Thunder boomed in a continuous roll overhead, quaking the floors of Draevensett beneath their feet, as Aken grabbed Cy's hand and hurried out the room and into the corridor.

Bak came skidding out of his room, wearing polka-dot pajamas. "Whatisit—*whatisit?!*"

Instead of answering, Aken hurried over to the window in Bak's room. There, he saw it: crawling up the spiral walk's roof just beyond and to the left.

"What's going on?" Bak tried again.

"I think it's a Corpsed," said Cy.

"Corpsed are attacking the school?" Bak shrieked.

Zartin rushed to them in black pajamas, his normally shy demeanor overpowered by fear. "Did you say *Corpsed?*"

"I'll stop it!" Aken said. He yanked the window open and leaped out onto the spiral walk's roof. Cy's shout to wait faded behind him. Thunder boomed.

Wind and rain battered his sides as he landed on the arched roof. The Corpsed turned with a hiss, its shredded cloak flapping. It straightened, body emaciated and differently shaped from the one Nephryte had battled. Smaller too, if you could call seven feet tall small.

"You're not getting inside this school and hurting anybody!" Aken shouted and charged, tossing clay birds that flew forward and exploded in the Corpsed's face.

The Corpsed reared back its hooded head, and an extra pair of long, multi-jointed arms burst from its chest—all bone and black silver claws. Aken faltered as the arms shot forward. If it really was black silver, a strike from that could kill him.

Aken leaped out of range and landed up on the edge of Floor Harlow's roof. The creature cackled as if laughing, and used its bone-and-metal arms to climb up after him. Aken debated what to do; with no dirt present, he couldn't create lava spouts.

More clay birds blew up simultaneously like firecrackers, attempting to knock the Corpsed off, but its grip was strong and it easily reached the roof.

Aken tried to think, as the Corpsed's leathery skin and bone mask grinned. If he could just make the creature fall to the ground, then—

Claws flashed for Aken's right side.

He dodged left then forward, using his speed to run at the Corpsed, his fist ready.

◦

Cyrus rushed back into the corridor, Bakoa and Zartanian on her heels. "We need to help Aken, and wake the school!" she shouted.

In the floor's entryway, Bakoa found a red lever set into the wall, broke the glass encasing it and yanked the lever down. "Fire alarm should do the trick!" he said.

Bells in the highest tower came alive, bonging harshly, and sprinklers in the ceiling went off, showering them all.

As Cyrus opened the door leading outside onto the courtyard's spiral walk, stirrings and shouts from students could be heard. It wasn't long before vempars were flooding out of their dorms and down to ground level in a confused panic.

Cyrus balanced on the banister, trying to reach the walk's roof. She was too short, couldn't get a foothold, and her muscles weren't trained to lift her own body weight. But there was no way Aken could take on one of those horrid Corpsed alone!

Bakoa rushed past her and, shifting his legs into a sand tail, he flew, picking her up by the armpits and lifting her with him. They plopped onto the roof, and she craned her neck trying to see through the wind and rain. Thunder sent tremors through the structure beneath them.

A flash of lightning revealed two figures, high on the dorm roof.

She tried to call out and crawl closer.

Aken was charging at the Corpsed, his fist forward and glowing red. But the Corpsed arced a clawed foot through the air, hitting Aken's head and sending him rolling and tumbling over the roof.

Aken's fingers scrambled and gripped the rooftiles above the eaves, his legs dangling.

"Hold on!" Cyrus shouted, and the Corpsed looked her way, eyeballs rotating. Bakoa came up beside her, just as the creature vanished to the other side of the peaked roof.

Aken hoisted himself up and hurried to chase after it. And just then, the silhouette of Master Nephryte landed beside him.

"What on eartha is going on out here?" he demanded.

"A Corpsed is attacking the school!" Aken said, and he ran up the roof's slope to stand at the peak and point. "It's right there…!"

The Master followed. "I don't see anything," he said as his

gaze swept the many peaked roofs. "Are you sure that's what you saw?"

"I just fought it!" Aken squinted, trying to spot where it had gone. "It has to be here, somewhere."

After one last eye sweep, the Master ushered them down off the roofs. The school was in chaos as students ran to get outdoors, drenched from the sprinklers inside and then from the raging storm outside. The staff and Masters were hurrying up and down the castle-sized levels, attempting to restore order and find the cause of the alarm.

"There's a Corpsed on the loose! Run!" Aken shouted once back on the spiral walk, and students rammed down doors and crashed over one another in a stampede.

"Silence! You're making things worse," Master Nephryte snapped. He grabbed Mamoru's shoulder when the boy appeared, "You're in charge, Mamoru. Make sure they stay put while I resolve this." He indicated Aken, Bakoa and Cyrus, before he flew down to the central moon courtyard and vanished inside the first level doors.

"But—!" Aken began.

Mamoru gave him a stern look—the kind when you've woken someone who really needed their sleep.

Aken's mouth snapped shut.

17

The storm moved on, and was soon followed by a fair Sunday morning—though it was anything but fair inside the principal's office as Floor Harlow stood awaiting their punishment.

Master Nephryte loomed off to the side with the four other Masters, his eyebrows drawn low. The students kept their heads down before the large desk, though their glares stabbed at Aken, who they assumed was to blame.

"But we *did* see a Corpsed, sir," Aken kept insisting.

"It's true," Cyrus spoke up. "I know it sounds crazy, but it was there, and he saved me from it."

Two of the Draev Masters snorted, and the principal shook his head.

"The roof has been thoroughly examined for evidence of what you claim, but nothing but a few scratches were found, and those most likely made by you leaping about the roof like monkeys," said Principal Han. "Corpsed cannot breach this city's well-guarded walls—they never have. So, can you see how ridiculous this all sounds?"

"But it was—" Aken tried.

"How are we to know this isn't some new prank of yours, hm? Should we believe the word of a middle schooler who delights in getting attention through misbehavior?" The principal leaned forward, his fingers laced together on the desk.

Aken's mouth opened, then hesitated. "It wasn't a prank; I fought it," he murmured.

"And did anyone else besides you and Cyrus see this Corpsed?" asked the principal.

The other Harlow students shook their heads. But Bakoa spoke up, "It left before I could see it, sir. But I'm sure Aken was fighting some creature. He wouldn't make a prank out of that."

Aken looked over his shoulder at Bak, surprised.

"Well, there's nothing to prove that it was a Corpsed, or anything dangerous. It was either a trick of the wind, or a large bird seeking shelter from the storm that you saw," Principal Han concluded. "I hear you were reading ghastly picture books during the night—it'd be no wonder if you woke with a fright and started imagining things."

"They weren't ghastly, and it wasn't a dream!" Aken protested, but with a warning look from Nephryte, he shut his mouth and stared at the floor.

"Setting off the fire alarm is not something to be taken lightly. There was no fire, there was no emergency, yet you created panic throughout the school and caused sprinklers to damage student property and staff offices," said Principal Han. "If there had been a true threat lurking about, then you should have first gone to your Master, instead of leaping out windows and climbing rooftops." The old vempar snorted.

Aken's lips pressed together tightly.

"Principal," interrupted Dr. Zushil, "We have to consider what we are dealing with, here. The last Scourgeblood is a source of trouble, and should be locked away before more incidents like this happen—or dare I say, something far worse happens."

Aken's neck heated in anger.

"I am well aware of *all* that we deal with, Doctor Zushil,

having run this school for years." The principal looked at him pointedly. "This incident was unintentional, however, and does not require such extreme measures as that."

Aken exhaled.

"But punishment, indeed, is in order..."

Floor Harlow was released from their scolding and they filed out of the office, sullen and silent. Before them, Draevensett's hallways were lined with angry students and staff, who looked as if they were awaiting Harlow's execution. Mattresses, rugs, and any book or homework or project that hadn't been tucked securely away was now being aired out to dry on the lawns and on every windowsill. Choice words and glares flung Harlow's way.

Aken kept his arms in, making himself small as Nephryte herded them forward. Denim was among the glarers, a bruise mending on his cheek.

"Isn't this where the saying *Dumb blond* comes from?" Denim coolly commented to his lackeys.

"That Scourgeblood is nothing but trouble," said another.

Nephryte's firm hand on Aken's back forced him onward before he could comment back. He wanted to smack that demeaning look off of Denim's face.

Nephryte bent to Aken's ear as they exited the main doors, his voice lowered. "Be grateful I haven't taken that picture book collection of yours away permanently. One more incident out of you, and I might. But that's the least of your worries. You don't want to be expelled and locked away as an uncontrollable Ability user, do you? Keep playing pranks, and that's where your future will be."

Aken's ears burned red as he focused straight ahead. "Be honest. They don't want to lock me away—they want me dead, just like the rest of my kind," he growled.

Silence ticked by for a moment. "Then, all the more reason for you to straighten up and avoid causing trouble," Nephryte replied.

Causing trouble? He was just trying to keep Cy and the school safe!

Causing trouble…

No one believes me.

I mean nothing to them.

Heheh, end them all.

The darkness he'd locked away before now lurked at the edge of his subconscious—a cockroach trying to pry free from its cage. He mumbled bitterly, "I did see a Corpsed out in the storm, and it tried to grab Cyrus."

He glanced sideways, and Cy gave his hand a brief squeeze.

The madman of darkness slowly shrunk back inside the cage in his mind again, falling silent.

Nephryte glanced down, but didn't reply.

At least Cyrus had his back. As for the rest of Harlow, though…it would be wise if he kept a low profile until this incident blew over.

"Corpsed in the school? What a childish prank! He should still be in the crib, drinking from baby bottles," said Hercule.

"Perhaps Scourgebloods are monsters for their foolishness," sniffed Lykale.

Aken dug his fingernails into his palms.

Once the school premises fell behind, the atmosphere was less menacing as they walked through Uptown on their way to church.

"Master, I have projects to finish. Let me skip church, this time?" Lykale was asking.

Nephryte shot him down. "My answer is no, and it will always be no. Nothing is more important than church. Every student of mine will attend. And after church, you will be carrying out Harlow's punishment serving in the kitchens."

Lykale turned his head and made a face.

Down a cobblestone street, which ended in a cul-de-sac island of flowering trees, stood a quaint church. It wasn't like the grand, cold cathedral of the Church of Draeth that towered over the city, where the king and most prestigious of citizens attended. Aken could make out the looming gothic spires not far away.

In contrast, this small chapel on Pordenone Street radiated warmth and welcome, its walls a rosy brown, and stained-glass windows charming above the sidewalk. Faceted stone posts and rusted limp chain made a fence marking the property.

There were a lot of old stone fences, chains, and odd gates in Draethvyle that no longer served much purpose. Cy commented how unique it was, though Aken had never really thought about it.

Twin bronze bells in the steeple *bonged*, spooking pigeons who flapped away. Inside, the church was as cozy as its outward appearance promised. Nothing fancy but a tiled floor, some petunias in pots, and the small, old organ humming music. The air was cool.

The pews were filling up. Aken recognized the female Master Seren-Rose and a handful of Draevensett students. He also spotted humans, fox-like kitsune, and faeryn—all of them slaves who for some reason or other were allowed time off on Sunday mornings.

Harlow took seats along the second-row pew. Aken made sure to sit next to Cyrus, far from Lykale and Hercule. The dragon-eyed noble had yet to stop seething, and curls of steam were rising from his ears.

The first service soon began: the Lord's Supper, when cups of red juice were handed out—symbolizing the blood Jesus shed to cleanse people of their sins—and handed out bread—symbolizing Jesus's body, His death and resurrection. It wasn't a religious ritual or something you had to do for salvation, but a reminder of what Jesus had done, and that He would one day return.

In the next service, the church speaker for this week continued a study lesson of the book of *John*. Aken found his mouth involuntarily yawning; between Cy's nightmare and the Corpsed mayhem, he was barely awake. His eyelids sagged lower and lower with each tick of the clock.

A warm bed and pillow sounded so nice. He imagined sailing through the sky on a fluffy cloud, the ground below melting into a tranquil sea...

"Aken-Shou..."

He ignored the voice.

"Aken." It came louder.

"Go bug somebody else's ear. I don't wanna be in class," he mumbled.

"AKEN!"

Something smacked him.

He jolted awake and got to his feet, shouting the answer to what he thought was a teacher's question: "Epidermis!"

The church fell silent. The elder at the podium startled.

Everybody turned to stare at Floor Harlow.

Nephryte's face fell into his hand. Cyrus's mouth gaped. The Harlow boys flushed red in humiliation, and shifted, ready to skin Aken alive.

"As if last night's trouble wasn't bad enough!" Cy hissed at him.

Aken blinked, turning his head this way and that at the mass of staring faces. "Oh..." He scratched the back of his head. "*Eh-heh*, I thought I was in—erm, y'know—in health class..." The sentence trailed away, and he croaked: "Carry on!"

He dove underneath the pew, but not before pairs of angry Harlow shoes kicked at his backside.

Afternoon found Harlow scrubbing pots, pans and floors in Draevensett's kitchen maze, drenched in slimy soap water.

Master Nephryte paused before entering the open doorway. Punishing all of the boys for Aken's troublemaking wasn't what he wanted, but other Floors would hold a grudge against Harlow and cause problems if they felt no justice had been served. As it was, except for Hercule, his students were considered the odd ones, a pack of homeless strays; and having the last living Scourgeblood among them made it harder.

They had potential, though, and could become a great Draev Guardian squad in the future. He was determined to believe in the youngsters, even if no one else would. But if Aken couldn't graduate, if he couldn't learn to be more responsible, then nothing would be left for him but a future locked away. Uncontrollable Ability users were too dangerous to let loose in society—and he was the most dangerous breed of vempar.

Nephryte craned his neck. Harlow was scattered about the connected network of rooms, at every sink and floor, scouring away. They'd been at it for hours. "That's enough punishment for today," Nephryte's voice carried. "I'll let you off easy, this time."

Bakoa heaved a grateful sigh.

Aken rested back on his heels, until the Master coolly added: "All except for Aken-Shou, that is." Nephryte beamed a smile for the other boys. "Go enjoy what's left of the day."

"Wha—!" Aken started in protest.

A warning shadow crossed Nephryte's face, and Aken shut his mouth tight.

Harlow bustled out, while Aken stared glumly at the massive brown cauldron twice his size before him. He'd been scrubbing at the thing for hours, and it was no closer to getting clean. Aken groaned, sitting on his knees on the tiled floor, in the corner where drains made for washing out pots too large for sinks were; his shirt and shorts were thoroughly drenched, and his feet sloshed grossly inside clogs.

Nephryte observed from the doorway. He noted fondly that, while the other students had left, Cyrus remained cleaning away at a sink. He turned and left them to their work.

Cyrus scrubbed a gritty sponge along the sink's yellowed sides. Needle pains stabbed at her wrists—due to all the abuse she'd put them through the past two days, no doubt. At least the fingerless gloves helped shield from the arduous work, though they felt gross and wet.

"Cy, you don't have to stay," Aken told her, sounding touched but not wanting her to suffer hot, soapy slosh any longer. He flashed a reassuring grin. "I can finish this up in no time!"

"You saved me from that Corpsed—or whatever it was. Friends stick together," she said.

"And you have, buddy; thanks. But c'mon, at least one of us should enjoy the day. Maybe you can even, um…convince the others to stop hating me?"

"Don't ask for miracles."

He gave her a thumbs-up. "Just go. I got this."

Disbelieving that, Cyrus finally kicked off her water-filled clogs, shrugged on her shoes, and headed out the doorway, waving a hand back. "See you later."

A loud *CRASH* rang behind her—it sounded like a stack of pans had fallen, followed by a frustrated: "*Grahh*, fang it all!"

She winced and didn't look back.

18

Cyrus shifted from foot to foot before the door.

Now that she was a member of Harlow, it was a good idea to get to know better the comrades she'd be spending the next handful of years training with—providing she survived that long.

Her hand rapped lightly on the door.

"Come in," spoke a voice from inside.

Mamoru didn't look when she entered, seated on a wood stool at work on something. Light olive skin showed through random tears in his dark vest. He raised his head, "How are you liking Draethvyle so far, Cyrus?"

Somehow he knew it was her without looking. She closed the door behind her, leaving it a fraction open. The scent of amber oil and wax hung in the air.

Cyrus took a step near. Within Mamoru's artsy bedroom was an extra, dimly lit chamber with a sliding door blended into the wall—puppets, tools, limbs and other parts crammed shelves and display cases inside.

"Is it very different from your old home?" He rotated on the stool to face her.

Her cheeks flushed. "Y-yes! It's very different from what I'm used to. But I like it here."

A ghost of a smile crossed his lips.

She mentally rebuked herself for stuttering like a nervous idiot. "I'm so socially challenged…" she muttered under her breath at the floor.

Mamoru blinked.

Darn, she forgot vempars had sensitive hearing!

Mamoru broke into an amused grin. "Being social was never my strong point, either." He rose from the stool and chuckled, a sturdy hand built from years of craftwork resting on his hip. His fingers should have been worn and calloused, but instead looked smooth as wax. "I can handle small groups, but anything more than that is stuffy. I find more enjoyment working on my sap-wax puppets." His chin nodded to the secret chamber.

"I've never seen anyone with puppets like these," Cyrus said, nearing the work table.

Mamoru's left hand splayed, and thin amber threads rose from each fingertip. The threads glimmered like tree sap, and flew and attached to the skeletal puppet. The jumble of joints and limbs suddenly sat up.

"They're made of hardened wax, a *special* kind I create using tree saps," he told her. "I call it sap-wax. I'm of the Terravis class, like you. My Ability can manipulate sap and amber."

Cyrus poked at the puppet's knobby, glossy hand.

He pulled out a rock of amber from his pocket, similar to the one he'd used the other day. "I store puppets inside amber, like this."

Light from a window reflected off the hardened sap's facets like a gold jewel. A dark shape was trapped inside.

"I coat layers of sap over an object, soaking it in *essence* sap until it breaks down and becomes flexible enough that I can twist and fold it as I please." He set the amber rock down. "That lets me shrink a puppet down to this convenient size."

She swallowed. "But it'd be a flimsy puppet then, right?"

"My *essence* activates the amber and sap-wax of the

puppets, making them strong while in use; you'd be surprised how tough they are." He winked.

She nodded, pretending to understand. "Those strings…"

"Hm? Oh, these puppet strings?" He twirled one. "They extend from a layer of sap coating my body."

Cyrus resisted the urge to gag. "Your…skin is covered in sap-stuff?"

Mamoru held out his arm. "My secret protection." His hand clenched the stool, and a coating of sap moved down his arm to cover the seat. "I can grab my enemy, shift a layer of sap from my skin and wrap them up like a pretty package with it." He snapped his fingers, "Amberfied, instantly." The sap on the stool hardened. "The enemy fast suffocates, and will become a new addition to my amber collection."

Cyrus stiffened. She debated whether or not to maintain her fake smile or run for the door.

Mamoru chuckled, waving both hands. "A joke, a joke! Haha, you take me too seriously. I would never do something so cruel. Then again…" his face turned up to the ceiling, "perhaps if it were a very evil person…"

"And that makes it okay?" she squeaked.

Mamoru touched the back of his hand to her palm, and she gave a start. "My skin still feels normal, see?"

Surprisingly it did feel muscle-firm, not sticky; but still too smooth to be natural.

"I don't mind if you have a look around," he said, and leaned his elbows back against the table. His vest rode up, showing more olive skin.

A look around his abs?

"But keep it secret." He winked. "My workshop is the only place where I can get away from the world, and from certain needy students."

Obviously he meant the puppet chamber—not his abs. *'I'm such a dweeb.'*

She eyed some of the puppets that were hanging up. Had

any of those been real people, once? *Eek*, even if it had been a joke, the thought was unsettling.

He let out another laugh. "They were never alive." When his mirth subsided, he fiddled with a rip down his vest. "I'm sure you've been wondering about my unique style of clothing, too?" he asked.

Unique was putting it mildly.

"Because of how my Ability works, I need clothes that won't hinder my use of sap. I need skin exposed in order to use it properly."

"Aren't short sleeves enough?"

"Maybe. But if something happens and I can't use my arms, then I'll need other skin. And besides, exposed skin makes me dangerous to touch—for an enemy, that is." He hooked his thumbs in his pants pockets and studied her. "But enough about me. How about you? You don't seem to handle your *essence* very well."

She flinched.

His eyes closed in thought for a second. "Meet me in the grasslands at sunset—and bring Aken along. I'll teach you the basics of Draev *essence* then."

Cyrus recalled Master Nephryte had asked him yesterday to teach her Landing—whatever that was. Now they had a training date. With a nod and a "Thank you," she made her way out. He gave a casual wave.

Down the Harlow dorm corridor, she came to Lykale's room next. The door had been left ajar. She peeked inside. "Hello?"

Silence. She took a few steps in, pushing the door farther.

It looked more like a haphazard lab and clothing shop than a room. One half of it hangers and hooks of paired outfits, the other half littered tables and shelves of test tubes, pipes dripping solutions, bowls and vials of contents ranging from seeds, ground plants, powders, to bubbling liquids.

Lykale was either a clutterer or a hoarder—she couldn't

tell which. Vents let in fresh air through the ceiling, otherwise fumes from experiments would be unbearable to live in. Yep, all of Harlow was strange, she decided. The taunts from other Floors were making more sense.

"Hello?" she tried again.

Cyrus weaved her way about, scanning table contents. One bowl held halves of putty-like orbs the size of walnuts, like what he used during volleyball the other day.

"Snooping around my laboratory, when you're barely two days new?"

She jumped with a squeak, turning to face the tall, lean boy, who today sported a collared plaid shirt and tan trousers layered with pockets. He knew fashion, and she noted with irony how almost-human that fashion seemed.

Lykale's intense aqua gaze studied her from behind the glasses perched on his long, falcon nose.

"Sorry, I just wanted to get to know everyone in Harlow better," she piped, trying to muffle the fright in her tone.

Lykale sniffed disdainfully. "You're not going to become another troublemaker like Aken, are you? Because I *really* don't have time to deal with such nonsense." A finger by habit adjusted his glasses, and sunlight reflecting off a lens made her squint. He half-turned aside. "No, no. There is not a single person in all of Eartha who can cause as much trouble as *him*. You seem better mannered, at least."

Cyrus smiled—a cute smile unbefitting of a boy. "Thank you, Lykale. I hope we can be friends!"

Lykale looked startled; a shaky hand adjusted his glasses once more. He cleared his throat. "*Ahem*...erm-erm...perhaps." He turned to a congested table. "What is it you wanted?"

"I want to get to know my Harlow comrades better," she replied. His hair was so white; did he bleach it?

Lykale's brow pinched. "Better? Well, my Ability is of Armavis class, though unlike most, my weapon isn't a blade but chemistry." He held up a vial of purple powder, swirling it. "I concoct smoke bombs, poison fogs, paralyzing liquids and such." A sweep of his arm indicated the brimming bowls and mugs. "This was the smoke bomb you saw me use—it has a putty texture, one side flat so it can stick to any surface." His thumb flipped one of the halved orbs.

She poked the putty.

Lykale pulled out a syringe, twirling it from finger to finger as a knife-thrower would knives. "I can also throw these toxic darts at enemies." The syringes he called darts varied in shape, with feather wings in different positions. She shuddered at the thought of needles flying through the air at her.

"What about your Ability?" he inquired.

She didn't have much to say, except it was Terravis class, related to metal. "I think it only works on certain metals, though. I can't seem to do anything with gold."

"Hm, curious..." Lykale had the sort of inquisitive expression a scientist might give a dissected bird.

Since he was open to talking, she pointed at the choker padlock he always seemed to wear, and asked, "I like your choker. Does it have a special meaning? I noticed you always have it on."

Lykale's gaze wavered for a brief second, then his hand rose to clutch the padlock defensively. "What do you care? It's none of your business. Being in Harlow doesn't mean you should know *everything* about everyone."

She stepped back in surprise at the outburst. "I should get going and leave you to your work, then," she said, moving toward the door.

Once outside, she took a breath. *'Note to self: never ask about the choker.'*

Now, who was next to see?

Hercule—ugh, the Harlow boy she dreaded most. Should she skip?

She made up her mind and headed for Zartanian's door instead. What sort of Ability did the shy boy have? And why did he seem to have a problem with touching people?

Her forehead bumped into something that rattled her teeth. She backed up. There was a lavender shirt in her way, and the head atop it turned a fraction.

Hercule had been looking out one of the corridor's fanciful windows. He looked over his shoulder to what had disturbed him.

"Sorry! I wasn't paying attention and..."

Hercule studied her up and down with one glance. "*Hmph*. I'd expect nothing else from a country bumpkin. Rather scrawny and short, aren't you?"

Country bumpkin? Short? What a smug pig! Hercule may be handsome, with his smooth features and fine clothes, but his attitude ruined it. She forced a polite smile. "Well, I'd rather be that than some ungrateful snob."

Hercule's eyebrows rose, then slanted down icily.

Oops, that just slipped out—she didn't mean to actually say it!

Hercule stood tall, a vempar ten-times stronger than a human. Her mind raced to think of a way to ease the mounting tension. "You little..." he growled through clenched teeth.

Hercule's golden eyes glowed like flames, and tendrils of steam rose from his ears and fang-clenched mouth. She flinched back a step. Human instinct screamed for her to run, but at the same time she knew she had to stand up for herself.

Hercule's gaze flicked away momentarily to something behind her, and the steam dispersed.

A hand clasped Cyrus's right shoulder from behind, and her soul nearly leaped out of her skin in fright.

"Tell me, Hercule. Are you so spoiled that you forget how to be civil?"

Cyrus craned her neck back to see Mamoru; his chest brushed her shoulder from behind.

"As Draevensett students, we are equals, even if you are the son of a Noble House." Mamoru's gaze held his firmly.

Hercule stuffed his fists in his pockets; his all-important expression remained unperturbed. "*Hmph*," he snorted, and with his chin held high, he turned on a heel before stalking off to the stairwell.

"He's never been the friendly type," Mamoru said once he was gone, and side-stepped back from her. "But for him to be so outright aggressive...I don't know what's gotten into him." He stood with his arms akimbo, and shifted his weight on one foot.

Cyrus frowned. If only she wasn't so short—she hated being short and weak. The sooner she mastered her Ability, the safer she'd be. Maybe.

Images from the nightmare flashed up, and she fought them down.

'*Stop being this way,*' she growled in her mind. '*Everything is fine. I'm fine.*'

"I'm going to the Harlow study room." Mamoru's voice cut through her thoughts. "It's our Floor's hangout. Would you like to come?"

The study room was a color scheme of gray, white and grape red, with dark wood furnishings. Paintings hung wherever space allowed between bookcases, and on her left stood a rose-marble fireplace. White leather sofas and armchairs sat around the unlit fire.

Light poured in from windows at the back, around gray curtains, showing a view of the school grounds and a tall oak—one branch reaching toward the glass like a hand. A second door blended into the wall near it.

Lykale was there scanning book titles. Master Nephryte

reposed in a high-back armchair, the side table beside him weighed under a stack of books and a gilded lamp—its bronze base in the shape of a lion's paw matched the tall stand lamps in the room. He was speaking to Bakoa, who sprawled on the rug before the fireplace listening with a carefree grin. They looked up when she and Mamoru entered.

Master Nephryte motioned, "Feel free to borrow any books. They're from my personal collection, gathered over the years." He smiled. "I've always believed that a world without stories is bleak and bland. Books fill the imagination and make dreams come alive."

Cyrus marveled at the impressive collection, but she was more surprised by his enthusiasm. She hadn't seen this side of the Master—she didn't know he was capable of it. "Thank you. I will," she replied, and eyed the books eagerly.

Stories were her guilty pleasure, despite the sad fact that she wasn't very good at reading. What took an average person one hour, took her twice as long.

She swept over to the right wall bookcases and began browsing titles: *The Seas We Never Traveled*, *Inglish: The Universal Language*, and *The Protector's Legacy*.

Movement caught her eye. A feather bobbed and swayed behind a short bookcase jutting perpendicular from the opposite wall. She made her way near, pretending to browse more books.

The feathered hat came into view, and hunkered beneath it a mop of curly black hair—Zartanian, huddled on the other side, walled-in by books and the windows.

Cyrus backtracked and took a sofa seat near the Master. The white leather had a surprisingly luxurious feel, with its wide arms, short swirling legs and dark wood lining. She waited until the Master was looking, then sent him a silent questioning nod toward Zartanian—or rather, his blue hat.

Master Nephryte blinked in acknowledgment. "Give him

time. He's a bit shy because of his past," he said, softer than a whisper. He gave no more than that and a flash of sympathy.

Cyrus rose again, and this time wandered closer to the low double-sided bookcase. She recalled how Zartanian had drawn back from the farmers' children, as if afraid they'd touch him. So instead of heading toward him, she pretended to look out the windows. The oak's branches were full of new leaves.

Zartanian's gaze flitted across the space to her, then hid beneath the hat's wide brim and focused on a pad of paper he was busy drawing on. She tried but couldn't see what he was drawing.

Kraw, kaw-kaw! Cyrus turned as a raven rose from its nest, snug in the crook of the oak's branch, side-hopping before taking flight in search of food. "Look, baby birds. So cute!" she exclaimed.

"Ooh, I love baby birdies!" Bakoa leaped to his feet and rushed to come see. His silly grin widened when he spotted the tiny, fluffy things peeping and crying. "They're smaller than my hand. *Awww*," he swooned.

Cyrus stole a glance at Zartanian, but the boy did not move an inch. Her lips pursed. If he could see how cute and innocent those baby ravens were, maybe it would help bring him out of his shell. She unlatched the window and a warm breeze blew in.

Bakoa's orange eyebrows shot up. "What're you doing?"

She stood her knees up on the windowsill and grabbed around the nearest branch with both arms, putting the pressure on her forearms instead of her wrists. "You'll fall!" she heard Bak yelp at her back. But she inched her way forward along the bark like a giant inchworm, and soon got within arm's reach of the nest. One curious chick hopped toward her, ogling her fingers as she weaved them through the leaves to scoop the birdling up.

Sitting upright, and scooting backwards to the window, Bakoa helped her as she crawled back inside. He gave a squeaky gasp of delight, "*Wao!*" his eyes large watery bowls of joy beholding the bundle-of-cuteness cupped in her palm. "You're a cute little baby-waby, doobie-doo, aren't you?" Bakoa fawned. "*Yes* you *are!* My wittle bitty, teenie-beebie googie-goo…"

Hercule wandered in, frowning at their exuberance. "Please. Bakoa. Do us all a favor and cut your vocal cords, before you kill us off with that high squeak baby-talk of yours. It's a bird—not a freaking baby." His glare shifted from Bakoa to see that *she* was there too, holding the bird.

Bakoa gawked. "You meanie! I tolerate stuff from Aken, but I'm not gonna from you."

"Oh?" Hercule's tone dared him.

Bakoa's hands became sand and grabbed up books, flinging them at the noble snob. "Meanie, meanie, *meanie!*"

Hercule dodged easily and stuck his nose up in the air. "Pathetic. Are you even trying to hit me?"

One of the flying books hit Lykale, and he turned, growling, "Which of you rodents did that? *Which?* I'll pulverize you!"

Master Nephryte rubbed an aching forehead before rising to intervene.

Cyrus inched away from the commotion, moving to hide where Zartanian was in the alcove, as books sailed overhead. The shy boy drew back at her approach.

She showed him her hand, "A baby raven. See?" Zartanian peeked from under the hat's brim, and she scooted forward on her knees.

His eyes were like twin pools of winter ice—she'd never seen a shade of blue so fair. He watched her warily.

The raven chick peeped and its cottonball head looked around Cyrus's fingers at the noisy world. Zartanian glanced down to the chick, then back up to her face as her hand moved toward him.

The raven chirped, tilting its fluffy head sideways. Tiny bead eyes blinked and scruffy wings stretched, as the chick tried to balance on its wobbly feet.

Zartanian slowly put down the pad of paper and reached out to the chick. He eyed Cyrus one more time, and she smiled back, motionless. His fingers lightly brushed against her hand as he scooped up the raven. Zartanian's breath seemed to freeze, as if his nerve sensors spiked coming into contact with someone else, but the soft, cute bundle now nestled in his palm lifted the clouds from his spirit.

Cyrus took the opportunity to glance down at the paper: He was drawing a rose, the petals looking velvet soft, and beside it was…a skull.

The shy boy liked to draw morbid things.

'Yep. Harlow really is strange,' she thought to herself.

19

Aken strode into the study room, wiping both palms together as if he'd done a full day's work. He stretched noisily before plopping down on a sofa, arms spread out and both feet propped up-and-over the sofa's back like an upside down bat. "Whew, what a load of pots that was! But no labor is too great for these here biceps. Right?" He flexed his arms. But showing off failed to work upside down, his hair spilling across the floor.

Mamoru rolled his eyes to the ceiling. "Yes, what a fit princess you are."

"*Princess?*" Aken exclaimed.

Master Nephryte commented without so much as a glance, "Hanging upside down is dangerous, Aken-Shou. You'll fall on your head—not that much would spill out."

Aken pouted and stuck out his tongue.

Hercule snorted, while busy thumbing through a thick green book from the shelves.

Aken glanced in his direction. "Fall in a pile of ashes, did you, Hercule? Oh, sorry, that's just your natural hair color, isn't it?" He grinned sardonically.

Cyrus watched from a chair at the alcove's study table. Across from her, Zartanian eyed the growing tension with unease as he let the raven chick run about the tabletop.

Lykale was absorbed in three books and refusing to acknowledge anyone's existence.

"Ever thought of playing old Santa Claus in the next Christmas play?" Aken continued. "You wouldn't need to wear the wig." He rocked his body side-to-side, "Just wear a smile and get that jolly *Ho-Ho-Ho*-ing a going!"

Steam swirled out of Hercule's ears and grinding jaws, the hazy vapors filling the room.

"Oh no, the dude's gonna blow!" Aken feigned worry. "Quick, get a bucket of water. Call the Guard!"

Aken halted and spun back around. "On second thought, you'd make a much better Scrooge than Santa."

"I'll beat the snot out of you!" Hercule bellowed.

"*Aken-Shou.*" Master Nephryte intervened, giving up on any further peaceful reading for the day. His gaze beat a stern warning into both of them, and Aken shut up and put on an exaggerated apologetic face.

The Master tried not to facepalm.

Hercule stomped out of the study room, growling under his breath as he went, "Stupid no-good *nrgrg*, wanna…*strangle*…stupid…*khrgr*." Angry mutters trailed out the door and down the corridor.

Cyrus shook her head. Seriously, how childish could boys be?

Zartanian made his way over to the window. He didn't seem as shy as before, though he did keep an arm's length of space between himself and her. At the open window, he looked from the chick in his hand to the tree.

Cyrus was about to scoop it up and climb back outside again, when Mamoru took out an amber rock. The rock grew, and something unfolded itself and crawled free: a winged puppet, half-dragonfly half-grasshopper, knee-high tall.

Cyrus watched, creepily fascinated, as human-puppet hands at the end of two insect limbs scooped up the chick.

The device glided on dragonfly wings out the window to the nest. The chick hopped into its home and chirped at its siblings.

Relief washed over Zartanian's face, and he turned to Mamoru with a grateful smile. "Thank you, Mamoru."

He had such a pretty smile. Cyrus wished he'd use it more often.

The older boy dipped his head. "You're welcome. Don't be afraid to ask for help."

The day was nearing sunset beyond the glass already, the sky blooming sherbet orange and pink along the horizon line, with golden cloud wisps fanning outward.

Sunset? She'd almost forgotten! They had a training date with Mamoru. Her gaze cut to him. He ruffled his hair back with a hand before heading for the door and motioning her to follow.

She bumped her elbow on one of Aken's lounging legs as she passed by, startling him awake. "Mamoru said he's gonna help us with some training. Let's go, *now*."

"Wha? But I just— Aww, man. No rest for the weary."

"Weary? What about the kitchen staff who *every single day* do that work?" She let irritation take over without thinking. He faltered, and everyone in the room hid grins.

She didn't mean to snap at him. She just…wasn't in the mood for whining, and wanted him to stop causing trouble. "Toughen up! I'm going," she said and made her way out.

"Ah! Wai-wait—!" Aken struggled to turn himself upright. "I'm coming. *Oof—!*"

Legs falling up and over his head, he hit the floor hard.

To the side, Master Nephryte commented, "I said you would fall on your head."

Aken glared through his disheveled bangs, and scurried out the door.

"Hold tight to my back," Mamoru instructed her, outside the school gate. "Draevs use their *essence* to travel quickly through the city."

"Travel how?" Cyrus asked.

"I'll show you."

She clung to his back, feeling like some giant parasite. Starting from a clear spot on the street, Mamoru bent his knees and—*Vwoosh!*—they were leaping into the air, headed for the nearest rooftop, landing atop it. Without pause, he crossed the rooftiles, and was leaping out to the next roof.

Cyrus held on, trying not to get vertigo, as the streets passed beneath them.

The city wall soon appeared, but Mamoru didn't stop. He bent his muscle-toned legs, knees brushing the ground, and they shot up into the air with physically-impossible power, vaulting in one wide leap which carried them up and over the wall. So high that, as they began to descend, they were clear on the other side. A sentry atop the wall waved, recognizing the Draev students-in-training.

Cyrus squealed as the ground came rushing up to strike them. But their fall slowed before the blurred ground and, like magic, he landed on the grass as if it were a stair step.

"Wo...wow..." She gulped in air, her hair windswept into an afro. Her arm-hold around Mamoru's middle released shakily.

"How did you...?" she began. Then saw Aken arrive.

⌣

High from his perch on Limitless, Aken managed to catch up in time to witness Mamoru's impeccable talent. Honestly, was there anything the guy couldn't do?

Landing the bird at the Outer Woods edge near them, Aken held his chin high and strode forward. "Yo there. I'm ready for anything ya dish out, Scar-face bro," he said.

Cyrus and Mamoru stared at him blankly for one drawn second.

Maru's sigh broke the silence. "Not even bounty hunters speak that way, Aken. Hercule would be having a fit." Amusement twitched his lips.

Aken chuckled, rubbing his nose with a thumb. Cy didn't smile but looked uneasy about something. "Hm? What's wrong? Did you get better acquainted with the Hercule grump, yet?" Aken inquired.

Cy's mouth opened and closed, hands wringing together. "He…I don't think he likes me very much."

"*Tch*, that snooty-pants doesn't like anybody but himself."

He caught Maru and Cy sharing a look. That couldn't be good.

"Did something happen?" he asked more seriously.

Their slow response was answer enough. His fist clenched and unclenched. "That rotten— He better not mistreat you. I'll teach him a lesson if he does!"

Maru rolled his eyes to the sunset sky. "I don't need you making things worse, Aken. Leave matters to Master Nephryte." His hooded eyelids lowered halfway. "He knows what's best."

Aken grumbled under his breath.

"Anyway, let's start with why I called you here," Mamoru said, and then ordered Aken and Cyrus to climb up the nearest tree: a high oak with sturdy limbs. "I'll be teaching you how to Land from a high fall—otherwise known as the Landing Technique. And pay attention, Aken, because I won't be helping you with this again. You should have learned it in E.M. Study already."

"Eh, I don't get what the point is," Aken shrugged, unmotivated to climb. "I mean, it's not like I'm gonna go jumping off cliffs or anything—"

"You fly at incredible heights with that swallow, don't you? What if you fall and an enemy takes Limitless away from you? What then—*Ker-Splat?* Could your body Heal fast enough to save you?"

Aken crossed his arms. In truth, he was being stubborn because he didn't want to risk looking like a failure in front of Cy. But failure was a necessary part of learning.

"I'm sure you're aware that Draev Guardians travel by rooftop to avoid hampering civilians? So yes, Aken, this does have a point. It's called Leaping and Landing Technique—and if you ever hope to be a Draev Guardian, you'd better master it."

Aken folded his hands behind his head and leaned back to eye the sky.

"Leaping," Cy contemplated. "That's what you used to jump over the city wall?"

Maru nodded.

Aken leaned close to Cy's ear, "Hence the name Leaping—I'd imagine Leaping would have something to do with leaping."

Cy's cheeks burned. "Don't make me smack you!" Aken chuckled as the redhead boy scratched at his ear. "You pudding-head." Cy focused his attention back on Maru.

There was a ghost of a smile on Maru's lips as he watched their banter, though it vanished and his back straightened. He pointed to the oak's third branch up, "Climb to there."

As they finally climbed, Mamoru instructed: "Leaping and Landing both use *essence*. All lifeforms have a surplus amount of life-energy, and that surplus is what we call *essence*. In case you were wondering, Cyrus, a Draev's *essence* is different from that of regular vempars and other races—they can't use theirs in the same way we can."

Mamoru tapped his chest, "That's why we call it a gift, or Ability."

"But all vempars Heal."

"Healing has nothing to do with *essence*. That's an entirely different subject."

Once they were both perched on the branch, he had them close their eyes. "Now, imagine all of the energy—energy from the core of your being—collecting and flowing like a stream through your veins. Flow that stream down, down to the soles and heels of your feet."

Long minutes of trying passed. It was easier said than done.

"Once you have *essence* gathered in your feet, it will act as a cushion—a cloud—to slow your fall and soften the impact of landing." Mamoru lectured. "Remember: the more *essence* stored in both feet, the stronger of a cushion you'll have, and from a greater height you'll be able to land safely."

Aken's eyes closed. He pictured the flow of energy running through his core and limbs. His mind strained, and beads of sweat dripped.

He knew what Maru was saying. If he wanted his dream of becoming the world's greatest Draev Guardian to come true, he had to master this basic technique. Something so basic that every student could do it by now—even that smug Denim.

Aken let his eyes pop open, hoping he'd gathered enough *essence* in his feet. '*All right, time to test this out!*' Observing the ground below, his legs unsteady on the oak branch, he jumped.

The ground rose to meet him. His hair whipped back.

He fought but his legs wouldn't stay under him, instead splaying out like flags. When he impacted the ground, it was flat on his stomach, slamming the air out of his lungs—*GUh!*

Pain roiled his insides. He yanked his chin out of the ground, and watched as Cy faltered but landed on his knees—a fail, but at least Cy had managed to keep his legs under.

"Decent for a first try, Cyrus." Mamoru clapped, then turned to Aken as he scrambled to stand. "Your *essence*-cloud was off-balance: too much in one foot and not the other.

Stabilize it," he ordered. "As for posture: keep your knees closer together and bent slightly forward. Anticipate the land. When you're about to touch ground, stretch your legs and bend to meet it."

"I *was* anticipating," Aken muttered. "But I'll get it right this time, Puppeteer. Watch and see! I'll be the best darn Leap-Landing vemp you ever saw!"

Back aboard the branch, Cy was rubbing at his knees.

"You okay?" Aken asked.

Cy nodded. Sunset light cast gold flecks into the lilac pools of Cyrus's eyes, just like the human princess in the starlight orb.

The human princess…the Swan… Why did they look so similar?

"Hurry up!"

Aken jolted back to his senses. What was he just thinking? Something about a swan? What the heck. What a time for him to space-out. Cy had already jumped and Landed—and better than the first time.

'Focus, pudding-brain!'

Aken jumped—this time hitting the ground with his knees before falling flat on his stomach.

It was well into dusk when Mamoru ended their practice session, the first stars emerging overhead. By then Cyrus was able to Land on wobbly feet. But Aken…well, he was able to Land like a flying lizard: arms and legs splayed down, catching himself with hands and feet before slamming against the ground. At least it wasn't on his stomach anymore.

"Yes!" Aken pumped a fist, "I've mastered Lizard Landing Technique!"

Maru wiped his brow. "There's no such thing."

Aken tutted, "There is *now*."

Maru snorted, his frame silhouetted in the fading light. "Now that you get the basic idea of Landing, practice until you can Land down from the city wall, as I did." Finished with them, and waving back a hand, he turned on his bowtie shoes and headed for the city.

Aken put on a dark, theatrical façade, waving a hand and pretending to toss an invisible cape over his shoulder. "Land down the city wall, Aken-Shou, as *I* did. The Great Mamoru, the mysterious and creepy anti-hero."

Maru's head turned slightly, one mulberry eye gleaming at him darkly.

Aken hurried to get on his clay swallow before Maru decided to make a mannequin out of his skin. "You coming?" he held out a hand for Cy. But the redhead was still by the oak and peering off into the woods.

"Hm?" Aken leaned sideways, trying to see what Cy was looking at. But, scanning the tree line, there was nothing he could make out. He opened his mouth to ask, when Cy quickly spoke: "Go on ahead. I…want to practice some more."

He looked back, checking that Maru was gone. "I don't mind waiting. Maybe I'll pract—"

"No! I mean," Cy's voice caught. "Dinner's already started. I need someone to save me food before it's all gone," he spoke in a rush. "You know how gluttonous we boys can be, *haha*."

That laugh was so forced.

"True enough," Aken played along. "Okay, but don't take long. It's not safe out here in the dark alone." A piece of him hesitated before steering Limitless away, taking one last look over his shoulder.

A troubled feeling grew in the pit of his stomach.

'*It's not like Cy can't take care of himself, though. I'm just being paranoid,*' he thought.

It was silly to worry, and yet he couldn't help the feeling, after having lost so much already. The madman stirred restlessly inside the cage of his mind again.

20

Cyrus watched Limitless disappear over the city wall before she turned to face the night-shadowed trees. She took several steps forward.

She was sure there'd been a presence observing them from the shadows as Mamoru left. Someone well trained in the concealing arts of the Argos Corps, that even a vempar as vigilant as Mamoru had missed. It was clear she never would have noticed the person unless they'd meant for her to.

Could it be someone from Elvenstone, come to bring her back for sentencing? Maybe she should've had Aken stay...but if this was an Argos, she couldn't put his life in danger. "What do you want from me?" she asked the darkness.

Warm breezes rustled the grass, and blinking fireflies drifted away. A shape emerged from the trees, the outline of a boy not much older than her and clothed in Argos gear.

"Huntter! How in the world did you find me?" The silhouette came into clear view of the moonlight. The boy known to her as an elusive wolf regarded her, his eyes twin copper coins, his brown bangs swept forward.

"I've come to take you home," said Huntter, to the point. "People say you left willingly, but I know better." His hard gaze softened a fraction. "I know you didn't... you *wouldn't* just leave. That vempar prisoner forced you to come here because of your Ability."

Cyrus's chin dropped a fraction, guilt upsetting her stomach. Huntter, the one person in Elvenstone who had never resented her for what she was. The shadow who had watched over her from a distance over the years, yet rarely ever spoke. He was the last of the Shoshana Clan—a breed of humans said to have the strength able to rival that of vempars. He must have been away training with his mentor the day she fled from Elvenstone.

Moonlight played across his angular features and furrowed brow.

"I had to leave..." she said, unsure how to answer him. "I'm sorry." She gripped the hem of her shirt to stop her hands' trembling. "They were going to kill me, and— I can never go back." She swallowed. "But that's fine. It's not like I ever belonged there."

She met Huntter's gaze, though it wasn't easy. "You know how the town treated me when I was just a half-blood. Now, with my Ability awake, can you imagine how they would...?" She couldn't finish. "This city is where I will stay. I can't be anywhere else but here. That's just the way it is." It hurt to say the words which rang true, and to watch as any hope Huntter held inside faded.

"But to live *here*?" He couldn't speak Draethvyle's name, not without disgust. "Why not choose the Human Republic's capital, instead? It's our largest city—nobody will know who you are there."

She had thought of that, many times while walking Elvenstone's streets. But it would only be a matter of time before her secret got out again and she'd have to move on. Even if she could move from house to house, place to place, within the city, what kind of bleak life would that be? Hiding her Ability, never learning more about Mother, never exploring the vempar side of herself...

Here, among those who shared the same blood and gift as her, she was accepted. Not feared or loathed. She could belong, have a life. Aken, Bakoa, Mamoru, Master Nephryte, Zartanian—she finally had something like friends. Friends she could cry and laugh and train with, some who even shared the same beliefs. This was where God had led her, even if she wasn't sure she could be brave enough to become a Draev Guardian.

Cyrus's heart beat fast and she rested a hand on her chest. Until now, she hadn't realized how strongly she felt about them. How did that happen? When?

"Huntter," she spoke past the pain, "You don't want me here because you fear I'll become like *them*, don't you?"

The crease in his brow told her she'd hit the mark.

"I tried being human, and I failed miserably at it. Now, I'm turning to the other half of me." She watched his controlled expression, and said quietly, "Vempar blood will always run in my veins."

His jaw worked.

'Darn, why do you care?' she wanted to ask.

"As will the blood of humans," Huntter countered, "which is the race you take after most. Lacking fangs and Healing, vempars won't consider you one of them. Do they even know, yet?" He neared, and she shrank back a step. "Do you think they won't shout: *Enemy*, when the truth comes out? The only human they like is one drained of life."

Her hand moved to her throat instinctively.

Fangs...shrieks...a woman with scarlet hair slumped in the grass...

"They'll suck your life away. Drain every ounce without a care."

Scarlet hair...

"They will always need *essence* from others. A vempar's need never ends."

Mother…

"Stop it!" she shouted. She clenched both sides of her head, trying to shut out the nightmare's images. Tears blurred her vision. "I can't——" A sob caught in her throat.

Huntter fell silent. The grass rustled and crickets chirped. He took a hesitant step closer, raising a hand as if to console her.

"Back off, human!"

She and Huntter both looked up, just as a figure fell down from the sky and landed between them.

"Aken!" she cried. How much did he overhear? Would Huntter give her secret away?

Aken's gaze glowed fiery blue, as Huntter's flashed fierce hate. Each sized the other up in one cutthroat scan.

"You." Aken's hands fisted, his tone a threat. "Stay away from my friend."

"Don't tell me what to do, *vempar*." Huntter's tone was an equal threat, the last word spat out like rotten fruit. A gun was already in his hand.

"A weakling human is threatening a vempar? Seriously?" Aken's voice rang superiorly, and the veins in his hands glowed lava-red.

"Vempars are not immortal," Huntter coolly replied. He held the gun expertly, as if the weapon were a part of him. "Let's see you Heal from a black silver bullet through the heart."

Aken smirked, ready for action. "If you can aim it right."

Click.

K-boom!

The instant Huntter's gun *clicked*, the ground erupted under his boots in a bright flash of lava—dirt melting to burning liquid as it spouted upward.

Huntter back-flipped away from danger, landing in a crouch and ready to move again. "So that's your Ability: Terravis, soil to lava."

Aken sneered. "Oh, I can do much more than *that*, human."

Huntter grimaced. "Don't you know anything about combat? Never give away what you *can* and *cannot* do, until you know what your opponent *can* and *cannot* do."

"Like I got time to care about battle strategies. I'll whip your butt to Kingdom Kong!"

Huntter's frown tightened at Aken's misplaced choice of words, then he spotted the clay bird that was coming at him from behind. The bird exploded in a firework of yellow, and Huntter somersaulted high, landing neatly on a branch clear of the blast.

Blam!

Aken barely had time to whirl out of the way as a black silver bullet grazed past his cheek. The human had just alighted the branch, which meant he'd fired the shot while in midair—a good aim, and unexpected. Aken's hands glowed in red aura.

Huntter alighted a branch above the vempar. That Ability wasn't one to take lightly, but his gun Bloody Thistle could do more than fire bullets. "*You have to be ready for anything when facing those monsters,*" his mentor always said. This vempar seemed like an idiot, though, so it shouldn't take much to finish him off.

A flock of clay birds swooped toward Huntter's left and right sides. He leaped from branch to branch, avoiding the blasts, and used the next branch to launch himself head first, gun-arm held straight at Aken. A dark blade protruded above the gun's barrel.

Aken readied *essence* through the ground beneath his feet for another lava spout, hoping to strike the human before either the bullet or blade reached his chest.

Huntter pulled the trigger—

Ground bubbled up red—

"Enough!"

The shout rang. Cyrus's forearms became metal: one fist knocking Huntter's aim off, the other knocking Aken off his feet.

Both boys hit the dirt.

Cyrus felt a sting in her hand and saw a cut across one finger. Huntter's gun blade had cut her skin before the metal formed. She hid the injury behind her back, fisting the hand.

Two surprised faces blinked up as Cyrus planted herself between them. "Stop trying to kill each other!" she growled. "It's wrong, and it could start a war, you dolts! Argos and Draevs hate each other enough without you adding more bloodshed to the cauldron."

She knew what Aken was about to say and cut him off, "I know you think you're protecting me, Aken, but stop. This person wasn't hurting me; he was just asking questions." She could only hope that he hadn't overheard her and Huntter's conversation.

Aken's eyebrows drew down and he side-eyed the human boy. "Snooping around our city, were you? Looking for weaknesses you could report back to your Argos Corps buddies?" As he rose, Aken clearly made an effort not to rub his sore backside. "Get back to your giftless race, while you still can," he spat.

Huntter snarled, ready to beat the cheeky vempar to a pulp. Cyrus sent him a pleading look, and he refrained. "I'm sure we'll meet again, idiot vempar," he replied instead. "Do be more of a challenge for me next time, will you?"

In three strides, Huntter melted into the woods like a shadow, leaving Aken to fume. Cyrus looked on, guilt sagging her shoulders. Huntter had come all this way to make sure she was safe—all this way into Vemparic territory for her. She let the metal vanish and fought off a wave of fatigue.

"That—*that*—!" Aken's face scrunched up. Taking a deep, cooling breath through his nose, he half-turned toward Cy. Had Cy seen the human nosing around and stayed behind for that reason? But then, why not say so? Why keep it secret? It was odd. Everything about it was odd.

"You sure surprised me with those metal fists." Aken barked a laugh. "Y'know, I almost didn't come back to check on you. Glad I did. *Erm*, that is, I know you're tough enough to take care of yourself and all, but you shouldn't take on dangerous humans on your own… I'm not saying you aren't capable or anything." He waved up his palms. "Just that…that…" He searched for the right words. But when he looked again, he could tell Cy was only half-listening, staring absently beyond the trees.

He gave up talking.

"So much for dinner, huh? It's too late," Cy mumbled suddenly.

Aken broke away from his thoughts, and couldn't hide a wry smile at the redhead's appetite. "Heh. Yeah. For a small person, you sure eat a lot, y'know?"

21

Huntter's boots trekked lightly through the undergrowth of the Outer Woods. Insects trilled in the tops of the canopy. The serenity of the night forest was lost to him as emotions stormed in his mind. Cyrus couldn't be left to live in such a dangerous city! If the vempars found out the truth about her, it could mean her life.

He understood her refusal to live among humankind, but at least she would be alive, not a corpse left in some forsaken ditch.

His right fist tightened. Cyrus was sweet, yet naïve when it came to the ways of the world. Just because you hope for something doesn't mean it will turn out right—he had learned that lesson well, years ago. Fist loosening, he raked his fingers across the back of his head.

He recalled the day he first met her. He'd been four years old, and was captivated by her large eyes the shade of lilac flowers, surrounded by a messy sea of scarlet. She hid behind her dad's leg, shy and afraid ever since the loss of her mother. The memory was stamped in his mind like permanent ink.

He had decided, from then on, never to let her feel pain like that again—never to let her cry like that again. He promised. She was his betrothed, decided by their parents when they were toddlers. It was his responsibility to take care of her, and he'd been watching over her from afar ever since. He doubted she remembered their betrothal; no one else living did, except for her dad. But one day, he would have to bring the matter up.

Huntter slowed his pace and closed his eyes. He would keep that promise to her, as best he could. But he also had another promise to keep: to become an Argos and take revenge for his massacred family. It wouldn't be easy keeping both promises at the same time. He raked his hand through his hair again.

He could give Cyrus some time to enjoy whatever happiness she thought she had found in Draethvyle. Maybe it would benefit her to learn how to use her Ability. And who knows, with time, she might decide on her own to leave, when things get too tough. *They won't accept her any more than Elvenstone did,*' he thought. And she would grow tired of it, tired of the malice, and leave—and he would be there, waiting to take her wherever she wished to go next.

"Aken…" Huntter growled at the mere thought of the vempar who seemed to have a friendship with Cyrus. He wasn't about to let it go any further than that. No *life-sucker* was going to lay a hand on her while he still breathed.

Huntter edged around a cluster of ferns and climbed over a fallen trunk, orange fan mushrooms sprouting from the bark's rot. It would be more than difficult to check in on Cyrus regularly. Draevs made their rounds around the city perimeter and the Outer Woods edge, day and night. He'd almost been caught twice already. He was only an Argos apprentice—he wasn't ready to take on a full-fledged Draev.

A frustrated sigh escaped his parted lips. It would take a lot of risk and effort, but he would check in whenever he could.

Ff-sssshh!

Leaves in the canopy whistled as something rushed through the air. Something fast. A dark blur, high above him in the trees.

Huntter ducked low, one hand wrapping a camouflage cloak around himself. But the *thing*, whatever it was, had vanished as quickly as it had appeared.

It wasn't a Draev, he was sure of that. But from the brief glimpse of a shape and cloak, it was no creature of the forests either. An almost humanoid thing, yet not. Corpse-like…

He was about to uncloak and continue on, when a faint rustle in the underbrush reached his ears. He kept low near the fallen tree and slowed his breathing.

A long wait of complete silence passed, and then he could hear faint footsteps.

For the steps to be so quiet, almost non-existent, it had to be a Draev. The patterned two-foot stride told him it was nothing four-legged, and the few two-legged animals there were would have heavier steps and breathing. A vempar's breath was deep…calm…silent as death.

From his concealed crouch, he spotted a dim figure as it strode through the trees and underbrush. A top hat, a stray moonbeam reflecting off of white gloves—that was all Huntter could make out before the woods and shadows swallowed it.

Only one vempar? Were they going after that corpse creature, or…?

Huntter breathed in through his nose and hurried on. Whatever was happening, it wasn't any of his business.

22

"**W**hoa, hold on. You mean Scar-face actually *let* you see inside his workshop?" Aken exclaimed. "He's never let me see it, as much as I beg him!"

Cyrus muffled a laugh in her palm, as they made their way up the spiraling walk outdoors that ringed the moon courtyard, its ceiling blocking the stars from view. Warm night air spilled past the rails and narrow support columns to moisten her skin. Reaching the fifth floor, they went through the grand door leading into Harlow's entryway.

"I only peeked inside for a second," she said. "I didn't see much. I was kind of nervous to, honestly."

Aken guffawed. "Maru can seem creepy with that weird Ability of his. Did you know he can trap people inside that sap-wax and turn their bodies into amber?" He mock shivered. "I don't think he's ever done it; but then again, who knows. Some of his puppets do look too real..."

Cyrus elbowed him in the gut. "Stop trying to scare me!"

A grin parted his lips. "Anyway, I can't figure why he'd let you—*someone he just met*—see secret stuff he won't let me or Bak or any other comrade see! So not fair."

An image of reckless Aken and Bakoa tearing through the workshop, with Mamoru freaking out in the background, crossed her mind. "I think I understand why," she murmured. Aken looked at her, and she coughed. "I mean, the workshop is Mamoru's solace away from people—especially loud, troublemaking people."

She waited for him to understand, but he just blinked. "Never mind."

Reaching the dorm rooms, Aken looked ready to say something, but then his gaze dropped and he exclaimed, "You're bleeding."

Cyrus raised her left hand: A cut on her index finger leaked red. "Sheesh, take better care of yourself. What's it from?" he tutted.

The cut from when she'd stopped Huntter's gun blade had reopened. "M-maybe the dinner knife?" she mumbled. Master Nephryte had graciously saved leftovers for them.

A red droplet trickled, and a sudden surge of anxiety rushed through her before it could be suppressed.

Blood...

The nightmare flickered awake.

"Are you okay?" Aken's tone was concerned, and she realized her shoulders were shaking. His hand moved to take her wrist and guide her. "It's no big deal. C'mon, I'll Heal it for you."

He led her inside his messy room, a disaster zone that he tried but badly failed to keep clean. She sucked in a breath. *'Aken isn't a monster; he'd never hurt me. What Huntter said is wrong,'* she told herself.

"Sorry about the mess," Aken's voice cut in. He paused at the foot of an unmade bed, kicking two shirts and a pair of boots aside. His hand took hers, and he raised the bloody finger to his lips.

Cyrus's heartbeat thrummed like a woodpecker in her ribs. "W-what are you—?"

"Your Healing must be real slow, Cy," he teased. "Cuts like this should be easy for you to Heal on your own."

"Why your mouth?" She struggled not to let him feel how

much her hand was shaking.

He tsked like a teacher. "It's easier to transfer Healing super-cells through saliva. We've been learning about it in class. You really don't know anything, do you?"

Clenching her free hand up in a knot, Cyrus tried to think of flowers and pretty sunsets to keep the nightmare's claws at bay.

His lips closed around her finger.

She held her breath as seconds ticked by, and then Aken released her hand. A strange look of reluctance flashed across his face.

She cupped her hand to her chest, and eyed the cut: every trace of it was gone. Incredible; if only she could have inherited Healing from Mother. Her genes took after her human side too much. Oh well, moping about "If only" never made a difference.

She looked up to thank Aken, and found him staring at her. His forehead creased, as if debating something.

She tensed, fear sparking anew, fueling the panic she'd tried to suppress.

"Your blood." Aken took one measured step toward her. "It's not normal. It's so…sweet."

Her heartbeat pounded like a mad drum in her ears. "What?" She couldn't get out words. She took one unsteady step back.

"Sweeter than honey. How's that possible?" Aken continued, and she tried to wet her dry lips.

He stepped closer. She backed away farther.

"Where are your fangs?"

She barely heard the question above the rapid pounding in her ears. She raised a shaky hand to the fake fangs in her mouth, and found them missing.

After dinner, she'd rinsed them out in the bathroom sink, and must have forgotten to put them back in.

"Cyrus…what are you?"

The question echoed, and the room seemed to tilt around her.

Huntter's words repeated inside her mind: *"Do you think they won't shout Enemy when the truth comes out? The only human they like is one drained of life."*

Her back pressed against the wall, trapped—how did she wind up trapped?

Aken's shadow loomed. His blue captivating eyes, once friendly, held hers. She couldn't look away.

"You're not…a vempar…" He paused, and the world fell still around them. "Are you?"

She couldn't read his expression or gauge his feelings.

All of her careful planning had come undone and been for nothing. She was a liar, a fake, to be seen as a possible human spy—a threat to Draethvyle.

She let her hand fall back to her side. There was no point in fighting Aken. She was no match for him or any vempar in her untrained state. If he was going to kill her as a traitor, he could do it easily. As if that wasn't pathetic enough, fear wouldn't even let her focus to make her fists metal.

'I should have known better.'

Aken planted a hand on the wall beside her shoulder. She squeezed her eyelids shut, back and arms pressing against the wall in a futile hope it might open and allow her an escape.

'Huntter was right.'

Something pressed against her forehead. Her breath trembled.

A long moment passed…and nothing happened. She peeked one eye open.

Aken's forehead rested against hers, his slow breath warm on her cheek. Then he stepped back, holding her by the shoulders at arm's length. His steady gaze glowed in the dark of the room. "Tell me the truth. What are you, really?"

Cyrus blinked several times, making sure she was still alive. "I'm half-human," she admitted, no more than a whisper.

"Half-human…" Aken repeated. She thought back to the bitterness in his voice the last time she'd heard him say the word *human*. He stared sidelong at the wall for a while. "Ah, who am I kidding?" he finally said. "I'm a Scourgeblood, the worst of the worst. What right do I have to judge you for being born different? Besides, we made a promise. I don't go back on my promises."

Aken's finger rose and flicked her forehead.

"Ow." She rubbed the spot.

"That we'll keep moving forward, despite everything. That we'll never let the past weigh us down. That we'll look out for each other, to the end," he recited.

She couldn't speak—surprise and relief, confusion and tears, mixed together in a messy torrent. All the fear and tension she'd been holding inside for days wanted to burst out in a flood.

She fell forward into Aken, hugging him. Her dripping eyes and nose buried in his chest, soaking his maroon shirt.

Aken let out an awkward laugh, lightly patting her back. "Didn't mean to scare you, buddy," he told her. He tried easing her tight grip.

"Are you mad?" Cyrus mumbled without looking up from his shirt.

"I don't know. It's not like you were trying to hurt me. I get why you kept it secret," he said, then had to swallow. Maybe a part of him hurt, after all? "Hey, Cy." He gently pried off her squeezing arms. "You're from a human town then, right? How did your parents end up together: a vempar and a human? And what made you come all the way up here?"

Rubbing her eyes and nose dry, Cyrus backed away.

The truth gradually poured out: how her mother had pretended to be human when she married her dad, and how the town despised her for years after once they found out the truth. How Mother was found murdered one day, and how Cyrus—being a half-blood child—had to put up with the town's malice. She told about freeing Gandif, who in turn brought her here for a chance at a new life and a place to master her Ability.

Cyrus felt like a tense rubberband that was finally starting to unwind, relieved to let out the truth to someone. Aken listened to every word, sitting cross-legged on the bed across from her.

"It feels like I don't fully belong anywhere," she concluded. "I'm stuck in between worlds, forced to pretend to be something I'm not, whether I'm with humans or vempars."

Aken pinched at the fabric of the bedspread, dorm life beyond the window making background noise. "There's something I should tell you… Something that everybody else knows." His head lowered until his ears touched his shoulders. Cyrus waited silently. "When you asked me before what a Scourgeblood was, I said it's just something people called my family, but…there's more to it."

He sucked in a breath. "Scourgebloods were a different breed of vempar, a breed that no one wanted around. And I'm the last one left." He paused. "When you came along, for once there was somebody who didn't know what I was, who didn't judge me, and it was nice. That's why I didn't want to tell you." He fell silent.

"Were they that bad?"

He shrugged. "I haven't bothered to research—don't really want to. But if you need an example, you know that evil Emperor from the Swan legend? Well, he was a Pureblood, what people now call a Scourgeblood. In other words, I'm the last in a legacy of monsters."

After he said it, he couldn't look up. Seconds ticked by on the nightstand clock. "Are you…afraid of me?" he asked, as if not wanting to hear the answer.

Her hand moved to pat his. "I won't pretend to understand what Scourgeblood means. But I'd be a real loser if I dumped my friend just because of some old legend, or because others don't like you." Cyrus smiled. "If you can accept a pathetic half-human, then I can accept a pudding-head Scourgeblood."

"Pudding-head?"

"You know you are."

Aken lifted his chin, chuckling. "Sounds like a good deal to me, buddy. Sounds good to me."

Aken flapped his shirt collar to cool off from the warm night air, while they sat lost in thought listening to the crickets and random laughter carrying across from the other dorm levels.

"You never said who killed your mother," Aken said carefully. "I felt too bad to ask earlier, but was it other humans?"

Cyrus took a moment, shutting out unwanted images. She spoke in almost a whisper, "I heard it was a vempar, one or two of them." She swallowed. "But the culprits were never found."

"Your mother was killed by her own race?" Aken exclaimed, then lowered his voice. "That's a crime punishable by death! Only an authorized Draev can carry out executions—and it has to be approved of by the big guys in charge, as ol' Nephryte said. Unless..." He mulled over it further. "Maybe it was a Draev who went rogue, turned criminal?"

Cyrus looked startled. "Are you saying the killer could be a Draev Guardian?"

Aken tapped his cheek in thought. "It's possible. I mean, your mom had an Ability like you, didn't she? She could defend herself against an ordinary vempar. So, the culprit had to be someone powerful."

Cyrus rubbed at her wrists. Images from the repetitive nightmare whirled along the rim of her subconscious. Why had Master Nephryte's face shown up in her nightmare? Younger, with a blood-stained shirt.

Maybe this nightmare—as much as she didn't want to admit it—was more than a figment of her imagination and an actual memory. A memory of that day. Had her two-year-old self witnessed Mother's murder, and survived?

'How did I survive?'

She shook her head. "Until there's solid proof, I can't be suspicious of every Draev." Aken side-nodded in understanding. She slumped back against the wall. "Let's change topic." Sweat dabbed her brow and neck, her stomach queasy. The thought of a Draev murdering Mother was too much to bear.

For now, she was just grateful Aken didn't turn on her for being secretly half-human. She doubted the city would be as accepting if they found out.

"Are you sure you're not mad?" she asked again, and averted her gaze. The lamp's dim light made his eyes glow like pools of mountain sky.

"It's the world we live in that I'm mad at. Why can't we all just get along, and forget where we came from?" he said.

She watched the floor, pondering that. "The darkness inside won't let us—sin won't let us."

Aken leaned toward her.

She tensed. "What?"

"Hmm, I was just thinking." His head cocked to the side. "For being a different race, you don't seem all that different from me."

"It took you how long to figure that out?" she stated sarcastically.

He laughed. "By the way, who was that human? That broody boy who tried putting bullets through my chest?"

Cyrus sucked in a breath. "Yeah, Huntter. He came to see how I was doing."

"And to take you away?"

She gave him a brief look, then tugged on a red strand of her hair. "Growing up, Huntter was the only person who never despised me for being a half-blood. Though, I still don't know why..."

"*Hmph.*"

She tried to read what Aken must be thinking, but he hid it well. "There's something else we should talk about," he said quietly, as if the walls had ears. "Other people don't need to know your secret, but you should tell Harlow the truth."

She gave a start, feeling like she'd been slapped.

"*What?*" she screeched, then covered her mouth, hoping no walls had heard. "Are you serious? I can't— No. No no no!" From her seat on the bed, she grabbed the nearest pillow, hugging it tight to her chest and shaking her head vigorously.

"Don't worry. They'll accept you, same as I do," Aken assured, his smile trying to ease her nerves.

"How can you be so sure?" she snapped.

"I've been with them long enough to know," he tried to appease. "They've never been hateful toward slaves, and they don't say mean things about other races. I know they won't hate you. And besides that, none of their families were killed by humans—they've got no reason to hold a grudge against you."

She eyed him doubtfully.

"We're on the same Floor—we will be for years. They need to know you can't do all the things vempars can. Like not being able to Heal yourself or others: that's a weakness Harlow's gotta be aware of, to keep both you and us safe."

She looked down at the rug, rubbing her left wrist.

"*Erm*, not that you can't take care of yourself in a fight or anything. I just mean, if you do get hurt, then you'll need somebody there to Heal you. And when we have to fight humans…I know it won't be easy for you."

Cyrus gripped her arm, leaving a red mark. Aken was right, being realistic. The way things were now, she was more of a burden than a comrade to Harlow—and secrets only made it worse.

She chewed her lip. There were only two options: Let Harlow find out the hard way one day while putting them at risk, or tell them and get it over with.

'Which is the right choice, Lord God?'

She released her arm and faced Aken. "I want this to be my home. I'll defend it." She tried to sound firm and unwavering. "I'm gonna work my behind off. No matter who we face, even if it is other humans, I'll support team Harlow any way I can. I want to live as my mother did, and accept the vempar half of me."

Aken watched the new determination set on her face, and she watched the moonlight play across his cheek.

"I believe you, Cy."

She brightened. "I need more time until I'm sure Harlow will accept me. Then I'll tell them," she said. "We're still in training, so it's not like I have to rush and say anything right now."

Aken looked up to the ceiling. "Or…"

"Or what?"

"Or you could win a request from the king to give you citizenship."

"Huh?"

"At the Festival Duel: the winner is granted one request from the king. If you become a citizen of the Kingdom of Draeth, then you'll have equal rights same as any vempar, and you won't have to live in hiding."

She stared at him. "Enter the Duel, are you *crazy*? I'd be squashed like a bug!"

However, becoming a citizen did sound smart. No one could enslave her or throw her out of the city, then.

"At least try," he said.

Cyrus rubbed at her wrists nervously. "I don't know…"

Scrtch.

Something scratched the door, and they both went still.

Aken inched forward on tiptoe. Soon as he reached the door, he flung it open.

There, leaning against the door frame, was Lykale.

The older boy adjusted his glasses with a tell-tale smirk. "Been keeping a secret from us, have you, Cyrus?" he said. "I couldn't help but overhear a few things…"

23

It was almost curfew, yet all of Harlow was in the study room when Cyrus and Aken entered. Lykale stood like a towering wall behind them.

He'd given her the choice of either telling them the truth herself, or letting him. And so, here she was, about to spill the truth beans. But what if Harlow didn't want a half-human among them? She'd need to flee the city before they could alert the authorities.

Cyrus spotted Zartanian at a little chessboard table, opposite Mamoru, considering his next move. Bakoa busied himself learning how to use watercolors, and leaving a mess on the alcove table. Some warmth filled her at the quaint sight, but not enough to quell the fear pounding in her chest.

The only person not present was the Master, and she wasn't sure how to feel about that.

"Go on." Aken nudged her forward before Lykale could say anything.

She tried not to appear nervous—that was the last thing she wanted them to see. "Um, hey guys." Her voice came out timid and shaky, betraying her. She wanted to melt into a puddle on the floor and disappear.

Only Mamoru and Zartanian turned in their chairs.

"Listen up!" Aken shouted, nearly giving her a heart

attack. "Our comrade's got something to say. Yeah, I'm talking to you too, Snobby-pants."

Hercule glared from near a window.

All eyes were on Cyrus now—vempar eyes. Being the center of attention stinks, but this was far worse. *'To think I came here hoping to lay low and be invisible,'* she thought wryly.

She fumbled for words. "I sort of…lied to you all." It was the only way her frazzled brain could think to begin. She gripped her arm, vision focused on the grape-red carpet underfoot.

Lykale folded his arms across his chest impatiently.

Her dry throat tried to swallow. "I have Elemental Manipulation Ability, as vempar blood runs through my veins. But the truth is, I'm not fully vempar." She spoke the last part in a rush, as if to lessen the blow.

Their pointed ears twitched, catching every word. The room fell silent as a graveyard.

"I am…"—she cringed with every fiber of her being— "…half-human."

In the following silence, a single cricket chirped beyond the windowpanes. *Cricket. Crick-cricket.*

Bakoa's jaw dropped to the floor.

Zartanian went wide-eyed as if struck by lightning.

Hercule looked as if he'd discovered a cockroach.

Mamoru showed the faintest curl in the corner of his lips.

The silence seemed to drag on. The stares, the cricket…she wanted to go outside and smack that stupid bug, and then run as fast as she could out of Draethvyle.

"Human? He's tainted with human blood?" The first to speak was Hercule, and the way he said it— Cyrus took a step back.

"Really?" Bakoa sounded uneasy.

"Does the principal know of this?" questioned Lykale. She couldn't move to shake her head. "Well, this is a very serious matter then, isn't it?" Lamplight reflected off the lens of his glasses.

"I...I just..." She tried to speak, but every jaw muscle stiffened in fear. They watched as she swayed and almost lost balance, gripping the door frame.

"I'll go and report this. Lock him up, in the meantime," said Hercule.

No...no no! She turned, shoes squeaking as she hurried out into the hallway. Aken was wrong—they hated her just as much as the people of Elvenstone did!

She raced across the carpet and tiles, her steps echoing down the corridor.

The redhead vanished down the corridor, out of Aken's sight and his outstretched hand. He clenched his fist and rounded on the room and those inside.

"What the heck was that? *Lock him up?* Cyrus hasn't done anything to deserve that! If anybody here has a reason to hate humans, it's me—my parents were killed by them, in case you forgot. But I'm not blaming Cy for something he had nothing to do with."

When no one reacted, Aken urged them, "C'mon, give him a chance! Isn't that one of the things Nephryte's been teaching us: not to judge based on race?"

He confronted the sand boy. "Bak. Cy's been nothing but friendly and accepting of you and your hyper-happy ways. Hardly anybody else in this school does."

Bak hung his head in regret. "He's been a good friend, even if I haven't known him long. I'd like to know him longer."

Aken turned beside him. "And you, Zartin. Cy went out of his way to cheer you up and be a friend. Did you even show him why you wear a hat all the time? Were you afraid he wouldn't accept you if you did? Yet here you are judging *him?*"

Zartanian tugged his hat closer around his head. His gaze didn't lift from the floor. "Cyrus seems like a kind person. I—I want to trust him and give him a chance. I just wish he hadn't lied to us."

"He didn't lie! He just…didn't say things upfront. And for good reason—he knew *this* would happen," Aken gestured. "Lykale, Cyrus takes your fashion advice and pretends to be interested in your science stuff, when no one else is."

"No one else is? Science is knowledge! How can no one else be interested?" Lykale snorted. "Well, I will confess that Cyrus has more potential than *you* when it comes to brain usage and Ability—that's for certain."

"I'll ignore that snide remark." Aken smirked. "So, shouldn't we keep a member who likes science and who has great Ability potential?"

Lykale frowned, fidgeted, and frowned some more. "I suppose I could cast my vote to keep the little half-blood, but only if everyone else agrees."

Aken gave an approving nod.

"Look at you lot," Hercule spat, "fawning over a human as if he were some little brother. How repulsive. He should be turned over to the Guard."

Mamoru, having been quiet until then, rose to face the nobleson. "What did you say?"

"Humans are the enemy, more so than any other race—and I refuse to harbor an enemy." Hercule held his chin high.

Mamoru's eyelid twitched. "More so? You should read up on your history books before speaking, Hercule, or have you forgotten the Goblin Shadow War?"

"Why are you defending a boy who lied to us—who lied to the entire school?" Hercule demanded.

Zartanian shifted uncomfortably, Lykale looked to the ceiling, and Bakoa rocked on the heels of his feet.

"He's part of Harlow, that's why! Cy's one of us," Aken

shot back.

"A human can never be one of us."

"He's half-vempar! You can't just dismiss that."

"Enough!" Mamoru's command brought the room to silence. "If anyone outside of Harlow finds out about this, Cyrus's life will be in danger. The higher-ups might assume he's a spy for the humans, and who can say what they would do?"

Aken swallowed. Bak and Zartin shared a look.

"Those in favor of keeping Cyrus in Harlow, and keeping his secret safe, raise your hand," said Mamoru.

All hands steadily rose, except for Hercule's.

"The majority wins. Follow through with it, Hercule, unless you no longer wish to be on our Floor," Mamoru told him. "I wonder what people might think of an unstable student who switches Floors, though? Couldn't be good for the noble image."

"Don't threaten me..." A tendril of steam escaped Hercule's ears, and he crossed his arms and turned his chin away. "Fine," he said at last, "Keep your rotten secret."

⸺

Cyrus grabbed the handmade bunny with its hidden pouch and necklace contents and stuffed it into her backpack, along with an extra set of clothes, before pulling on a jacket and opening the window.

She climbed out and landed on the spiral walkway's roof just below, then hastily followed as it spiraled down to the moon courtyard. At the end, there was a tumble as she dropped down and rolled to the courtyard grass.

Picking herself up, she entered the nearest door and hallway, and tried to picture the map of the school in her head. An exit door came up, and she hurried out into the school's front courtyard.

Several servants were moving about, but preoccupied

with chores; none paid her any mind as she slipped past and down the paved path, making her way to the main gate.

"Cyrus!" A voice called, and she tensed just before a hand caught her shoulder. "You don't have to leave."

She spun to face Aken. "Yes, I do." She reached for the gate, and he stopped her again.

"We just talked it over. We voted to keep your secret so you can stay in Harlow," he insisted. She gave him a look, and gripped one of the gate's curled iron bars. "Only Hercule protested, but don't worry. He won't tattle—it'd be too embarrassing for him."

"Oh, so I'm an embarrassment now?"

"What? No! That's not— Why would you think that?" he floundered.

She pulled on the gate, and his hand covered hers to stop it opening.

"Please, Cy, don't go. We need you here—*I* need you here."

"Did you see the way they looked at me? Afraid, disgusted, as if I wasn't the same person anymore. As if I didn't belong in this world—as if no one would miss me if I left it." Her cheeks were damp. "Do you have any idea what that feels like?"

Aken's features softened, and he steered her by the shoulders to embrace her. "Of course I do. That's been every day of my life." His chest was warm against her cheek as her tears rolled onto his shirt. "But you can't give up. Things can only get better if you keep working at it."

Her shoulders shuddered involuntarily. "It's too hard…"

"I know." He patted her back. "But you don't have to struggle through it alone. Lord God brought you here for a reason. I know that's a very Nephryte thing to say, but I believe it's true. You have value."

Cyrus looked up at him. All this time she'd hated herself for being different, for being ridiculed by others. She had let people determine her value. But God had given *her* life just as He'd given *them* life, and that meant she had value, no matter what anybody else thought. Why had it taken her so long to acknowledge that?

"Thanks, Aken. You know, sometimes you actually sound smart."

He grinned.

A buzzing sound drew near them. The cotton pixit came out of its nest. "Noisy! You noisy! Go away, go away!" It swatted at them.

24

Cyrus re-entered the study room, with Aken flanking her. Mamoru was the first to meet her, bowing his head. "We apologize for frightening you, Cyrus. You've been a kind friend, and we want to give you a chance to belong here. Some of us just needed a little time to think it over."

Her nerves eased a small bit. "Thank you, Mamoru. Thank you, all of you."

Bakoa bounded up from the floor. "So, you're like one of those creatures that's two things mixed into one, right? Like a turtle-dove, fire-ant, or toad-hog?" One finger reached to poke her arm. "What should we call you? Vemphu? Humapar? Vehuman—?"

"*Baka*," Aken slapped the finger away. "Stop saying stupid-*baka* things."

The desert boy blinked in response, completely oblivious.

Lykale studied her ears closely before stepping back and taking a quick up-down look. "How could I miss it? I'm supposed to be the genius here. I've brought shame onto myself and my brilliant intellect."

Cyrus was starting to feel overcrowded.

Chair legs scraped back as Zartanian rose and his pale, thin form came to a stop before her. His eyes fair as winter's morning briefly met hers. "Will you still be our friend, Cyrus? You won't resent us?"

Her heart melted into a puddle of feelings. "I'd love to stay friends with you, Zartanian. Always."

The shy boy smiled back. Not a full, beaming smile like Aken's, but for someone who kept smiles hidden, it may as well have been the biggest.

Hercule was watching, arms crossed and leaning against the left wall. "Answer me this, Cyrus," he spoke, and she felt a stab of heat cross the room. "If you had been honest with the school from the start, would they have harmed you?"

She stared at him.

"You have a powerful Ability, and that makes you valuable. Both Principal Han and the Draev Grandmaster might have taken you in and let you become a citizen—if you had been honest."

Her mouth slackened as Hercule's words sank in. Had she gone about all of this the wrong way? Her hand gripped her forearm.

She shouldn't have lied…she should've trusted God was in control, and been honest. The realization hit like a mound of crushing rocks.

Mamoru fixed him with a hard glare. "You don't know that."

"No, we don't," Hercule said with a faint smirk, and glanced her way. "And now, we never will." He turned and strode out the study, hands in pockets.

Mamoru watched him leave, then turned to her. "Ignore him. He's just trying to upset you. But there is one more person who should know your secret, if you're up to it now."

~

Cyrus tapped her fist lightly on the wood-paneled door.

At a "Come in," she ventured inside the dorm flat, hands trembling.

The door let into a small kitchen space. She crossed the tiled floor, until it melted to carpet inside a living room, decked in gothic and elegant furnishings, like most of Draevensett.

She waited, searching for the owner. To the left of the kitchen stood an open doorway, leading into what looked like the insides of a dimly lit tower. She poked her head inside. The curved walls resembled a miniature library—it wasn't a large space, yet books packed every curve of the stone surface more than nine-feet up. She craned her head back; there was no ceiling as the tower rose up and up, old as an attic and dotted with little windows along the way. An iron rail staircase spiraled up the wall to vanish at the tower's top.

She was tempted to climb it, but spotted the Master waiting patiently for her at a desk that had too many drawers and stacks of paper, which he thumbed through—those were probably Harlow's test results, and work from the older grade classes he sometimes helped train. A small rhombus window showed the night sky above the Master's head.

Without looking up, he spoke. "A good evening to you, student Cyrus. I hope learning the Landing Technique was not too difficult?"

How did he know it was her, without looking or hearing her voice? Mamoru had done the same thing. Was there something odd about the way she walked? She pouted.

"I'm sorry I wasn't able to teach you properly in an E.M. Study class. But my other students have gone over the exercise so many times, it wouldn't be fair to start them from the beginning."

Cyrus nodded, rubbing and massaging her wrists to keep calm. Watching the Master's long fingers flip through paper after paper, she wondered again: Could he know something about her mother?

"I think I got the hang of it," Cyrus answered. "Mamoru's a patient teacher."

"Hm." Master Nephryte straightened. "What did you come here to discuss, Miss Cyrus?"

She swallowed. "I'm…" Then swallowed again, leaving his steady gaze to eye the floor of the little tower-turned-library. "There's something I need to tell you."

She paused, and her lips went dry. Did he just call her *Miss* Cyrus?

Dumbstruck, she lifted her head slowly. The Master had laced his fingers together, elbows propped on the desk, a knowing smile curving his lips. "Yes, I know," he replied to her unasked question. "I know *both* secrets."

The gears in her brain malfunctioned. All this time he *knew*? He knew she was a female and half-human? "B-b-but…" Her tongue wouldn't cooperate.

The Master leaned forward. "People have tried to keep secrets from me my whole life. That is why I learned well how to discover the truth that others strive to hide."

Cyrus gripped her arms, feeling the urge to flee again. "You sensed it, didn't you? By touching my shoulder. Is that how you found out?"

Master Nephryte shook his head, and fair brown hair spilled over his lean shoulder. "There are many ways in which we use Touch," he told her. "I can steal a person's *essence* for myself, or I can channel my own into them—transferring super-cells to Heal their wounds. Touch has many uses, but it cannot reveal a person's race or gender. We are all born of ancient humankind, and are much more similar than we'd care to admit."

"So…?"

He smirked. "I've always been good at making Dr. Zushil talk. It's impossible for him to keep anything from me, much to his frustration."

"But the doctor doesn't know I'm half-human."

"You gave yourself away the day you arrived, when you started asking odd questions. Thankfully for you, I was the only adult who heard you asking." The Master rose, moving around the desk toward her. "But why did you come here? Is it worth risking your life to master your Ability?" He halted before her.

She squeezed her arm. "It's because...I don't have anywhere else to go," she admitted, voice hushed. "Humans don't want me, and I doubt faeryn or anybody else would either, with these freak powers."

Master Nephryte lowered to one knee so that he wasn't towering. The enduring blue river in his eyes met with the insecure lilac petals in hers. "You can belong with us," he said. She searched his face, every crease and angle. He wasn't lying. He meant it. His finger lightly tapped her jaw, "And I can get you better fake fangs. Wood must taste terrible."

Her lips twisted to the side—*It did.*

"I'm allowed to stay?" She masked any note of hope in her voice. It was too much to believe that Principal Han and the D.G. League authorities would be fine with this.

"Yes, you are, because I'm the one letting you stay and no one else needs to know," Master Nephryte said. "I've already taken you under my wing. You're my responsibility, and no one can say otherwise." He tapped the tip of her small nose. "You are God's creation as well as any of us. To me, your life has equal value."

Cyrus fought back tears. "Master?"

"Yes?"

"Should I have been honest from the start? Should I have let the school know the truth?"

The Master regarded her. "Vempars outside Draevensett would despise you either way. But...it's possible that the school would have accepted you, because of your Ability."

Cyrus hung her head.

"Don't dwell on *What if's*, Cyrus. It's far too late to change anything now."

She gave a halfhearted nod.

Master Nephryte rose. "A difficult road lies ahead of you. You can choose to keep your secrets, for now, but I've a feeling they won't stay secret long."

She tried to keep her back straight and look resilient.

Lamplight made the outline of his hair golden, and glinted off a silver ring on his hand as he reached for a drawer. "Someone or something will give away the truth. And once the school knows, then all of Draethvyle will know." He drew a billboard in the air with his free hand: "The Human Training To Be A Draev Guardian—that will be the headline on every front page in the kingdom."

She groaned. Hopefully those secrets would stay secret long enough for her to complete the training.

The Master took something from the drawer. "Vempars will be shocked, some horrified, but with time I believe many could grow accustomed to having a half-human as a Draev Guardian. As long as you work hard." He winked. "Anything labeled *different* is frowned upon, until people realize its value."

Cyrus turned her head away, unconvinced. "What if the principal disagrees when he finds out what I am, and throws me out, or worse?"

Master Nephryte arched an eyebrow. "What did I just say about *What if's*? Listen to me, don't give up your future here just because some can't see past the shape of your ears." He ruffled her hair teasingly.

She pushed his hand away with a giggle, trying to comb it back down.

"Here, I got these for you." His palm revealed a pair of metal bracelets. Lamplight played along their decorative feather design. "Wear them and use the metal for your Ability."

She slipped them on, one each around her upper arms. They looked like a string of swan feathers. "Thank you."

The Master's smile became a little more serious and he cautioned, "Never leave the school grounds without me or a Harlow member with you. It's best we be on the safe side, until your combat skills improve. And keep practicing your Landing."

She nodded.

'Why is he in my nightmare?' The same face, a younger version. If only she could muster the courage and ask him straight out, right now. But asking such a grim thing—*"Were you there when my mother died? Did you have something to do with it? She was murdered by someone powerful, you know."*—how could she ask that to his face? He'd been nothing but kind. She shouldn't suspect him based solely on a dream.

"You look ready to keel over," he voiced. "Off to bed with you; go on. We can talk another time." She rubbed her eyelids, emotionally exhausted.

Later, as night lengthened beyond the window of her bedroom, Cyrus snuggled into her fluffy pillow. Her thoughts turned to Huntter in the quiet. Was he okay? She felt so guilty for sending him away...not that it could've been done any differently.

The stars were bright, glimmering like a wolf's coppery eyes around the curtain folds. She slowly drifted into the realm of sleep.

Part 4

The

Trial

25

Clouds bled rose and lavender across the dawning sky, and a soft hum of music drifted in through the window. Cyrus yawned, sat up, glimpsed the cat clock on the nightstand which read 6:00 am.

"*Nuhh*…why am I awake?" She turned and swung her legs down, bare feet contacting the plush rug before she stood. Stretching her arms, she peered out the window. The faint music was beautiful. Piano—no, organ. The way it was being played, though, almost resembled piano, each note filled with mystery.

Too curious to go back to sleep, she quickly dressed and tiptoed outdoors onto the spiral walkway, there following its curve down to the fourth floor. The morning air was slightly cool. She paused at a door where the music hummed clearer.

She turned the handle and crept inside. If she remembered correctly, this wing of the floor was made up of music rooms and art classes, with a branching section leading to the grand library.

She swept across the polished floor and made a right turn, following the melody. Who could be so dedicated to music that they were up this early practicing?

There were no more windows as the hallway became a

dim, narrow space; the walls either side a maroon wallpaper with scroll-work patterns, broken only by closed doors and dark frames.

Tap-tap-clak.

Someone else was roaming these corridors, not far behind.

Her pulse quickened, and her feet hurried the pace.

Tap-clak-tap.

She practically dove into the nearest unlocked door—which happened to be the last door, as the narrow maroon world dead-ended.

She scrambled to her knees and waited.

No footsteps followed. Silence, as if they'd never been.

The mysterious melody swirled around her ears now, and she let the notes turn her head to look beyond the little entryway she'd hidden inside. A set of double doors were propped open, and she inched her head through.

The room beyond was like a miniature ballroom. The marble floor a rose, ochre and ivory mix that shimmered as light slanted in through ceiling-high windows. The windows themselves were works of art in metal tracery. A curving set of stairs just beyond her feet waited to lead her down into the tucked away realm.

A separate little staircase ran up the wall to a balcony on her right, its glass door shut. A place for private chats and gazing at the moon after dancing.

Cyrus unpropped the doors, letting them close behind her—just to make sure no one could sneak up without her hearing. She made her way to the marble dance floor, and there the music's source came into view.

Fluted pipes climbed like vines up the wall from a silver organ. Ivory inlays resembling spiderwebs and ancient symbols covered the instrument's framework.

It looked as enchanting and mysterious as the song being played.

A lovely sorrow seeped into the music. She listened as pale, nimble fingers carried the song without a hitch. She recognized the boy on the red velvet bench—his buttoned-down blue vest and white blouse with lacy cuffs, the too-big hat with its plumes on the seat beside him.

"Quite the talent," she said to herself.

The music trailed to a stop; his pointy ears twitched. The black, curly ponytail shifted as Zartanian turned to look behind him. "Cyrus?" His timid voice echoed in the near-emptiness of the ballroom.

'Why's he surprised?' she thought. *'Playing the organ early in the morning—of course people are going to come investigate.'*

She found an ounce of satisfaction in being able to sneak up on a vempar, for once, though the music had probably masked her approach.

She crossed the space to the bench. The shy boy drew his hands back from the keys, resting them on his knees instead. "I h-hope I didn't wake you," he stammered. "I s-sometimes play this. It makes the world feel better."

Her mouth opened to ask what he meant, when he added: "It's better to play early. People don't come around; most hate mornings, so even if they do hear, they ignore it and sleep." He hesitated, looking both apologetic and nervous. "I don't play every day, though. I won't be a bother."

Cyrus frowned sideways. "That's a shame. I liked hearing you play. It felt like I was being wrapped in a lullaby." Her hands covered her heart as she imagined, "As if I were the Spring Maiden from the fairytale, waiting for the Frost Prince to find her."

There was an odd look on Zartanian's face. She stumbled, "If I were a girl, I mean! Which I'm *not*, of course." Her laugh came out awkward. She ruffled the sides of her hair to appear more messy.

Zartanian's head tilted quizzically, but whatever he was thinking, instead he asked, "You really liked it?"

She nodded brightly. "M-hm! I've never heard an organ sound so beautiful. Actually, I've never heard one at all—I've only ever seen them in picture books."

The boy's cheeks dimpled in part of a smile. "Thank you for the compliment. I get nervous, though—playing around people."

"We'll have to work on that." She sat down beside him—well, beside the hat; and even then he flinched.

Light glinted off something above his ear, and she realized with a start that Zartanian had a small pair of antlers growing from the sides of his head, just above the ears, sharp as an elk's and gradient black to white.

He felt her staring and nervously averted his face.

"I w-was going to tell you," he said quietly, almost embarrassed. "I'm mostly vempar, but a part of me is rehfabel."

She was tempted to ask why Harlow could accept him so easily, yet had had trouble accepting her.

"I wasn't judging you for being human, Cyrus," he said, as if guessing her thoughts. "I didn't know if we could trust you, if you were really here for the right reasons. I was afraid—I think we all were. Humans and vempars have always been bitter enemies."

She turned to face the organ. Now his hat made sense.

"Are people mean to you?" she asked.

"…Sometimes," he replied.

"Where are rehfabel from?"

He smoothed his curly hair. "Across the sea, in Bergvolk."

"Really? How did you end up here?"

"Well…I wasn't born there. I was born in Draeth. It was my male parent who moved from Bergvolk to here."

Male parent? Another way of saying father, as if he wanted to avoid the word completely. His expression turned dark and overcast.

"Does this mean you're a fan of the Three Bladeers

books?" she asked, indicating the hat, which looked like a replica of their style.

Zartanian hesitated, then nodded. "We both were. I want to become a swordsmaster, like them, one day."

"We?"

"…My brother."

"You have a brother?"

Zartanian's mouth hung open, as if the words were stuck in his throat, and he turned his face away.

Cyrus suddenly felt awkward. Maybe she'd asked too many questions. Pressing her fingers to the ivory and ebony keys, she tried playing a few piano ditties she'd memorized from watching Heily play: *The Bunny Who Was Bald* and *Twinkle Little Star*. The silly tunes carried round the miniature ballroom.

Zartanian's hands joined in, adding extra notes and flourishes, as his faint smile returned.

The morning kitchens bustled, working to get school breakfast ready, when one woman suddenly cried out.

"What is it, Head Baker?" The chef came running at the sound.

Head Baker Bel dashed out of the baking rooms, clogs skidding across the floor, hands waving smoke away wildly. "It's *him* again, I know it! He's using the smoke for cover," she said.

Head Chef Burly scanned the area with her dagger-eyes. "Yes, I can sense his presence—his conniving little pastry-eating soul."

Just then, Aken ran out of the baking area, zipping through the connected doorways and into the central kitchen hall.

"THERE HE IS!"

Aken scurried toward the exit doors at the far end,

snatching up a cake slice *here*, a strawberry tart *there*, and whatever else came close to hand.

The floor pounded with footsteps. The heavy-set form of Head Chef Burly came up behind him, charging like a mad bull. Aken picked up his pace.

He barely made it out the swinging entrance doors and into the dining hall, where he quickly blockaded the doors with chairs, just in time.

Furious fists pounded the doors, striving to burst them open. "Pastry scoundrel! I'll have your hide for this, boy! I'll whip it RED!"

Aken quelled his racing lungs. "I'll make up for it and bake something later," he hollered, stuffing down the last bit of a blueberry scone before strolling out the dining hall and off into the hallways.

Classrooms were still empty at this hour. Just ahead, he spotted Master Nephryte vanishing around a bend. Aken stiffened to a halt, licking berry juice off his fingers.

This was his chance! The moment when he would best the famous hero Draev and catch him off-guard. Aken flexed his muscles in anticipation.

～

Master Nephryte savored the calm atmosphere. The hallways were quiet in these early morning hours. Such a tranquil serenity—

"*Hee*-yah!"

—except for the occasional blond howler monkey, who frequently made it his goal to disturb the peace.

Aken came with lightning speed around the corner behind him, shoes barely grazing the floor.

～

Aken aimed his rushing fist, the gap between himself and his target shrinking—ready for the full impact his strike would deliver. Nobody was as fast as Aken; none could dodge his speedy punch!

He struck.

Then winced.

His vision grayed and went dark. A numbing pain threaded through his body.

Something hard had blocked his face, smashing his nose and forehead in, and he wriggled until one of his eyes could see around the painful object.

There was Mentor Nephryte, staring down at him. He had turned to face Aken at the last moment, with three thick books in hand: *Psychology of the Mind & Body* volumes 1 & 2, and *Encyclopedia of the Known World*. He'd held them up for Aken's face to meet—halting Aken's outstretched fist well short of its intended target, his young arm not long enough to reach past the painful collision.

"Hmm? Oh?" Nephryte blinked as if just realizing Aken was there. "Aken-Shou, you're here a bit early, aren't you?"

Aken glared around the book covers.

"How rare of you to be this eager for class. My, at this rate, you'll even be on time. What a miracle."

Aken growled. He'd lost the element of surprise, but he wasn't about to back down just yet. Yanking his swollen face free of the books, he lowered into a crouch and fell backwards: kicking both feet out, aiming to knock Nephryte off his legs. "*Hyah!*"

But Aken found himself kicking empty air. The Mentor had vanished.

"Huh?" He looked up in time to see the heels of fine shoes coming down on his head.

"Crud!" Aken fast rolled aside before his skull could be dented in.

Instead of landing on the floor, Nephryte hovered just above it, and began reading the first page of *Psychology of the Mind & Body*.

"Look at me when I'm fighting you, you show-off!" Aken charged again. This time, he circled his quarry, zipping clay birds at the Mentor's unprotected sides and activating the *essence* stored inside.

A firework chain of clay-to-lava set off.

Nephryte's left hand moved, giving a dismissive wave while he continued to read, and a gust of air whipped the clay birds up—tossing them back at Aken as they exploded.

Kr-Pom-Pom-BOom!

Coated in cinders, Aken coughed. "I cwasn't expeckting dat…"

Mentor Nephryte closed the book and regarded him coolly. "Learn to expect the unexpected. You cannot survive in combat unless you plan ahead for what can go wrong." He tilted his chin down at Aken, his gaze icy.

Sweatdrops beaded Aken's forehead.

"You were in the kitchens again…"

More sweatdrops beaded.

"You called me a *show-off*…"

Frantic sweatdrops trickled down.

"I cannot let that slide."

Trickles became streams.

Before Aken had a chance to bolt for the nearest exit, a current of air ripped open a maintenance closet and hefted out a broom.

Aken yelped and ran as fast as he could away from the broom as it soared after him, threatening to swat his backside.

26

yrus waved. "See you in class."

Zartanian nodded, remaining seated at the organ as she left.

Today would be her first of Draevensett classes. She had no idea what to expect.

"Both Principal Han and the Draev Grandmaster might have taken you in and let you become a citizen—if you had been honest." Hercule's words rattled through her, again.

"—if you had been honest."

She shuddered. Navigating out of the music and arts wing, she exited onto the spiral walkway—and then pivoted back on her heels to avoid a collision.

"Excuse me!" Cyrus began to apologize.

"No, no, it's fine. I was moving too fast," said a clear, female voice.

Cyrus stared, speechless.

The girl's full lips formed an understanding smile. "You must be the new transfer-student? It's nice to meet you."

"A...a girl," Cyrus blurted out. She wasn't alone in this sea of testosterone!

The vempar blinked, trepidation tinting her forehead. "Yes. Girls do exist."

"Sorry. I mean, of course they do. I'm just..." Cyrus's

face flushed.

The girl's smile returned. "Well, at least you have the decency to be polite. The way some of these boys behave, you'd think they'd never seen a girl before in their entire life! I hate standing out like a sore thumb in this school."

Cyrus gave a nervous laugh.

The girl's hair cascaded down her back like a snowy waterfall, a section pulled back into a silver-and-sapphire hair comb high on the back of her head before dangling down in a braid. Bangs hid her forehead, longer bits framing sharp cheekbones and a mole at the corner of her left eye; her eyes were a deep amethyst.

But she was in a wheelchair, and Cyrus couldn't help staring. The girl gestured with a hand, "Don't start pitying me. I don't need this thing all the time—just when I stress my *essence* too much. My Healing doesn't quite function the same way as everybody else's." She started to lift herself up off the seat, and Cyrus almost moved to help. But the girl managed, standing up to extend her hand. "My name is Cherish."

"Cyrus." They clasped hands.

Cherish had on a stiff black dress, with burgundy seams and lace. Sleek braces fit around her forearms and elbows. Leg-braces around her knees and ankles, peeking out from her puffy shoe-boots.

Cyrus glanced at her own wrists. This girl had it harder than her, yet here she was, training to become a Draev.

"I like those fingerless gloves you're wearing," said Cherish. "They remind me of last year's fashion trend. Is it by *Marina*? They've been incorporating human fashion into their clothing a lot lately."

Cyrus didn't know what else to do but nod. "I like your dress. It's very pretty the way it fits you," she said in return.

Cherish's cheeks turned a shade pink, and Cyrus started. She'd better be more careful while role-playing as a boy.

Footsteps clacked up the walk behind them, and Master Nephryte came to a pause. "Cyrus, do you need help finding your way to class? Draevensett can be easy to get lost in." He leaned on one foot, books under an arm.

Cyrus shook her head, "I'll find my way." She thanked politely.

The Master nodded. "You have the same schedule as Aken-Shou. I'm sure he'll help you." His attention turned to Cherish, bending down a bit so he wasn't towering over her. "And how are you feeling since that accident?"

"Much better," Cherish said brightly.

"Good. Very good." He patted the chairback instead of her shoulder. "I know Master Seren-Rose is very proud of how far you've come."

Cherish blushed slightly.

Something skittered across the floor by the girl's shoe. Cyrus squinted, then saw what it was and screeched, pointing. "Spider! Spider!"

They both looked at her, then at the eight-legged bug scurrying across the floor. The Master raised a finger, and the spider was lifted up and flung over the rails.

"Disaster averted," he said.

Cherish tried not to laugh.

Cyrus suddenly felt embarrassed. She hated spiders.

More students were up and about now. And when she looked, she thought she'd glimpsed Aken.

Leaning sideways to see past the Master, she spotted sun-gold hair among the current of students flowing down the spiral walk, ducking low. What was he doing?
She called out to him, "Aken!"

He froze, as if hit by an axe, then sped up—diving through the nearest open window before Master Nephryte could turn.

"What's gotten into him?" She frowned, then glanced sideways. Had there been a ghost of a smile on the Master's lips?

"Well, I'd best be off," Master Nephryte told the girls. "I have my own homework and Draev chores to do! I'll see you later, after the Trials. Happy Swan Festival week!"

With a wave, the vempar man disappeared down the walk. A herd of students was rushing past. The older boys walked with friends, while those younger hollered and horse-played—what a difference age made in boys.

"I forgot today's the Duel Trials..." she mumbled.

Cherish nodded. "Will you be entering?"

"Um..."

～

Behind the bench of an alcove, lined with potted plants, Aken peeked out, making sure he hadn't been followed by Mentor Nephryte.

"What're you doing?"

Aken jumped as a head of orange hair rose up and over the bench back, Bakoa's expressive face full of curiosity staring at him.

"Are you trying to give me a heart attack? Keep quiet!" Aken snapped.

Bak frowned for one puzzled moment, mouth scrunching up, then grinned and snapped his fingers. "Aha! You're running from Master Nephryte again, aren't you? What'd you do this time?"

"*Tch!*" Aken stood up, so fast that Bak had to lean back out of the way and fell backwards. His legs turned to sand and he floated himself upright. "It's none of your beeswax," Aken huffed.

"But I don't have any beeswax."

"It's a form of expression, *Baka*. Another way of saying: *It's none of your business*."

"Ohhh." Bak paused. "Why didn't you just say that the first time, instead of being confusing?"

"Shut up!"

Bak hovered forward, a knowing smirk on his lips. "You were being a naughty and sparring with Master again, weren't you?"

"I said, shut up!"

Bak's sandy-green eyes laughed. Though Bak didn't have a mean bone in his body, he liked to pry and get in the way far too much. The world was happy sunshine and kittens, as far as Bakoa was concerned—and he liked nothing better than being just as nosy as one of those kittens.

Aken's fist swung for the sand boy's stomach, but instead of hitting flesh, his fist went *through* Bak's torso—the flesh and shirt molecules now grains of sand, while still maintaining their original appearance.

Bak's silly grin looked from his stomach to Aken's arm. "What were you trying to do?"

Aken punched again and again.

Bak scratched his chin. "Um...I don't really know what you're trying to do. When I'm in *sand-mode*, you can't hit me."

"It's therapeutic. You're a sand punching bag."

"Oh. Could I make a living off that?" Bak thought. "You owe me food, now. So I want one of those fancy turkey sandwiches, with extra salt."

Aken ceased punching. "You really think you're invincible in *sand-mode*?"

"Sure! I mean...hey, why do you have that look on your face? It's ominous." Bak took one nervous step back. "I don't know what's going on in your head, buddy, but...we *are* still buddies, right? No need to be jealous, right?"

Aken whipped out a long-nozzled dust-sucker from a maintenance closet, the oilpowder engine roaring to life in his hands.

Vr-Vr-Vroom!

"Where'd you get that?" Bak squeaked as the dust-sucker

approached.

"Draevensett always has the latest vempar tech. Say hello to your demise."

VrrROOM!

"AaaH!" Bak fled, his legs now a sand tail propelling him through the air. But the nozzle sucked away at his sand as he struggled to flee. "Nooo! I'm shrinking—*shrinking!*"

The more sand sucked up, the smaller Bak's body shrunk—his off-kilter voice shrinking with it. "It's a cruel world!" He became the size of a chipmunk, diving and zig-zagging away from the nozzle, squeaking, "Cruel world—Creeul world—Creeeul weeerld!"

Ploomp.

The last bit of orange hair was sucked up.

Aken turned off the switch with a satisfied grin, listening to the rhythm of tiny thumping fists and yelps coming from inside.

❧

"Look what we have here, boys."

Cyrus and Cherish ceased chatting when a group approached them.

Denim sauntered up, his cocky smirk ever present, and a pack of Floor Tathom boys followed. He stopped beside the wheelchair, casually resting an elbow on one of the arms. "I see you met the newbie. Cly or Chai-something?" He made a show of trying to recall.

Cyrus watched Aken's nemesis warily.

"The name's Denim, of House Sivortsova." He combed fingers through his hair as though he were hot-stuff. "In case you didn't know."

"The name's Cyrus Sole, in case you didn't know," she said back.

He raised his chin. "You're friends with that Scourgeblood, aren't you?"

She bristled. "So what if I am?"

"Please, Denim." Cherish cut in. "Don't start something, again."

"Start? Ha! My dislike for that misfit started years ago. So keep your fragile nose out of it."

Cherish's lips tightened together.

"Why can't we take it easy?" A burly, overweight boy stepped out from the group; he was heads taller and three-people wider than any boy Cyrus had ever seen, and snacking on a bag of cheese chips. She instinctively shuffled back. "I mean"—*munch*—"we shouldn't stress Cherish out, y'know?" he rumbled. "I'm Billsbury, by the way. But the nickname's Doughboy." The huge boy flashed a chubby grin.

Cyrus offered a smile, though her brow furrowed. At least he seemed more friendly than his companions. She wondered how she could've missed his presence earlier.

"Guess who's gonna enter the Duel Trials today?" Doughboy nudged the wheelchair.

Cherish clapped in surprise. "Really? You'll win a spot in the Duel, for sure! But don't hurt anyone too badly, okay? Hey, is your Floor entering, Cyrus?"

Denim rolled his eyes. "Enough with the random chit-chat! You ruined the menacing mood," he barked. "Listen, Chai. Don't go thinking you're some privileged guy being at this school. You ought to know your lowly place here. I'm the prince's cousin, see. So if I hate Harlow, everybody hates Harlow. Which means, don't get on my bad side. Got it?" He jabbed a finger at Cyrus for emphasis.

"Second cousin," Doughboy corrected.

Before Denim could snarl at him, a sharp note peeled through the air and courtyard below—a noise so terrible that all of their ears trembled.

"*CherISH!*" the high-pitch note called.

Cyrus glanced about for the source. Denim, Doughboy and the Tathom gang shivered, and Cherish shut her eyes with a dreadful sigh.

"Time to go," said Denim, suddenly in a hurry. He pointed a finger back at Cyrus as he and his followers scampered off. "We'll be seeing you and the doofus later. You won't stand a chance in the Duel Trials."

The high call came again, and the boys practically barreled down the walk in their haste to get away.

The call was nearer, louder, parting through the sea of students like a knife.

'What dreadful thing approaches?' she thought, as anxious sweatdrops chilled her neck.

The answer soon came barreling towards her.

"Cherishy-pooh!"

A wiry beanpole of a man held both arms outstretched, as he leaped across the floor space between them. "Cherishyyy!" he cried, wrapping long arms around Cherish and the wheelchair. Dramatic tears flung from his eyes, splashing onto his rectangle glasses.

The girl grumbled against his hug. "You know I love you and all, but please don't make such a scene every time."

"Not make a scene?" he exclaimed. "Not call your sweet name? And give you as big a bear-hug as I possible-possibly can? Cherishy-doo! Is that any way to treat your big brother, who loves you as infinitely deep as the deepest ocean in all the universe?" He sniffled, his dark hair curled up at the edges.

Cyrus realized her jaw had been hanging open, and she shut it. Now she understood why Tathom fled.

"Oh! Oh-hohoho, I see we have a new student!"

Cyrus cringed as the big brother swung his attention to her. His narrow, odd face made a drastic grin as he leaned forward, and his crazy eyebrows fluttered—dramatic off-shoots of eyebrow hair that angled out as if he'd glued a pair of wings on his brow. She wouldn't doubt he could use them to fly. Maybe he did.

She leaned as far back as she could, her mouth in a tell-tale sour frown, but he didn't appear to notice or take the hint.

"From one of those far away farming communities, I hear!" the old brother chattered on. "My, your hair certainly is red, isn't it? I guess they weren't exaggerating when they said it was a bowlful of cherries!"

Her frown broadened.

"Um, brother?" Cherish said, "You scare people when you act like that."

"Oh!" His eyebrow wings flapped and he took a step back, much to Cyrus's relief. "Ah-haaha! I didn't mean to shock you with my electrifying personality, there, Cherry-boy! It's a habit. I can't help but be curious about new things. Haaha! I'm Professor Kotetsu Cuore."

Cherry-boy? Cyrus wanted to say a few choice words, but held her tongue.

"Are you harassing people again, Chickenwings?" Aken arrived, an hourglass tucked under his arm. Cyrus almost laughed out loud at the nickname.

"What! I do *not* harass people." The quirky guy grimaced, eyebrow-wings fluttering.

"Then learn the basic personal space rule," Aken pointed.

Kotetsu's mouth became an impossibly curved smile. "As one of your prominent teachers, you'd best show some respect," he countered the boy. "Did you complete your homework?"

Aken faltered.

'A teacher?' Cyrus thought. What on eartha did he teach?

"Well, either way, I appreciate you taking care of that pesky dragon for us. The House Cuore business gets its wool from those farms. We must repay you sometime!" said Professor Kotetsu.

They were aristocrats? Cyrus bobbed her head, "Glad we could help."

The brother beamed. "Today are the Trials that decide which two students will be in the Festival Duel tomorrow— I'm sure you haven't forgotten about that? Good luck with it! A happy Swan Festival to you both!"

"Of course I haven't." Aken glowered. "And I'm gonna win it. Just you see."

"Ooh! Look at my watch—the time," Kotetsu gasped. He grabbed the handles of the wheelchair. "Time for claaass. Onward we go, Cherishy!"

Laughter bounced off the ceiling and balustrade as brother and sister sped away, wheels squealing. Cyrus and Aken shared a look, and he scratched the back of his head. "It's the sister I feel sorry for."

"Yep." Cyrus wiped her forehead. With that over, she regarded the hourglass in his arm. She lifted one eyebrow in question.

But before Aken could answer, a tiny noise squeaked "Heeelp meee!" followed by thumping.

She stared. "The hourglass is talking?"

"Oh yeah, I forgot." He held the object up and peered through the glass.

Tiny fists and a tuft of orange hair rose from the sand as it poured down the hourglass funnel and into the bottom half. "Heeelp!" cried a blubbering face. Small fingers clawed desperately not to be sucked down the funnel.

"Bakoa?" she realized. "Aken, how could you!" On impulse, her hand turned metal and she slapped his arm— so hard that he tumbled over backwards. She snatched the hourglass away, breaking it open, and let the sand pour out, and mini Bakoa pour free.

The frazzled boy grew to normal size, absorbing sand back into himself. He plopped on the floor as if he'd run a marathon, "Thank-you, Cy-rus."

Aken rose from the floor where he'd fallen and clamped a hand to his arm. "*Ouch*; you sure give a fierce slap."

"Bakoa is your friend. You shouldn't bully him."

"I wasn't—"

"Meanie!" Bakoa interjected and ducked behind her, sticking out his tongue.

Aken made a face back.

She was about to knock some sense and maturity into their childish skulls, when Bakoa pointed at an antique clock hanging on the walk. "We're late for class. Again."

"Aw, shoot!" Aken grabbed Bakoa by the shirt and wrapped his other arm around Cyrus's waist. Before either of them could yelp or protest, he dove into a run—speeding down the spiral walk towards class, their legs waving like flags.

⟡

Zartanian rose from the organ bench. The silver pipes reflected dappled morning light across the walls. He made his way over and pulled open the lower half of the nearest window, a gust of warm air breezing in as he did.

Perched on a nearby maple, a young raven regarded him, fluffing its feathers. He observed the bird for a while. He'd never seen a baby raven up-close before Cyrus handed him one. It was very cute; the tiny feathers of its stubby wings softer than silk. Soft, helpless, fragile. Unable to tell friend from foe—who would be kind and who would abuse. Unable to trust anyone.

'To trust is a dangerous thing,' he thought.

Those who should protect you may turn against you.

Zartanian reached his left arm through the window, a piece of bread in his palm. The raven tilted its head, peering sideways at it.

Traumatic experiences could be like chains, wrapping around the mind and constricting all that you did, haunting every waking hour, becoming a never-ending nightmare. He wondered if he could ever be normal like Cyrus, or brave like Aken. If he could ever be free of those chains.

The young raven hopped closer, skeptical yet curious.

To trust is a dangerous thing, and yet…

He held out his palm, steady. The bird was a beautifully morbid creature. Feathers black as coal, except where sunlight streaked them violet. He wanted to embrace it, soak in the night of its perfectly dark, round eyes.

The raven made up its mind, and with a clumsy leap flapped off the branch to land on his wrist. Like two dainty fingers, its ebony beak lifted the piece of bread.

Zartanian smiled. "See? I want to be friends with you, little raven."

The bird cocked its sleek head.

The wariness of the raven made him recall the first day he'd arrived at Draevensett, the first moment he caught sight of its towers and dagger spires, how beautiful they were and how intimidating. And his fear of what it would be like to live in a new place, alone without Elijob.

But life before had been…an endless pit of pain.

The twin bells rang, *bong-bong bong-gong* from the high tower, signaling the start of school. The raven squawked and flapped off, and Zartanian wiped a tear spot from his eye. Best not to think of things that could no longer be changed; the past was a door best kept sealed shut.

Without wasting another second, Zartanian grabbed his books up off the floor and hurried out the tucked-away ballroom.

27

Cyrus pored over her 6th grade class schedule—every other day was different. Here, students of the same grade were divided into groups, with each group going to the same classes but at different times of the day.

She took a front-row desk for Math class. Aken on her left, and Bakoa at the desk behind hers, tapping a pencil and swinging his legs back and forth. To her surprise, Hercule took the desk right of hers, though he didn't bother once to glance in her direction, and his expression said *Everyone here is a low-life.*

She twisted her mouth to the side. If he wanted to pretend she wasn't there, then why sit next to her? Noble snob.

"—if you had been honest."

She swallowed, then craned her neck as Zartanian darted in and took the desk behind Aken. Denim and his gang owned the back rows, and Cherish rolled up to a table.

"Okie-dokie!" Professor Kotetsu hopped into the room. Cherish's crazy brother taught math? The room visibly cringed at the wavy voice that made her think of an exaggerated clown. "It's fun math-time with Professor Kotetsu and Sir Happy Squirrely." His hand held a squirrel muppet, which wore a little bowtie, suit, and clown shoes, and a stitched U-grin that matched its crazy owner.

Professor Kotetsu waved the squirrel's arms enthusiastically to the students. "We're here to make math fun," the squirrel sing-songed.

Cyrus looked for a plaque somewhere—making sure this wasn't kindergarten.

Bakoa practically bounced in his seat, shouting, "I'm ready to learn!"

"And so you shall, my eager jumping-bean," said the Professor. "Turn to chapter twelve in your textbooks."

Kotetsu Cuore's muppet hand wrote out a math formula on the board for them to solve. Through the hour, he told them stories of how he'd used that formula to solve real life problems. It was useful to see what purpose math had in real life—most teachers never showed that bit. Maybe he wasn't as crazy as he'd first seemed.

The next class would be their last for the day, since the Duel Trials were taking place right after, and they waited for the teacher to arrive. She turned to eye Bakoa's legs, swinging back and forth and making the chair squeak.

"Ooh! I wonder what our new history teacher will be like?" said Bakoa.

"New?" Cyrus cocked an eyebrow. "But aren't you far through the school year?"

"Yep, but the other guy got fed up with us." Bakoa fingered his chin, shooting a tell-tale glance Aken's way.

Aken stood his elbows on the desk, chin in hands. "It wasn't *my* fault. Not completely..."

The door creaked as it swung open, and everyone shifted in their chairs to see. Cyrus had to leaned forward as nothing but a very tall top hat strode into the room.

The green velvet hat came to a halt before the large desk at the head of the room. It took several blinks to discern that the whole shape wasn't just a hat. Half of it was the shortest man she'd ever seen, with red tufts peeking from under the brim, and a short red beard trimmed into a two-pronged fork. Complete with green blazer, pants and bowtie, and shiny shoes that came to curly points.

Aken's mouth twitched; she knew what he was thinking.

The professor's green gaze narrowed up at the class, taking them in one at a time fiercely. "That's right," he boomed. A deep, husky tone that made up for any loss in height, and flavored with the northern mountains accent. "Ah'm short, but Ah'm alsoo older and wiser than you lot, soo Ah don't want tae hear et mentioned. You will shoow respect." He paused for emphasis. "Es that understood?"

The class nodded respectfully, while Aken's lungs were bursting at the seams. The fierce gaze shifted, and Aken quickly buried his face in the big history book on his desk.

"You will address me as Professor Ponairi." The short teacher marched with surprisingly loud footsteps for his weight, stomping to a halt before Aken's desk. "What are you snickering aboout, laddie? *Hum?*"

"Nothing, Professor," Aken mumbled, not daring to peek over the edge of the book.

"Poot that book doown!"

He did so, quickly replacing it with a sheet of paper.

"Ahnd the paper!"

Aken replaced the paper with his hand.

"*My Auntie's crying potatoes*," Ponairi swore, "And the hand too, you wee brat!"

Students snickered. Aken hesitated before letting the hand fall, revealing a face as red and huge as the sun.

"Es there something you find amusing?"

Aken shook his head vigorously.

"Then keep quiet and wipe that grin ooff."

As the professor returned to the front of the class, Aken hid his face back in the book, trying to muffle his chuckles. When Ponairi's monologue on history began, Cyrus perked her ears to listen.

He began discussing how little was known of the ancient

world, how few records and scraps were left of Eartha's past before The Disaster—the event said to have fractured the world, making it into the divided place it was today.

What The Disaster was and how it had happened, though, remained a mystery wrapped in legend. In particular the legend of the Swan Princess, when the Emperor used a weapon of mass destruction during his attempt to steal the Pure Light.

Most historians today dismissed it as nothing more than a fairytale, and believed The Disaster to have been caused by natural forces. The truth, whichever it may be, still remained unknown.

In the months following The Disaster, vempar kind became a scattered, scavenger race, wandering Eartha as they hunted for *essence* to survive. The Time of Wandering, when vempars no longer had a rooted home and were viewed as monsters as they stole people's *essence*. They were hated and murdered by other races, which made them retaliate in return. Vempar kind was trapped in a downward spiral towards destruction, until one vempar rose to put a stop to it.

Protector Draev, later given the title The Protector of Peace, founded the Vemparic Kingdom. He united the vempars and put an end to the Time of Wandering. He established the Draev Guardian League of Ability users to restore order, with the help of his Twelve Legendary Knights—whose descendants were now the twelve Noble Houses.

Peace was found, and the Protector established a monarchy to reign over the new kingdom. The D.G. League was given the task of gathering *essence* for the kingdom to live on, without killing. Hunting would no longer be necessary for the people—the League would do it for them, and within a controlled set of rules.

The Draevs would also protect and serve the kingdom as

its most powerful military force. It gave those with Abilities a purpose, and was a way of keeping them in check.

Some of the tension between vempars and the other races eased. But the humans were unforgiving and refused to lay the past to rest. Skirmishes and raids occurred frequently, and became the way of living between the two.

The Protector lived to be the oldest vempar ever recorded, his youth and strength never once failing. Until on one bleak day, when the Protector was found murdered.

The most powerful vempar of their time suddenly dead, and the culprit never found.

The centuries following the Protector's death were filled with conflict against humans and goblins. The most recent being the Goblin Shadow War, which ended just seven years ago. Master Nephryte would have been fifteen when it finally came to an end.

The war had been a crusade for the goblins' advanced society to "cleanse" Eartha of those they considered inferior—paying special attention to the Vemparic Kingdom and Human Republic.

While vempar and human armies moved to face the threat, they had run-ins with one another resulting in petty skirmishes. It was the forest faeryn who intervened and begged for a truce between all of the races until their common enemy could be defeated.

Minor truces were made, lasting long enough to drive the goblins back to their land across the sea, the victory coming at a heavy price of lives.

Cyrus recalled seeing the soldiers pass through Elvenstone on their way back to the capital city, and the

celebration as her town's own soldiers and Argos returned from war...

Professor Ponairi smacked his hands together sharply, making sure everyone was still awake. "Now will come further studies, quizzes and tests before the school year ends!" he bellowed.

Cyrus heard groans rotate the classroom.

28

The Trials were about to begin—deciding which two Draevensett students would partake in this year's Festival Duel and win the granting of one request from the king. Cyrus followed as Aken, Bakoa, Zartanian and Hercule crossed the green lawns toward the school's training arenas.

Aken leaned close, asking in a whisper, "Did you make up your mind? Are you gonna enter, and try and win your Draeth citizenship?"

Cyrus wasn't feeling confident, but she nodded. It was worth a try. "But if we both win, won't that mean we'll have to fight each other?"

He waved that aside. "Just focus on passing the tests."

She looked around. "Where's Lykale and Mamoru?"

He shrugged. "Guess it doesn't appeal to them."

The small Harlow group clustered with other waiting Floor groups around the gate of a tall arena. A muscular vempar, who could have been part dwarf with his hefty stature and thick beard, stomped to the head of the crowd.

"For those who don't know me, I'm Master Brangor, the authority of these arenas. This year's trials to enter the Duel will be focusing on speed, accuracy and endurance. Students who are participating, come forward! Those just here to watch, get to the bleachers."

The gate opened, revealing a great rock wall running the length of the arena; no ceiling to shield from the elements. Ropes tied at the wall's top suspended across a huge gap to a long platform on the opposite wall. "The speed trial is this: Scale the wall, cross the chasm, and grab one of the red ribbons on the platform," ordered Brangor. "The last ten to finish will be eliminated. Now, line up!"

Cyrus approached the steep wall, craning her neck back. Footholds speckled about, and there was a dangling rope, but nothing more.

"Ready—*Set*—Start!"

The vempars to either side of her climbed the footholds in a burst of speed. Some didn't bother but used the Leap Technique to spring high up onto the wall top. Brangor didn't say they had to *climb* to get there. Only those more experienced were good enough to Leap such a distance.

Cyrus used the rope, turning her hands and forearms metal to protect her wrists, and put most of her weight on her legs, finding each foothold with her toes.

She tried to hurry. Her time climbing trees was somewhat useful, but the strain on her legs and hands was different, harder. Out of the corners of her eyes, she could see she was falling behind.

'Don't think. Keep going!'

Even with the metal, her wrists were stinging in pain. She tried not to let her mind feel it, focusing on moving each foot to a new purchase.

Once she did reach the wall top, lungs wheezing, a pair of ropes ran across a steep drop before her—the chasm—to the other side.

Once again, those who could Leap crossed the chasm easily, while the rest traversed the ropes as fast as they could. Cyrus balanced her shoes on the lower rope, and gripped tightly to the rope above her head. She closed her eyes and breathed in, shutting out thoughts of the steep drop below, then placed one foot in front of the other at an angle across the rope. It was only thanks to the upper rope that she didn't unbalance and fall—even then, she had to go slow. Wrist pain screamed more and more.

She glimpsed one student fall. There'd be no surviving *that* for a human.

She paused to steady her trembling muscles and breathe. Then pressed on.

Not much farther now.

A dagger of pain tore through her left wrist. Her teeth clenched. Not much farther.

Pain lanced through her other wrist down to the elbow. She almost let go. More daggers stabbed at the left. She bit down hard, every muscle in her tightening.

Three more steps...two more steps...one...

She collapsed onto the platform on the other side, landing on her shoulder and gripping her wrists in a failed attempt to stifle the pain.

"Cyrus!"

She pushed up and with one last effort grabbed for a dangling red ribbon.

Except...there were none left.

A whistle pierced the air. "Trial 1 is over!" boomed Master Brangor. "Those who were too late and didn't get a ribbon, failed. Those who passed, make your way to the next arena!"

Failed...?

She...but she'd tried her best. She needed to become a Draeth citizen. She needed to win this more than anyone else here! Her fist wanted to pound the platform.

Aken helped her stand and led her down a flight of steps to the ground floor. They all exited the arena. "Are you okay?" he asked, studying the way she was holding her wrists.

Tears pricked her eyes. All she could do was shake her head. What was she thinking, trying to compete against vempars? Could she even become a Draev Guardian, or was she just kidding herself? She thought back to the dragon mission, how good it had felt being able to help others. She wanted that. She'd thought it was what Lord God wanted her to do.

"Don't worry, Cy. I'll win this for you."

She looked up at him.

"I'll win, and I'll ask the king to give you citizenship." He smiled brightly, eyes blue as the sky. "Now, you go and have the doc look at your wrists," he said, giving her a slight shove.

"But…" she started.

"People don't think I can become a Draev Guardian. Many don't even see me as a person. I've got to change that. I can't afford to lose this, for either of our sakes." He motioned her a thumbs-up, then trotted to catch up with the students at the next arena.

Cyrus clutched her hands to her chest and hurried back to the school. Master Nephryte was in the front courtyard when she got there, and she told him timidly about the pain. "I'll be fine with just some pain reducers," she said, as his Touch tried and failed to Heal her. He led her to Dr. Zushil's office.

Zushil inspected the state of her wrists, then placed his hands over them to channel Healing. After a while, his brow pinched as if puzzled by something. "Does it feel any better?" he asked.

She shook her head.

He took out pills from a green vial and plopped them into her palm. "An analgesic," he said. "It should work and numb the pain. I don't understand why your own Healing hasn't kicked in, though. And these scars are curious."

Cyrus turned her face to the side, hoping her unease

wasn't showing.

"Perhaps it's malnutrition," offered the Master, steering clear of the truth. "Cyrus did just arrive to a new environment, and has probably been stressed. I'll see to it she eats better." He ushered her out of the office before Zushil had time to think on the matter more.

"Thank you, Master. I should hurry and see how Aken's doing in the second trial." As she turned to go, she noticed an odd look of concern cross Master Nephryte's features, though he said nothing.

Cyrus hurried off and soon found Zartanian, who had also failed the trial. They climbed flights of stairs to reach the bleachers high above the second arena. She watched as Aken, Hercule and Bakoa lined up with the large group at the gate.

~

Brangor positioned himself before the grand gate of the second arena. "The accuracy trial is this: Navigate through the obstacle course environments and strike down one of the cardboard villains, then return here with the villain in tow. But harm even one civilian, and you fail instantly. When you become Draevs, you'll be facing all sorts of environments while tracking down criminals—this is giving you a taste of that." Brangor's mustache curled with a dark grin. "There are only fifteen villains in the obstacle course, which means only fifteen of you can pass."

Aken flexed his fingers.

The Master had them line up in rows, and then he opened the gate: Steep roofs and balconies rose, facing them on the other side. Aken had to look hard to make sure it wasn't part of their real city but a recreation.

"No maiming or killing each other, and no harming cardboard civilians—those are the only rules."

Aken lowered into a crouch, ready to sprint. Hercule did

the same. Bak's legs made a sand tail.

"Ready—*Set*—Get your backsides out there!"

The group charged forward as one mass. Aken sprinted to get ahead, then had to slow to climb over a balcony. He jumped from building roof to roof.

He glanced left and right: Some students were lagging behind, but the older ones traveled with ease in wide jumps that carried them across several buildings at once, using the Leaping Technique he hadn't learned yet.

"Thirteen villains left!" shouted a speaker device from the arena walls.

Aken shook his head, reminding himself this wasn't a foot race, but a race to find the villains. He peered down an alley as he vaulted across.

There, a cardboard person! He halted when his shoes touched the opposite roof, and spun around, readying a clay bird, shifting to throw the bird at the target.

The cardboard moved mechanically, painted in a dress and gray hair. An old lady. Aken just managed to stop himself from hurting the civilian cardboard. Another student wasn't so lucky, though, as the boy lunged at the old lady without thinking, and realized too late his mistake.

"You're out!" came the speaker voice, and the student hung his head.

Aken continued along the rooftops, spotting nothing but civilians as he went, until suddenly the roofs fell away to a stretch of open swamp.

He halted and got out Limitless, and rode the swallow low over the green-tinted water. He glimpsed Bakoa, with his legs a sand tail, gliding through the tall swamp grasses. Those who could were using their Abilities to navigate the environment. Aken pushed the swallow faster.

A figure rose from the grasses: another civilian. He'd almost took it out.

"No luck, eh?"

Aken glanced down to see Denim running over the swamp, the water freezing beneath his shoes with each step. Aken didn't bother to reply.

Another cardboard rose inside a thicket of reeds, painted in dark clothes and shifty eyes, a dagger in one hand.

A villain! Aken dipped Limitless into a dive. Denim saw the cardboard figure too.

"Oh no you don't!" Denim charged.

Limitless swooped over the villain. Aken caught it by the neck, hoisting it up. But then the villain tugged down. Aken looked to see Denim holding onto its feet and pulling. "You'll tear it. Go find your own!"

"It's not against the rules to steal one. Anything goes!" Denim shouted and yanked.

Aken gripped the cardboard hard as he could. Limitless flapped higher and higher, as the other boy held on like a tick.

Denim tried swinging the villain back and forth, and he formed an ice spear in his hand and threw it. Aken ducked his head to the right.

The cardboard suddenly tore from Aken's hands, and Denim fell into the green water, as a buff vempar ripped the villain away from them both.

Aken righted himself, but the vempar had already dashed off into a jungle—the next environment. He steered Limitless into the moss-covered trees, as Denim splashed and hollered in rage.

"Seven villains left!" announced the speaker.

Vines, moss and shafts of light through the jungle canopy made it hard to see. Aken slowed the bird down and hopped off. The jungle was too thick to fly while keeping an eye on the ground. He jumped over logs, and shoved foliage aside in a hurry.

There were two students he spotted who had caught villains, and they were being attacked by others trying to steal them. Aken moved on, peering around boulders and any hiding places. Someone passed him by, with another villain in hand. Aken couldn't turn back—the villains back at the roofs and swamp would have all been found by now. He pressed on, pushing back a tall bush, and came out into a field of snow and tombstones—vents in the high walls of the arena blowing fake snow down around him.

"Four villains left!"

Aken raised an arm to shield his eyes, and peered through the blizzard as he moved forward in a crouch through the cemetery. This was his last chance, here or never. From the looks of it, not many students had reached the snow environment yet.

He skirted around a mausoleum and spotted three civilian cardboards moving mechanically along a snow-covered path. Their clothes were thick, hoods and a hat concealed their faces. Hands gloved, carrying a purse. One carrying a suitcase that was cracked open at the top and showing gold pieces inside. That was a strange thing to have one of the figures carry.

He inched forward, and that's when a dagger became visible in the cardboard man's coat.

Aken darted forward, bypassing the other two cardboard people, and grabbed the villain. With Limitless, he carried his prize up through the snowy air before any competitors could see.

"One villain left!" crowed the speaker.

Aken still had to get the villain to the gate and out the arena to win.

The snow, and then the jungle leaves, provided some cover, but once he emerged into the open sky over the swamp and rooftops, the many students who were still searching desperately for a villain began chasing after him.

"He has the last one!"

"Knock him out of the sky!"

Projectiles of rock, ice, wood and more tried to strike him down. He took evasive maneuvers—flying in a zigzag pattern, keeping Limitless high and moving fast towards the gate.

A spear almost ripped the villain out of his hand. He glanced over a shoulder to spot a boy flying after him. The boy held onto the pole of some flying device, as its wood propellers spun and buzzed, his Ability manipulating the wood. He threw another spear at Aken, and Aken dove to the left to avoid it, then quickly rose high as students below sought to grab him.

Reaching into his pocket, Aken pulled out a stash of clay birds. He tossed them one after another, and activated the *essence* stored inside. A chain of lava explosions filled the air in a trail behind him, knocking his pursuers back.

He urged Limitless forward in a wing sprint for the gate, pouring every ounce of energy and will-power into the bird. The gate drew closer, and Limitless began to descend as his *essence* started fading. He leaped off the bird, landing on the last rooftop, and dashed for the gate.

He barely made it through and out as the flock of students followed on his heels.

"All of the villains have been brought back!" announced Master Brangor. "Aken-Shou is the last to win round two."

The losers cursed, some collapsing, some kicking at the dirt.

Master Brangor clapped his hands together, loud as thunder. "You fifteen winners, follow me! The rest of you can either leave or continue watching."

Aken sat on his knees on the ground, catching his breath, and pocketing shrunken Limitless.

"Awesome, you won too!" Bak slapped his back.

"You made it?" Aken said, incredulous. "You too, Hercule?" The noble sniffed, as if there were never any doubt he would.

They followed the winning group over to the next arena, and he spotted Cy and Zartin following with the crowd of onlookers to watch the final trial.

Bars hoisted high on poles above the dirt floor space of the next, smaller arena glinted in the sun. And nearby, large watermelons were stacked in a pyramid. Master Brangor strode over to pat one of the massive fruits. "The endurance trial is this: Whoever can hold these watermelons the longest wins a spot in the Festival Duel."

Students shared looks, and some laughed.

"Think that's easy, do you?" Brangor's thick mustache and beard twitched. "Then try holding them on your stomach while hanging upside down by your knees from these here bars." He waved at the high bars, and the laughter ceased. There was nothing that looked easy about *that*.

"Contestants, line up and grab a watermelon!"

They stood in line; each picked up a watermelon that was almost half their size. Aken hefted his, and waited under one of the parallel bars until all fifteen students were ready. When Master Brangor gave the signal, they each climbed a rope to reach the bars, and positioned their knees to grip the metal before hanging upside down. They curled their torsos, shifting the large watermelons so that it rested on their stomachs, forming an almost sling with their bodies to keep the fruit in place.

"If your watermelon falls, you fail; plain and simple. The last two boys left are the winners," thundered Brangor gruffly.

Aken hugged the huge watermelon to his stomach. This was a test to push every leg and abdomen muscle to the maximum; and after twenty minutes passed, students were quivering against the heavy strain as their bodies fought to hold on.

After another twenty minutes, he heard several watermelons hit the ground in a burst. Those who failed dropped down, panting, slick with sweat.

Aken shifted the watermelon against him, holding tighter.

An hour passed, and more fell. Hercule dropped out, his shirt soaked and legs trembling as he stalked off.

Aken's thighs and knees burned as if on fire, and the hot sun beat down on the arena. Beads of sweat dripped into his eyes, stinging, as he tried to blink them away. The watermelon was getting more slippery in his arms, the weight of it crushing his stomach muscles with each passing minute.

He had to hold out. Failure was not an option.

More students began dropping like flies. Aken gritted his teeth against the pain, summoning every ounce of stubbornness inside him.

He wasn't sure how much time had passed when Master Brangor finally blared, "Six contestants left!"

Aken turned his head, neck muscles stinging, to see who was left: smiling Bakoa, Doughboy, a grim reaper-like boy, a buff student, and a gnarly-looking kid. "Better up the task, or we'll be waiting here all day!" said Brangor with an eagerness that made them all shudder.

Aken tried to watch as Brangor picked up another watermelon and tossed it to land on Doughboy's stomach. The large boy grunted but held both heavy fruits. Brangor proceeded to toss one to each of the remaining boys, and when the second watermelon fell onto Aken, atop the one he was already struggling to hold, he almost dropped both.

Lifting his chin back to give more room, he shifted the watermelons so that they were side by side on his stomach and cupped by both his arms. The weight was nearly unbearable.

Failure was not an option.

Aken gripped the fruit, his stomach feeling as if it were being crushed and split in two, knees burning so hot it felt like they might tear off at any second.

"I can't anymore." Bak dropped down, off to his right.

Four students were left to beat.

The gnarly boy snarled before throwing his watermelons down.

Three students left to beat.

Doughboy wasn't budging, and the grim reaper looked calm and steady.

The buff boy sneered his way, "Give it up. You don't have what it takes for the Duel."

Aken shifted his focus to the sky and to hugging the fruit tightly.

"Come on, stop putting yourself through pain," the buff student continued. "Nobody wants to see a loser and a chubby boy in the Duel. People cheer for muscle and good looks, something fine they can admire."

The biceps in Aken's arms twitched.

Master Brangor approached once more. "You lot have ridiculous stamina." He began gathering more watermelons. It was a struggle not to groan and give up.

Brangor had to use a ladder to place a third large fruit on top the two Doughboy already had. Amazingly, the heavy boy did nothing more but grunt.

"You're a bunch of sissies!" the buff kept saying. Until a third watermelon hit his stomach and he crashed to the ground with a *whump!*

Aken didn't have the strength to laugh, tightening his abdomen further, stretching beyond his capacity, as Brangor plopped a third watermelon on top the other two.

Aken's neck quivered and his breath wheezed as the huge melons, each almost half his size, threatened to rip his arms.

The sun inched across the sky. He tried to hold on, even as every part of him screamed pain and the watermelons slipped bit by bit. Doughboy and the grim reaper were still there. Aken's top melon began to slide.

He dug his fingernails into the rinds, and gathered the last ounce of strength he had, and stretched his neck the highest it could go, halting the watermelon's slide with his chin.

One minute passed.

Two minutes.

His body was fire.

He couldn't hold on, yet the stubbornness inside refused to let go of this one chance to help Cyrus and to make people acknowledge him as a Draev Guardian.

Something hit the ground, and for a moment his heart stopped, thinking one of his watermelons had fallen, but then the grim reaper guy grumbled and dropped down.

"That's a wrap! The winners are decided," boomed Brangor. "Aken-Shou and Doughboy will be this year's Swan Festival duelists!"

Aken let the watermelons fall and his body drop to the ground. He panted against the dirt. It hurt his cheeks to grin as he raised his arms in victory.

Doughboy broke one of the melons open and began eating it.

Brangor clapped a hand on both their backs as the onlookers cheered. "That's some fine monster-sized stamina you've got. Put on a good show for the city, tomorrow!"

Chants for Doughboy filled the training arena as he and Aken wobbled out. The crowd flowed down from the bleachers, filling the lawn.

Aken stood catching his breath, then weaved through the crowd. Students either glared or ignored him. His ears caught a few drifting comments:

"Why couldn't it have been someone more worthy of facing Doughboy?"

"I know right? Not some troubled Scourgeblood. The Festival Duel is ruined now."

Scourgeblood…

Something inside Aken twisted.

Cyrus cheered, and Bakoa gave a slap to Aken's shoulder. "You did it! You held out against all of them and won!" Cyrus could feel her face beaming, unable to contain her elation.

Aken gave a partial smile and rubbed his shoulder, not as enthusiastic as she'd expected him to be.

Harlow regrouped and headed back to the school, its soaring spires reflecting sunlight. They passed lawn tables, and at one of them sat Mamoru, at work finishing the hat of a pretty doll. Other dolls, dragon toys and puppets were grouped in boxes at his feet.

He noticed their questioning looks, and flicked his wrist. Amber strings floated from his fingertips to touch the doll and make it walk. "They're for charity—children who don't have the luxury of toys."

Cyrus fingered the doll's pretty shoe, as it curtsied. "It's lovely. I wish I could make things like this."

Zartanian took a seat, fascination filling his winter-ice eyes. Beside him, Hercule craned his neck to get a better look, and Bakoa hovered over Mamoru's shoulder to watch. A line of students leaving the arena also paused to see. Mamoru was one of those cool artist types, though Cyrus could tell he was uncomfortable with the growing crowd.

Cyrus turned to ask Aken something. He'd been unusually silent, his mouth twisted to the side and chin perched on folded arms. He looked cross, though she couldn't imagine why.

"You do charity work?" Cyrus talked to Mamoru instead. "That's very kind of you, very thoughtful. I'm sure it means a lot to the children."

Mamoru smiled but kept his gaze on the doll. "I'm simply doing my share to help out. Children in need shouldn't be forgotten."

Suddenly Aken's hand slapped down on the table. "I'll do charity work, too," he declared.

Every Harlow head turned.

"I will. Really! I'll…" Aken paused a moment, "make sculptures out of clay. Yeah. I'm good at that."

Hercule snorted in aversion. "Who would want *those*?"

Aken glowered. "Pardon me for not being blessed with wealth, like you. I'd buy up a toy store and groceries to give to the poor, if I had been. How many children's meals could that tie of yours buy?"

Steam rose from Hercule's ears.

Cyrus intervened before things could worsen. "Do you think the kitchens are still open? I could use another lunch after all of that climbing," she said.

Hercule rose and stalked away.

"Aken, congratulations on winning a spot in the Festival Duel," Mamoru nodded to him.

Aken turned his face to the side. "Thanks."

Mamoru shared a look with Cyrus, and she shrugged.

29

The sun lowered, casting gold hues through the clouds over the city, while Aken-Shou wandered the narrower streets beyond Draevensett. He didn't bother to look up as the swallows careened in graceful bliss above the rooftops.

His shoe kicked a lose pebble, sending it skipping through a crossroads. He made an irritated sound through his teeth, and several passersby eyed him.

Make them pay…

Something whispered from the back of his head, the madman in his cage, the darkness scratching at the door's lock.

No one cares about you. Make them pay. You did it once; you can do it again…

"No, I won't do it!" Aken snarled, clutching the sides of his head. He must have said it too loud—people were keeping at a distance.

His mind fell quiet, and he raised his head.

It was a typical spring evening, too light for the streetlamps to be on. A lady in a frilly dress walked arm-in-arm with her man, who smoothed a thick mustache and whispered something in her ear. An elderly woman in mix-match garments hobbled across to a produce shop, while a young girl—a faeryn slave with drooping wings—rushed past in a hurry to get last minute errands done.

The air was quiet and sweet, lacking the daytime bustle and musty scent of oilpowder engines. He strummed a hand along the decorative bars of a window guard as he passed.

A crew on ladders were out hanging up décor and banners for the Swan Festival, depicting white feathers against lush red backgrounds.

A chorus of children's laughter nearby made him pause on the cobbled path. At the crossroads corner, children were grouped in a semicircle around a boy in ripped black tank shirt and multi-pocket capris.

Mamoru moved the strings of dolls and puppets, dancing and twirling them about before the fascinated boys and girls.

Aken crossed his arms and observed for a while. These kids were lucky not to be stuck in the Outskirts beyond the city walls. Out there, if you became an orphan, you were on your own. Orphanages inside the city didn't go looking beyond the walls for more.

"Her name is Isabelle." Mamoru gave a doll to a bedraggled little girl with big green eyes. "Can you give her a good home?"

The child's smudged face lit up, reaching to hold the doll like a treasure in her arms.

Aken's chest tightened.

Once Mamoru emptied one box, he hefted a second and moved up the street to a new gathered group of children, close to where Aken was leaning against a streetlamp. Maru nodded his way, "Did you make any of those clay sculptures you mentioned?"

"Uh…" He'd forgotten about that. His vision took in the stained, tattered clothes and dirty elbows and fingers of the curious youngsters, who now shuffled about them expectantly. Their thoughts were not for the future—they didn't have much of a future to hope for. Their thoughts were for today and tomorrow, surviving however decently they could, whether they were orphans or had rotten families.

Having a special toy was a respite from that, an escape from reality's cold grip. They could be normal children whenever they played with it; a treasure for those rainy days in life. That's what his clay art had been for him—a respite, an escape.

Aken lowered his chin to his chest. Mamoru set the box down, shifting to take a seat on the curb beside him while organizing the toys. They watched the children skip and chat animatedly at each other.

"You're a better person than I am," Aken admitted at last. His side bangs fell forward, veiling his vision.

Mamoru watched him for a moment, then pushed up off the curb. "Better? What makes you say that?"

"Because," Aken stiffened and looked away, "Everybody likes you. No one judges you, or calls you names."

Maru tilted his head. "Well, Aken, the only person who can make people stop believing you're a monster is *you* yourself. It's hard to gain people's trust, but nothing ever comes easy."

"A Scourgeblood can gain people's trust?" Aken scoffed. "I won the Duel Trials, but they're talking about me like I'm a pile of crud, as if nothing I do matters."

Mamoru clasped his shoulder. "You still have Harlow on your side."

He shrugged the hand off. "On my side? Since when? I know you guys never wanted me on your Floor."

Maru glanced skyward. "You're a real pain in the backside sometimes, Aken. But even so, I wouldn't trade you for anyone."

Aken's breath hitched.

The children quieted, wondering what was going on. Aken turned aside, letting his hair hide the tears. When his shoulders stopped shaking, and the tension and anger left his muscles, he wiped his face with a shirtsleeve.

Mamoru lifted an armful of toys out of the second box. "Here," he pushed them at Aken. Aken stared blankly for a moment, but Maru simply asked, "Would you like to help hand these out?"

He blinked until his vision cleared. "Sure." Aken took the armful awkwardly, leaning this way and that not to drop anything. Children began crowding around him expectantly, all hopeful smiles. He could almost see his young reflection in them.

"No one is better than anyone else, Aken," said Mamoru. "Our lives and the trials we face are too different for us to compare ourselves to others." He grabbed more toys. "Don't beat yourself up, but don't go slacking either. You want your dream to come true, right?"

His dream, right. He had to stay focused if he wanted to become the greatest Draev Guardian.

Aken handed out a toy dragon, his thoughts shifting to how he should prepare for the Festival Duel.

30

Fluffing her wavy hair about her ears, Cyrus closed the iron gate of the school behind her with a metallic *clack*, ignoring the yapping pixit and the winged lion statues who seemed to watch her with contempt.

Master Nephryte's warning that she never go beyond school grounds alone pricked the back of her mind, but she had to see if Huntter had left or if he still waited in the woods for her. If he was still around, she needed to apologize for sending him away so coldly the other day, and…maybe take him up on his offer to move to the Human Republic's capital, if Aken lost tomorrow's Duel.

Much as she wanted to stay here, the Trials had proven just how incapable she really was. How useless she was.

Just as she left the gate, someone called out. She was tempted to ignore them, then saw Cherish rolling her way alongside a woman: the lady Master.

"Cyrus, I wanted to tell you how well you did in the first trial," said Cherish. "You're new and yet you really put up a fight."

"Ah, thanks. I don't feel like I accomplished anything by losing, though." Cyrus averted her gaze.

The attractive lady Master nodded to her, "I'm Master Seren-Rose, of Floor Tathom. Nice to meet you, Cyrus."

"And you, Master." Cyrus dipped her head.

"Cyrus, just because you lost once, doesn't mean you didn't accomplish anything," Cherish stressed. "I couldn't take the Trials. I may not be able to become the same kind of Draev as everybody else in the future, but I don't let that stop me. Instead, I look for the things I *can* do, and the different kind of Draev I *can* become."

Cyrus half-smiled. "Your heart is like a Draev."

"As is yours."

Cyrus lowered her head. "I have to go. See you later." She trotted down the street. Sinking back into the hood of her brown cloak, she boarded a tram, heading southward.

White feather banners were everywhere, and the shops displayed swan merchandise—all of it a reminder of her failure.

Shadows stretched across the decorated streets as she hopped off near enough to the southern gate. People went about their business, jackets and frocks brushing past. It felt different being out in the city's maze of streets alone. The air felt clammy and foreboding; and every vempar's gaze seemed to flick her way, from the youngest child holding her mother's hand, to an old man twirling a cane, their glowing irises following her steps, as if they could read her secrets—knew what she was—and wanted a taste...

She turned onto Main Street, heading south, and rubbed at her forehead. Paranoia, that's all it was. Maybe they stared because of the red hair peeking from under her hood. Not many vempars had red hair, though many humans did.

Twin boys slouching against a bakery window regarded her, and she quickened her pace. Soon the city's encircling wall rose above the rooftops, and the southern city gate came into view. Ignoring the prickly feel of eyes on her back, she rushed forward to mingle with the sparse traffic going in and out. Most were entering, and for the first time in her life she was thankful for being short—able to duck from sight under an empty wagon and follow its roll out into the grasslands and the dirt road that cut through.

The scenery brought back memories of Gandif. She wondered absently what he was up to as she trotted briskly toward the tree line, finding the tree where she'd practiced Landing the other day.

Twilight's first stars winked awake. The western horizon clung to the dying rose hue left from a departed sun. Stepping into the woods, she was about to call Huntter's name, when a stand of ferns and fire bushes was roughly shoved aside.

She froze as a pale body came stumbling out onto the open grass.

It panted, its head like a mop of pearl gray, tinted rose by the dying sky.

Her throat held in a scream, until with a start, she realized it was Hercule.

What on eartha was the nobleson doing out here, at this hour? His ragged appearance made her step back. Long slashes tore through his fine pants, his dress-shirt barely held together in tatters around his torso, the silk vest nowhere to be seen, and his shoes looked shredded by claws. Twigs and leaves made a mess of his hair, and dirt and scrapes marred his skin from head to toe.

Hercule's breathing came hard, as if calming down from a mile run.

"Her…cule?" she asked faintly.

His head jerked toward her, just now aware of her presence, golden eyes wide for a second before narrowing to glowing slits in the dim light. His thumb and forefinger nails clicked together. She had the feeling she'd found him in a place he clearly did not want to be found.

Cyrus moved back another step, slowly, trying to maintain a mask of calm. "I…had…" She searched for words to distract him. "Are you good at Landing? I was trying to learn here, earlier. Mamoru taught me."

The intensity of Hercule's gaze diminished a fraction, and he turned aside, striding stiffly past as if she weren't there. Cyrus didn't move until he was several yards away, then she released the breath she'd been holding.

She was a fool for coming out here alone. She should've listened to Master Nephryte. Huntter clearly wasn't here, and hopefully never would be again. Despite herself, a part of her wished he *had* hung around, at least to properly say goodbye.

She began to leave, thoughts shifting to Hercule and what he could've been up to out here.

The underbrush rustled. She stilled, listening. It was getting too dark to see more than shapes, but one of those shapes seemed to be inching closer through the leaves.

She walked several steps before breaking into a run.

Something burst out of the foliage; the dark shape came after her.

Cyrus screamed as she ran. Hercule was ahead, and she raced to catch up, shouting, "Something's after us!"

He whirled around, eyes glowing in the dark.

She reached his side and turned to face the creature.

It came, a black blur through the tall grass. Hercule sucked in a deep breath and released a roaring exhale of fire. Gold flames shot from his mouth at the creature circling them.

The firelight made visible dark gray skin, bones and metal. Hercule rotated with its movements and released a second blast of flames, this time catching the creature's cloak on fire. It swatted at the burns, and lunged for them.

Cyrus channeled the metal of her bracelets into two blades and flung them, forcing the creature to halt and draw back. Bone peeked from under the creature's hood. A Corpsed, just like the one Aken had fought. Her knees weakened. Fear threatened to break her focus.

The creature crouched, ready for another attack. Then a strange bird call sounded.

The Corpsed lifted its head. With a chilling hiss, it retreated into the woods, and all fell silent.

"What the heck?" Hercule stared after it, the air steaming around his mouth.

"It's that same Corpsed—what me and Aken saw during the thunderstorm," she said, shuddering, retrieving her bracelets. She'd almost failed again, letting fear get the better of her; she really wasn't cut out to be a Draev.

Hercule's brow crinkled. "Aken wasn't just making that up?" She shook her head. His lips pursed in thought, and then he was marching off again. She wasn't sure if she should give him space, but there was no way she was walking alone.

"What's going on out here?"

A vempar in blue-and-white Draev uniform landed nearby. He shined a lampstick on them. "Draevensett students? Ha! Up to mischief, are you? I remember those days," he mused.

"Some creature attacked us," Cyrus blurted out and pointed back at the woods. She was about to call it a Corpsed, then thought better of it, considering the school's previous reaction.

"Creature, eh? Well, the beasts of the land have to eat too, you know." The Draev chuckled.

She frowned, and Hercule turned his nose up and continued on ahead of them toward the city gate.

"Get going, kid. I won't let the boogie man come after you."

Cyrus's frown became a pout. Some adults just didn't take things seriously.

～ට

Hercule's fist squeezed the ripped fabric clinging at his sides. What was Cyrus doing out here? He snorted in disgust. Humans were such a deceitful race; he doubted Cyrus was even from a farming community, the little liar!

He picked up the long coat where he'd left it on the grass, shrugging it on over his battered physique. Worry nagged at him. The half-human had found him in such a suspicious state.

Cyrus would talk. Rumors would spread. Master Nephryte would ask questions, and someone would be sent to trail Hercule's every move. Then people would find out about his secret, and they'd—

He stopped that train of thought and took deep breaths to calm his temper. Anger had gotten the better of him *once* today; he didn't want to have to turn around and hide in the woods for a second time.

He rolled his shoulders back. There was only one thing he could do before Cyrus had a chance to gossip. The best way to stop a rumor was to start an even bigger rumor.

"*Hmph*, let's see how well you like people learning *your* secret, liar-human." His bruised lips curled.

31

"Cy, where on eartha have you been?"

Having used Draevensett's coat-of-arms on the back of her shirt to be let back inside the gate, Cyrus wasn't far up Main Street when she heard Aken's shout and saw him coming out from a narrow side street.

His shoes screeched to a halt, anxiety written all over his features. "You're not supposed to wander off alone! Plus, it's dark out. What were you thinking?" Aken rebuked like a parent. "I was worried that— What I mean is, Mentor Nephryte told you not to wander off alone, didn't he?"

She tilted her head, a small smile creeping up. It was an odd feeling to have someone worry where she was and how late she stayed out. "I wasn't gone *that* long. And since when do you care what Master Nephryte says?"

He rubbed worry creases from his brow. "I just want you to be careful."

She punched his shoulder lightly. "I'm not some fragile butterfly. Are you over whatever was bothering you today?"

He glanced at the river on their left, as they walked back through Downtown. "Yeah…*un po' triste*."

She arched an eyebrow at him. "Since when did you learn Fluire phrases? Isn't that what faeryn speak?"

He shrugged. "My brain remembers odd things."

They caught a late tram ride, then walked the rest of the way to Draevensett. The city was beautiful at night, with every streetlamp and hanging iron lantern lit, painting the masonry and polished doors in soft yellow pools of light against the darkness.

A fountain bubbled in the center of a street they passed; lamplight played off the Moon Maiden statue and the water that poured from the vase she held.

With almost no one on the streets, Aken began a song:

"She stole my heart
The lady did
Standing upon the bank,
And though I said hello to her
Her willow branch she did not shake.

The townsmen laughed
They jeered at me
For falling in love with a willow tree,
But alas, I know she's in disguise
And the willow will again become a lady.

A lady-ee
A lady-ee
Oh I know my willow is a fair lady.
Just you wait
When the early dawn breaks
I'll catch her and make her my lady-ee."

A shoe flew out a third-story window as they passed by, hitting Aken square in the back of the head.

It was followed by a loud "Shut up!"

Cyrus's lips twitched while Aken rubbed his sore head.

Aken stretched all fours out on a sofa, and Cy took the armchair beside Nephryte as he had them gather after dinner in the study.

"Is story time normal for kids our age? Not that Harlow's ever been normal," Aken mumbled, then yawned, eyelids drooping. It was one of Nephryte's ordinances to have story time twice a week. It "strengthened Harlow's bond" and "encouraged love of reading," supposedly.

Hercule looked to be in a fine mood, as cheerful as a badger with a toothache, sitting as far away from everybody as possible, back propped against the farthest end of the opposite sofa—arms crossed and shoulders sulking.

'He changed clothes,' Aken noted. The nobleson changed clothes more than a dog shed fur. Showing off his fancy wardrobe, maybe?

Bak and Zartin plopped on the rug before the empty fireplace. Bak rocked back and forth, knees bent in a butterfly-pose, and holding his feet. Zartin sat quietly, arms wrapped around shins, Bladeer hat on the floor, his small antlers visible.

Mamoru took up the second sofa, head propped against an armrest. Lykale leaned against the sofa back, content to stand while thumbing through a botany textbook, the choker padlock still around his neck—Aken had yet to see him take it off.

"What's the story?" Cyrus had both elbows on the chair arm, chin cupped in hands, feet drawn up and tucked.

Nephryte flipped the pages of an old red book. "*The Last Princess*, a fairytale that was written several centuries ago," he began.

Aken made a half-hearted attempt to stay awake as the Mentor read, his consciousness fading in and out, in and out.

The human princess appeared in his mind suddenly. Her hair like scarlet roses swirled, just like the image within the starlight orb.

She moved towards him, collapsing on her knees.

She was crying, screaming, clawing at his hand for him to wake up. White wings, bright in the gloom like a swan's, rose at her back.

The soil beneath him as he lay on the ground churned damp with rain.

There were ruins of buildings everywhere, all around them.

"Get up!" she pleaded.

"Run…" he tried to tell her. "Be free. *Run*."

Enemies drew near. And suddenly he saw a sword swing at the princess.

"Stop!" he called feebly as his body lay dying. He struggled to reach out to her, to stop the sword, but it came regardless.

"Cyrus!" he shouted…

And blinked awake.

The familiar ceiling of the study room came into focus— no ruins, no rain.

It had been a dream…

A dream that felt all too real.

Off to his right, Bak was sniffling, wiping tears from his drenched cheeks. "That was so sad," he was saying. "How can the story just *end* like that? The hero gets killed along with the bad guys. All so his true love, the princess, can live on and be f-f-free!" he spluttered. "What kind of story *is* that?" Twin rivers cried from his eye sockets, and Zartin scooted a few inches away from him.

Aken rubbed at his temples, trying to collect himself.

Did he shout Cyrus's name? There was a vague feeling he had.

Lifting his head to look across at the redhead, he took a moment to imagine longer hair and a white dress.

Cy could be a perfect replica…if only he were a girl.

Were most human boys that feminine?

"It's a fairytale, you dunce," Hercule commented irritably from the sofa end as Bak's blubbering went on and on. "It never happened. Why are you crying over something that *never happened?*"

"Because…!" Bak hiccupped and couldn't finish the sentence.

"It was tragic," Zartin reasoned softly.

"Eh?" Aken sat all the way up now, head groggy. "Traffic? What traffic? Is there an ice cream sale this late?"

"Tragic," Zartin repeated.

"Oh. My ears must've fallen asleep, too."

Mentor Nephryte made an effort not to roll his eyes skyward; he closed the book perched on his crossed knees.

"You were sleeping?" said Cy from the armchair. "Shame on you! It was a really good story! Even if tragic. Is it based on a real story, you think?" Cy looked up at the Mentor, as if half-hoping it wasn't, yet half-hoping such a grand tale could be true.

"It's possible," Nephryte considered. "Every legend is based on some ounce of truth, some occurrence of long ago, even if it barely resembles the original event itself."

Aken stretched his arms with a loud yawn, and everyone in the room scowled his way. "Can we call it a night, now, *jiji*? A vempar needs his beauty sleep."

The line of Nephryte's mouth slanted. "While I am glad of your odd talent for memorizing other languages, I am not an *old man*. Where did you learn that Hanasu word?"

Aken gave a blank shrug.

Nephryte reached over to ruffle his bangs. "How about you call me *onii-sensei?*"

"*Brother teacher?* Nope." Aken scooted out of reach.

Off beyond the windowpanes, a peel of thunder rolled— a new spring storm was brewing over Draethvyle. Aken turned to watch. "Do Corpsed like thunderstorms?"

Nephryte massaged his temples.

"So help me, Aken-Shou, you will not go off chasing imaginary enemies during a thunderstorm for a second time. If it's work you need, to get out all of your excessive energy, then I'm sure the kitchens will be happy to have you."

Aken turned away. "Never mind."

32

A ken tried to sleep while the storm rolled past throughout the night, muffling his ears with a pillow. When it finally calmed, there was just an hour left before his alarm would ring. He shut his eyelids tight, seeking sleep…

Ro-hoo ro-hoo.

"Nhhhr," he groaned and gripped the bed sheet in a fist, then burrowed his head deeper to block out the solo act of a dove who'd so wonderfully decided to use his windowsill for a stage this morning. Its cooing, owl-like warble rippled through the glass as it strutted back and forth, greeting the dawn.

Ro-hoo fro-ho-hoo-hoo.

"Aw sheesh!" He pounded the pillow with a fist, and when that didn't work, he threw it at the window.

The dove looked at him, startled by the pillow's *thump*, then continued warbling.

He let out a vexed sigh, got out of bed and opened the window. "Did you have to choose *my* windowsill? Go bother Denim Dunceface!"

Instead of being spooked, the dove fluttered and landed on his head. *Fro-hoo!*

Aken gave up, letting his shoulders slump forward, his eyelashes wanting to droop to the floor.

"The only person who can make people stop judging you and stop believing you're a monster, is you yourself."

He held onto Maru's words from yesterday. He would make people acknowledge that he wasn't a monster and see the person he really was.

His nose felt wet suddenly. He wiped it with a hand, then paused mid-wipe when he realized what it was.

"*Gah!* Bird poo!"

The dove took off, and Aken could've sworn it laughed at him.

"Yuck! What'd I ever do to you, rotten bird?"

⌒

Cyrus checked once more that her fake fangs were intact and her ears lined. Students in the hallways kept glancing her way and whispering—and it was putting her nerves on edge. Why were they eyeing her as if she'd grown antlers? (No offense to Zartanian.) Her gut refused to settle.

She glimpsed Hercule: Healing had erased all traces of damage from his body. No one else but her knew of the nobleson's secret excursion last night. She hoped he wouldn't hold it against her.

A group standing just outside the classroom door whispered fervently. And they paused to watch as she passed by.

The hair on the nape of her neck stood on end as she took a seat.

The teacher for Physical Ed marched in, none other than the perpetually miffed Dr. Zushil himself. "Buttocks in your seats, this instant!" he commanded, and every student hurried to sit. "Let me make this very clear. No silly behavior or interruptions will be tolerated in this class, such as last week's disturbance."

Cyrus whispered out the side of her mouth to Aken, "What's he mean by *disturbance?*"

Aken groaned. "I sort of…caused some trouble."

"Like what?"

"*Erm*, well, drawing him as a hedgehog on the chalkboard, and throwing an eraser at his hair—it's so spiky it actually stuck."

Cyrus raised her eyebrows.

"It wasn't my finest hour. But I'm a reformed vempar, now."

"Uh-huh. Sure."

"No, *really*. I'm trying."

But before he could convince her, class began. "Today's chapter in *Health & Body*," read Zushil from a lesson planner, "is on the topic of birth. The final stages: From womb to newborn."

Unease and disgust rustled through the room.

Aken grumbled, "The last three chapters were bad enough. I really don't think we need any more info on this stuff."

The doctor clasped both hands together, and a malicious grin parted his lips. "Oh, but I have a video to go along with it!"

The classroom stilled.

Oilpowder lights flickered out, and window shades rolled down to darken the room. A sheet above the chalkboard unfolded and a projector turned on. Zushil's glasses became glowing rectangles in the projector's light. "This is payback for last week. The class has *you* to thank for it."

The class muttered angrily, and Aken ducked his head, making himself small.

"*And now*," spoke the video, "*let us explore the details of the birthing process…*"

When class came to an end, they all rushed outside in a flood. Harlow scurried down the hallway toward the cafeteria, in hopes that lunch would rid them of the memory. They nearly ran into Master Nephryte's torso around the next corner.

"Whoa—slow down there! The world isn't ending, just yet."

"Yes, it is!" cried Bakoa.

Zartanian struggled between breaths, his face green, breathing in and out through a paper bag.

The Master raised a questioning eyebrow.

"Scarred—I'm scarred for life!" Bakoa repeated like a broken record.

"What on eartha did Zushil put you through?" mused Master Nephryte.

Cyrus hung back, content to let everyone else do the talking, as Bakoa tried but could barely speak. "B…"

"Hmm?" Nephryte leaned an ear forward.

"B…Bi…Birthing process!" Bakoa squeaked out.

The Master's forehead creased upward, and a hand conveniently rested across his mouth.

"You're laughing. You're *laughing* at us!" Aken scowled.

The Master's shoulders shuddered with muffled sounds before he coughed, keeping a straight face. "*Ahem*. I would do nothing of the sort."

"Yeah right," Aken spat. "Why do we gotta learn that stuff? It's got nothing to do with fighting or being a Draev Guardian."

"It's to prepare you for the biggest fight of all, Aken-Shou: the fight known as Growing Up." Master Nephryte's hand came down, tousling Aken's hair roughly. "Life isn't all about having powers. And besides, it was only a cartoon video, right?"

"We don't need that stuff!"

The Master's head shook, and Cyrus wondered if it was laughter. "My, my. How will you survive the *real* thing when you get married and have families of your own?"

Zartanian made odd noises trying not to throw-up. Cyrus lightly patted his sleeve, though the boy flinched away at her touch.

"No chance of that, Nephster. My sole goal is mastering battle skills." Aken threw several punches in the air. "I'll need them to become the greatest Draev Guardian. Who's got time for romance?"

"Greatest Draev Guardian, indeed," Hercule mocked.

Aken was about to say something back, when Bakoa gave him a funny look and said, "Then how come you were happy when you thought Cyrus was a girl—?"

Aken clamped a hand over his mouth quickly. "It was a joke, Bak, *duh*. Who could ever mistake Cy for a girl?" His laugh wavered. "I'm glad he's my best boy bud. It wouldn't work otherwise!"

Cyrus faked a smile but rubbed at her gloved wrists and shifted to watch their reflections in the polished floor.

"*Nephster*—so creative with alternate names, aren't you? Or is that your way of avoiding calling me *Master*?" Master Nephryte gave Aken's head a hard pat, nailing down each word like a hammer. "Know this: in addition to battle skills, you'd better master people skills, because it's key in becoming a valuable Draev. And also, consider yourself blessed if a girl should ever happen to like a troublemaker like you."

Aken's face sunk into a wide frown; but then a sly grin tweaked it back up. "Really? Do you happen to know something about girls liking you, Mentor Nephryte? Does her name have the word 'Rose' in it, by any chance?"

Cyrus recalled the female Master: Lady Seren-Rose.

The Master's jaw twitched. "Why should I discuss it with someone whose highest grade is an F+?"

The sly grin melted.

Before any more snark could be exchanged, a loud "Master Nephryte!" down the hallway grabbed their attention. Cyrus watched the caller: a pear-shaped man with a long beak of a nose, as he slid to a squeaky stop before them.

"Assistant Principal Pueginn?"

The assistant paused just long enough to say, "Principal Han wishes to speak with you in his office. Urgently. Do not delay!" Then he was off, shiny shoes squeaking across the floor tiles.

Cyrus stared after the man. His skin was a unique charcoal gray, and his beady eyes like boulder opal. Something about him didn't feel right, though no one else seemed to notice. He was soon out of sight.

Worry flashed across Master Nephryte's features, and he fixed his gaze ahead. "I best be off and see what this is about. Behave yourselves. And yes, I mean you, Aken-Shou."

Aken made a sound between his teeth and stalked toward the cafeteria.

Lunch and recess came early as the school day cut short for the Festival Duel. In the cafeteria, Aken got caught trying to sneak a second dessert—which made for laughs when he was forced to eat broccoli instead.

Aken washed down the green taste with cold milk. Students at other tables kept glancing their way and talking in hushed tones, more so than usual. Cy looked to be on edge about it, rubbing his arms. But Hercule held his chin high, looking smug about something.

The madman began prowling restlessly in the back of Aken's mind. He tried to ignore it. He cleaned up his plate and stood. "Come on, let's get some fresh air. I'll race you guys outside!"

Once out on the green field, he dove, rolling down the slope like a bowling pin.

His roll came to a stop, and he sprawled on the spring grass, laughing. Bak and Zartin followed. "Try it, Cy!" he called out, his fingers rubbing over the grass-clover mixture under him; he breathed in the warm air and rich earthy scents. But when no one answered, he sat up. "Cyrus?"

Bak and Zartin sat up too, sharing a look. Cy walked instead of rolling down the slope and halted several feet away.

"What's wrong?" he asked, a pit of concern growing in his stomach.

Cy's mouth opened halfway, then faltered. "I feel like people are talking about me. Like they know something…"

Cackling laughter rose around them.

Aken bristled, every hair on the nape of his neck stood on end, as Denim's gang approached, circling Harlow like eager feroce on the hunt.

33

The cocky royal relative and his lackies leered as they surrounded Cyrus, Bakoa, Zartanian and Aken.

Denim let his head tilt back as he strode with exaggerated footsteps around them. His knowing smirk made Cyrus's gut sour. "I heard a rumor," he sing-songed, strutting like a proud rooster who knew a tantalizing secret.

"Buzz-off, chicken brain. Or did you come hoping for lunch scraps?" Aken confronted, kneeling up from the grass.

Denim shook a finger, "Tut-tut-tut. You won't even ask me what the rumor is?" His strutting came to a halt several feet from Cyrus. "The whole school—maybe the whole city, by now—is talking about it. The rumor's been circulating since first class." His gaze narrowed. "Why aren't you curious? Unless…you Harlow boys already knew?"

Cyrus's heart hammered against her ribs.

Denim combed a hand through his jet-black hair, grinning darkly. "It appears that *someone* here isn't who they *say* they are," he sing-songed again, and this time with a threatening undertone that made her breath hitch. "*Someone* here," Denim snarled, "is a human."

Cyrus's knees gave out. The words felt like they echoed across the field, across the school grounds, across the world, as she knelt. Cold hatred seeped through the air, freezing her bones—vempar hatred, as if her hands were stained in their brethren's blood.

Something slapped her mouth, and she jolted back. Denim dangled the fake wood fangs between his fingers for all to see. She shrunk, covering her mouth. This moment was destined to come; Master Nephryte had warned her. But for it to happen now...she wasn't ready. *Darn it*, she wasn't ready!

A hand clasped her shoulder. She forced her head to turn, finding Aken beside her. His focus on Denim was dangerous.

Zartanian moved to place himself between her and the circling gang, holding a stick as if it were a sword. Bakoa shifted into a ready stance opposite him, arms becoming large hammers of sand. Together the three made a triangle barrier around her.

Hercule hung back a distance away, observing, as if curious how the situation would unfold.

"You took one friend away from me." Aken's tone grew harsher with each word. "I won't let you take another."

Denim leaned forward. "Are you siding with a human? Betraying your own kind? I don't think that's very Draev-like behavior."

"I will *not* let you take Cyrus."

Instead of backing down, Denim smirked. "Guess I should've expected you to take in another stray pet, after losing that sabercat."

A fierce glow lit within Aken's eyes, replacing the blue with lava red.

"You know the school won't let you keep a pet. In fact, I'll be surprised if they don't expel you along with it. Oh, wait." Denim held up a finger. "With that Scourgeblood of yours, you're too dangerous to expel, aren't you? They'll have to lock you away. Yes, that's what they'll do: lock you away for good."

Aken dove at him with a shout. The veins down his arms glowed as if flowing with lava, and his fists heated and swung forward.

Denim blocked the punch with a shield of ice growing from his forearm. He made the shield grow wider and thicker before the second punch came.

He laughed as Aken's attacks chipped away at the icy barrier. "You'll never become the greatest Draev Guardian. And after today, you'll never see that half-human friend of yours again."

A roar tore from Aken's throat, and Cyrus watched as his right fist became a gauntlet of obsidian. He punched straight through the ice shield, shattering it to pieces, and connected with Denim's shoulder—sending the boy flying backwards.

Silence followed as Aken panted and waited for Denim to get back up.

The bully clutched his dislocated shoulder, then pulled back his shirt to see red burn marks in the shape of a fist on his skin. "It's not Healing..." Denim stared, breathing hard. "It's not Healing!"

Aken looked at his armored hand for the first time and came back to his senses. The obsidian crumbled away as he stumbled back, and his irises were blue once more.

"He used his evil Scourgeblood power on me!" Denim shouted.

"I didn't mean..." Terror filled Aken's features. "I didn't mean to..."

Everyone backed away, even Bakoa and Zartanian.

"He's a monster," someone voiced. "Lock him up before he kills us!"

Aken's hands shook. He glanced back once, meeting Cyrus's gaze. But she didn't know what to do, her soul still in turmoil.

Footsteps approached from across the field, a Master's cape rippling behind.

"Master Eletor!"

Cyrus watched as the vempar man raised a hand to forestall the students' flood of accusations. "That's a nasty wound, there, Denim," he said and inspected the red mark.

Denim pointed, "He attacked me with his Scourgeblood power! It's against Draev rules to attack the innocent."

Master Eletor pressed the wound, and Denim flinched. "Are you really that innocent?"

Denim's jaw worked.

"Still, this is serious. Even I can't Heal it." With a *pop*, Eletor relocated the shoulder, ignoring Denim's yelp. He rose and approached Aken. "You have to come with me."

Fear streaked Aken's face.

"Where are you taking him?" Cyrus forced her throat to speak. When the Master hesitated, she knew. "No, you can't lock him away!"

Master Eletor grabbed Aken's wrist, and Aken didn't fight back.

"You can't!"

"If he's a danger to the citizens, then there's no choice but to keep him contained. And only special dungeon cells can hold someone like him."

"He's not a danger—he was protecting me!"

Master Eletor turned toward her, Aken's wrist in his firm grip. "I don't think you have much time to argue with me, half-human. You should leave before the other Masters and school staff come looking for you."

Sweat beaded Cyrus's brow.

"Since I'm busy with Aken-Shou, here, I'll give you this chance to escape."

Escape? Was that all she could do?

She moved to block Denim and the Master from leaving. Denim held his injured shoulder and raised his head in contempt.

"Tell him the truth!" she demanded, "You were

threatening me, and that's why Aken hit you."

"So what if I was threatening you? You're not a Draev student anymore." Denim smirked.

The Tathom boys fanned around her and Bakoa and Zartanian—Doughboy among them, looking grim despite how friendly he'd seemed yesterday. Humans were the enemy here; it was Argos who fought and slayed them. She wouldn't doubt each one of these boys could name a relative who'd been killed by the Argos Corps.

This was all her fault. If she'd been honest about what she was from the start, then maybe none of this would be happening. Just like Hercule had said.

'Guide me, Lord God,' she sent a silent prayer and gathered courage.

"I'm half-human, but I'm also half-vempar," she said, "born with Ability, same as each of you. Which means I have just as much right to be at this school. I will become a Draev Guardian and stand alongside Harlow, no matter what enemies we face."

"Cyrus…" Aken started, but she silenced him with a gesture.

Denim leaned on one foot, raising his chin further. "You want to be one of us and leave your human side behind, is that it?" He paused, and his frown was replaced by a sly chuckle. "I know how to solve this. It's simple."

Denim spread his good arm wide. "You say you're a Draev student like us? Well then, let's have you prove it." He spun on a heel, arm sweeping to indicate the Tathom boys left and right of him. "You'll prove it by accepting our challenge: to fight and win against one of our own. Only then can you truly be accepted here."

"Don't listen to him," Aken shouted. "Just run, get somewhere safe!"

Cyrus considered the challenge. Fight a Tathom boy, who would no doubt know how to use his Ability better than she did hers. Chances of winning were slim, if any. But…

"The Swan Festival Duel takes place today, and since Aken won't be taking part in it, how about *you* take his place and face off against our contestant, Doughboy?" Denim flourished his good hand for dramatic effect.

Incredulous gasps and whispers circled the field, and Doughboy thudded his fists together, accepting the challenge.

Cyrus had to shut her lips to halt a hiccup of fright. Billsbury Doughboy stood huge—the biggest boy in their grade, and maybe the whole school. The fat making up most of his body thick and tough, something that'd be difficult to land a damaging punch on, especially for a short, scrawny girl like her.

"Liars and spies get punished," said Doughboy. "You won't escape me, sneaky human." His height loomed, a shadow obscuring the sun.

"Hold on, Doughboy," Denim said before the boy came at her. "Wait for the Duel, where everybody can see the half-human lose."

Cyrus kept her trembling fists at her sides. "If I win, you will free Aken and explain this was all a misunderstanding. That way, he can stay and keep training," she said.

Denim regarded her. "I can't *make* the Draev Guardian League free Aken, but I'll do what I can to convince them, if you win. But then I'm raising the stakes for you, too: If you lose, not only will you never come back to this school, but you'll become a slave to my family's Noble House, and serve me."

Bakoa and Zartanian made sounds of shock.

Aken froze, then released a heated stream of name-calling as he tried to launch himself at Denim. Eletor's grip held him back.

Cyrus's throat was too dry to swallow, and Denim's leer sent spiders crawling up her spine.

She stiffened and didn't give herself time to think, but said, "Deal."

Denim chortled, then winced as he clutched his shoulder. "Go hide, and meet us at Central Plaza for the Duel at one o'clock," he told her.

The school bells *bong-gonged* the end of lunch, and Master Eletor began leading Aken away. "You said it was a rumor," Aken growled at Denim over his shoulder. "Who started it? Tell me!"

Denim coolly glanced back. "We overheard some older students talking about it. No clue who it was that first tattled, though." He waved his fingers, "Bye-bye. Hope you enjoy your new prison life. Maybe I'll send you a letter now and then."

Aken snarled as he was pulled by the wrist. "Cy, don't worry about me. Just get out of here while you can!"

She stared after him, tears blurring her vision. "I'll free you. I promise I won't lose," she whispered.

Master Eletor led him away to a bolted door holed in the slope at the edge of the school grounds, a door that must lead to the depths beneath Draevensett. She pressed a hand to her aching chest.

Denim swaggered back to school, lackeys following in his wake, though his path deviated towards the front courtyard and most likely the doctor's office.

Cyrus's insides burned. A hand tugged on her elbow.

"You shouldn't be out in the open. A teacher might see you," said Bakoa, coaxing her out of the field and under the cover of trees. Zartanian kept a watchful eye at their back. They were anxious, and she stared at her own shaking hands.

How had things come to this?

⁓

A rush of cool air rippled Aken's shirt as Master Eletor yanked open the old door, revealing a stone spiral staircase leading down into the darkness. He followed rather than be dragged down the moldy steps.

Reaching the base, Eletor raised his free hand and snapped his fingers. An electric current weaved through the air, touching and igniting the oilpowder sconces along either walls, bringing the underground dungeon beneath the school into gloomy light.

Aken tensed his shoulders as they passed empty stone cells, the smell of mildew permeating the air. The cell bars and doors gleamed, unmarred despite the age of the place. Master Eletor stopped at one cell; the hinges made no sound as he pulled open the door.

"Black silver; never dulls or ages. And it's the one thing no vempar can break—to my knowledge, anyway," Eletor explained, and then he looked down at Aken pityingly. "This is a temporary holding place. If things don't work out in your favor, you'll be moved to the Morbid Dungeons, far from Draethvyle."

Aken didn't meet his gaze but clenched his fists instead. The cell awaited, and it took every ounce of courage to step inside. The door clanged shut behind him, his view of the world now crossed with bars.

"Don't let Cyrus get hurt. Please, help him escape."

"You know I can't do that. I'm being nice enough not informing the principal of Denim's scheme," Eletor stated. "Cyrus has a chance at winning his life here—and maybe your freedom, too—if he wins the Duel and the prize of one request granted by the king. I'm curious to see if the little half-human can win." Master Eletor moved to leave.

"What are the Morbid Dungeons like?"

Eletor paused. "You don't want to know."

As he left, the sconces went out and the darkness flooded back in. Aken shivered against the damp slabs underneath him, and drew his knees up as he hugged his arms for warmth.

A future locked away.

A future locked in darkness.

A future of being alone, forever.

He shuddered. He couldn't face that loneliness, even if it was what a monster like him deserved. He'd rather die.

Aken raised his hand, thinking of the obsidian armor that had wrapped around it—wondering and fearing how he'd summoned the Scourgeblood power.

"Please be safe, Cy."

The *plip* of water dripping was the only answer in the dungeon's silence.

34

S tay calm.

Ba-thump.

Stay alert.

Ba-thump.

She had to do this.

No room for failure.

No matter how her limbs trembled and her knees threatened to give out. She had to save Aken, and prove to everyone—and to herself—that she deserved to be in Draevensett. That she could become a Draev.

Ba-thump.

She would win this, or die trying.

Cyrus's heart pounded in her ears as she stood on the pavestones of Central Plaza, taking deep breaths. The wide city square was decorated for the Swan Festival with banners and white bows and roses, and an assortment of white feathers on every possible thing, including the hairdos of some ladies. Most everyone in the crowd wore some piece that was white, whether it be a hat, bowtie, or swaths of lace.

In the center of the plaza, a ring had been set up for the Festival Duel, and the crowd was already taking seats in the mechanical bleachers that surrounded it. At the head of the battle ring, and elevated, stood a canvas pavilion, where beneath it, seated in elaborate chairs, were two royal figures.

Cyrus gazed in awe, her first time seeing the king and queen of the Vemparic Kingdom. Their garments stately, trimmed in gold, their expressions immovable. To the right of the king stood an important-looking man trimmed in laces, his countenance ghostly pale gray, his hollow eyes and cheekbones deeply shadowed, hair a straight black curtain. Principal Han was present in the adjacent row, along with the numerous Draev Masters of the D.G. League. This Duel must be an even bigger deal than she'd thought.

Ba-thump.

"What are their names again?" she whispered.

"King and Queen Magnovska, and Viceroy Deciet," replied Mamoru.

Cyrus waited at one end of the ring, Harlow among the first row of spectators behind her, Floor Tathom and Denim at the opposite end behind their broad champion Doughboy, smug and confident as ever, though Denim was still nursing his shoulder. Cherish was present, too, in her wheelchair off to the side, her expression somber. Flocks of Draevensett students filled the bleachers alongside the wealthy citizens. The lower class had to sit on the ground at the ring's edge to watch.

The announcer, a rotund man with a bowler hat, made his way to the center of the ring. "Ladies and gentlemen!" he blared, "The Duel of the Swan Festival is ready to begin!"

Applause resounded.

"However, there has been a slight change to the match." Murmurs rustled through the crowd.

"The Scourgeblood was forced to cancel his part in the Duel, for as of yet undefined reasons. However, Draevensett's first half-human student will be taking his place!"

Murmurs turned into shock and incredulous sounds. The king's dark eyebrows rose, and the pale Viceroy Deciet leaned forward. Masters and others of importance stirred in their seats, some standing to get a better look as the two contenders entered the ring—Cyrus thought she glimpsed Master Nephryte among them.

"This is absurd! The next runner-up should take the Scourgeblood's place, not some half-human," spoke up one of the members of the D.G. League. Others agreed.

"Humans don't belong in Draevensett."

"He shouldn't be allowed to compete—he should be executed!"

Cyrus rubbed at her wrists nervously.

"According to the documents, he is still a student. You've yet to change that fact, even if you were planning to," spoke Master Nephryte. "And Principal Han has already signed off that Cyrus is allowed to take Aken-Shou's place in the Duel."

All eyes turned to the principal, who shrugged without concern. "I thought it curious. Can you blame me for wanting to see how such a match would turn out? Besides, it was the prince's cousin who made the proposal to me."

More protests rose, but the Viceroy lifted his hand and spoke, his voice like scratching sand. "His Majesty says the Duel is to commence. If Draevensett did not want a half-human among its students, then they should have done a better job in exercising their vigilance."

The Draev group unceremoniously shut up.

"Come forward, contenders!" called the announcer.

"Be careful, Cyrus," said Bakoa.

She turned to them. Zartanian was pinching the lacy cuffs of his sleeves. And Mamoru had his fist clenched in a hand behind his back, though he flashed her a reassuring smile and said, "Go show them what you're made of."

Cyrus closed her eyes, gathering strength from God and

from Harlow's support, before she stepped forward to face Doughboy.

The crowd cheered as Doughboy took slow, heavy steps toward Cyrus, the fat of his stomach and limbs rippling. A grin split his chubby cheeks, eager for battle, a headband tight around his forehead.

Taunts and shouts for the large boy to teach the human a lesson blared. Cyrus kept calm, trying to come up with a plan.

Not everyone in the crowd was making noise. Scattered among the lower class were slaves—faeryn, humans, kitsune. Their silent faces focused on her, as if she were a miracle, a ray of hope in their chain-bound lives.

"And…begin!" shouted the announcer, and he quickly scurried out of the way.

Cyrus readied her stance, channeling *essence* through the metal feather bracelets, and wrapping the hard material around each hand up to the elbow, knitting it to her skin.

As Doughboy drew near, his body and clothes changed color and consistency, his height rose and mass doubled in size. Bread-colored, bouncy, wobbly limbed and squishy… She stared, transfixed in horror. He literally became a boy made out of—

"Dough?"

"It's my code name for a reason, baby human," Doughboy boomed, now looming over her.

She had time only to suck in a breath before his stretching dough arms lashed out, and she fast dodged to the side. Her knees skinned across the pavestones.

Huge fists on trunk-thick limbs flattened the stones where she'd stood—*baM!*

How flat would her body be if those fists pinned her to the ground?

'*Stay focused!*'

Back up on her feet, not far from Doughboy's turned

back, she leaped high. Both hands coated in metal, she gripped them together in a double-metal fist and swung it— striking the back of his head.

"*Wohg!*" Doughboy roared.

But her double-fist attack merely made a dent in his dough head—after several wiggly shakes, it swelled back to normal—but her double-fist bounced back at her, knocking the breath out of her lungs as it struck her chest. "*GwuH!*"

She fell back, rolling across the plaza ring.

"Cyrus!" Bakoa started. But Mamoru's arm held him back: "If you interfere, it's all over. He has to win this on his own."

Back stinging, chest burning with each breath, Cyrus forced herself upright. She watched as Doughboy rolled himself into a giant ball, legs and arms wrapped behind him. Using his stomach, he bounced—pounding the ground like the world's largest ball.

"Stomach Pancake-Maker!" he roared.

She scrambled out of the way. The last thing she wanted on the menu were "Cyrus pancakes."

'*That could kill me, that could kill me!*'

"Run right! Right!" She could hear Bakoa call out amidst the jeering crowd.

Doughboy bounced, like a dough moon rising and falling.

"Above you—he's above you! RUN!"

Doughboy had been at the opposite end of the ring just seconds ago. Bouncing had brought him closer much faster than she'd anticipated. Now he was overhead, coming down. No time to dodge.

Planting both feet, crossing her metal arms overhead, Cyrus braced for impact.

Ww-BOSH!

Dough stomach crushed down on her raised metal arms.

Her knees buckled.

Using the ground as a brace, she shoved with all her

might: using the weight of her metal to bounce the huge body aside—making him skid away like a beachball. Her hands and knees hit the ground, exhausted from the massive effort, raw scrapes bleeding down her arms and legs.

Ignoring the pain, she got back up.

'I have to win! Please give me the strength, Lord God. Not for me, but for Aken, and these slaves.'

Doughboy rebounded toward her. She raised her metal forearms once more, as his wide girth came down on her defense. She struggled and strained against the weight crushing down on her.

A dough fist freed from behind his back—it curved a punch into her exposed gut.

"*GHah—!*"

The world moved and blurred.

Her body tumbled and skid clear to the opposite end of the ring.

Face down, agony burned every inch of her. She jerked, trying to lift her head—pain searing the effort.

"Cyrus." Mamoru's voice. "You can do it. Get up! He's coming—*Get up!*"

Blocking out the shooting pain, she rolled on her side, shaking as she pushed up off the ground.

It wasn't fast enough.

Doughboy's stomach came down. At the last moment, he freed his hands and swung them forward—grabbing her legs out from under her.

She yelped. He rotated to land on his back, and in the same motion raised his arms high and flung her up into the air like a rag doll.

Cyrus screamed, limbs flailing in the sky. As gravity pulled her back down, the ground rushed up to meet her.

She couldn't survive a fall this high. Death opened its jaws beneath her.

'Think!' her mind shrieked.

An image from memory opened: of her clinging to Mamoru's back as he carried her in one leap over and down the city wall.

She ceased flailing, and concentrated.

Essence gathered in the soles of her feet, an invisible cloud, and her fall slowed.

Her feet met the ground with a hard stumble, but she straightened, chest heaving.

Noises of surprise traveled through the onlookers. A human had done what only Draev Guardians could do, right before their eyes. Doughboy appeared momentarily surprised, too. But with a shake, he charged at her once again.

What to do? She needed a plan! How do you defeat something made out of dough? She couldn't keep this up for long, fatigue and pain from who knew how many injuries threatened to drag her down with each breath.

Punches rained down from Doughboy's fists, pounding the pavestones with the force of a mace. She tried to spin out of the way. Three blows grazed her shoulder, ribs, and lower back as she dodged—one direct hit and that'd be the end of her.

Again and again she threw herself out of the way and got back up, sprinting and dodging, blood dripping from a split lip and countless more scrapes.

She desperately tried to make the metal spread and cover more of her body, but her *essence* wouldn't hold out long enough. She couldn't focus to keep more than her arms steady.

How can metal overpower something so elastic and bouncy as dough? Picking herself up for what felt like the hundredth time, from the corner of her eye she saw a slave child: Compared to other faeryn he was odd, with blue skin and wispy darker blue hair. The child was watching her, and she could feel his hope fading into disappointment, resignation—acceptance that nothing in this world would ever change.

Bile soured her throat.

She had to change how these vempars viewed and treated other races. She would start by showing them what this half-human was made of, that this half-human wasn't much different from themselves when it came down to it!

'Guide me…help me win…for them!'

"C'mon, Cyrus! Show that piece of unbaked bread what you're made of!" shouted Bakoa. Her mouth grinned despite the blood. That was all the encouragement she needed.

Piece of unbaked…piece of metal…? An idea hit her, from back in Elvenstone when she drew needles out of the death-cage's metal post.

She needed something metal. But she shouldn't use her bracelets when they were her only defensive shield, or iron blood when it would make her weak.

Scanning the plaza, while running to keep distance between herself and Doughboy, a glint caught her eye: sunlight reflecting off a streetlamp. There were several of the lamps spaced around the plaza, and all blocked off by the crowd. But one was less obstructed—she could push past to it.

Using her legs' last ounce of strength, she sprinted toward the streetlamp.

Behind her, Doughboy's stomach bounced, gaining on her with each bound.

Onlookers scurried aside as she barreled through.

She reached out.

Fingers caught hold of the streetlamp's pole. She recreated the same thought, same feeling, that she'd had back then—willing *essence* into the pole, drawing metal out, stretching it…

People gasped as metal spiked out from the pole's surface—countless needles—stretching, elongating. And all of them aimed at Doughboy.

Denim's face went wide. "Doughboy, dodge!" he yelled.

Cyrus willed the sharp needles out, and they streaked through the air like a shower of arrows.

Metal pierced dough-skin—arms, legs, hands, ribs, in and out the other side.

He was dough on the surface, but somewhere underneath had to lie a skeleton and nervous-system, even if doughy; he would feel the pain.

"*AUGH!*" Doughboy roared.

Now was her chance, while he faltered, and dough flickered back to real skin.

Sprinting one last time, right arm and fist steel, Cyrus rushed in to deal the final blow.

Kr-PNCH!

Metal fist connected with Doughboy flesh, striking the side of his head with a right-hook swing.

The crowd fell silent. The only sound to be heard was that of Doughboy's body colliding with the ground, unconscious.

Cyrus collapsed to her knees, exhausted beyond her body's capacity. She could barely make out the faeryn child and the new spark of hope there.

"I…did it," she murmured against the agonizing pain.

A half-human had used Ability, and won against a Draev student.

It was Harlow's cheers that broke the silence. Then the plaza came alive with exclamations of disbelief, applause and protests—a buzzing cacophony.

The announcer stepped forward into the ring and waved an arm in grand gesture toward her. "We have our winner! Cyrus Sole, the half-human, has won the Festival Duel!" Cheers and boos mixed together loudly. The announcer came forward with a crown made from swan feathers, setting it upon her head. "The prize of one feasible request to be granted by the king is now yours, Cyrus. Step forward and proclaim what is your request!"

Cyrus could barely move her feet towards the pavilion and the royals seated beneath it. She gathered all the air she could into her lungs and forced her voice to carry loud enough, despite the stabbing pain in her ribs, her joints, her wrists. "Your Majesty, my request is that Aken-Shou be allowed to continue his training in Draevensett, to become a Draev Guardian."

Commotion stirred among the school faculty and the Masters. "The Scourgeblood is too dangerous! Keep him locked up," one of them disputed.

"He's done nothing to prove he's dangerous. Don't be rash and assume things," she heard Master Nephryte say.

The king raised his hand, and silence fell.

"I hear your request, Cyrus Sole," spoke the king. "For as long as Aken-Shou does not pose a serious danger to this kingdom and to those who live within it, he may be allowed to continue his training."

She could hear grumblings of unease throughout the bleachers.

"But this is not what I expected. You could have saved yourself and asked to remain at Draevensett, or even become a citizen. But instead you spend your request on a fellow student?" The king stared down from his ornate chair. "A selfless act deserves some reward. I want the Draev Guardian League and Draevensett's principal to consider keeping you on as a student. Your Ability could serve us well."

A wave of murmurs rippled through the crowd.

Cyrus bowed as best she could. "I am grateful, Your Majesty."

Tathom hurried to Doughboy's side, while Harlow trotted across the ring toward her, their arms raised in victory.

"I won…" Cyrus tasted blood, feeling faint. "Thank you, Lord…"

Everything turned blurry and gray, the world fading in and out. She felt her shoulder and left hip slump against the sun-beaten ground, and the feather crown roll away.

Zartanian's worried shout was the last thing she heard.

~

Hercule stood transfixed as the plaza's crowd dispersed, bustling past him, going back to their daily routine now that the show was over.

Separate groups chattered about the outcome. Others shook their heads and stalked off. While yet more looked back at the dueling ring, mystified and eager to spread new gossip.

Mamoru was cradling the half-human in his arms. "He's exhausted his *essence* tank," Lykale was saying, while Bakoa and Zartanian fretted and fussed. "He needs to see a doctor and be Healed, right away."

Hercule watched as Mamoru traveled quickly over the rooftops, the half-human secure in his arms.

"I can't believe it," Hercule mouthed to himself. Amazed, then angry with himself for being amazed.

Cyrus's duel had been admirable. He'd gone against a formidable, more experienced opponent, and didn't once give in to fear. He'd kept going, despite bleeding all over the place. "How? Why?" Why go so far when he couldn't Heal? Cyrus could have been crushed to death or impaired for life. Why risk so much to stay here and rescue Aken? Why not run away, leave Draethvyle behind?

"I don't get it." Rubbing the frown line from his forehead, a separate thought occurred to him: The reason he'd let on about Cyrus's secret was to divert the school's attention away from himself, in case Cyrus had tattled on his whereabouts the night before.

But there were no rumors or whispers going around about a nobleson alone outside the city at night. Had the redhead not mentioned it to anyone?

If that was the case, then Cyrus wasn't a snitch like he'd assumed. Instead, Hercule had become the real snitch himself.

His hand paused from his forehead to move to his stomach, a nauseous feeling taking hold.

35

Earlier, before the Festival Duel:

Nephryte hurried to Principal Han's office, and when he entered, Master Deidreem was there waving a finger as if to a naughty child, and both Zushil and elder Master Brangor wore the deepest of scowls on their faces.

"*Tsk-tsk*, I would think that of all people, you, Nephryte, would know better than to bring in a human. How disgraceful."

"Enough, Master Deidreem," Principal Han cut the young Master off, then laced his fingers together on the desk, paper stacks and pens shoved aside. "It has come to my attention, Master Nephryte, that one of your students is half-human. Did you know of this?"

Under the principal's thick-browed scrutiny, Nephryte gave one slow nod. "Yes, Principal Han."

Master Lady Seren-Rose wasn't meeting his gaze, and Eletor remained expressionless.

"Tell me," Han continued, his gaze as piercing as an owl's, "At what point in time were you planning on informing me of this? If at all?"

Nephryte opened his mouth, but Han went on. "Why did I have to hear of this from one of your students, instead of from you? You said nothing to me—*nothing!* This is my school, Master Nephryte. The students, and everyone connected to this place, are my responsibility. Their safety and well-being rests in my hands. And yet you allowed an enemy to live among us. A human, who could be a possible spy, a possible terrorist sent to kill off some of our valuable Ability users!" His wrinkled hands pressed against the desk. "I demand an explanation for this."

Nephryte maintained his cool composure and flicked a glance Zushil's way. "Principal Han, if I had suspected, even for a moment, that Cyrus posed a threat to—"

"It is not your place to decide who *is* and who is *not* a threat to Draevensett and this city. That is *my* job, and the job of the Draev Grandmaster."

Nephryte dipped his head. The old man's frown slanted for a moment, as he added, "In case you are wondering, Zushil has already received his tongue-lashing. He shares some blame, being a doctor who failed to examine and confirm Cyrus's race before admittance."

Zushil busied himself with analyzing the ceiling.

Nephryte bowed his head in acknowledgment. "Forgive me. It was not my intention to deceive you, Principal, whatever others may accuse me of." His eyes flicked toward Deidreem, who merely smirked and tilted his top hat. "I was searching for the best moment in which to discuss the matter with you. I was hoping that, if given the chance to get to know Cyrus, you would see he is an innocent boy who simply wants a place to belong. But clearly I went about this the wrong way; forgive me."

Han regarded him.

Nephryte straightened, his chin level in resolve. "Whatever your decision, though, Cyrus's home is with me. Even if I have to leave this city and bring my students with me. I will not abandon a child of God."

"Oh puh-leeze!" Deidreem rolled his eyes. "Ever the

drama king, this man."

Han scrubbed a weary hand across his temples and gray mane. "Don't, Nephryte. Don't. There's no need for such drastic talk, as that. I will have a chat with the half-human myself, and determine what he is like."

Deidreem started, but Han nodded his chin toward Nephryte. "I've always trusted your judgment. You've never failed me—and that is the only reason I will meet with this Cyrus before making a final decision."

Finished discussing the matter, the principal rose to his feet. "That will be all for now. Find Cyrus and bring him to me at once. You can go back to your Masterly duties and what not—whatever it is you whipper-snappers do nowadays."

Master Seren-Rose chuckled as she, Brangor and Eletor filed their way out of the office. Deidreem stalked out, and Zushil marched with his face flushed in humiliation.

Nephryte bowed his head in thanks before departing.

A half hour later, just as Han was about to retrieve a hidden box of cookies from one of the drawers, a student shoved open the door to the office.

"Ah, Denim, what a surprise. Is there something you need?" asked Han half-heartedly, concealing the box from sight.

"Actually, there is. It's about the Duel and a change of plans..." said the boy.

From a rooftop facing Central Plaza, Master Nephryte observed the aftermath of the Duel, his arms folded, back leaned against a gothic spire.

A sharp breeze blew back his hair and Draev cape. Most of the plaza had cleared. Tathom worked together to carry Doughboy away, while Mamoru was hurrying in the direction of the Infirmary with Cyrus.

At first, Nephryte had thought of protesting the Duel, but this had been more than just a fight for Cyrus. It was the only way for her to be accepted and acknowledged by the other students and by the people of Draeth. She'd had to prove herself.

Nephryte sensed a presence beside him, but continued observing as if Master Eletor wasn't there.

"An interesting match...then again, Cyrus is an interesting student," Eletor mused, bare arms crossed, his short hair and thin ponytail swaying in the breeze. He had on another of his colorfully patterned vests in the Arah Desert style under his cape. "It doesn't surprise me you took him in. But you're too caring for your own good, you righteous bean. It will get you into trouble one of these days. You know that, right?" Eletor's glance cut sideways.

"*Hmph.*" A smirk touched Nephryte's lips. "So you've been telling me, over and over since middle-grade. Go mind your own business, and keep out of mine."

Eletor huffed, mock offended. "Life is easy for you. Most of your Floor is the same age. But me, I go back and forth between mentoring the younger, and those ready to graduate, and then the eldest who already graduated and are now learning the ropes of being a Draev squad out on the field... *Heh*, one nearly got himself killed in a skirmish with Argos the other day. I'm beginning to doubt those green horns will ever be capable of harvesting without me! I can't afford to keep playing babysitter, like this." He rubbed his temples, chin raised to the wind. "You have it so easy. Your students haven't reached that age yet."

"You say I have it easy, but I do my share of city patrols in between school duties."

"Ah, yes. The great hero Master Nephryte. What would the city do without you?"

Nephryte sniffed. "It's your own fault for taking on such a big Floor, and not dividing it up. Didn't I tell you to let

Master Brangor handle the older ones? He's the most experienced among us." He flicked hair out of his eyelashes. "He's raised some fine Draevs. He's a true warrior, and I hope when I reach old age I'm just as spry and alert."

"Sure, Brangor's great, minus all the ale." Eletor guffawed. "I'd bet a thousand gold coins the man is part dwarf the way he drinks the stuff." He feigned a disgusted face, and Nephryte chuckled.

"He *is* part dwarf—a fraction, anyway."

"Oh…that explains it. He does seem short and stocky." Hands behind his head, Eletor peered down at the square, following Nephryte's line of sight to the Harlow group. "I should go release that boy, now. You aren't still angry with me, are you?"

"Aken-Shou needs to face the reality of his power and the need for self-control. Perhaps this has taught him something. Though, in the future, talk to me before you go jailing one of my students."

Eletor shrugged. "I was just doing what the Grandmaster would have done. That kid shattered through Denim's Ability as if it were glass. That wound he got will take weeks to Heal—something that should've Healed instantly, but because it was made by a Scourgeblood it couldn't."

"Yes, I'm well aware of how dangerous a Scourgeblood is."

"Are you?"

Nephryte glanced at him sideways.

"Is that why you haven't told Aken the truth? Will you ever tell him that what happened to his parents wasn't an accident? That it wasn't an attack by humans?"

Nephryte had to let the silence linger before replying. "Never. Not as long as I can help it." His inhale wavered. "That is something Aken-Shou can never know."

Eletor watched him, eyes glowing like citrine quartz. "Secrets never stay secret."

Nephryte shifted his weight, arms crossed over his chest.

"That kid is a ticking time bomb. You know Scourgebloods don't belong in this world anymore. They were wiped out for a reason." Eletor turned back to view the plaza below. "When the day comes—when he grows up to be like his parents—I hope you can put aside your feelings and do what's necessary."

"Aken-Shou will never be the murderer his parents were."

Eletor fiddled with one of the leather bands around his wrist. "It's in a Scourgeblood's nature. He can't escape it. Poor lad…he never should have been spared to live. And it's your fault that he was."

The image of an innocent smiling baby in diapers surfaced in Nephryte's memory. The day he first met Aken—a time Aken would never remember.

"I had my reasons."

36

Aken shifted his seat on the gritty, damp stone floor. He could feel the bits of mold with his fingers, but couldn't see through the heavy darkness. He tried to stay positive, but fear crept in regardless—fear that this was all life would be for him now. Alone. In darkness. Just because he was born with a power he never wanted.

The dark pressed in on him, choking oxygen out of the moldy air.

So still, so quiet, everywhere.

Was Cyrus okay? Would they ever see each other again?

He prayed that his friend had fled, had gotten as far away from Draethvyle as possible.

Aken had made a real mess of things. He could be out there helping Cy right now, if he hadn't lost control of his power.

Regret after regret swam to the forefront of his mind.

Mom, Dad, Sabe, Cyrus…he'd failed them all. Instead of becoming the greatest Draev Guardian, he would live imprisoned far away.

Perhaps that was the only destiny a Scourgeblood could ever hope to have.

"He's a monster. Lock him up before he kills us!" The student's words swirled in the suffocating black of the dungeon.

The madman scratched at the locked cage door inside his mind, whispering *Punish them, punish them*.

Aken fought to block it out.

A distant door creaked, and a faint shaft of light from the stairwell made the cell bars and stone surfaces suddenly visible.

Footsteps drew near.

A sconce glowed to life beside the cell door. Aken blinked, and a familiar face took shape. "Quite a gloomy place down here. Are you all right?"

"Nephryte…?"

The door unlocked and swung open. "I'm sorry I wasn't there to keep this from happening," said Mentor Nephryte, and Aken leaped to his feet.

Aken paused at the edge of the cell frame. "What happened to Cyrus? Is he okay?" He couldn't mask the desperation in his tone.

The Mentor nodded. "He'll be fine. In fact, it seems he won the Duel."

Aken's face went wide, and he sunk to his knees in relief for a moment. "Really? He won? He's okay?"

Nephryte's hand gently grasped his shoulder. "Are *you* okay?"

Aken realized he was on the verge of tears. He rose, embarrassed, but Nephryte wrapped an arm around him in something like a hug.

"I wouldn't have let them lock you up down here, if I'd known."

Aken wiped his nose. "I'm dangerous. Nobody wanted me here, and now I know why. I've been an idiot to think I could live normally, to think I could become a Draev."

Nephryte's arm tightened around his shoulders. "I brought you here, and Harlow is better because of it. Don't give up just because you made one mistake," he told him. "With practice, you'll learn to keep your blood Ability under control.

"But you know, Aken-Shou, becoming a Draev Guardian is something that comes from the heart. From the deep well of love inside you. The love that makes you willing to lay down your life for others. As long as you have that," he ruffled Aken's hair, "even a Scourgeblood can become a heroic Draev."

Aken considered that, then pushed free from his arm. "I don't blame you anymore—*well*, not as much. You may be a hero, but you can't be there to save everybody. I know you would've saved my parents if you could have. I just…needed someone, something, to blame."

A sad smile crossed Nephryte's face. "I appreciate that, Aken-Shou. Come on, let's get out of this miserable pit."

Reaching the top of the stairwell, sunshine poured over Aken, warming his skin. He breathed in the free air through his nose.

High above, a flock of swallows soared past on a swift gust, reminding him of that long ago day as a child perched on a rooftop, full of dreams as he watched the birds soar.

37

Doctor Zushil jolted in surprise when Mamoru suddenly showed up in Uptown's infirmary, bearing Cyrus unconscious in his arms. They brought the half-human into a care room, and Zushil went to work on the injuries— Healing an ugly bruise the size of a fist on her lower back, raw cuts and scrapes on her shoulder, elbows and knees, and another bruise that had nearly fractured her ribs.

Zushil placed his hands lightly over each spot, using his *essence* to sense for damage and to transfer Healing super-cells into her, carefully repairing muscle and tissue, and to strengthen injured rib bones.

His attention shifted to her wrists lastly, and the white scarring that encircled them. He concentrated on the scars, sensing them, before transferring the vemparic super-cells through his *essence* to Heal.

There was no change in the scars.

He tried several times, but the scars refused to stay Healed and kept coming back.

"Strange…" He frowned to himself, then pulled out a series of plates and equipment for an X-ray, to make sure everything was in proper order according to human anatomy.

After a series of clicks and whirs as the equipment did its

work, he removed the images and held one up to the light. His glasses nearly slipped off his nose in shock...

Master Nephryte arrived to check in on the half-human minutes later, and he cast a glance at the folder Zushil had just stored the images inside. "Anything to report?" he asked.

"This." Zushil handed him the folder, and watched as Nephryte examined the images that, instead of showing a detailed skeleton and organs, showed a bright light where the chest should be—so bright that only the farthest parts of the body could be made out.

"What does this mean?"

Zushil shrugged his shoulders, arms akimbo. "I've never seen anything of the like. A well of *essence* energy that's more powerful than any of ours combined. It shouldn't be possible, especially for a half-human."

Concern knitted Nephryte's brow. "And yet she tires, has limits, and cannot fully use her Ability."

"Like I said, it shouldn't be possible...and won't be for long," Zushil stated, and Nephryte's head snapped up. He elaborated: "Her body cannot sustain containing whatever this *power* is. It's eating her away, slowly. I suspect the condition of her wrists is merely the beginning sign of this, and is why they can't be Healed."

Nephryte studied the folder's contents for several long moments, then handed it back. "Keep this secret. I don't want any more attention drawn to Cyrus than she already has."

"You and your secrets! I will not allow myself to fall into trouble with Principal Han again. I need this job, and I refuse to do anything that could jeopardize it."

"Fine, fine." Nephryte waved his hand. "But let me be the one to tell Han."

Zushil shoved his glasses farther on his nose. "Cyrus herself has a right to know, as well."

Nephryte paced the room, his bent index finger tapping his chin, as he often did when in deep thought. "Yes…but I'm concerned what this could mean—what this energy could possibly be."

〜つ

"…Hnn-*nnn*…"

Cyrus's eyelids cracked open. She squinted against a bright window light. She didn't recognize the pillow and blankets around her, all white. Had she passed out after the Duel? She vaguely recalled feeling an icy tingle like that of ice cubes traveling underneath her skin, fanning out through her body, little icy rivers running along her limbs, ribs, chest… Like something Healing her? She blinked the rest of the way awake.

"Hey, buddy. How you feeling?"

She sat up and turned her neck; the room was in an infirmary. Aken was lounging in a chair as if he'd been there a long time. He rose.

"You were sleeping deep—deep as a frog on a log in a wine bog."

She swung her legs over the edge of the bed. Surprisingly her body didn't hurt, though her wrists did sting with pain. "Oh shut up," she said as she wrapped her arms around him in a friendly hug. He hugged her back, and she could feel his body shudder slightly from held-back tears.

"You almost got yourself killed." His cheek rested against the top of her head. "Why would you do that? I told you to leave."

"Some friend I'd be if I had. I knew it was the right thing to do, something I needed to do." His chest rose and fell against her cheek.

"But you could've used your request to the king for yourself, to get citizenship and keep training here," he protested. "That was the whole reason you tried out for the

Duel, in the first place."

"But the reason you were in trouble was because of me; I couldn't not do anything. And besides, it was worth seeing the shock on people's faces when I won."

"Well…don't go risking your life for me again. Next time, it's my turn."

Cyrus pulled away, and he flashed a smile. "I'd rather neither of us have to risk our lives," she said, then yawned. "My head aches…I think I could sleep for a month."

Aken leaned against the bed. "Not as much as Doughboy's head is, I bet! I hear that was one amazing fight. Wish I could've seen it!" He grinned. "You gave Denim's pride a real slap in the face for treating you that way—acting like you're less of a person just because you're different. Arrogant toad," he scoffed.

"You hated humans, too," she reminded.

Aken's scoffing took a stumble. "Well, I…*erm*…I learned better."

She wanted to laugh, but there was something she had to know first. "What happened after? Do you know if Denim kept his word or not?"

Aken's shoulders shook with a chuckle. "He was sure sore about it, but he finally admitted to provoking me." He fist-bumped her arm lightly. "I'm proud of you, Cy. You did great."

Her cheeks dimpled and she looked away. "Thanks, but I only won because Lord God showed me how. Who knew something I learned in Elvenstone would prove useful?"

Aken chuckled. "Now you're being a humble bumblebee."

"A what?" She suppressed a grin. Winning the Duel had been like finding the vempar half of herself, the gray half that had been hidden away all these years. If only Mother were here, she'd…

"Oops—a bruise was missed."

She flinched as Aken's hand rose to her face, one finger brushing down her cheek, Healing a bruise there. She flushed red.

Should she tell him her final secret? A part of her wanted to. But a cautious feeling kept telling her to wait, whispering that it was important she keep silent about being a girl. Averting her gaze from Aken, she reluctantly heeded the warning and closed her mouth.

Aken drew back his hand. "You look sad," he said with a question.

She gave a nervous start. "I'm just tired." She grabbed a hand mirror on the bedside table and combed her fingers through the messy nest her hair had become, then looked down at the drab infirmary garments she wore. Who'd changed her clothes? How was she clean and not bloody? It was disturbing to think someone could do all of that without her knowing, even if it was just the infirmary staff.

A heavy curtain that acted as the door to the room *whooshed* aside suddenly, and Dr. Zushil crossed the space to her bed.

He stuck a thermometer in her mouth before she could make a sound. "It's good you're awake. We have much to discuss."

Something odd in his tone made her anxious. He checked the thermometer, "Body temperature normal."

"What do you mean, *discuss?*"

Zushil took a seat in the chair near the bed and leaned so that his elbows rested on his knees, his fingers steepled. "Aken-Shou, would you step out for a moment?"

Aken looked uncertain but made his way to the curtain door, slipping outside.

Dr. Zushil cleared his throat. "While restoring your health, something abnormal was discovered."

A chill ran up Cyrus's arms and she braced herself.

"Every humanoid has a core at the center of their being

made up of *essence*. It varies from race to race, and most cannot access the energy directly, if at all, except for Draevs. Here's an example of what it typically looks like." The doctor handed her a slick paper bearing the X-ray image of a body. She noted the white dot like a little sun in the chest. "And this," he handed her another image, "is of yours."

A bright light almost blotted out the shape of her body, a sun that was more than ten times greater.

Her jaw fell slack.

"A core of *essence* like this should not be possible for any lifeform," said the doctor. "I regret to be the bearer of bad news, student Cyrus, but whatever this energy is, it's slowly killing you. Currently it only affects your wrists, but with time it will spread and affect more of you. I don't know how long this will take—could be until you reach adulthood, if you're lucky; but your organs will eventually shut down, and you'll…"

"…I'll die."

"To put it bluntly, yes."

Cyrus bunched the bed sheet in her hands, then drew the sheet close, leaving the glossy images at her feet. "There's nothing you can do?"

"Unfortunately, no. But I can help to manage the symptoms." Dr. Zushil placed a bag of little stoppered bottles on the table by the bed. "Medication to help manage the pain and any swelling. As more symptoms appear, we'll deal with those. I can also prescribe better fingerless gloves for you that will act as sturdier guards for your wrists."

Cyrus nodded numbly. She didn't register when Master Nephryte had entered the room until his hand touched her shoulder, then she looked up.

"Let's get you back to your dorm room, where you can be more comfortable," the Master said. She stood and allowed him to guide her out. "Don't fall into grim thoughts of death just yet, Cyrus. None of us can foresee the future, and it may be that in time we'll find a solution for you."

She gave that some thought as they exited the infirmary building. Lord God had brought her this far, and she knew there had to be a reason even if the answer seemed invisible now. She couldn't afford to worry about the future—there were enough things to worry about in the present.

It did make her wonder, though: What was this great energy in the core of her being, and had it always been there?

Once back at the dorm, Aken was already at the door waiting. He didn't ask about what the doctor said, but she could tell he was itching to know. Master Nephryte left promptly, and Aken perched on the edge of the bed beside her in silence.

Neither of them spoke for a long moment. And then,

Knock-knock-knock!

They both turned their heads sharply. "Come in?" Cyrus said as the door swung open.

A nose like a bird beak poked in, then talon hands shoved the door further. Mr. Pueginn, the principal's assistant, bobbed his head and flashed unnaturally white teeth from his dark gray face.

"Student Cyrus," Pueginn said with a voice that spoke through his wide nostrils, "Your presence is required in Principal Han's office."

Worry iced down her spine.

Pueginn's gaze fixed on her, as if she should be up and running that instant. "And I do mean *now*," he said when she didn't move.

Cyrus barely stood before the man grabbed her elbow and pulled her hurriedly along. "I'm sure the office will still exist if we're a few seconds late," she protested.

"Watch it, Penguin, Cy's just recovered!" Aken called out.

Down a stairwell and crossing tiled hallways, Cyrus soon

found herself steered to a halt before a set of twin mahogany doors that reached as high as the ceiling—Draevensett's coat-of-arms at the center, and twin horned lions bearing wings framed the woodwork.

Assistant Pueginn yanked one double door open, quick as a bird, and shoved Cyrus through.

The door clanked shut behind her.

38

Pueginn turned on heels too small for his body, humming nasally as he went off to his next order of business. Aken caught up and halted before the tall doors. He huffed and resorted to pacing the stretch of hallway, worrying what would become of his friend. After overhearing what Dr. Zushil told Cyrus from behind the curtain, his chest couldn't stop aching.

Clep-clak clep-clak. A second set of footsteps echoed the silver and white marble tiles. His ear twitched, recognizing the gait.

There wasn't much else to do besides worry and wait, so he tiptoed forward to where the hallway curved, leading down a set of steps to meet with adjoining halls. There, he spied Nephryte, midnight blue cape swishing as he entered a set of grand doors with the engraved word "Library" overhead.

Stopping one of the doors from closing all the way with his shoe, Aken crept inside and down a little staircase to the floor. It was a cavernous room, rising three levels and full of branching roomlets. Among the countless rows of bookcases, shelves, and air-tight glass resided the majority of Draeth's literary collection. Newer books filled the accessible spaces, while those very old were kept tucked behind locked glass doors inside well-ventilated roomlets.

Careful as a heron stalking a fish, Aken approached the man from behind. Clay birds readied in the palm of his hand.

"Did you finish your homework?" Nephryte spoke without looking.

Aken stumbled. "Do you have eyes in the back of your head?" He pocketed the clay.

The Mentor smirked. "Maybe I do."

Aken looked to the ceiling. "Everybody's got a weakness. I just have to find yours."

Nephryte thunked the top of his head with a book. "*Baka.* No loud talk in the library."

"I'm not a *baka.* Bak's the only *baka.*" Aken rubbed his head.

"If you don't have questions about homework or something else worthwhile, I have better things to do than play cat-and-mouse with you." Nephryte turned down a book aisle.

Tempted to say something snarky, Aken instead asked, "Are they gonna let Cyrus stay?"

Nephryte's lips parted, but then he halted whatever he'd been about to say.

"Cy proved he's one of us. What more do they want?" Aken protested. "I won't let them lay a finger on—!"

Nephryte pinched his lips shut, silencing him. "Cyrus is a part of Harlow, and Harlow is my responsibility," said Nephryte. "Leave matters to me, and don't worry."

Aken pulled away, arms crossed and foot tapping. "Not worry? All I can do is worry! What if I use Scourgeblood power by accident again? What if I really am a monster and can't stop myself? What if Cy dies from the weird energy inside him? What if—"

Nephryte pinched his mouth shut again.

"You're making me dizzy. Tell me, did you mean to use your blood power?" asked Nephryte. Aken shook his head.

"Then you can't be a monster. A true monster hurts and kills on purpose. That isn't you, Aken-Shou." He released Aken's mouth and flicked his forehead.

Aken grumbled, but deep inside he was glad to hear those words: *That isn't you, Aken-Shou.*

"But do work on restraining that temper of yours—I've a feeling that's what flamed your power. And as for all these other worries, worrying gets you nowhere fast, but it will give you a massive headache. When something is out of your control, what is it you should do instead?"

Aken chewed his lip and crossed his arms tighter. "Pray—that's what you always say."

"And patiently look for the solution, too. Lord God won't help you if you sit around doing nothing. But for now, wait and see how things will play out. The king has asked that Cyrus be allowed to stay, and I doubt anyone is willing to go against what the king wishes."

"...Fine."

"That's not what you're really worried about, is it?" Nephryte confronted him at eye-level. "Were you eavesdropping on Dr. Zushil's conversation with Cyrus?"

Aken's mouth twisted to the side.

Nephryte sighed. "That was a private talk. I trust you'll keep the information to yourself?" Aken nodded. "I understand you're worried about your friend, but don't jump to conclusions. You can't let thoughts eat away at you."

"Fine, fine." Aken heaved a breath, letting his mind relax. The scent of old books in the air was somehow soothing. "I've been wanting to ask something, and I know it's out-of-the-blue, but...you know a lot of stuff about other races, right?"

Nephryte nodded slowly.

"Well, do other races have—um—does their blood taste different?"

Nephryte's brow furrowed. "I suppose so, yes. Why?"

"Eh, nothing, it's nothing. It's not illegal to be curious, is it?"

The Mentor cocked an eyebrow. "Are you curious about Cyrus?"

Heat rushed to Aken's cheeks. "I... I once Healed his finger, and his blood tasted sweet—abnormally sweet. Kind of freaked me out."

A dark shadow fell over the Mentor's face. "You should never put blood in your mouth, Aken-Shou! Even if it is only to Heal. It's—" He paused to inhale, and brushed back his bangs. "It's not always safe, especially for someone so young as you. Don't ever do it again. Understand?"

Taken aback by the outburst, Aken avoided meeting his gaze.

Nephryte's emotions cleared and he straightened, all calm again. "Finish your homework, Aken-Shou." Nephryte's boots continued clacking down the path toward the library's roomlets, cape swishing.

Aken's stare followed. "He's never said that before. I've never heard anybody say blood is dangerous." He exhaled through this teeth, then moved to exit the way he'd come.

Nephryte wasn't one to lie, so why did he feel like the Mentor was hiding something?

～

"Cyrus Sole." A deep voice echoed off the rosewood walls and arched niches inside the principal's office. Cyrus tried to swallow but her tongue stuck to the roof of her mouth.

Shelves everywhere displayed an assortment of exotic beetles, frozen in time. She eyed one specimen: a horned green beetle the size of her head.

A bay window at the far back let in muted light, highlighting a mahogany desk with legs carved like a giant insect, and two rows of chairs either side against the walls.

A scent of age and musk hung in the room, quite like the gray mustached vempar within it.

Beard reaching to his belt, it swayed side to side as the principal glided across the floor toward her. He bent his towering frame. She'd yet to see a vempar this old. Years of knowledge and strife dwelt behind the elder's deep wrinkles and sienna-brown eyes. His bony frame and hands flexed, strong and capable, as he regarded her.

"Y-yes, Principal, sir?" she asked, then jumped when he chortled.

"*Heh-heh-heg.* Your movements are as cautious as a swan," he mused, and stroked his hidden chin.

Swan? Strange analogy to use. Why not beetle? He seemed to like collecting beetles. She inched sideways from a blue specimen's long tusks.

The elder's knobby finger pointed, almost touching her nose, and her eyes crossed staring at it. "I was suspicious about a human possessing the gift. It seemed like a clever ruse for a spy, except that you've proven your Ability is real. Tell me, which of your parents was vempar?"

"My mother, Nancy," Cyrus replied.

"And she had Ability?"

Cyrus searched but couldn't decipher what his intentions might be. His question lingered, and she quickly nodded.

"You wouldn't think to betray her by betraying us, your vempar half?"

She shook her head.

"Or do you favor the human in you?"

She shook her head again from side to side. "I will favor what's right, and I won't betray my comrades."

"Well, that's not quite the answer I asked for. I can't tell whose side you're on based on that."

She didn't know what to say. Her gaze focused on the curly end of his beard, until his strange chortle came again.

"Your battle with Doughboy was quite something; a Duel

to be remembered. You have the makings of a Draev." He straightened, his fingers drumming against his robed chest.

"Either way!" Principal Han said so suddenly that she jumped, elbow bumping a cluttered shelf. The principal studied her. "I'm usually a good judge of character, Cyrus Sole. You deceived us about your race, but I sense no malice or evil intentions in your heart. And Master Nephryte seems to trust you—he has vouched on your behalf. I do wish you had come to us openly about your heritage, but I understand that fear often makes mistakes."

Cyrus rubbed her wrists and tried not to let her hopes rise.

Han combed two fingers down his moustache thoughtfully. "The King has granted Aken permission to remain a student, as you've requested, and he's asked that the same permission be granted to you, as well. Though, if I detect any falsehood in you, I could object." He paused, and she panicked. "You were willing to sacrifice your freedom to save Aken-Shou, and for that reason, and for my excellent judge of character, I won't object."

The words washed over Cyrus like a flood of relief and mixed emotions. She could stay on as a student!

"Not everyone in this city will be pleased, and you'll have to be very careful to give no one reason to accuse you of anything," Principal Han warned. "You must master your Ability and grow strong."

"But, Principal sir, won't the D.G. League be against me staying?"

Principal Han readjusted some of the beetles that had been jostled by her elbow. "Against it or not, they have no say in the running of this school. I was once the League's Grandmaster, you know, before I retired and took on this role."

He pointed to her gloved wrists. "Your Master told me about the doctor's diagnosis. Oh don't look so worried, I can keep a secret," he assured. "We'll try to help you as best we can, and keep it just between the four of us." He patted her head. "Such a curious name for a child: Cyrus, after the Swan constellation."

She scrunched her nose, wondering what that had to do with anything.

"Tell me, do you know the legend of the Swan Princess?"

"Yes, a little bit."

"They say the Pure Light trapped within her body causes her to be brought back to this world, time and time again, reborn." He spoke quietly, as if it were a secret. "She could be anywhere. In this kingdom, in this very room, even as we speak."

Cyrus glanced left then right—it didn't look like anybody else besides the two of them were here. "Do you believe the legend?"

"I'm old enough to believe that *anything* is possible." His eyes twinkled. "But that would mean the old Emperor is real, too, and that he will one day return to find the Swan and finish what he started."

His gaze drifted upward, lost in some distant thought, and Cyrus watched him, chewing her lip in the silence.

Han shook himself awake, then took her thin right hand in both of his large, bony palms. "It is both concerning and a wondrous mystery how such a powerful energy came to be inside you."

Cyrus shrugged uncomfortably. "Yeah, it's a mystery."

His moustache rose with what might have been a smile.

Releasing her hand, Principal Han made a shooing gesture. "Enough with my prattling then; I won't bore you any longer. I'm sure you've much that you're eager to get back to. We old folk can be dreadfully boring."

She tugged one of the tall doors, pulling it open the rest of the way with her foot and elbow. "It was nice to officially meet you, Principal Han." She flashed a smile before exiting, and the door clicked shut. That had to be the strangest talk she'd ever had with a grown-up.

Swan Princess, what did that have to do with anything?

At least she was allowed to stay in Draevensett.

39

The evening sun was a bright orb in the low sky, though dark clouds were slowly rolling in for battle. Cyrus and Aken lay sprawled on the grass of Cherryblossom Park, pencils in hand, scribbling through homework.

The inner reaches of the park became thicker woods the farther you went. Most people didn't venture there, and they missed the tucked away meadow dotted with wildflowers.

A stream meandered nearby, and a pettirosso trilled merrily. It was as if she'd escaped from civilization.

"Math, oh my aching *fangs*," Aken whined, forehead hitting the ground repeatedly. "I can't figure this stuff out. Why do they call these square-roots? There's nothing root or square about them!"

"Oh my aching ears. If you don't stop whining, I'll box those fangs out of your head."

Aken squinted, mock-shrinking away from her. "You're getting scarier by the day."

Cyrus hid a laugh, then turned more serious. "I hope you won't shun Hercule for what he did."

The humor paused as he regarded her.

"Just don't, please; it won't make anything better. I'd rather leave it to the Master."

He sighed and turned away. "I wasn't planning to. Sure, I'm mad at him, but if he's really sorry, I can let it go."

Cyrus stared at him, speechless. "You'd forgive him, just like that?"

"Why do you look so surprised?" Aken mumbled. Then he asked, "Will you forgive your family for how they treated you?"

Her mouth slackened at the sudden mention. Could she forgive them?

"Have you forgiven yours?" she asked him instead.

He nodded. "Mom and Dad each had their own issues, but you know, they provided a roof over my head and food on the table—and that's more than some kids have ever had. I wish they were still here."

They rolled over on their backs to gaze up at the gathering clouds, and she thought about his answer.

Aken cupped his hands behind his head, and she propped the back of her head on his shoulder. He pointed at a cloud that resembled Professor Kotetsu.

Cyrus found her eyelids starting to droop, drifting into a doze from the warm sun and the sound of Aken's heartbeat like a rhythmic lullaby in her ear.

The breathing of a vempar was slow and deep, chest rising and falling like rolling waves in a sea of calm. The rhythm reminded her of Mother—conjuring images of her holding Cyrus to her chest, rocking her to sleep. No solid memories, but a familiar comfort.

She silently wished they could stay this way, forever.

Plip…Plop… Plip-plop plip-plop.

Her forehead felt wet.

She rubbed it with the back of a hand, opening one eye in time for a thick raindrop to *plop* right inside.

She jolted up.

Thick drops descended in a sudden torrent, and Aken snatched her hand, his hair and shirt already plastered.

"Run!"

They hurried and laughed, stomping through puddles and a rain rivulet as they exited the park, oblivious to overhangs they could have hidden under to wait out the storm.

He skipped with her, arm-in-arm, up a cobbled street.

"Rain comes down from the mountain top
Raindrops fall, ker-plop ker-plop,
The mists will rise to whisk you up,
Hurry on home while you can…

The brewing clouds turn day to night
Roaring loud the thunder's might
Pounding the ground as giants fight,
Hurry on home while you can…

Lightning spears the heart of the sky
Splitting cracks vast, far and high
Shattering glass behind your eyes,
Hurry on home while you can…

Rain comes down from the mountain top
Hurry on home while you can…

It's coming and it won't be stopped
Hurry on home while you can…"

"Better watch out, Aken, or another shoe will come flying at you," Cyrus warned.

Back inside Draevensett's shelter, Cyrus was toweling off her hair in her room when she discovered an envelope on the bed.

The tidy script read:

*I thought you might appreciate
having this. She was a dedicated
student and a compassionate soul,
not much unlike yourself.*

~Principal

She held her breath as she opened the flap and reached inside, pulling out a single photograph.

It looked old, the fringes long since yellowed. In the picture was a group of students gathered shoulder-to-shoulder, most of them boys. But one girl stood out, her wavy hair dark in the black-and-white image, a color she knew must be red.

"Mother…"

Something dripped onto the photo and she wiped it off, holding it away from the tears.

She studied the petite face, the smile with a dent in the lower lip, the brightness in her young eyes. And for the first time, Cyrus's memories became a shade clearer.

She held the photo to her chest, and didn't move until Aken came for her.

After changing soaked clothes for dry ones, Aken sat on the study room rug before the lit fireplace, drying his hair and chatting with Bak and Zartin about the day's events. Cy drew the curtains back to watch the rainstorm.

"Dude," Bak was saying, "You were all alone in that creepy dungeon. What's it like? No one's been down there for ages!"

Aken snorted, ignoring the chill that ran up his arms. "Who cares about that? Cy just won the Festival Duel. That's all anybody should be talking about." He jerked his head to the side defensively.

The room fell into an uncomfortable silence. The others glanced at him then pretended to focus on something else.

Aken regretted it; he didn't mean to dampen everyone's mood.

He got an idea: he scrubbed at his hair, making it part and arch similarly to Nephryte's, then put on a calm, serious façade. "Young ones," he imitated the Master's tone, "You better behave yourselves and be good little students, or no story-time for you. I'll send you to bed!"

Bak blinked for a second before catching on, then he fell over in a fit of giggles, rolling on the rug. Cy doubled over, Zartin hid his face inside the blue hat, and Mamoru openly laughed. Even Lykale chuckled at his chemistry book.

"Aken-Shooou!" he continued the act. "That's right. I draw out the *Shou* part of your name when I'm really upset with you. You are a brat!"

Aken flipped his hair back over a shoulder like some fashion model. "You must mature and become like me. Your hair needs to *flow* and *wave*, like mine. See how gorgeous and luscious it is? How it flutters in the breeze?"

By now, everyone was laughing themselves sick.

Then they suddenly froze, staring beyond Aken at something.

Aken raised an eyebrow at them. "What, it's not working for you? How about if I gracefully glide across the floor as I walk?" He slid along on his socks. "Reminds you of some ballerina, doesn't he?"

He missed the vocal grunt behind him.

"Or should I swoon my undying love for the Lady Seren-Rose?" Cupping hands over heart, and gazing up at the ceiling starry-eyed, Aken lamented: "Oh Seren-Rose, Seren-Rose, how I pine for thee! My love, my life, you are in my dreams—even when it is day—and lo, how I longeth for you-eth. But no!" He raised fists high to the ceiling sky, a soul in torment. "Alas, my love, we cannot be together!

Because we are both Masters in the same school, and I guess it would be weird or something—I don't really know the reason why!" He hung his head in defeat. "But what I *do* know is that you will always be with me in my head. As I perish from broken-heart syndrome, I will be thinking of you…in my head."

His voice lowered to a whisper, kneeling, "…In my head." Several seconds passed to allow the final words sufficient echo through the room, before three sharp claps sounded behind him.

Clap—clap—clap! "What a talented actor and drama king you are," said a too calm voice.

Aken visibly cringed, blood draining from his face.

"Aken-Shooou."

With a yelp Aken dove behind a sofa for protection. Nephryte's gaze quivered like a boiling river that would soon melt him, and the floor along with him.

"You are a brat, indeed." Nephryte lifted a finger.

"*Uwah—!*"

Aken found himself hanging upside down in the air. "Gah! Lemme go—*lemme go!*" Limbs flailing, he tried in vain to right himself.

"I am not a ballerina." Nephryte's brow twitched. "And I am not some love-sick character from a romance drama. I and Master Seren-Rose are childhood friends. *Friends.*"

"Sure, sure." Aken folded his arms and grinned deviously—an odd feat upside down.

"And furthermore," Nephryte fixed his rebuke on the entire room, "I hope that each of you realizes the seriousness of what could have happened today, that Cyrus could have been killed. You should have come to me, and let me resolve the matter, instead of letting Cyrus risk his life."

Every head hung, reprimanded, and Aken resorted to swimming through the air like a belly-up fish.

"I know you felt there was no other choice. But never do

something like that again. Ever. Instead, you come talk to me—that's what I'm here for."

⸏

Hercule rolled his eyes, while leaning against the door frame outside the study room, eavesdropping. Normally he would go in, find a spot on the rug for his school work, and brood while tuning out everyone as they whined and bickered over the lamest of things. But now things were different. Cyrus was in there, and it was too obvious *he* was the one who'd let the half-human's secret out.

Cyrus had lied to them, which was wrong, but putting Cyrus's life at risk was also wrong—and all so Hercule could hide his own dark secret. The gravity of what he'd done hadn't fully hit home until he saw the redhead fighting for his life. He hadn't wanted Cyrus to die—he wanted him thrown out of the school, but not to die...

Hercule sucked in a breath before daring to creak open the door, just wide enough to poke his head through.

Students were required to let their Master know before spending the night some place other than the dorms. He didn't want to break a rule on top of the trouble he'd already caused.

"Master Nephryte." He tried to keep his tone passive and out of earshot from the others.

It failed. All heads turned in his direction, a mix of condemning frowns.

"I'll be at Dragonsbane Mansion for the night," Hercule said more clearly. "My father wishes to see my latest grade report."

"Again, hm?" Master Nephryte considered, tapping his chin. "Why the man won't simply let me mail the reports to him, I'll never understand. Such an overbearing and controlling—" He stopped himself short, and shook his head. "Very well," he dismissed with a gesture, "Be on your way."

With a slight bow of the head, Hercule withdrew.

Cyrus tried not to grin as Aken continued dancing upside down around the ceiling, once Hercule had left.

She decided to take this relatively quiet moment to ask Master Nephryte something that had been bothering her for a long while now, since she'd first walked the city's streets. "Master, why is slavery allowed here?"

She noticed the others pause to listen.

Master Nephryte inhaled as if it were a heavy subject. "As you know, Draev squads are sent out each week to harvest—gathering *essence* from whoever they can, in order to keep the Vemparic Kingdom alive," he began.

His fingers laced together upon his crossed knees. "While searching for people to harvest from, if those they find resist and pose a danger, then Draevs are allowed to use different measures."

Cyrus cocked her head.

"It can become a serious problem if too many escape before *essence* can be collected. For this reason, those who resist or flee can be brought back here as captives to make up for the loss."

Cyrus shook her head. "So you're saying that non-vempars are supposed to obey, not run away or fight, or they'll be taken as slaves?"

"Basically, yes. And personally, I hate the method. It breeds hatred between our race and others. But we have no other solution, and it's getting harder and harder to harvest *essence*. Towns are stronger, and not as many people venture far from their homes; and when they do, they hire Argos for protection."

Master Nephryte bent a finger against his chin. "I don't blame them for wanting to protect themselves, but the less we harvest, the less *essence* we have to share around, and the more danger the civilized world will be in.

"A famine in Draeth would spell disaster across the continents. It would force vempars to abandon the kingdom and harvest for themselves. Vempars would go back to the old way of living, to the Time of Wandering. Imagine desperate Ability users and starving vempars running rampant—no more laws or boundaries or a king to hold them back? A nightmare, that's what it'd be. All of the progress we've made up to now would be for nothing."

Cyrus gripped her arm, Bakoa clasped his feet, and Zartanian huddled further inside the shelter of his blue coat.

"Those are the worries of the future we face," Master Nephryte surmised. "So, to answer your question on slavery, Cyrus: Because it is harder to collect *essence* today, many feel it's easier and more efficient to bring back captives—some to sell as slaves, and most to keep for the city's *essence* reservoirs."

Cyrus's fingers left red marks on her arm as she considered the problem. "But, you said they only take captives if too many escape or resist, right?"

"Yes, that's supposed to be the case. But that rule is abused," he acknowledged. "I've tried gathering evidence for the Grandmaster and king to take notice, but the problem of possible famine is not the only one.

"The upper classes want slaves, simple as that. I don't know of a single lord, lady or moneybag whose house doesn't have a handful." He massaged the lines creasing his forehead. "No, that's not entirely true. House Cuore doesn't have slaves, but that is only because of the kind nature of Professor Kotetsu and his little sister. They hire their servants. Other than *them*, though, I don't know of anyone."

Master Nephryte closed his eyes for a brief moment. "There are Draevs who make false accusations, claiming a faeryn tried to attack them or a human posed a danger—lies, all of it. Only Argos pose a real danger. Not these children and young people they keep dragging in. As if a child could be dangerous, *tch*! How many have been made into slaves purely for the rich and powerful's greed?"

The Master let his hand fall from his forehead, gaze fixed on the fireplace embers. "Aristocrats are bribing certain Draevs into capturing slaves for them—giving them their *shopping list*. I know it's happening, even if I can't prove it."

A sad heaviness permeated the air. Zartanian gripped his hat in his pale hands, and timidly murmured, "But I thought Draev Guardians were supposed to be the good guys?"

Master Nephryte smoothed away any trace of anger from his voice before reassuring him. "Draevs are heroes to their own kind, willing to sacrifice their lives so that our kingdom can live in peace. But not many care for the well-being of non-vempars."

Cyrus drew her knees up to her chin.

He continued, "Hating a person for no reason but that they're born in a different place and race from you…in the end, you hurt yourself with that way of thinking. We are all Lord God's creation, and He will punish those who hate."

There was a *thud* as Aken dropped from the ceiling. "I've got my work cut out for me, then!" Aken straightened, now free. He jabbed a thumb at his chest, "Once I become the greatest Draev Guardian, I'm gonna change people's way of thinking, and solve this harvest problem."

The group looked at him, full of skepticism.

He pointed to Cyrus, "But I'll need the greatest Half-human Draev's help to pull it off."

A laugh bubbled out of her. "Sure thing, if I survive that long. Changing the world sounds *so* easy." She made a face.

Dear diary,

It's been a crazy day. I still can't believe I won the Festival Duel. Maybe I can be brave enough to become a Draev Guardian, after all? Lord God has given me an Ability that I know I should use, and I want to help others.

I haven't had much confidence in myself, in who I am. I've been hiding behind a mask without realizing it. It's hard to change, it's hard to break out and just be me. I was never allowed to be me back in Elvenstone.

The pen paused as Cyrus thought.

Did Dad or Heily miss her, stop to think of her? What were they doing at this moment?

She didn't forgive them for their cruelty, but she realized that the anger—the hate she'd held inside—was fading.

If Aken could let go of his resentment toward his parents, then so could she. She made the choice to let the anger go, and be open to forgiveness if a day ever came when they regretted their actions.

Let's see, what else has happened? Oh, Dr. Zushil offered to prescribe me medicine that would help me look and sound more like a boy. But I said no. I gave myself a chance, and now I like the boyish girl that I am.

I don't need to change—I'm a girl that's not very girly, and that's okay. I can be that. Even as I grow up and physically change more and more, it doesn't mean who I am has to change with it. I'll always be me.

My body is fine the way God designed it, even if I complain— everybody complains about themselves a little bit, right? I think it just takes time to grow comfortable with yourself.

That said, I wish I could stop pretending to be a boy altogether, but something keeps warning me to stay quiet. A voice in my head telling me it's very important I keep pretending.

I don't know why...but for now, I'll listen.

I just hope I'll get the chance to reach adulthood and make a difference here. I don't understand this strange energy that's eating away at my body, but at least I have an answer for what's been causing the pain.

Simply knowing that, is a relief.

40

Hercule buttoned up his finely cut ochre coat against the rain as he exited the school's main doors, out to the drive where a motor carriage hummed, waiting for him.

Father insisted the son of a nobleman should always look the part, wearing the best of attire at all times. Even during E.M. training, no matter how hot it was or how much he sweated, he must always look his best.

Seated inside the carriage, Hercule flipped out a hand mirror to check that his pearl-gray hair and countenance was presentable. He didn't want a repeat of last time, when a windy day had tousled him messily and Father gave a lecture on how his son's appearance reflected on the family House name. Hercule exhaled sharply, and watched as the streets glided by.

It wasn't long before the carriage pulled up to Dragonsbane Mansion: an impressive structure adorned with balconies, balustrades, fluted columns and intricate windows. A beauty that smelled of wealth, complete with a wide driveway circling round the front yard pond—a round, marble-lined pool speckled with lily pads, pink lotuses, and colorful fish. A fountain of green marble rose in the pond's proud center, carved in the image of a woman running a dragon through with her blade—the representation of their Dragonsbane ancestor, one of the Twelve Legendary Knights.

The back yard sprawled beyond: part garden paradise, and the rest lush field and a natural pond, running to meet with Cherryblossom Park's forest off in the distance. The mansion was a lovely place to behold on the outside. But the inside was cold, the people indifferent. Very un-homelike, not that Hercule knew what *homelike* should be.

Hercule waited until the footman opened the carriage door, holding high an umbrella for him to duck beneath. "Greetings, milord," spoke the suited servant. "His Grace Dragonsbane awaits in his study, when you are ready."

"Understood, Footman Vayn." Hercule followed under the umbrella, careful to keep his hair from frizzing.

Once through the main doors, embellished with the Dragonsbane crest, in the entrance hall he handed over his coat to the waiting head butler. "Good evening, milord."

Without a reply, Hercule stalked up the grand staircase. When Father called, you didn't waste time; the Head of the House must never be kept waiting.

Sliding the grade report from an inside pocket, he stopped before the gilt-framed doors. He knocked, then entered at a stiff "Come in."

"My grade report for this month, sir." Hercule walked the length of the study, lined high with books on one side, old family portraits and tall windows on the other. He halted at the grand desk, whose legs were dragon limbs and sides chiseled scales.

Hercule plopped the envelope down, opposite the looming red-velvet chair that was not unlike a throne.

Lord Renald of Dragonsbane lifted his chin to regard his son. Everything about the man was pristine and precise: The Dragonsbane crest pinned to a freshly pressed suit, his pearly beard trimmed to a sharp point below a thin mustache, hair combed neatly to one side, with nothing to show his age but a few darker lines under the eyes. He was in every way the perfect, stark image of a Head Noble. He opened the envelope and inspected each inch of the report.

"Mm-hm. Hmph." The nobleman grunted as he scanned the grades of every test, every quiz. "Right here."

Hercule looked as Father tapped a finger on one of the scores, frowning as if it were a squashed bug on the paper. "Merely an *A*?" he said, "Not an *A*+?"

Hercule's brow crinkled slightly. "It was a pop quiz, sir. But you do see that my results for everything else is *A*+?"

"Not the Harlow Missions grade. You still have a *C*."

Hercule sucked in a breath. "I cannot control the actions of others during missions. It's a group grade, unfortunately, sir."

"A blemish on the grade of a nobleson, no matter how small it may seem to you, is still unacceptable."

Hercule held his tongue. There was no reasoning with Father; his ideals as to how things should be were set in stone. Being the only son, much was expected of Hercule. He was to be a model member of high society in every way, and surpass the other Noble Houses' heirs.

Rivalry between the twelve Houses of the Vemparic Kingdom had been playing out since the founding of Draethvyle. And Hercule was the only heir to Dragonsbane, the only one who could uphold their House's future—a more than heavy burden.

"I will try for better next month, sir," said Hercule, straight-backed.

"There is no *try*. You will *do* better," Lord Renald stated matter-of-factly. Hercule tried not to look skyward at Father's favorite saying: *"There is no try to do, but only will do."* A decent saying, perhaps. But a person must also accept that there will be times when they fail to *do* no matter how hard they *only will do*.

Hercule turned to leave. There would be no speaking

with Father until next month's report, too busy and wrapped up in his Head position to spend time with his son. And when there *was* any time spent together, it was only to lecture.

Back out in the hallway, Hercule exhaled through his nose. Why dwell on it? He shouldn't. It wouldn't change anything, except fuel his anger further—and he didn't need a repeat of rage like the night before in the Outer Woods, after which Cyrus had found him. He had to keep a firmer leash on his anger, or else the curse would...

"Hercule, daaarling."

His shoulders tensed as the swishing sound of a dress approached, announcing Mother.

Her lips puckered in a smile, her body swathed in layers of periwinkle silk, trimmed in black lace and pearls. Her long dark hair was done up in silver pins and combs. She breathed of wealth, to the point where she could barely breathe air.

Mother took him in with her acorn-brown eyes. "How is everything at school? Is my little growing sprout popular with the ladies? Oh, silly me, I forgot it's mostly boys at your school. *Hahaha*," she giggled to herself. "But you must have many friends, yes? Do tell me, daaarling. You never say much—at least, not enough for your loving mother's ears."

Hercule stared blankly forward. How could he say much when she talked non-stop, blabbing on and on until his ears fell off? Mother wasn't one to hear what others had to say. She simply wanted someone to share gossip with, while jumping from topic to topic like a grasshopper.

"How is Master Nephryte? Such a handsome young man. If only he'd been the same age as me, and of wealthy descent, when I was a youth!" She fanned her face with a hand. "I might've married *him* instead, *hahaha*."

Hercule's insides cringed. That brought up a bad memory, the day Master Nephryte first met his parents:

Mother couldn't take her eyes off him, standing there talking his ears off for a good three hours, winking and giggling, before he managed to come up with an excuse to leave.

The poor Master never came back. Most men never did, not if they could help it, fearing the ridiculous flirtatious attempts she made: Pretending to brush a dust-speck off their shirt while feeling their shoulder muscles and chest, clinging to their arm like some playful baby monkey for an excuse to inch closer… It was enough to drive any sane man running. Not to mention her way of speech, drawing out *daaarling* and other such words in a sultry voice. Hercule had to banish the memory for a moment and cool his heating face.

As if that list of embarrassing things wasn't enough, Mother had a reputation for the most wild, outlandish hairstyles in the kingdom; the renowned hair of aristocracy. Every day it was done-up to resemble some fantastical creature, flower, or structure. Mother's hairdo today resembled a giant lotus flower. Huge swoops of hair wrapped in the shape of floppy petals, ribbons woven through for added pops of color, pins and combs with giant pearls on the ends for a flowery center—a massive creation that dwarfed the woman's head.

'How does her neck move under that?' A sweatdrop beaded Hercule's temple as he stood facing it, and Mother continued chatting about who-knew-what. His head ached, and it was well past dinner. He was used to the dorm's schedule, not the mansion's anymore.

"Your Grace Chatsalott? Lord Hercule?" A soft note spoke from the staircase behind them. Hercule turned to the faeryn slave, who was barely a year younger than himself.

Her eyes were mint green, pupils a deeper green, set in a petite face like angel-cake. Honey-hair, a mix of flaxen highlights and amber streaks, was tied back in a thick, intricate braid down her back. A handful of loose bangs trailed down her left cheek, shading one mint eye.

In the middle of her back, wings like a green luna moth's shimmered in the hallway lamplight. Though pretty, they hung limp and lifeless, folded behind her like wilted petals—nothing of how alive they'd once been when she first arrived at the mansion. He often wondered what had made them change.

"The dining room is prepared, dinner is waiting to be served…when you are ready, Your Grace, Milord." The slave girl added a curtsy to each of them.

Mother paused from her ceaseless chatter, confused at first, then realized what time it was. "Oh! Oh gracious me, look at the time, a half-hour late! Why wasn't dinner ready sooner? It's past the proper time, in my standards." She huffed.

"The chef has been in mourning for a relative these past few days, Your Grace, but he's been trying his best," the faeryn cut in, eyes lowered respectfully.

"Oh? Is that right? He's— Ah, I remember now! But I do not think that is a good enough excuse to skimp out on one's duties. Why, if noblewomen sat around every time they felt dreary, nothing would *ever* get done around the house."

Hercule held in a snarky comment. Noble ladies never did *anything* around the house—it was servants and slaves who did all the work.

The faeryn, Marigold, cut in once more, this time her expression flat as stone as she added quite bluntly, "…And because you told him to wait until later. You were full from your evening tea, I believe were your words."

"I most definitely did not—! Oh, I did? Oh, yes, yes. I did. Ahaha! But I'm well and ready for dinner *now*. Not too much, mind you. A lady must keep her figuuure," Mother prattled.

"Of course, Your Grace." Marigold's expression

remained flat.

Hercule hid his amusement. He left Mother to chatter on and on to the air, silently thanking Marigold for the distraction as he slipped away.

It was time for a quick meal, then off to bed.

The dining table sparkled with extravagant dinnerware and a three-course meal.

So much for it being *quick*, Hercule thought. He ate in a hurry, even if it was improper, while Mother babbled on about the day's gossip, and Father was lost in his own thoughts, mechanically forking the cream pasta.

Hercule paid them no attention, until Mother suddenly mentioned the Festival Duel.

"What a dreadful thing! A human, can you believe it? A creature like that wanting to train as a Draev Guardian? How's such nonsense possible! It shouldn't be allowed, in my opinion—and in my friends' opinions, too. It's been the gossip all day. I'm surprised a riot hasn't started," said Mother.

Mother's faeryn slave and Marigold both waited by the wall, alongside the head butler, ready to refill glasses and take away finished plates. Their very long ears were tilted forward to listen.

"Do you know that human person, daaarling?" Chatsalott craned her neck.

Hercule averted his gaze. "I've…seen him around," he replied impassively. No reason to get Mother in a fit. She didn't need to know the half-human was in Harlow with him.

Father spoke suddenly, "I have decided. It is not proper."

Hercule choked on his potato-leek soup. Did he mean to do something about Cyrus?

"Not proper for the heir of Dragonsbane to be away

without his personal slave-attendant," Father finished. "A House slave to do your laundry, serve meals and such, instead of using servants from Draevensett whom we know nothing about."

Hercule paused mid-chew, and from the corner of his eye noticed Marigold stiffen. How this topic had come up, he had no idea, but at least it didn't involve Cyrus. Perhaps Father had tuned out Mother's voice and hadn't heard a word she said. Neither of them had attended the Festival Duel.

"Several of the other noblesons keep their House's personal attendants with them in Draevensett," continued Father.

Hercule frowned; he knew where this was going.

"It is a sign of sophistication these days. Without it, a House may be viewed as too cheap to provide the best of comfort for its heir. And I will not have the Dragonsbane House talked about as being cheap. Therefore," Father's tone firmed, and Hercule swallowed, "I have arranged for your personal slave-attendant to live in Draevensett among the school's servants. She will be responsible for your care and daily chores."

A faint gasp escaped Marigold, in the same moment that a frustrated grunt escaped Hercule. "Father, I don't need—"

"End of discussion. For House Dragonsbane's image, this is how it will be. That is final."

Hercule's jaw clicked shut, struggling to hold in his rising temper. He knew it was no use arguing.

Why did this nonsense have to come up *now*? What idiot noble started this trend? He'd ring their silken neck!

Hercule could just picture it: Aken laughing his head off, and all of Harlow shooting disdainful looks at the snooty nobleson with his faeryn slave-attendant doing his laundry… What an embarrassment!

He was already labeled the "rich brat" enough. Imagine what they'd call him now?

'Why can't I just have a normal life?' he silently wished, and not for the first time.

41

Cyrus couldn't sleep, couldn't rest, not after the wild ordeal she'd survived through. Images of Doughboy kept flashing in her head—flashbacks of pounding fists and near misses seeking to flatten her. And then the images of something *else* surfaced, like bubbles rising from her mind's darkest depths: the nightmare showing Mother's lovely hair and pooling blood, and the mist parting to reveal a boy standing over her...

Cyrus sat up.

Why did she see young Master Nephryte in that nightmare of mist and murder? She scooted the rest of the way out of bed, shouldered on a robe, and padded her way silently down Harlow's corridor, cast in the patterned shadows of the windows as moonlight crept between the dwindling rainclouds.

It was time to learn the truth. Now or never, she had to ask.

Her knock was faint on the door, but his sharp ears heard all the same and he let her inside. Master Nephryte motioned she take a seat by the lit fireplace. He adjusted a lavender robe over his pajamas. "I see something is troubling you," he noted, and took a seat opposite her. His eyes glowed like rivers in the dull light.

Cyrus fingered the white scarring around her wrists, visible now without the gloves on. Her heart was a thumping rabbit's foot, and she couldn't meet his gaze directly.

The Master laced his fingers, leaned back and waited. Her mouth opened and closed several times, before she finally let the words spill out. "Did you know my mother?"

It shocked her ears to hear herself finally say it out loud, and fear built up in her chest.

Master Nephryte regarded her for one lengthy moment, then straightened. "You remember me, then?"

Her breath held, her ribs freezing up, she could do no more than nod.

"I won't pretend with you, Cyrus," Nephryte said carefully. "I was there. Though I'm surprised a young child could remember… Then again, traumatic experiences do tend to stick in the mind, no matter what age, don't they?"

She couldn't reply.

"Should I recall that memory more clearly for you, now?" He crossed his legs and folded his hands, ready to recount that fateful day.

⤜⤏

The Outer Woods, 10 Years Ago

The first rays of dawn slanted color through night's grip on the land, and thirteen-year-old Nephryte was jogging through the cool of the early woods.

He came around a cluster of birch trees wreathed in mist, when something red caught his eye.

He slowed and then pivoted, almost stumbling over a woman lying on the ground. After catching his balance, he saw that the woman was motionless, her scarlet hair mingled with a pool of blood.

Nephryte kneeled beside the body, the shock of it making him choke, and he quickly felt for a pulse.

There was none.

Horrified, he sat back on his heels and scanned the surrounding trees. All was quiet, still as death in the woods, the person responsible long since gone.

Blood seeped from the woman's chest, a strange wound etched in black. What could cause this? The work of an unusual Ability? But that meant this was the work of a vempar.

He found a spot showing two different sets of tracks: More than one vempar, then.

Nephryte rubbed his eyes, contemplating what to do.

Who was this woman? How could someone do this to her?

Uh…uhu…uhu…

His ears twitched to the side. That sound, it was like whimpering.

Nephryte rose, careful not to make noise, and followed the whimper to the base of an old tree, where there was a dug-out tunnel of an animal den.

He hesitated, not wanting to get bitten if it was an animal—he'd Heal, but it'd still hurt.

Uh…uhu…

Animals couldn't whimper like that, though, could they?

Nephryte tensed and reached his arm down into the murky darkness of the den. His fingers brushed against what felt like fabric. And the fabric shuddered, drawing back farther.

He retracted his arm and sat back, instead trying to coax whatever was down there with his voice. "Is someone there? It's safe now. You can come out. I won't hurt you."

He peered inside the dirt tunnel as something shuffled about, and then a mop of curly red hair appeared. A head poked out of the den, and twin lilac eyes looked up at him. Nephryte swallowed his surprise, and reached to lift the child the rest of the way out. She couldn't be more than two years old.

He held her for a moment, fascinated, and then she cried. "Mommy! *Uhuuu*, I want Mommy!"

A lump caught in his throat. He wasn't sure what to do with her, and so set her down. But she crawled faster than he expected and headed toward the still form of what had been her mother.

He stopped the child just in time, holding her back by the shoulders.

She tugged and squirmed, her attention fixed on the body. Nephryte noticed blood on his shirt, and hoped it hadn't frightened the child. What should he do? Was she too young to understand the situation?

He sat down, and forced her to sit too, using air to hold her in place. "You can't go to Mommy. She's passed away."

"Mommy's there. I want Mommy!" the girl struggled.

Nephryte inhaled. How could he explain this?

"Have you ever seen a butterfly or bumblebee stop moving?" he asked, and the child turned her head to him. "They get hurt, and don't ever wake up?"

The child's head bobbed a little.

"That happens to people, too."

"Mommy won't wake up?" Panic filled the girl's voice, and he wondered if he'd made a mistake letting her know.

"Ah, I'm not the best with kids..." he mumbled, scratching his head. Then he leaned down to her height, "Do you have other family? A daddy?"

"Daddy," she repeated.

Something seemed off about her. He brushed her upper lip back and noticed. "No fangs?" He freed an ear from her red waves. "And these aren't vempar ears. They're more like...a human's? But your mother is vempar."

He pondered. "Oh no. Is your daddy human?"

She cocked her head, not understanding the question.

"This'll complicate things..." He sighed.

Nephryte let the child say goodbye to her mother—letting her get close enough, but not too close. It took a long time of waiting and staring at the body before she finally said, "Bu-bye, Mommy." She hiccupped, little hands scrubbing tears as they wet her face. She didn't want to leave, didn't want to say goodbye, and he still wasn't sure she fully understood. It was an effort to pull her away.

"I'll take care of your mother later, I promise. But you can't stay here. You need to see your daddy." He ruffled the back of her head. Whether she understood or not, she didn't protest when he picked her up.

Nephryte held the child in his arms, sheltered under his cloak, and he activated his Ability, manipulating the air to carry them up above the woods. The nearest human residence he knew of was Elvenstone, and it was with much caution that he flew and approached the border.

The moment he came within view of the town rooftops, a volley of bullets fired.

With a wave of his free hand the bullets were stopped midair and left hanging, as he glided down to the front gate, alighting with grace.

Human guards held gunswords at the ready, all except for one human, whose attire he recognized to be that of an Argos. The Argos approached him at the gate with a harsh scowl.

"Just because there's a temporary truce between our races, while battling those goblin vermin, doesn't mean you're welcome here. *Vempar*." He spat. "But I'm guessing you'd already know that?"

Nephryte nodded curtly and unwrapped the child from his cloak. "I'm searching for this child's father. I found her in the woods near her mother's body."

The Argos's eyes narrowed, neck craning to get a look.

"She's half-human. You must know who her family is?" asked Nephryte.

"Half-human?" The Argos spat. "Is there a name?"

Nephryte sat the child up in his arms, meeting her lilac gaze. "What's your name, hm? What did Mommy call you?"

She flopped her head from side to side. "My name Swyrus," she tried to pronounce.

"Swyrus?" Nephryte gave her a funny look, and she giggled. "Oh, you mean Cyrus, like the constellation?"

"Swyrus constetashen~!" she sing-songed.

"Cyrus…" The Argos considered, then commanded him: "Stay put," as he vanished back inside the gate. Long minutes passed until he returned, and this time with another human in tow. "That her?"

The grim expression of the human he'd brought with him could have melted stone. "Yeah. Looks like her," the man said. He stopped ten feet from Nephryte before motioning with a hand. "Let her down. I'm her father."

Nephryte didn't like the look of him. "I can show you where the mother is, if you want to bury her," he offered.

"How'd she die?" the man asked instead, with bitter intensity.

Nephryte hesitated. This wouldn't sound good coming from him. "It looked like she was murdered…by vempars."

The father didn't seem fazed by the news, just a twitch in the jaw. "Vempars killing vempars. Guess you hunt your own kind as much as you hunt others," he snorted. "Keep the body with your own people. But hand over my child."

A part of Nephryte held Cyrus closer. He almost didn't want to hand her over, which surprised him. The child clung tighter to him, too, pouty cheeks ready to cry. If only he could keep her…but he was young, and still in school. He could never give her the time and attention she would need—children were not pets you could just leave at home and come back to.

With a heavy heart Nephryte set her down, standing her feet on the grass. "There's your daddy, see? Go on. Go to him," he motioned.

She took a few wobbly steps, and Nephryte quietly backed away.

But then she turned and ran back to his leg, hugging him. He patted her back. "Don't want to say bye, hm? But he's your daddy. This is your home, right?" For the second time he wondered if he was making the right choice, if a half-blood child would be taken care of or hated here among humans.

He ruffled a hand through her hair. "Maybe we'll meet again, someday. Anything is possible." He smiled down fondly. "I know another child, a rambunctious blond who you'd be good friends with." He chuckled, thinking about him. "Let's meet again, okay? It's a promise." Her small hands fit in his.

He let her go then, hurrying up into the sky before she could chase after him.

She cried, hand reaching for his vanishing form, before the human picked her up.

Nephryte didn't turn back. He couldn't.

PRESENT DAY

The first streaks of dawn gave color to the darkness, while a nightingale trilled to finish its song, and Cyrus approached the gravestone.

There was no name but "Loving Mother" engraved on the front. A small vase for flowers stood beside, and a creeping vine sought to climb the stone as it already had over other graves—she yanked chunks of it away.

"Why didn't you tell me sooner?" she had asked Master Nephryte, and he looked down at her with something between fondness and sadness.

"And bring up bad memories for you?" he had replied. "I couldn't make you relive such a painful scar, Cyrus. Though I admit," a smile tugged at him, "I am glad you didn't forget me. I certainly never forgot you." He'd then ruffled the top of her hair.

Now, he waited several steps back, as Cyrus reunited with her mother for the first time since that tragic day.

She'd been there when Mother died, hidden safely in an animal den. Mother had tried to protect her—and succeeded—but she hadn't been able to protect herself.

Cyrus wasn't sure before today if she'd been there in the woods with Mother, always assuming the killer would have ended her life, too, if she had been. But now the truth rested before her—if only it could help catch the murderers.

Cyrus held in a breath, and fiddled with a handful of daises and daffodils before fitting them inside the little vase, getting on her knees.

"Hi, Mom." Her fingers reached to brush the stone, still damp from the morning dew. She smiled through tears. "I finally made it back to you."

As the sky cast off night's dark cloak, warm light caressed her cheeks and the gravestone. So many years of wondering and heartache, and getting no answers, but at last, she'd found her. The memories of Mother's love were renewed in her mind, even if blurred at the edges.

Draethvyle was Mother's home. She wished she could ask her if she'd been happy growing up here, what life had been like, and why she later chose to leave...

"Is this where I belong?" she asked the air.

"Well, how do *you* feel?" Master Nephryte turned the question around. She kept forgetting how sharp vempar hearing was.

"I feel..." Cyrus wondered. "I don't know how I should feel."

The Master raised his head to the dawn as sunlight breathed across the cemetery. "Well, ultimately we belong with our Creator." He winked. "But while we're stuck on Eartha, where your family is, is where your home is. And

I'd say you have a good-sized family here."

She looked back at him, then up at the clouds. Harlow had stood up for her when no one else had. They wanted what was best for her, and weren't afraid of being honest. That's what family was, wasn't it?

"Harlow is a nice home," she said.

She recalled Cherish's words. *"I may not be able to become the same kind of Draev as everybody else in the future—but I won't let that stop me. Instead, I look for the things I can do, and the different kind of Draev I can become."*

A different kind of Draev, that's what Cyrus would have to be. And after winning the Duel, that finally seemed more possible.

EPILOGUE

The young human ran, her feet dodging littered branches and jutting rocks strewn across the woods. Trix didn't know what monster was chasing her, only that she couldn't trip or it would all be over for her.

She hurried in the direction of Elvenstone, legs pumping, desperately trying to move faster. Twigs snagged at her billowing shirt.

She scolded herself for coming out here alone, all for a basket of mushrooms that she'd had to cast aside in her haste to run.

The monster hissed at her back, and out the corner of her eye she could see tatters of black fabric, the glint of metal claws, and a bone face beneath a hood.

Her heart seized in fear, and her foot caught on a root.

She fell, slamming her knees in the ground, and scrambled to rise, before a clawed hand gripped the back of her neck. She tried to scream.

"Easy, now. Don't kill her just yet, my Hound Corpsed."

Footsteps approached, and Trix tried in vain to shift and see. Who had the power to control a Corpsed? She didn't have long to think or panic before her vision went dark...

The air was cool, with the dampness of an underground

cave. Trix trembled as she walked—a hand and knife point at her back steering her. A cloth around her head blinded her; wherever this was, it wasn't the woods or anywhere familiar, and by the sound of it, many others were walking with her.

The hand gripped Trix, making her halt in place, and her knees shook in fear. The blindfold yanked off.

It took many blinks to adjust to the green fungus light ringing the walls of the cavern. She was standing in a line of other girls, their hands bound like hers, but the similarities didn't end there: All of them had red hair, and all of them were human.

She tried to get a look back at the darkly garbed figures behind them, who held them captive, but the cloaks and hoods kept their faces concealed.

A stone platform jutted from the cave wall like a stage before the gathering, and a willowy figure soon strode across and took a seat in the large chair at the center.

"The Impure Nights greet you, Leader," spoke the cloaked persons in unison.

The willowy vempar popped his wrists and cracked each of his fingers. "This is all you could find this week?" he said. His deep voice scratched like sand rolling in the wind.

"Forgive us, Leader," spoke the cloaked figure behind Trix. "The new Corpsed haven't been able to sniff out the Pure Light, just yet. But they are finding female humans of red hair. If the Swan Princess is somehow cloaking her power, we still have a chance at finding her *this* way. The girls need only be tested, one by one."

"Very well, Deidreem." The vempar on the throne, who they called Leader, let his long hand fall forward before flicking it with a pop. "Proceed."

The first girl in line was dragged forward. Tears streaked her face as she begged for mercy and was made to kneel before the man. His fingers shot forward, gripping her neck, nails digging in as she screamed. The skin under his palm glowed for one painful moment, and then he released the girl with a shove. "The Pure Light is not in this one. Next."

They went down the line, and when it was Trix's turn and he grabbed her by the throat, she lost all control of her body and almost passed out. She barely felt the pain when her head hit the floor as he shoved her away.

"None passed the test—none of these are the Swan." Leader growled. "Take them away, and put them to use in the experimental chambers."

"Yes, Leader," said Deidreem. "Don't worry, we'll find her. And when we do, the Vemparic Empire of old will rise again."

Trix tried to sit up. "N-no..." she tried to say, tried to cry, as a dark cloak swept forward, and gray hands dragged her into the underground tunnels.

⟝

Cyrus looked down one of the meandering paths leading out of the large cemetery. The Master had left to pick up some iced lattes at a nearby café, and told her she could take her time in the meanwhile.

She stayed there before Mother's grave, until she could gather her emotions and get her head back into gear, sending a prayer to Lord God before she left. It was a quiet walk, the air still, as if the eartha had taken a breath and now held it in. Too quiet.

K—krnch, k—krnch.

Cyrus stilled. What sounded like footsteps were dragging from somewhere ahead of her—a slow, uneven drag.

Just as she was about to hurry down a different way, a young figure dragged itself onto the path. Its head turned, and the ragged state of the body made her think it was an animal at first, until she recognized red hair and human ears.

A girl, no older than herself, stared back at her, and the

whites of her eyes grew. With a stumble she came at Cyrus, mangled hands reaching out.

Cyrus backed away, fear jolting through her. But the girl limped forward, reaching.

"Red hair…female…human…"

Words that were barely audible spilled through the girl's bleeding lips, her damaged fingers reaching. Chains dragged behind her ankles, as if she'd broken free from someplace.

"They're looking for…looking for…"

The girl collapsed.

Cyrus cautiously approached her side. "What do you mean? Who's looking for what? Here, I'll help you."

"Hide. Don't tell anyone. Don't let them…find you…"

"Who?" Cyrus persisted.

"…Impure Nights…"

The girl's eyes glazed over, and Cyrus realized there was nothing she could do. She was dead.

Trembling, Cyrus rose and hurried down the path to find Master Nephryte.

There came another dragging sound through the underbrush of the cemetery, and she turned back, fearing to see what else might have come. But when she did, the girl's body was gone.

"Don't let them find you…"

Cyrus hurried away as fast as she could. That girl had looked so much like her; it was unnerving.

Looking for who? For *her*? Who were the Impure Nights? And…what would they, or anybody, want with her?

⌣

"You called?"

It was late evening when Nephryte let Mamoru inside his dorm flat, and indicated the living room table where tea had been set. "Please, have a seat."

As they each took a spot on opposite settees, Nephryte

filled the cups with floral grey tea. "I need to speak with you about Cyrus," he said. He began by recounting what Dr. Zushil had discovered in the half-human. "What could this great force of energy be that's inside her? Lord Mamoru, you're the oldest in the kingdom; surely you have some idea of what this could be?"

Mamoru took a sip from one of the fluted tea cups, his expression careful. "Some things are best left in the dark, Master Nephryte. Take care of Cyrus as your student, but do not pry any further."

Nephryte took out a piece of old parchment and slid it across the table. "This prophecy, *The Song Of The End*, is a warning of the future:

Arise, three Ghosts of distant past
Save us with the Pure Light vast,
War has begun, the dice are cast
The Swan must live, or none will last.

Is the Pure Light real? Have you seen it? Could this power be what's inside Cyrus?"

Mamoru narrowed his eyes at the table. "I strongly urge you to keep this to yourself, Master, and not ask any further questions."

Nephryte carefully folded the parchment back into its secure place within his journal. "I understand your caution," he said, "though, I do hope you remember that I'm the one who found and freed you."

Mamoru perched his elbows on the low table. "And I am ever grateful that you did. I trust you more than anyone else here. But there are things that no one should know—not even you—if it can be helped."

"...Very well," Nephryte finally acquiesced.

"Let's switch topics to the other matter," said Mamoru, and he swirled the tea cup in his hand. "Do you believe it's true that Aken's parents were murderers?"

Nephryte regarded the curious scar down the lord's cheek. "Several murders have been linked to the couple. Though only a select few in the kingdom know of it," he replied.

"Then they could be the ones who killed Cyrus's mother?"

Nephryte gave a regrettable nod. "The king gave the order for their execution. We were to eliminate them under the cover of a human terrorist attack—which was one of the hardest things I've ever had to do."

It had taken a surprise attack, and every ounce of his Ability and other Draevs, to take down the Pureblood couple—the explosion was the last thing to finish and conceal the job. But it was the emotional scar it left behind that now ached.

"Aken-Shou has a good heart. I know he won't become like them; that's why I pleaded for his life to be spared," Nephryte said, staring down at his reflection in the brown tea.

"I wanted him spared, too," said Mamoru. "But you must keep in mind that Purebloods are easily tainted; and Aken-Shou could become very powerful."

Nephryte's fingers clenched the cup.

Mamoru finished his tea and rose to leave. "Let's be vigilant," he said, turning. "And be prepared."

Extra Bites

Mamoru's Scar

Cyrus approached the mysterious puppeteer. "Mamoru?" He turned from his work on a long-nosed puppet, and motioned for her to join him.

"What's on your mind?" he inquired as she took a stool.

"Well...I've been meaning to ask, how did you get that scar? I mean, if it's okay to talk about," she added hastily.

"This?" His finger trailed down the vicious vertical red slash down his right cheek, just beneath the eye, black fringing the edges as if burned. He considered the question, then flashed a secretive smile. "It was many years ago. Back when I stumbled upon the *creature*."

"Creature?"

"An angry dragon with razor claws. It was camouflaged so well in the woods, I didn't know it was there until it was too late. I had climbed onto its head, thinking it a giant boulder, and then it moved. I tried to jump off and get out of the way, but that's when a nasty claw swiped me and— I had to run for my life."

Mamoru looked up, as if reliving the horror. "My poor companions, though...they weren't so lucky. Chuck has to go about on stilts for legs, now, and sad Luck has to drink his meals through a straw."

Cyrus gasped, hands over her mouth. "That's terrible! I had no idea dragons could be so fierce, and camouflage themselves so well. But why didn't your injuries Heal?"

"Yes, poor Luck." Mamoru stared up at the ceiling, eyebrows drooped. "Or maybe…" His forehead creased, and he tapped his chin. "Maybe I got it wrong, and it was a knife-throwing accident? Or maybe that time I tried peeling potatoes?"

Cyrus blinked.

"I'm quite fond of potatoes. I bet that's when it happened. My knife slipped."

She stared up at him flatly, realizing she'd been duped. "Luck and Chuck, my foot. You're not planning on telling me the *real* story, are you?"

Nephryte's Pin

"Hey, Nephryte! What's your Master identity pin-thingie supposed to be?" Aken came near for a closer look, narrowing his eyes and analyzing the pin on the vempar's tunic.

"A cloud with moving air currents," replied Mentor Nephryte. "It represents my Ability with air."

"It looks like the cloud is farting," Aken stated.

"You brat, it does not!" Nephryte covered the identity pin with his hand and stalked away.

Later that day…

Nephryte stared silently at the pin and its wind representation, solemn and long-faced. "I can't look at this pin the same way, anymore."

Master Seren-Rose touched his shoulder, offering small comfort, while Master Eletor fell on his side laughing his head off: "It does—*bahahaa!*—it does look like that!"

"No, it doesn't!" Nephryte snapped.

A NEED TO BE REMADE

Aken-Shou finished the final touches to one of his clay masterpieces: a hawk proudly perched upon a branch, its head held high as though it ruled the world.

He gave a proud nod at his hard work before yawning and rubbing tired eyelids. "It turned out perfect! Mmm, but now it's bedtime… I'll leave it in the study room, for now."

He trundled off to bed.

Morning came. Aken rose to check on the statue, thinking of a good spot to display it, when he noticed something was wrong. "NO! My lovely hawk!"

The clay's paintwork was flaking, slivers of color peeling off as if it were shedding. He'd accidentally used the wrong kind of paint and created a nasty chemical reaction.

Aken eyed the statue with a disappointed glower, hands on hips. He heard the door open and recognized Mentor Nephryte's gait without having to look.

Nephryte came up beside him and tilted his head at the peeling paint. "I guess the created thing cannot be long-lasting and perfect like its Creator. It will always fall short."

Aken let his hands fall from his hips with a groan. "You always have to make a life lesson out of everything, don't you?"

Nephryte shrugged as if he didn't know what he meant. "It is merely an observation that happens to be true and pertain to life."

Aken stared sidelong at him. "You do it on purpose. Admit it."

"Are you going to fix that poor bird or not? As the Creator, you can easily help what you have created."

"Ugh, there you go again!" Aken grabbed some new paint bottles, appropriate for clay, while the Mentor stood aside watching.

"The Creator can refurbish and renew his creation, remaking it so that it will no longer flake or fall apart. A wonderful depiction of how we need our Creator in our lives."

Aken grumbled. After an hour of careful work, the statue was fixed, and its glory shown brighter than before. "There!" Aken folded his arms with a satisfied grin, "Now my creation is *truly* perfect." He regretted it the moment he said it, though, as Nephryte applauded.

"That's exactly right, Aken-Shou! I'm so proud of you. We are not perfect, and make many mistakes in life. Our paint work peels and flakes away. But if we let our Creator into our lives, He can remake us. For only the One who made you can cleanse and rebuild you."

Aken evaded a hug. "Enough, *enough!*"

GENETIC DISORDERS

"Dr. Zushil?" Cyrus inquired during a brief doctor visit. "Why do you need glasses? Can't Healing make your vision perfect?"

"Kids these days really are ignorant, aren't they?" Zushil sniffed. "Vempars can be born with genetic disorders and defects, same as any race, though it isn't as common. A disorder is different from an injury. Healing only kicks in to heal something that has been damaged. It does not fix something you were born with."

Cyrus listened, working her brain to follow along.

"An arm that does not fully develop into an arm, while inside a mother's womb, is not an injury, and so will not Heal. The same goes for many genetic disorders. I was born with distorted vision, and therefore require glasses."

The doctor made a show of placing his damaged glasses—

the ones she'd ruined—in a case, before taking out a new pair he'd just received in the mail.

"I trust that your control over metal is improving?" he asked, and his palms cupped the new glasses rather protectively.

Cyrus swallowed. "I'm working on it."

WHY AKEN ONLY MAKES BIRDS

"Hey, Aken!" Bakoa trotted up. "Can you make other animals and stuff with clay?"

"Hm, sure. As long as the clay is good enough," said Aken.

"I don't think I've ever seen anything else but birds from you, and rarely a snake."

"Birds are easy. I have a knack for them, since they're special to me. But here, take a look at this horse!" Aken pulled out a clay shape and set it on the table.

"Oh wow! It's…it's…" Bakoa squinted. "Are you sure it's a horse?"

"Obviously."

"But…it has an elephant trunk."

"That's a raised leg."

"Oh…where's the head?"

"In the front, duh."

"That's a head?"

Aken glared.

Bakoa shrugged. "It sure is a fat horse."

Aken threw the clay at him. "That's why I only make birds."

COUSINS

"Cyrus Sole."

"Yes, Master Nephryte?"

"I don't believe I've heard the full story of how you reached Draethvyle. Who was it that guided you here?"

"Oh, it was this odd vempar I freed from a death-cage in Elvenstone. His name was Gandif," she said.

"Gandif? He ended up in *another* death-cage?" The Master grinned, clearly amused. "I've been wondering what that bounty hunter was up to."

"You know him?"

He nodded, chuckling. "Since when we were younger. You two could actually be related, you know."

Cyrus looked up. "What?"

"His last name is Sole. His human grandmother was captured and made into a slave years ago; but before that, she'd been married to a human with the last name Sole. So, you and Gandif could be half-cousins."

She exclaimed, "I have a *living* vempar relative?"

Thank You For Reading!

This series has been a passion project of mine, inspired by the years I spent living as a middle schooler in northern Italy, surrounded by enchanting scenery and ancient architecture, which later on became the perfect setting for my fantasy vampirish tale. ;)

You can get the bonus stories to Strayborn: *Storm & Choice* plus another one of my books free on my website, in the Reader Insider Vault, where I hope you'll also come along on this author journey with me and follow my bookish updates!

Draev Guardians Book 2
NOW AVAILABLE!
And the stakes are higher than ever…

Dragons & Ravens
(Draev Guardians 1.5)
How did Hercule and Marigold first meet, and what is the secret he's so desperate to hide? Who is Elijob, and what drives Zartanian's goal to become a great swordsmaster? Find out this and more in the first Draev Guardians novella!

Frost, Winter Guardian and current resident of Boston. For centuries he's watched over the winter seasons, and now he longs to end his work and move on from this world. But for that, he needs a replacement, and the human artist, Norah, might be the one, and the key to thawing his icy heart.

A Jack Frost reimagining full of heart and wintery chill!

Madness Solver in Wonderland
"It's a crazy ride trying to keep the peace between both Wonderland and Earth, solving mysteries, but somebody's got to do it—and unfortunately that somebody is me. Welcome to my nonsense life!"

Beast of the Night

A one-armed, practical girl. A rude lord hiding a curse. A dark secret with the town's fate hanging in the balance…

A Beauty and the Beast retelling with an Austrian twist and a new breed of curse.

STRAYBORN

Discussion Questions

1. How does Cyrus feel about her Ability, and about her being half-human? How do her feelings change?

2. Cyrus is willing to give up her freedom for Aken's sake. How does this affect Aken? What would you be willing to give up for someone else's sake?

3. Aken despised Master Nephryte. How does the Master's patience and persistence with him finally pay off? Is there someone you know who is hurting similarly to the way Aken is?

4. Secrets play a big part in Strayborn. But should Cyrus have kept her race a secret, or been honest from the start? What are the pros and cons of each? What would you have done?

5. Cyrus hasn't forgiven her parents yet. Should she wait until they're finally sorry for what they did?

6. Aken and Cyrus eventually become close friends. What does true friendship mean to you? How can you work on being a better friend? What roles do trust and honesty play?

7. What does faith mean to each of the characters, and how does it affect the way they live their lives? Are there any contradictions they should work on?

How You Can Help

Reviews help boost a book on retailer websites so that it'll be found by more readers, which in turn helps support the author. *If you read Strayborn and want to share it with others, please consider leaving a review on Amazon and Goodreads*—this makes a huge difference for indie authors like me! It doesn't have to be much, just click on how many stars you want to rate the book, and maybe add a sentence or two on your thoughts.

8 WAYS TO SUPPORT AN INDIE AUTHOR:

See a list of all the ways you can help support my work, as well as other indie authors!
Scan the QR code:

AUTHOR

E.E. Rawls is the product of a traveling family, who even lived in Italy for 6 years. She loves exploring the unknown, whether it be in a forest, the ruins of a forgotten castle, or in the pages of a book. Her brain runs on coffee, cuddly cats, and the mysterious beauty of nature while she writes. *All thanks be to God, who makes her able.* To learn more about Him, visit **AnswersInGenesis.org/good-news**

Visit her online at **eerawls.com** and get free access to the Reader Insider Vault:

Reader Insider Vault

Here You'll Get Access To:
- My Curated **No-Spice Book Lists**
- Bookish **News**, *Recs & Merch*
- **Behind the Scenes** details + First Looks + *Fun Bonuses* of my books
- **Free ebooks** & more!
- My **Exclusive Newsletter** & Substack: *where you can follow my author updates & fun random finds!*

eerawls.com
Scan QR Code